To everyone past and present who have suffered when I wrote this book...sorry, until the next one! To all those who read this book watch out for the magic, you'll love this one!

Visit the web-site www.hunter-novel.com and let me know what you think.

Join the Facebook group.

This is just the start...Thanks.

HUNTER

P.A. SKINNER

iUniverse, Inc.
New York   Bloomington

HUNTER

iUniverse books may be ordered through booksellers or by contacting:

iUniverse
1663 Liberty Drive
Bloomington, IN 47403
www.iuniverse.com
1-800-Authors (1-800-288-4677)

Because of the dynamic nature of the Internet, any Web addresses or links contained in this book may have changed since publication and may no longer be valid. The views expressed in this work are solely those of the author and do not necessarily reflect the views of the publisher, and the publisher hereby disclaims any responsibility for them.

ISBN: 978-1-4401-3097-7 (pbk)
ISBN: 978-1-4401-3099-1 (cloth)
ISBN: 978-1-4401-3098-4 (ebk)

Library of Congress Control Number: 2009925103

Printed in the United States of America

iUniverse rev. date: 4/1/09

PROLOGUE

EXMOOR, ENGLAND

Mary Templeman had left the hustle and bustle of London for the quiet travelling life. Her plan was to hike around the southwest of England for a year and then be off to university. On occasion, if the weather turned bad, she would hitch a lift to the next town or village, where she would camp for the night. She had arrived on the moor later than she had anticipated; the weather was fair, but the evening was drawing in fast. She had not expected the moor to be so vast, its bleakness seeming to stretch into infinity.

The still evening air had given way to a chill sea breeze. It was refreshing, she thought, as it cooled the perspiration from her endless walking. She stopped briefly, took off her rucksack, and slipped on the jumper that was tied around her waist. It was at this point that she took in the aura of her surroundings. She turned a full three hundred and sixty degrees, not a soul was to be seen, no cars, no animals, and it really made her uneasy that there was no noise, not even a bird singing. The silence was near total apart from the wind buffeting against her ears. She shivered, and a sense of impending danger began to frighten her.

She scanned the gorse and heather that flanked her on either side of the road and could see nothing. But the feeling that she was being watched had her walking again, this time a lot faster, not so fast that she looked frightened, but fast enough to get her off of the moor quicker than she would have done at her normal pace. Her heels beat out a rapid march on the road surface, her eyes scanning every bush that she passed. Occasionally she gave a quick glance over her shoulder, but still nothing. Her lower leg muscles began to burn as her walk turned into a forced march. Danger was all around her, getting closer, watching her, and waiting its time.

Please let a car come, please, the thought screamed in her head. The countryside around her was minute-by-minute becoming undistinguishable in the gloom.

A twig snapped only yards to her left. She stopped. "Who's there?" A bush rustled the other side of the road. She spun round quickly. "I got a knife," she snapped, grabbing the six-inch blade from the sheath attached to her belt. The bush rustled again as if to mock her threats.

Behind her came the sound of movement. She turned, just catching a glimpse of something large moving through the gorse. Looked like a dog ... no, it was a lot bigger. The movement was all around her, getting closer as if gaining confidence from her fear.

"Nice dogs." She pulled a half-eaten sandwich from her pocket and threw it in the bushes.

Visibility was now down to just yards, and then came a stroke of luck. In the distance a set of headlights cut into the oppressive gloom; a welcoming car's engine raced in the night's silence. It appeared over the horizon and then vanished. Her heart sank.

Please let it be coming this way. The lights appeared again ... they were getting closer all the time. The noise of the engine was getting louder. Her hope was becoming audible. "Come on, you beauty, this way."

For a second she forgot about the feelings of fear. Hope and salvation were about a mile from her. She walked quickly towards the lights; they disappeared and reappeared as the vehicle dipped in and out of the contours of the moors. She was running towards the lights, only perhaps a minute from her now. The feeling of danger was receding, and she knew that soon she would be in a safe, warm car and being driven from these godforsaken moors.

The car dipped out of sight again, and at that moment something heavy sprang onto her, knocking her off the road and into the bushes on the opposite side. She could not see what it was; she just knew that she had to find her feet and get back onto that road. She gasped for air and was scrambling on all fours towards the road when a searing pain lanced through her ankle. She did not want to look back, but she had to.

Its eyes glowed like molten metal; it seemed to be playing with its catch as it wrestled with her, pulling her farther from the road. The pain became unbearable; she screamed and kicked at it with her free leg, but to no avail. Sheer terror and desperation was the only thing keeping her going.

The car, I must get to the car.

She spun round and lashed out with her sheath knife, slashing the creature across its muzzle. It let go of what was left of her ankle. Blood spewed from the torn limb as she made a last dash for the road. The glow of the car's lights grew on the pavement in front of her. She was nearly there.

~~~

Simon Homewood nodded in time with ZZ Top blasting from his car speakers. He was doing eighty miles an hour in his Ford Escort and was desperate for his dinner. He drove across the moor every night on his way home from work. He had never needed to stop here and never planned to; the place gave him the creeps.

A woman scrambled on all fours from the bushes into his headlights. Or so it seemed. He suddenly swerved and slammed on the brakes as two large Things ran across the road in front of him. They were like big dogs immediately sprang to mind.

The front wheels of the car just caught the grass verge, and the back end was swinging all over the place, but he managed to keep control of the vehicle. He stopped the car, snapped off the music, and opened the door.

"Bloody dogs, I'll run ya down next time," Homewood shouted into the blackness in front of him. He jumped back into the car and left with a screech of tires.

~~~

Mary Templeman heard Homewood's remark, only yards away from her, but her life was near to over. The creature had its large crushing jaws around her throat. Its weight held her body still, and she could feel its teeth popping through her flesh. She took her last gasp of air and with it tried to scream. Not a sound came from her mouth.

CHAPTER 1

Hunter swung his Land Rover out of the barracks, pausing at the gate. The civilian guard glanced at his pass and waved him through. A large red striped barrier lifted out of his way, and he passed out of the gate. As he stopped at the main road, he glanced up at the watchtower, a new addition to the camp, standing some twenty feet in the air overlooking the main road and front perimeter fence. His mate Jock was on lookout. The sinister-looking tower would have seemed more at home at a prisoner of war camp, but it was a necessary evil in the days of terrorism. Most road users would not have even noticed the construction, since it blended in so well with its backdrop of ash and elm.

Jock pushed aside the camouflage netting and gave Hunter the thumbs-up for their meeting that night, down at the local pub. Hunter replied in the same manner, feeling the scopes of Jock's SA80 rifle on his Land Rover as it disappeared out of sight towards the town.

Hunter did not live in married quarters, to which he was entitled as a married man with a child. However, Jenny wanted better. She hated the marines and all they stood for; she hated the forces full stop. With his low wages, they had just managed to buy a small terraced house in the nearby village of Norton. It was nice, but claustrophobic, with only two small bedrooms, a bathroom upstairs, two similar rooms and a kitchen downstairs, but it did have a pub just up the road, and that was a godsend for Hunter.

He pulled the short wheelbase Land Rover to a halt on the hard standing just outside the front door, its bumper nearly touching the small bay window. The hollow slam of the car door closing brought the old woman next door to her window. The curtain twitched, and an eye peered out through a small gap in the lace. Hunter grinned at his onlooker, the sort of grin that said, *Piss off, you nosy old bag.* He slammed the Georgian front door behind him, stepping into the tiny dark hall. The musty smell of damp filled the air in this little cubicle of a room. He had planned to get it done, but somehow it seemed to have slipped his mind, just like all the rest of the little jobs around the place.

The sound of something knocked against the living room door brought a smile to his face as he hung up his jacket, on the last remaining hook on the wall. The rest had snapped or had just fallen out of the plaster. Hunter opened the door slowly crouching down on his knees as he did so. The knocking became louder as Hunter peered round the other side of the door.

"What are you up to then?" Hunter said looking down at a toddler with a plastic play brick in his hand, banging it against the door. He snatched up the giggling little bundle, tossing him into the air and catching him again.

"Watch what you're doing, you'll bloody knock his brains out one of these days!" a shrill woman's voice shouted from the sofa.

"He's all right; he's a Hunter, isn't he," Hunter proclaimed, tossing the boy into the air once again.

"Yeah, don't I bloody know it?" Hunter's wife stood up from off the sofa, straightening her clothes.

She was a plain but pretty girl and did not need any

makeup to catch the eye of the opposite sex. She had a very Nordic pale complexion with fair hair. Her piercing blue eyes would captivate onlookers in a glance. Hunter thought she had an air of naughty innocence about her, and that was partly what attracted him to her. The bad boy image with the good, pretty schoolgirl. This summed them up as a couple.

Her jogging bottoms sagged round her bum; the material had lost its clinging power. She was a shapely girl, not showing the signs of childbirth that most mothers had to bear. Her figure was trim from constant diets and binge fitness. She feared gaining weight as her mother had done and never lost it again. Presently Jenny was happy with her body thinking it firm and made for pleasure. She had married Hunter at the age of eighteen, and now at twenty-one she wished she had waited. Carl their son appeared on the scene a year or so after the marriage, now eighteen months old, father and son were inseparable.

Hunter presented a contrast to his pale, pretty wife. His dark leathery complexion and dark cropped hair made for an intimidating look, reinforced by thick eyebrows that met in the middle of his face. Although both Jenny and Hunter were roughly the same height at five feet, ten inches tall. Jenny could never really put her finger on what attracted her to him, other than she liked the bad boy image and a bit of rough. She indeed got that from him.

Hunter held the boy in his arms as he followed Jenny into the small kitchen. The sink was crammed with dishes from the night before and a pot full of last night's curry still untouched on the draining board.

Hunter looked back into the living room. The place was a mess. Things had not been that good between the two of them lately; arguments had become more frequent, even sometimes leading to a fight. Like most arguments, it was down to money. He was due to leave the Royal Marines in seven days, with still no real job to go to. Therefore, her worry was money and where they would get it.

Hunter placed the boy on the floor in the living room,

next to a pile of his plastic bricks, then stepped back into the kitchen, closing the door quietly behind him. She knew what was coming next as she wound a tin opener round a large tin of baked beans.

"What've you been doing all day?" Hunter asked in a quiet but stern voice.

She slammed the tin down on the drainer, sending some of its contents into the air to land in splatters all around.

"Go on, start again! Every day's the fucking same." She squared up to him with one hand on her hip and the other ready for a fight.

"Yeah." He leant towards her till his nose was an inch from hers. "Well if you'd done some fucking housework, just tidied the place up, maybe I'd keep my mouth shut. But you don't, and every night when I get home, you're stretched out on the fucking sofa."

She had no answer or excuse for him, just a plain "Piss off."

Hunter curbed his anger, thinking, *It's like water off a duck's back.* He went back into the front room and wrestled with his boy. Within an hour, things had cooled down, and Jenny had started to speak to him again, even cuddling up to him. She sat on the sofa with her legs apart and him on the floor between them. She massaged his knotted muscles. He relaxed with the boy asleep on his lap. It was times like this Hunter knew why he had married her. She was a good girl at heart, but the pressure of not having any money would get to her; and he couldn't blame her. He was just glad he was not the same.

Jenny carried Carl up to bed; Hunter followed them up the stairs. He wanted a bath. He turned on the two chrome taps and stepped into the bedroom to get undressed. Stripped down to his underpants, he went back into the bathroom.

Steam billowed through the brightly lit boxlike room. Jogging bottoms, knickers, and a T-shirt lay in a crumpled heap on top of the toilet seat. Hunter peered round the bathroom door, seeing Jenny soaping herself in the bath. She smiled at him as she ran the soap over her firm breasts, leaving a white lathery trail in its wake.

Hunter needed no instruction; he pulled down his underpants and climbed into the bath behind her. Snatching the bar of soap from her, he started to massage it into her soft, white skin. He nibbled at her neck, licking off the watery residue.

She reached behind, feeling through the soapy water, and found what she was looking for. Hunter slipped his hands easily between her legs, sliding his fingers along her flesh, rubbing the most sensitive areas. She gave a sudden shriek of pleasure when he had found the right place. Her legs thrashed uncontrollably as his hands seemed to control her very soul. Water splashed up the walls and drenched the carpet.

Finally she lifted herself and turned. Facing each other now, they were coupled as one. Hunter let Jenny do most of the work. He watched as she moved her firm, supple body rhythmically on to his, gasping in ecstasy with every push of her loins. Watching her pleasure turned him on. Seeing her as she was now confirmed his love for her. To him she was a beauty. She was in another dimension with her whole body in rapture. These were the good times he remembered.

Her movements grew faster, and her pleasure became louder. Her head rolled from side to side as Hunter scrutinized her every move. She would look at him and then to the heavens, her green eyes ablaze with passion. Their crescendo came to a climax with Jenny collapsing onto him. He kissed the top of her head, its taste clinging to his lips. Then within moments, she uncoupled herself and stepped from the bath.

Back to reality, Hunter thought.

Jenny stood looking into the small bathroom mirror and rubbed the towel across her boyish short hair, then sauntered out of the room.

They sat on either end of the sofa downstairs. *Where's the passion now?* he asked himself.

He gave a quick glance at the clock on the wall, but not quick enough to avoid a wary scowl from her. Seven o'clock; the pubs must be open. He was restless, and Jenny had noticed.

"If you want to go down the pub, go!" she said, not even looking at him.

Hunter could not believe his luck. He did not need telling again. The drive to the Fox and Hounds public house did not take more than a few minutes. Hunter pulled into the car park, bringing the Land Rover to a halt on a small patch of grass by the entrance.

In the darkness, he studied the other parked vehicles. Jock's car was not among them. A cold north wind was gusting, not forecast by the weather service. The wind rattled Land Rover's canvas roof and threw down the odd heavy drop of rain with a thump. Hunter stepped from the cab, losing grip of the door as the wind slammed it against the car's front wing. He grabbed it again and slammed it shut with vengeance.

He shrugged off the chill night air as he turned to face the cottage-type pub; it was homely and welcoming but still had an aura of mystery about it. It was the oldest building in the village, even having a mention in the Domesday Book, but no one knew how old it really was. Now it served the community as a pub and had done so for many years, but folklore had it that the dreaded Judge Jeffries used it as a courthouse, after the Pitchfork Rebellion, and hanged many of the villagers, guilty or not. It was said that was the very same gibbet now bore the pub's sign.

Hunter stepped into the warm atmosphere of the bar.

"Evening, Hunter, the usual?" the landlord asked.

"Yeah, thanks, Fred." Hunter sat himself on a stool at the bar and watched the landlord pull his pint. Fred had been the landlord of the Fox and Hounds for fifteen years. He was a portly man with beetroot red cheeks and a grey handlebar moustache. Now in his late fifties, Fred was still going strong and still fancying his chances with the harem of young girls he employed. The pub was divided into two sections, the larger being a sixteen-table restaurant which took most of the trade.

"Cheers, Fred!" Hunter said, taking the pint from the bar and lifting it to his lips.

The landlord twirled his moustache with the tips of two fingers. "Where's Jock tonight then?"

"Should be here in a minute," Hunter replied.

One of the waitresses from the restaurant came into the bar. She smiled at Hunter as she sauntered past the landlord, then bent over and plunged both hands into a box of salt and vinegar crisps. Her meaty buttocks threatened to burst from the material stretched round them. Fred gave her a firm slap on the rump; she gave a friendly protest, then sauntered back into the restaurant. The landlord always boasted of his conquests with the girls, who were all young and all good-looking, but Hunter could not blame him.

Lonely old bastard. I would do the same.

Come eight o'clock the Fox and Hounds had livened up, but still Jock had not arrived. Hunter thought it unlike Jock to be late for a booze-up. He thought about ringing round to see where he was, thinking he had probably been held up at the camp. He would give him another hour and, if Jock still hadn't arrived, take some bottles home for Jenny. At least then he would not feel so guilty about going out tonight.

~~~

Jenny sat curled up on the sofa in her dressing gown. It was the usual Friday night crap on TV, quiz shows and a repeat showing of *Columbo*. A sudden gust of wind rattled the sash windows in the house. The lace curtain twitched above the TV at a draft from outside. She shivered as a cold tingle ran up her spine, and the hairs on the nape of her neck stood on end. Carl had woken a little earlier, she could only guess because of the wind. There was another gust, and this time the closed door to the kitchen shook. The atmosphere change brought a chill to the room. She checked to make sure the electric fire was still on.

She had an uneasy feeling that someone or something was watching her; she looked up at the darkened window covered by a thin curtain of lace. She stood and slowly walked over to the window, pulled back a corner of the curtain, and peered into the darkness. She tried to see the long garden, where a central access path led to the other houses in the row. However, all she could see was her own transparent reflection in the glass.

The neighbour's bathroom light partially lit up her small yard, and then she saw that her back door was wide open. She dropped the curtain, opened the kitchen door, and walked into the dark room. The stale smell of food hung in the air, and a biting cold dampness seemed to be all round her. She reached the back door and slammed it shut.

"Must be the bloody lock," she murmured aloud and scrutinised the latch on the door. She switched on the kitchen light, and then someone grabbed her from behind. Jenny swung round just as the fluorescent tube flooded the room with brightness.

"You stupid bastard, you scared me to death!" she said, pushing herself away from Jock, then punching him in the arm.

"Well that'll teach you to keep your door locked, won't it?" He burst out laughing.

She switched out the light, and he followed her into the front room. Jock was much taller, just over six feet, and of a bigger build than Hunter, with fair hair, green eyes, and a light skin. He was also one of life's practical jokers. He would never take things too seriously, as he thought life was too short. He was a typical Royal Marine who lived for the moment and didn't take tomorrow for granted. Work hard, play hard.

Jock closed the kitchen door as Jenny stood in front of him; he grabbed her by her dressing gown belt and pulled her closer. She resisted slightly, stumbling a few steps, then smiled up at him. "I thought you were supposed to meet Hunter down the pub?"

"There's plenty of time, I thought I'd come and see my bit of stuff first."

He loosened the belt, pulled the gown over her shoulders, and let it drop to the floor. Her youthful body on display before him, he dropped on to his knees and began to explore her intimate regions with his mouth.

Jenny gasped with pleasure and gripped his hair. "You're mad coming here and doing this. Hunter will kill us."

Jock looked up at her. "He's got to catch us first!" He pulled her down onto the carpet and once again quenched her insatiable appetite for sex.

~~~

Five pints later and Jock's hour was nearly up. Hunter was still sitting at the bar, and by now the pub was heaving. Sally, one of the other girls from the restaurant, came in behind the bar after finishing her stint in the kitchen. She said hello to Hunter and quickly scanned the bar; no one needed serving. Fred gave her a cautious glance, just to remind her that she was there to work.

Sally was a plain-featured but attractive girl about nineteen who liked a good time. She certainly dressed to catch the eye, wearing a tight T-shirt and white Lycra cycling shorts that left nothing to the imagination. Her lightly tanned legs curved down to a pair of virgin white socks and the same colour plimsolls, giving her an unmerited air of innocence. Sally sat down opposite Hunter and lit a menthol cigarette. She had a soft spot for the commando, of which he knew because one of her friends had told him. He naturally was flattered and had to resist the urge to play on his good fortune.

"Where's your mate tonight then, Hunter?" Sally asked, taking a seductive draw on her cigarette.

"Dunno, Sally luv, probably on top of a bit of stuff, knowing him." Hunter emptied his glass and placed it back on the bar.

Sally screwed her face up at Hunter's last remark. "Same again?" she asked, reaching for his empty pint glass.

"Yeah, thanks." She placed the glass under the tap. "Take one for yourself as well?"

She placed his pint back in front of him, then reached over to the shelves, pulling out a bottle of sweet cider. She took off its top and lifted it to her soft red lips, gulping back the sweet sticky liquid. A dribble leaked from between her lips, and she caught it seductively with her tongue, not once taking her eyes off Hunter.

The landlord indicated a group of young lads, and she went over to serve them. The lads ogled her nubile young body, along with several other men. One of them plucked up the courage to ask her if she was wearing any knickers. She answered no and told the group she was not wearing a bra either. The young men roared with laughter, erupting with wolf whistles and shouts of "Get your tits out for the boys."

The landlord shouted for them to keep the noise down or get out. They elected to leave.

Hunter was just thinking about following them when the door crashed open and Jock stepped in, sending a sudden cold snap through the pub.

Sally saw him before Hunter did, alerting him to Jock's arrival.

As Jock stepped to his side, Hunter glanced over his shoulder and asked, "Where the fuck have you been?"

Jock pulled a five-pound note from his pocket and waved it in the direction of Sally, who was serving another customer.

"Ah that'd be telling, wouldn't it?"

Hunter wanted to know. "Yeah it would, so tell me."

Jock had to think of something quick. He could not really tell Hunter that he had just been screwing his wife, and that she had begged him for more.

The two men had been in the marines for the same length of time after taking their recruit training together. They had both seen action in the Gulf War and helped each other through. Around that time, Jock started an affair with Jenny. Hunter was no angel, he had affairs, but not on his own doorstep, usually when away from home, when they were on exercise. These moments of weakness would be down to being drunk, but it was the accepted norm of a married man in the Marine Corps to play away from home with other women.

Hunter would know that he had been with a woman, so maybe he should tell him part of the truth.

"I had to go round and see this bird, didn't I." Jock's annoying waving of the five-pound note paid off, and Sally came to serve him. He ordered a lager, and she snatched the money from his hand.

"What bird's this, then?" Hunter asked.

"Ah just someone I thought was a nonstarter, but she turned out to be a right little cracker in the end."

Sally came back with Jock's change. Both men left the bar and found a vacant table.

By eleven o'clock most of the customers had left and Fred shouted, "Time!" Hunter and Jock were still at the small table, with Hunter now feeling the effects of the alcohol. Sally and three other waitresses darted about collecting empty glasses and tidying up. Snide innuendoes from Jock to the girls were starting to wear a bit thin.

Finally Fred took Sally aside and told her to get the drunken bums out of the place. She obliged, and the four girls coaxed the two marines outside. Fred slammed the door behind them and bolted it shut.

~~~

The wind had now died to a soft breeze, but black clouds floated across the moonlit sky threatening a storm. Hunter took a few deep breaths. Sally was at his side, and she steadied him to his Land Rover as Jock made a grab for one of the other girls. She gave a playful shriek as the other two hit him, then made a run for Sally's Mini, parked in the far corner of the car park. Jock gave chase, screaming like a crazy man and adding to their excitement, but they beat him to the car, jumped in, and locked the doors behind them. Jock contorted his face against the Mini's windows. Muffled screams came from the vehicle, and the girls seemed to love the attention.

Hunter laughed, propped against the door of the Land Rover, watching. Sally wrapped her arms round Hunter's waist and stood on tiptoe, bringing her lips to meet his. Her kiss was passionate and tempting, she rubbed at the crotch of his Levi's, and he knew she could feel his excitement growing.

The lights in the car park suddenly went out, plunging them into moonlit darkness.

~~~

Fred looked out from his upstairs living room window and saw the dark figures below. He watched them for a moment, especially Hunter in his passionate embrace, then closed the curtains.

"Why don't ya piss off home?" he mumbled to himself, then pushed in a video and turned on the TV.

He sat back in his chair, lit a cigar, and waited for the screen to come alive. Distorted music emanated from the television before the picture appeared—something that sounded like the music from a curry house or a cheap Chinese restaurant—and Fred took a long draw on his cigar while the picture brightened. He found himself watching a naked woman on all fours grunting and groaning as two men dressed in seventies-style clothing gave it their all, one at each end.

~~~

Hunter pulled away from Sally's passion, his lips moist from hers. Her pale white face was tempting, but he still had Jenny on his mind. He pulled himself into the cab of the Land Rover.

"Why don't you come back to my place for a nightcap?" she asked, still holding on to his arm.

He knew what she meant, even if he was drunk. "No, I got to go home, but thanks." He leaned out of the cab and kissed her on the forehead, then slammed the door.

"Fair enough, you know where I live, if you want to see me." She stepped back. He started the engine, smiled at her, and lifted his hand up to Jock as he left the car park.

CHAPTER 2

Hunter stopped the Land Rover half in the drive, but mostly in the road. It was 11:30, and Jenny had been in bed reading a book. She heard the car door slam and swung herself out of bed. Hunter lurched through the front door and stumbled over a pair of her shoes. He steadied himself to his feet again and lifted his gaze to the top of the landing. In his semi conscious state, she looked angelic, that was until she opened her mouth giving him a load of abuse.

She stormed down the stairs like a guided missile, grabbed him hold. He wrapped his arms around her, trying to cuddle, as they crashed through the door of the front room.

She dropped him on the sofa, then straightened her robe. Hunter sat up trying to get his bearings. His head spun, making him feel nauseous, and he struggled to gather his thoughts.

"You can't go out without getting pissed, can you?" she shouted. She was ready for a fight.

"Look, I just had a few!" he retorted.

His slurring voice gave the game away. "Yeah, sounds like it. You just don't understand, do ya?"

Hunter made a grab for her legs, evidently not hearing a word she was saying, and she kicked him away.

"We haven't a penny to our names, and you go down the pub and get pissed." She leant closer to him; Hunter thought his luck was in. "What's this?" She pointed to the lipstick on his face. "You bastard, you've been with another woman, ain't you?"

Hunter heard that, and his mind went into freeze-frame. Sally! He remembered the kiss back at the pub.

He thought of an excuse, but there was none.

"Look, it was just a joke! Jock put some bird up to it, I swear. Ask him, ring the bastard up!" He was sobering up quicker than anticipated.

Jenny lunged forward grabbing him by the collar. "You're a lying bastard, I've had enough of your bullshit, I wanna divorce, you ain't fit to be a father! You're a nothing; you always were and always will be!" She was inches from his face.

Hunter grabbed her wrists. His temper started to build. "Yeah, so why fucking marry me then?" His voice croaked with emotion. This was the first time she had said such a thing.

"I married you because I felt sorry for you. Just look at yourself, you're a bum, people always said I could do better."

"Yeah, then why don't you?" He pushed her away, sending her sprawling on to the floor.

"I will! I can get another man just like that!" She snapped her fingers.

"Yeah I bet you could, you tart, that's all you are is a little tart!"

She sprang at him, digging her nails into the side of his face.

Hunter winced with the pain. Not even the alcohol could stop that. She gripped him and worked her fingers into the flesh. Hunter saw the look of hate in her eyes. She was like a different woman, like someone possessed. Blood flowed from the open wounds as she grappled to do more damage. He could feel the warm blood trickling down his face and realised she was intent on seriously hurting him. He cuffed her on the side of the head and sent her crashing to the carpet once more.

She jumped up immediately attacking him once again. Tears ran down her cheeks, whether it was due to the last blow to her head or just her emotions coming out all at once, Hunter did not know. He just had to stop her. He fended off the onslaught of blows with his hands, trying to push forward as he did so. Her screams of rage seemed to fill the house. Hunter punched out again, this time landing the blow on Jenny's forehead. She dropped like a brick and lay stunned on the floor. Her eyes were open, but no one seemed to be in.

He swayed to his feet and staggered to the kitchen, grabbed a cloth, and laid it on the slashes on his face. Through the open door, he saw Jenny shakily stand up. The boy's crying rang out in the silence, and she went to his aid. She did not give Hunter as so much as a glance.

He switched off the kitchen light and sat back down on the sofa, feeling worse than ever now. The adrenaline was still pumping, and he was about to be sick. He dashed into the kitchen once more and heaved his heart up.

~~~

SUNDAY

The morning light gradually crept through the downstairs back window, making its way across the floor, then onto Hunter's lifeless face. He stirred on the sofa as the shafts of light warmed his skin. The blood on his cheeks had dried.

He opened his eyes, unclear about the time or the state of his appearance. Slowly he swung his legs off the sofa and onto the floor, sitting up. He had a foul taste in his mouth. Vomit was stuck to the front of his shirt and a pool of the same dry substance lay on the carpet. Rubbing his temples, he looked around the room. In the cold light of day it seemed a disaster zone.

A movement from upstairs made him look towards the

ceiling, where Jenny was sleeping. He wondered how she was and whether she meant what she had said last night.

He stood and slowly walked into the kitchen; he stopped at the sink and turned on the tap. The washing-up bowl was on the drainer from last night, and remnants of vomit still clung to the sides of the stainless steel sink. He wiped away the evidence with the dishcloth, then took a long, cold drink from under the tap. He splashed water onto his face. It stung where it worked into the cuts and sent small trickles running down his cheeks again.

Then he moved into the hall towards the dimly lit stairway. Resolutely he started up. Reaching the top of the stairs. he looked at the closed bedroom door. Should he go in? It was his house after all, he told himself, but first he needed to tidy himself up. The bathroom door was wide open, and the toilet looked welcoming.

He relieved himself with a shudder of satisfaction and a quiet gasp of relief.

Carefully he did up his zipper and turned to face the medicine cabinet, which had two sliding mirror doors on its front. He examined the damage on his face, lightly rubbing his fingers along the puffy red skin. The salty perspiration on his fingers seeped into the open cuts, and the sting was enough to stop him from carrying on.

Hunter slid one of the reflective doors back, took out a small bottle of antiseptic liquid, then pulled a couple of feet toilet paper off the roll. The pain of the liquid on his face was nearly unbearable and he barely kept from crying out. Instead, he bit into his fist until the shock passed. He stripped down to just his trousers, wiped down his upper body with a flannel, and cleaned his teeth. To his relief, he felt nearly human again. However, there was still the wife.

He stepped out of the bathroom onto the landing, within a few yards of their bedroom. Something held him back though, an invisible force that seemed to prevent him from stepping any closer. He gave a ragged sigh, not believing a Royal Marine Commando was bottling out of seeing his own wife. Here was a man who had fought in a war and been shot at on the streets of Northern Ireland. *You gutless peace of shit, get in there, now!*

As he slowly opened the door, the hinges creaked briefly in protest. He stepped into the dimly lit room, his eyes fixing on the bed straightaway. There she was, asleep, her bare body partially covered by the duvet, Hunter was transfixed for a few moments then put his mind back into gear. He opened his small wardrobe and pulled out a clean pair of jeans. Out of nowhere he felt as if someone was watching him. As he opened one of the drawers on the dressing table to get a T-shirt, he glanced across at the bed again, seeing that Jenny was awake and watching him.

He smiled at her, wondering whether it was the right thing to do. *Bollocks, he did.*

"Morning. Sorry, did I wake you?" His voice was low, calm, and apologetic.

She shook her head slightly in answer. Her eyes looked dark, from either tears or lack of sleep or maybe both. A dark shadow above her eyebrows made Hunter remember the punch, He shook his head, trying to forget and hoping that she would forgive him. Sitting on the edge of the bed, he clasped her hand.

"I'm sorry, love, I'm really sorry!" He pulled her hand to his lips and kissed it.

She stared at him briefly, then sat up. Putting her arms around him, she started to sob.

He held her tightly and kissed the top of her head.

"I'm sorry, I'm sorry," he kept saying.

She tried to talk through the tears, barely whispering the word "Sorry."

Hunter placed his hands on both sides of her face looking at her. "Let's forget about last night, it won't happen again."

She nodded. He kissed her tear-soaked lips. Abruptly she saw the damage that she had done and pulled away to take a closer look. He let her touch the puffy red gouges.

"I'm the one who should be sorry, I've hurt you!" Her voice was soft, broken with emotion. It seemed the damage frightened her. She kissed the inflamed wounds, smoothing his head as she did so. They lay on the bed for a few moments, in silence. A cockerel sounded off in the distance, probably from old Venner's farm.

Little Carl started to stir in the next room, the squeak of his teddy bear being bashed against the wall made Hunter want to go and see the little chap. He kissed Jenny on the forehead and swung his legs from the bed. Standing up now, he looked down at his wife. Her eyes were closed, her breathing heavy. Quietly he left the room, not wanting to waken her. Hunter opened the door to Carl's bedroom and stepped in.

The boy bounced frantically in his cot with a big smile on his face when he saw his dad. Hunter pulled the boy into his arms, then opened the curtains to let the new day into the room. He stood at the window and rubbed his hand across the condensation on the glass, and Carl tried to do the same. Hunter pointed out the hills in the distance to the boy, who also started pointing, at everything and anything.

"Shall we go out for a ride today, son, out in the country, eh?" Hunter looked at the boy, then out the window again. The boy laughed and slapped Hunter on his damaged cheek, making him wince.

It was nearly nine thirty in the morning when Hunter took up some breakfast for Jenny. She was still asleep, her naked body wrapped around the duvet, holding it like a lover. Hunter placed the tray of fried breakfast on the bedside table. He then opened the curtains slowly, letting the light cover her lily white skin. It seemed to glow, its whiteness nearly blinding.

"Come on, sleepy, I've done you breakfast!" he said softly, sitting on the edge of the bed.

She gave a semiconscious moan of pleasure, pushing her lower half under the duvet. Hunter stroked her bare buttocks, and she moaned again. She seemed to come back into reality.

~~~

Jenny's eyes opened, and she got her bearings, rolled over,

and then saw her husband. It definitely was back to reality: no Jock.

She smiled at him thinly, sat up, and looked at the feast. She wasn't in the mood for fried food, and she didn't like it at the best of times, but she'd make out it was a good gesture and eat the greasy shit. Jenny pulled the duvet under her armpits and across her breasts, then sheepishly took a piece of toast and started to nibble on one corner.

"Where's Carl?" she asked.

"In his playpen." He smiled, nodding towards the door, indicating that the boy was downstairs.

Jenny looked at him, almost staring. She put down her piece of toast. She had something to say.

"D'you think it'll honestly work from now on?"

Hunter frowned. "What d'you mean?"

"Us, me and you. Can we make it work? We do nothing but argue and fight all the time." She pushed the tray aside and swung her legs out of bed.

"Look, we do that because we're hard up. If we had a decent amount coming in each week, we'd ... well, we'd live like kings, and I'll bet we wouldn't even have a cross word!" Hunter smiled, hoping that for once he had it right.

She grabbed her dressing gown from the cupboard door and slipped it on, then sat in front of her dressing table and looked into the large mirror. She lifted one hand to her head and rubbed her fingers along the dark greyish blue bruise that hung above her eyes. You could almost see the shape of the knuckles. Hunter, watching from the bed, bowed his head, perhaps in shame. She looked at his reflection as she prodded the coloured flesh, contempt in her eyes.

"Look, if we're going to stay together, you better know one thing: if you hit me once more, I'm gone!" She turned to face him. "And you'd better get yourself a job pretty soon, because if you remember, you're out of the marines at the end of next week!"

Hunter knew that fact all too well.

"Yeah, all right, things will be different, you'll see. We'll be all right. I'll get a good job, earn plenty of money!" Hunter leapt over the bed and knelt on the floor, curling his arms around her waist. She gazed at her own blank face in the mirror; she had heard it all before. She chose to ignore his closeness and started to put on her makeup.

"Tell you what, how about the three of us go for a picnic today, eh? Little Carl will love that!" Hunter tried to make it sound exciting.

She shrugged. "The weatherman said yesterday it's going to rain!" She rubbed some foundation cream into the bruise and winced as she did so.

"Nah, it looks all right out there." He gave a quick glance out of the window. "A bit cloudy. but that doesn't matter."

She gave a deep sigh. She wasn't the outdoor type, but she thought it better than staying in all day, looking at the same four walls she looked at all week.

"Where were you thinking of going?" she asked, not bothering to keep the indifference out of her voice.

Hunter thought for a moment. "Leave it to me, it'll be a surprise!" He jumped to his feet and left the room.

Jenny listened to the sound of his feet disappear down the stairs and looked down between her legs. She pulled aside the dressing gown, tilting her leg towards the light. There on the inside of her leg, just below a few strands of wispy pubic hair, was a small red bruise, a love bite, which Jock had administered the night before.

~~~

Hunter checked the oil and the water in the old Series 2 Land Rover he owned. The bodywork on the vehicle was tatty, but the V8 engine was sound. He had bought the Land Rover mainly because it would be cheap on parts; he nicked them from the stores at the camp. They didn't care; just throw them a few pounds.

Jenny owned a small Mini, which was just about fit for the scrap heap. It was not road legal as it did not pass its yearly test, but she still drove it, saying it was her independence. She liked to drive to see her parents, who lived in the nearby town of Taunton. Hunter always let her go alone; he hated them, and the feeling was mutual. They kept telling her that she could have done better than to marry him. She might even think they were right. Hunter was not a local. He and Jock both came from Liverpool, so to the locals Hunter was a foreigner and did not fit in.

He was looking forward to this family picnic on Exmoor. He had been on stakeouts up there on numerous occasions with the marines sniffing out poachers and looking for the Exmoor beast. He liked the place; it was desolate, wild, and certainly mysterious.

Jenny had dressed up Carl ready for the big outdoors. The only part of him visible was his little red face, the rest of him wrapped in a thick fluorescent pink all-in-one snowsuit. Hunter slid the baby chair out of the Mini and into the centre seat of the Land Rover. Jenny slipped on her knee-high leather boots and put on her Barbour coat, then picked up the wicker picnic basket in one arm and Carl in the other, stepping out onto the drive. Hunter was waiting in the Land Rover with the engine running. She secured Carl in his seat, then jumped in and slammed the thin door behind her. She said nothing, just looked across at the neighbour's window, giving it a menacing stare.

~~~

Mrs Roberts of number 6 Hare Lane, who lived next-door, watched behind the relative safety of her net curtain as the noisy vehicle pulled out of the drive and up the road. She cocked her head as close to the window as she could, until they were out of view.

The old woman of sixty was the root of the village grapevine. Every bit of juicy gossip started from her, all that was worth hearing anyway. She was even known to place a glass to the partition wall so she could hear the Hunter's when they argued.

Her husband Fred sat in his favourite armchair. Silent as usual, he put up with his wife's nosy antics. He got on with Hunter, and he had a bit of a soft spot for Jenny, ever since he had seen her in the backyard sunbathing topless.

"I wonder where they're off to now. Probably taking that poor child down the pub, It should never be allowed." She left the window, scuttling back to her favourite chair by the window.

Old man Roberts put down his paper and looked across at his wife, who was back up onto her feet again twitching at the curtain. She had seen a movement in the garden opposite, and her eagle eyes were watching.

"What makes you think they're taking that little lad down the pub?" the old man asked wearily.

Mrs Roberts waved her hand at him signalling for him to shut up so she could concentrate on the burglary opposite. Her hopes of action were dashed when she saw it was only the owner of the house cleaning his windows.

"What did you say?" she snapped, sitting back down in her chair.

"I said how do you know they're taking the little boy down the pub?"

She gave him a reprimanding glare. "Well, it stands to reason, he's always down the pub, so he'd bring the boy up the same!"

The old man shook his head and lifted his paper again. He knew it was futile to argue. She would win; she always did, argument by attrition.

CHAPTER 3

Twenty minutes of noisy and uncomfortable driving and the Land Rover was in the splendid setting of the Exmoor National Park. The hum of the road through the rigid suspension and the droning of the massive V8 engine had sent the young boy into a deep sleep, his head resting on his mother's arm.

Hunter needed a nice spot for the picnic and had over twenty thousand acres to choose from. He swung the vehicle off the main road and headed for the heart of the moor. He wanted to see the real Exmoor and not the touristy side of it. The weather was still good, A few dark clouds threatened in the distance, but Hunter had his fingers crossed. He wanted a good day with his family, no rows, fights, or cross words. He just wanted to have a good time and hoped that Jenny might as well.

Carl woke up as Hunter drove into a little village called Oare, a place that had been untouched for hundreds of years and looked it. The road into the village was more like a track, wide enough for one car. The only new and modern things they could see were the signposts that pointed to various attractions on the moors, like Lorna Doone's farmhouse and the church where she got married. However, Hunter was not interested in that; he just wanted to get out in the middle of nowhere and relax.

Jenny pointed out a small herd of ponies to Carl. They trotted across the road in front of the car, looking as weathered as the moor. She lifted Carl onto her lap, to give him a better view. Hunter slowed down to a snail's pace through the village. The thatched cottages of whitewashed stone sat on the edge of the road with no paths, and no road markings, tourists or locals in sight. Jenny voiced her approval about a little cottage that sat amongst a backdrop of oak and elm trees. It had a little stream running through the garden and across the road. She pointed the stream out to the boy, but he was more interested in a goat tethered to an embankment outside the gate to another house.

"Have you ever seen a place like this? The land that time forgot." Hunter laughed, stopping outside what he hoped was a shop.

All three of them peered from the Land Rover into the window of the building; their own front room looked bigger.

"Is it a shop?" Jenny asked curiously, that being the first civil words she had said to her husband all day.

He looked back at her. "I think so ... well, there's an ice cream sign outside, so it must be." He stepped from the vehicle, glancing back at Jenny and the boy. "If I ain't back in ten minutes, call out the marines: they might have eaten me or something!" He smiled at her.

She conceded a little snort of laughter, and a smirk came to her lips.

"D'you want anything?" he asked.

She shook her head and watched him disappear into the gloomy building.

The door rang a small bell hanging on the frame above his head when he opened it. Hunter looked around the tiny room: Homemade shelves crammed with tinned food and household supplies cluttered up the wall; a long bench in the centre of the room was stacked to the rafters with boxes of vegetables and fruit. The dingy room had a musty smell, something stale with a tinge of mothballs, and it got stronger as he approached the worn and tatty counter. A garden fork, spade, and hoe leaned against it. Hunter propped both elbows on the counter and waited for some service. Maybe there was nobody home. He looked across the room and out towards the Land Rover. Jenny was still peering in. He gazed up at the ceiling, cobwebs as thick as net curtains hung from the low oak rafters, with spiders that oddly looked to him like toupees on legs. "Definitely not environmentally friendly, this place!" he muttered, inspecting the flagstone floor.

"Yes, me dear, what can I do for you?" a woman's voice said from behind him.

He jumped at the unexpected voice and spun around to face the woman. She was about five foot nothing, with black shoulder-length hair that was plaited at the back. She was a strange sight. Her face was pale, in fact deathly white, but wrinkled. The woman looked in her late forties, but something about her gave him the impression she was a lot older. Maybe it was her voice, which seemed tired, exhausted by life, but whatever it was, Hunter could not put his finger on it.

"Blimey, you frightened the life out of me."

Her dark lifeless eyes stared at him, not seeming to blink. "I'm sorry, I was in the back room and wasn't quite sure if it was the shop bell or not. So what can I do for you?" she asked again.

He composed himself. "Well, can I have three packets of salt and vinegar crisps, a can of Coke, and a couple of Mars bars?"

The strange woman shuffled back and forth putting the objects in front of him; he handed her cash and waited for the change. She walked over to a small table that stood beside the curtain-covered doorway that must have led to her living quarters. On the table sat a cigar box where she dropped in the money, taking out the appropriate change.

She was definitely strange, verging on the weird. Her long black dress stopped at her ankles then a shabby pair of leather shoes took over. They looked to be from the '50s and the dress looked older, but then again who was he to criticise, he still wore cowboy boots.

Her icy hand touched his as she gave him back the change; her fingers looked like claws, not those of a forty-year-old woman. Hunter thanked her, then remembered the wine. He wanted to surprise Jenny with a nice bottle of wine for the picnic.

"I don't suppose you sell wine or spirits?"

"No, my love, you'll have to go and see Eli for that sort of thing!"

"Um, who's Eli?" Hunter asked, picking up his shopping. The woman came out from behind the counter, and Hunter followed her to the door of the shop, then out beside the Land Rover. He dropped the goodies on the driver's seat and stood beside the woman.

"Eli's is just up this road, past Mrs Gore's cottage." The woman pointed, and Hunter peered in that direction. "You won't miss it; it's got a sign outside, the Black Dog Inn."

"The Black Dog Inn, there's a pub here?" he asked. This was music to his ears.

The woman nodded and looked over to Jenny and the boy sitting in the Land Rover. Her lifeless dark eyes lit up when she saw Carl. She shuffled over to the driver's-side passenger door and peered in through the open window. Carl pulled closer to his mother; Jenny smiled politely at the stranger.

"Ah, what a lovely boy," the woman said, her eyes widening, a smile creased her maggoty white face.

"Thank you," Jenny answered, just to make conversation.

Carl started to cry and tremble with fear. The woman just stared. Only God knew what she was thinking about, but it was almost as if Carl knew. His cries turned to screams, near hysterics as Jenny held on to him tightly and gave Hunter a pleading look. He got the hint and pushed past the old woman, then got into the Land Rover.

"Well, thanks for your help. Bye." Hunter started the engine and headed for the pub.

He looked in the rear-view mirror, expecting to see the woman still standing in the road. She had gone, and he thought nothing of it.

The pub was just up the road and round the corner as directed. He could feel a thirst coming on. Jenny scowled when she saw the faded pub sign hanging from an oak gibbet with the words *Black Dog Inn* in old English writing above and below a painted black creature, which must have been the dog. The pub looked as old if not older than the rest of the quaint cottages in the village, and about the same size. There was no car park, only a patch of grass across the road, which looked well chewed up by the odd vehicle or two. The wheels spun as he pulled the four-by-four on to the wet patch of ground, churning up what was left of the grass. Carl was only just starting to calm down, his sobs now turning into a whimper, with a little careful nursing from his mother.

"I thought this was to be a family day out," she snapped, "not ending up in the fucking pub!"

Hunter expected the outburst and was ready. "Look, just calm down, I'll be in and out in a matter of minutes. I'm only going to get a bottle of wine, that's all!"

Her lips stiffened, her face said it all, and she silently went back to nursing the boy. *Will wonders never cease.* He stepped from the cab and on to the sodden earth, slamming the door behind him, which made the boy jump out and start crying again. Hunter strode through the gate and up the short cobbled path to the closed pub door, where he glanced back at the Land Rover and then entered.

~~~

Jenny peered up at the sign hanging over the cobbled path, its rusty metal hinges creaking rhythmically in the westerly breeze. She stroked Carl's head to soothe him and studied the sign.

"It doesn't look nothing like a black dog, more like a ..." She paused. *What does it look like?*

The so-called dog was silhouetted against a huge full moon.

Its black shabby coat had a blue tinge to it, its hair thicker and longer along the neck, like a mane. However, the eyes looked almost real, even human, but cold, lifeless and moon blue. She thought the artist must have been on something when he painted it.

"A wolf, that's what it looks like, a wolf!" she said, looking down at the boy, almost as though she was telling him and not herself.

"Bloody thing gives me the creeps, Carl, the whole bloody place does for that matter!" She shook herself as a sudden chill ran through her body.

The boy started to tremble again, his whimpers turning to an all-out scream, his eyes wide as if looking for something or someone. Jenny tried to calm him again, but nothing worked. The boy was having a fit.

"Bloody Hunter!" she screamed. Her frustration was beginning to show. "What the fuck are you doing in there?"

She glanced over to the pub, trying to see him through the window, but nothing. Then she caught sight of a dark figure in the rear-view mirror, and her heart started to race. Some fifty yards away stood the woman who had given them directions to the pub, who had made the boy tremble with fear and panic at the very sight of her. The woman was standing on the grass by the turning in the road, just staring at the Land Rover.

Jenny spun round to face her, looking out of the rear window. Even at this distance she could swear that the woman was smiling at them, a malevolent smile that sent a shiver up her spine. By this time Carl had started to vomit, his excitement was that great. The woman still watched. Jenny sounded the Land Rover horn, and the woman started to walk towards them. She tried to mop up the vomit from the floor, keeping one eye on the boy and the other eye on the approaching dark figure.

~~~

Hunter strolled out of the Black Dog Inn with the residue of a quick pint on his lips and a bottle of wine grasped firmly in one hand. He crossed the road and opened the car door. The smell of vomit hit him at the same time as the abuse. He took a deep breath and climbed in.

"You said a couple of minutes! Not ten—"

"What's up with him?" Hunter cut her off; he was concerned about Carl. He looked down at the boy.

"This place, I expect it's enough to make anyone sick." The boy started to calm down. "And that bloody woman's lurking round back there." She pointed with her thumb over her shoulder; Hunter turned to look and then faced her.

"Where?"

"There ..." Jenny looked back out the window; the woman was gone. "Well, she *was* there, weird bitch!" The child's crying had stopped.

Hunter started the engine and pulled away, much to the relief of Jenny. He took them out of the village and onto a road that stretched across the moors, a bleak windswept place that had stood the tests of time, from the Stone Age and the Romans to right now, the place had not changed. It was raw and beautiful but merciless to those that did not respect it. Skeletal trees, sculpted by the weather, contorted themselves on the skyline, standing here and there like ghostly apparitions among the gorse and blackthorn.

It was a strange and eerie place, but something about it excited Hunter. A red post marked the turning he had to take. Jenny held the boy closer as the road faded into a track that led down to what looked like a wooded valley in the distance. Branches slapped against the front window making the noise nearly unbearable in the cab.

"Where the hell are you going, d'you know?" Jenny snapped, a little afraid that they might get stuck in the middle of nowhere. She strapped the boy back into his chair and then braced herself.

"This bloke back at the pub told me this is a right out-of-the-way place, he said it's the real Exmoor." Hunter looked at his wife. "And that's what we want, in' it?"

She could not care less; she just wanted to get out of this tumble dryer on wheels. The Land Rover had to be put into four-wheel drive as the track became a sodden mass of mud and grass, but it still laboured in places, the wheels slipping and sinking in the boggy conditions.

Finally they reached the woods. Hunter drove along the tree line and out onto the open space of the moor. "Here we are then, this'll do!" He stopped the vehicle and climbed out, stretched and breathed deeply.

"Just taste that fresh air!" he exclaimed, as if you really could taste it.

Jenny unbuckled Carl, lifting him out of his seat. Hunter pulled the picnic from the back and looked for a likely spot to set up camp. A small clearing surrounded by knee-high gorse and grass looked like the spot: the gorse was a natural windbreak, and there was not a piece of dog shit in sight.

An hour passed and the picnic was going well. The wine was having its effect on both of them. Jenny was starting to enjoy herself, and even the weather stayed clement, a miracle for the end of October. Hunter had taken a go at teaching the boy to play football, but it ended up more like rugby, with Carl picking up the ball and making a run for it.

Jenny watched, lying on the car blanket. Seeing how much Hunter loved the boy, she thought how it would tear his world apart if she separated the two of them, but living this lie was destroying her already. She loved Hunter but thought she loved Jock more, or was it just the excitement of having forbidden fruit? Whatever it was, it was clearly affecting their marriage, and the simple fact was that she wanted both of them.

The sun peered from the clouds, warming up the setting. Hunter came back to the blanket then sat, leaving the boy running around with the ball. He lay down beside Jenny, slipping his arm around her waist and gazed up at her profile, the sun giving her cheeks a healthy glow. She kept her eyes on Carl.

"This is nice here; we should do this more often!"

She looked down at him and smiled, raising her eyebrows to signify a weak yes.

"D'you know something? I love you!" He nodded as if in emphasis, then lifted the corner of her T-shirt and kissed her bare back.

He hoped for the same sort of response but got none. His hands slipped higher inside the shirt and fondled her breasts, and her nipples started to swell. Carl ran back over; he wanted his mum. She gave him his beaker of juice and cradled him in her arms, and soon the boy started to sleep.

Hunter stood up and thought he would explore this place a bit. He found a worn earth path not far from the picnic area that cut through the gorse and into the woods. It looked well used, but he saw no tracks or footprints. He would follow it, find out where it went.

The trees became thicker the deeper he went, and the track was now flanked by these ancient giants. A snapping of twigs from behind made him turn, looking into the dark shapes of the woods. He saw nothing but had the feeling that someone was watching him. He smiled, thinking maybe it was Jenny wanting to play games, so he carried on and ignored the slight noises that followed him.

He saw a break in the trees up ahead; it looked like a clearing, maybe a field. It must be right in the centre of the woods, he thought, daring to step on the lush green grass, but it looked so unnatural, like a manicured cricket pitch. Hunter stepped into the clearing, at once awestruck and uneasy. He followed the path nearer to the centre of this circle of trees, where it branched off in two directions around another perfect circle of stones that stood about five feet apart. The grey stones stood out of the ground about knee high. He reached down and touched one of the objects; its surface was smooth and felt warm to the touch.

"Must be the sun!" He followed the path with his eyes to the centre of the ring, stopping at a stone some six feet long and four feet across. This one, rather than standing, was lying flat on the ground almost like a table. At the head of the stone table stood the biggest of them all, a good nine feet high and two feet at its base, like a termite mound made out of rock. The earth around the bottom of the table stone was well worn, and it was the same with all the other stones except the tallest one. There was grass growing around the bottom, untouched and yet well cropped short. Hunter walked over to it, running his hand along the flat stone then up to the big one, which felt cold, icy cold. For some reason he wanted to keep touching it. He placed his other hand on its surface and felt every contour.

Who put them here? They must weigh a couple of tons each. He looked back to the flat stone. Blackened stains running down its side caught his eye, and he knelt for a closer inspection. The stains ran all the way down to the soaked earth.

The stain was everywhere, in every crevice of the stone; he ran his finger along some of the dried substance, resting his other hand in the soft wet mud at the bottom of the stone. A familiar smell seemed to be stronger the closer he was to the soil.

What is it? Bollocks; come on, Hunter. He knew the smell.

He shook his head in frustration and then examined the dried substance on his fingertip. Against the fleshy colour of his finger the powder looked brownish, maybe even red, and then he saw it *was* red. He rolled the red powder between thumb and forefinger, the moisture from his skin turning it a definite shade of red.

"It's blood!" he whispered. Another look at the table stone showed him the dried red stains were everywhere. Hunter stood up, studying the other stones that encircled him. He counted twelve in all, and all looked the same distance apart.

"Must have been here for hundreds of years, blimey!"

He leaned across the stone table, resting his hands on its surface, and wondered what use it might have had, and then thought of the time. "Shit!" he exclaimed pulling up his sleeve to check his watch and then he saw that the webs between his fingers were dark with blood. He looked at his palm, first thinking that he had cut himself without knowing. A thick crimson clot stuck to his palm, looking like a blood red oyster. He shook it off, letting it fall onto the stone table.

Then suddenly he realised what the fetid smell was. It was blood, but he could not be smelling only the stained table stone. He looked down to his feet where moments before his hand had been. A patch of soil about two feet long and six inches wide looked a lot darker than the earth around it. He pushed the toe of his training shoe into the wet mud, bringing up a red puddle around the sole. So much blood, and where did it all come from?

Maybe poachers used the stone table to cut up the deer they caught "Yeah that's it!" He had convinced himself.

Hunter took another quick look around, then hastily made his way back to Jenny. He wanted out of there. He left the mysterious clearing and jogged back through the darkened woods. He heard no one behind him.

CHAPTER 4

Coming out of the forest, he followed the path back through the gorse, his feet slipping in the wet mud. Now here were some tracks, his own. He could see the Land Rover and the picnic rug, but he could not see Jenny.

It was her following me, it must have been!

His pace steadied to a walk as he approached the blanket. Carl's buggy was facing away from him, and Carl was in it. Hunter smiled down at the sleeping face of his son. His bright orange dummy moved slightly as the boy took comfort from the rubber teat.

"Where's your mother disappeared to then, son?" he asked, scanning the countryside around him. He stroked the tip of his finger gently across Carl's chubby red cheek; the boy flinched slightly but did not wake.

"Where are you?" he whispered.

A large blackthorn bush shook slightly among the gorse; Hunter had seen it out of the corner of his eye. He dropped to the ground. Royal Marine Hunter P042516W was ready for action. He monkey-crawled into the gorse, then snaked through the undergrowth until he was close to the blackthorn bush. Slowly he got to his feet, peering through the black mass of sticks and thorns. Jenny had just pulled up her knickers and was straightening her jogging bottoms when Hunter announced his presence.

"What you up to then?" He jumped into full view, barking his question like a regimental sergeant major.

Jenny gasped with fright, quickly looking to see who it was.

"You stupid bastard, why don't you grow up." She started to climb over the bushes heading back to the picnic area. Hunter laughing did not help matters.

"What were you doing in here anyway?"

"What do you think I was doing?"

He viewed the ground where she had been standing. A rolled up piece of tissue lay on a glistening patch of grass.

"Ah!" He knew.

Hunter followed her back to the blanket. She sat first, then he flopped down beside her. The sun had retreated again behind the grey clouds, and it looked like a storm had erupted in the far distance, casting a black veil across the skyline. Slowly it advanced towards them, but Hunter was not in any rush to pack things up. He knew it would take an hour at least if not more to reach them, if indeed the wind did not change. Jenny had not seen the oncoming darkness, so he was not about to tell her. It was still hot even without the sun, a sort of tropical heat, humid and muggy, the worst kind of heat. This was God's way of telling you that an electrical storm was coming, so get your head down.

Hunter liked storms, the rougher the better. God could judge you in a storm, and it was the ultimate buzz to him.

Jenny was sitting up drinking the last of the wine; Hunter thought he would carry on from where he'd left off last time he was on the blanket, before the boy interrupted him. They were both in the same positions. He pulled up her T-shirt again, kissing her back softly, while his left hand gradually crept up the outside of her T-shirt and began to fondle her breasts. She gave no reaction—just drank her wine and viewed the countryside.

Hunter pulled on her nipples from the outside of her shirt. He knew she was becoming aroused; he knew her like the back of his hand, and this was the way she liked to play it.

Jenny glanced down at his hand massaging her breast, then pushed him away. "Your hands are covered in blood, and it's all over my T-shirt, look at it!"

Hunter had forgotten about the blood, just as he had forgotten momentarily about the stone circles. "Shit! Sorry." he said, looking at the red grubby pinch marks on the material around her nipples.

He pulled up several clumps of grass and wiped his hands in it. The blood seemed ground into his skin, but it came off with a bit of hard work, leaving his hands a tint of crimson and green.

"Have you cut yourself?" she asked, slipping off her T-shirt to give the garment closer inspection.

"No," he said, staring at her bare breasts; the delicate white handfuls needed some attention, he thought.

"Well, where did it come from?" She spat on a handkerchief and tried to wipe the blood from the shirt. "This is ruined!"

"Back there somewhere." He nodded towards the forest but did not take his eyes off her chest. "In the middle of the forest, there's loads of it in the grass; must be poachers got a deer or something. You know by the stone circle."

"Cruel bastards! What d'you mean I know?" She puckered her lips to spit again onto the handkerchief.

Hunter's eyes were transfixed on the now goose-pimpled flesh of her breasts.

"Don't come the old innocent with me," A smile hung on his lips. "You followed me in there."

She dropped the shirt onto her lap, looked at him, and frowned. "What d'you mean I followed you in there? I was here all the time, d'you think I'd leave Carl on alone?"

His eyes left her breasts, checking out her face. She looked serious. Maybe it was not her. He wondered who it could have been.

"No I don't suppose you would. Ah well, never mind."

He made a dive for her breasts, and she shrieked at the attack; both of them looked back at the boy, hoping that they had not woken him. They had not; he was still asleep, and they carried on the fight. She forgot about the blood-stained yellow T-shirt, throwing it aside as Hunter kissed and licked her chest. His hands slid under the elastic waistband of her trousers, into her knickers, and onto her moist, warm vagina.

She pushed him away. "Not here."

"Come on, there's no one about." He tried to continue.

"No. I said not here!"

He got up onto his knees looking for a suitable place. There was a clearing about twenty yards into the gorse just behind them.

"Over there then!"

Before she could agree, he had snatched up the rug, sending plastic plates and beakers flying across the ground. He headed for the love nest, pulling her behind him. They both scampered into the gorse, leaving the boy happily asleep in his buggy. Within minutes Hunter's grunts of pleasure could be heard.

~~~

Jenny stared at the sky between the branches of the small twisted tree that sheltered them. Slowly she let the pleasure engulf her body; he would satisfy her before she was done with him. Sweat dripped from his brow after about fifteen minutes, his pumping rhythm beginning to slow. She cocked her leg around his and rolled him onto his back. Now she was in charge, she was on top.

Her movement was slower but more satisfying; she rode him like a horse, squatting up and down on top of him. She knew it was a turn-on for Hunter just watching her; she was a performer, every movement tried and tested, and she loved it. She had a class act. Every look, every lick of the lips was to provoke orgasm. She nearly pushed him over the edge several times, but she had her ways of holding him until she was ready. She wanted satisfying, she did not care about him.

She began moving faster, moaning louder as she felt her climax coming on. Hunter squeezed her swollen red nipples, then held her taut, heaving body between his strong hands. Beads of sweat now lined her brow; she felt the flush in her cheeks.

She slowed down slightly, her attention drawn away from the lovemaking. She had the feeling that someone was watching her and had been for a while—since she jumped into the driver's seat anyway. Which did not bother her; she was used to a bit of voyeurism, in fact it was another turn-on for her. Back in her teens, she had ended up in bed with her girlfriend and four lads, all of them taking turns to shag the living daylights out of one another. At first she was a little shy but soon found out what a turn-on it was. Of course Hunter knew nothing of her past sex life—only what she thought he should know, which wasn't a lot.

She could not see her onlooker, but she knew someone was there.

I hope they like what they see, she thought.

She could picture the person behind a bush nearby, trousers round his ankles and giving himself a hand job, wishing it was himself underneath her.

Jenny felt Hunter's orgasm explode inside her, which triggered her own climax as she milked the last drips from him. She flopped down on top of him, and he pulled the rug over them both. The wind had a chill in it now, and the air smelt like fresh-cut grass. The rain was on its way. Both of them lay there for a while in a lover's embrace, neither one wanting the chill air to touch their damp nakedness.

Jenny uncoupled herself from Hunter, stood up, found her knickers and trousers, and put them on. She combed her fingers through her hair as she gave the surroundings the once-over, in case she could see the pervert, if there was one. However, she could see nothing.

Hunter too pulled up his underwear and trousers and sat up. "What are you looking for?" He was staring at her still naked top half.

"Nothing!" she said, but she knew he could hear the satisfaction in her voice.

At a distant rumble of thunder, Hunter glanced at the clouds. The storm was approaching, a demonic black regiment across the skyline ready to attack, the wind heralding its approach.

"Blimey, it's a wonder Carl never woke up then," Jenny said, starting to tiptoe back through the prickly gorse to the picnic area and the boy. "Usually a bit of thunder and he screams the place down."

"Yeah, looks like we're in for quite a storm," Hunter said, adding, "Better get things packed!"

Jenny reached the scattered plastic cutlery, gathered it up, and tossed it into the cool box, glancing at Carl's buggy, which was facing away from her. "Come on, sleepyhead, time you woke up!"

Hunter stood up rearranging his clothes, picking off the bits of grass and moss. Jenny had picked up her crumpled yellow T-shirt, examined the bloodstains once more, and slipped it on, mentioning once again how the garment was ruined.

She snatched up the cool box and the empty wine bottle and headed for the Land Rover. A bolt of forked lightning lit up the grey-blue sky, landing in the forest nearby with a deafening explosion of thunder. The black army was nearly on them, the wind shaking trees and bushes alike, heavy rain coming a hundred yards behind.

Jenny looked back at the boy's buggy expecting him to be terrified at the last bout of thunder. Her heart missed a beat; fear shook her whole body.

"Hunter?" she screamed, running towards the buggy.

The wind whistled around the bushes and trees, and the atmosphere was crackling. Hunter came bounding over the bushes until he reached Jenny's side. The boy was gone!

"He's gone, he's fucking gone!" Jenny was shaking and began shouting the boy's name.

"Look, just calm down," Hunter said, but his voice was unsteady.

"Calm down, calm down, your son's fucking gone!" she shouted hysterically in Hunter's face.

The noise from the wind, the sudden wind that made them yell, then snatched away their words, made the problem far worse, and the rain was also without mercy. The black curtain swept toward them across the moors, and the heaviest cloudburst she had ever seen instantly drenched them.

Hunter shouted, "How did he get out buggy? Did you strap him in properly?" He had grabbed her by the shoulders.

"Yes, I always do. Where is he? Where is he?"

~~~

Hunter looked at the path. It emerged from the gorse quite close to the buggy. He thought of the stone circle.

They had to brace themselves against the freak winds and shield their eyes from the cutting rain. The noise of both elements would drown out any child's cries—if there were any to be heard.

"You look for him around here. I'll go look down this way." He pointed to the track, she nodded, and they started their search.

CHAPTER 5

Hunter screamed the boy's name, but his screams were drowned out by Mother Nature. He fell several times, covering himself in black peaty mud. The path was now becoming a stream, and the water was making everything a quagmire. Hunter pushed his way into the blackthorn bushes and gorse, hoping that the boy was sheltering from the storm. The thorns tore at his flesh as he felt around the spiky foliage with his hands. He stumbled to the edge of the woods, trying impossibly to cover every piece of ground he could see. He looked for footprints, but the torrents of water running down the tracks wiped everything clean. Marine training was forgotten, and blind panic set in. A massive thunderclap above his head made him dive instinctively for cover, the deafening crash adding to his torment. Emotion welled up inside him, the frustration, the hatred of humanity and of God, the rage that impelled him to fight the world and the certainty he could win.

"Carl," he screamed, his voice becoming hoarse.

"Oh God help me." He looked to the mass of blackness above, raising his fist helplessly.

He tried to listen for the sound of the boy crying. He could hear nothing. Darkness was no more than an hour away; he had to find him before then. He went back to scanning the gorse around him and caught sight of something bright orange. Hunter scrambled on all fours towards the object. Large clods of mud weighed down his training shoes, and traction was nearly impossible on the slippery incline. It was Carl's dummy.

He must be here. Hunter shouted for him again, several times. There was no reply.

Lightning lit up the grey sky, strobing the dim countryside like a photographer's flash catching the setting forever. Another clap of thunder shook the ground. He clenched the boy's dummy in his hand, then saw the track that led into the forest, to the stone circle. He had to go in.

The trees shook around him, their bony claws reaching for him on the track. Now the forest was dark, a deathly darkness that engulfed him and every living thing inside, if indeed there was anything living there. He shouted to either side of the track, looking and searching, looking for the small pink snowsuit that protected his son from the wrath of God. Ahead he could see the clearing, the stones, and the forest beyond that. He felt like it was expecting him, drawing him nearer, willing him to come closer ... it wanted him.

Hunter kept shouting for the boy, stepping on to the wet grass of the clearing. There seemed to be a mist forming around the outside of the stone circle, a mist that crept across the ground at knee height towards the forest and Hunter. He skirted the edge of the trees, looking into the darkness and shouting Carl's name, sometimes stepping a few yards into the undergrowth hoping that the boy would be sitting among the leaves.

He was not.

Freezing cold bit into his ankles and frosted his wet trousers. He was just yards away from the circle, the mist all about him. He looked down to see what was causing the painful cold, then turned to look at the stones. The mist had covered the whole of the clearing floor but stopped at the end of the track into the forest and ventured no further. Hunter stepped into the middle of the stone circle, and the painful cold disappeared.

"What the fuck!" he exclaimed, forgetting about the boy for a moment.

The centre of the stones, where he was standing was free of the biting cold mist; it just lingered around the outer stones daring not to come into the middle. Something unnatural held it back. He thought no more of it and jumped onto the large stone slab. From there he could see the edge of the forest all around, a good vantage point to see the boy. The ghostly mist had him trapped, drifting as far as the edge of the forest. He could still see no sign of Carl.

"Where are you, son? Please." His voice broke with emotion; he slammed both hands into his face and fell to his knees. There was no justice in life he thought.

"Why me, you bastard? Leave my son alone," he gasped.

Hunter did not know if he was speaking to God; he did not care; he just wanted someone to blame. He thumped his fists into the stone slab at his knees, splitting the skin on his knuckles. Blood trickled from the open wounds, diluted by the rain and dripping onto the stone surface. He staggered to his feet, clenching bloodied fists at his sides. He looked to the sky once more, his rage at breaking point.

"Bastards!" he screamed. "Bring back my son!" His voice quietened at the strain on his vocal cords. He carried on in a low whisper, "Take me, but just bring him back."

Lightning forked from the black clouds above, striking one of the small outer stones. The force of the blast shook the ground. Hunter watched as the flash of electricity skipped from stone to stone, and static crackled on his shirt, the hair on his head stood on end. Hunter stood awe struck by what was happening, he wanted to move but could not, this was happening all too fast. Like slow motion he watched the lightning skip across all twelve stones, then kick off at a right angle striking him in the chest as he stood on the large stone table, throwing him about ten feet outside the circle. He lay stunned and shrouded in the mist.

~~~

Jenny fought against a head wind and the icy rain beating down on her face. Every drop stung, but she had to find Carl. At this moment she would not have cared if it was raining acid, she had to find him. Her soaking clothes clung to her body, her jogging bottoms hanging low in the crotch as the sodden material stretched. She screamed the boy's name repeatedly, checking every bush, every blade of grass, and visibility was getting worse. Now she could only see ten yards ahead; the blanket of icy water wanted her to fail.

Jenny carried on searching even though it was dark. Her body was tired, but she was not going to give up. Carl was still alive!

The wind and rain kept up their battle, pushing her to her limit. Her cut and bruised legs thrust through the tearing cover of the gorse and blackthorn. In the dark, the blackthorns came off better, and her cold, pale flesh tore like paper. By now, the darkness was total, and she had to get help. She had to make it back to the Land Rover.

Lights flickered in the distance, like candles blowing in a breeze. For a moment, she hoped that it was Hunter.

He would find help.

However, they seemed to be too far, some disappearing, then reappearing further along the skyline. Her heart sank when she realised that it was only cars in the distance, following the few roads that stretched across the bleak moors. At this moment she would have sold her soul to the devil (if he did not have it already) just to have her son back and in her arms and to be home in front of a nice warm fire. She was scared and hurt, and her limbs felt like jelly, every step now an effort. Nevertheless, she had to find help, so she had to keep going.

How she found the Land Rover she did not know, she just thanked God that she had. She stumbled towards the vehicle, her shoes covered with thick clods of mud, making her movements shaky and awkward. She took a few deep breaths, propping herself by her elbows heavily on the wing on the vehicle. She had no strength left. Her life force had been drained, so had all her emotions. She had only one purpose now, and that was to find Carl.

She shouted for Hunter, but his name came out as little more than a hoarse squawk.

She heard no response.

Tears of frustration ran down her cheeks, and panic shot through her as she abruptly realised that she might lose her husband as well.

The car horn, she thought, *he will hear that.* She opened the car door, pulled her numb body into the driver's seat, and leaned on the horn.

Then she waited in the sound of the driving rain, her mind racing in desperation.

"The lights, he'd see the lights"

She fumbled for the light switch, cursing as her wet hands slipped on the cold dashboard. She found the switch and turned on the headlamps, but they remained dark.

"Come on, come on." *Calm yourself down, Jenny, and think!*

She remembered the keys had to be in the ignition. Panic was starting to set in for good.

"Where are the keys?" Of course. Hunter had them.

She buried her head in both hands. She just wanted out of there. Then she remembered that Hunter always kept a spare key under the middle seat.

"Come on, be here, please."

She lifted out the baby chair and tossed it aside, then ripped out the centre seat. Her hands rummaged through the crisp packets, dust, and God knew what else, and then she felt it. The key!

She slid it into the ignition and turned it. A green and red light from the dash lit up the cab. She pushed the start button, and it fired first time, much to her relief. Then she switched on the lights. With one foot, she felt on the floor for the full beam switch. The two halogen spotlights plus the full beams tore through the shroud of darkness. She sounded the horn again.

Jenny peered out the front windscreen along the avenue of light. Rain distorted her vision, but something was out there. She could feel something or someone's presence, feel it watching her. She wiped the cloudy glass with her hand. Something moved, a dark shape in the distance. She could not see it clearly, just a vague outline. It did not seem to be the shape of a person, more like a large dog. It waited, waited on the edge of the light, waited for her to make the first move.

Two cold blue objects shone like mirrors, reflecting the cars lights, It was watching her, studying her, waiting for its moment. All Jenny could see were the cold blue objects hovering above the ground, like two small moons. It skulked closer, and she watched the thing advancing up the beam of light, transfixed by those lifeless hovering blue orbs. It had started its stalk. Keeping half in darkness, it advanced up the side of the beam of light. As it came closer, her senses came back, and she could see its doglike body.

That was what her brain told her, but her senses told her to get the fuck out of there, time was running out. As if the thing knew what she was thinking, its pace became faster with its thick strong paws thumping into the ground. As it reached within yards of the vehicle, its body came into plain view. This was no dog, no dog she had ever seen before. This *thing* had a thick black mane around its neck, the whole body looked black, the tail looked nothing more than a stump, and light flashed from the claws on its huge paws. Steam rose from the creature's body, as if it had sprung from the depths of hell.

Jenny glanced away as she reached for the door handle, but when she looked back, it had vanished.

Frantically she wiped at the glass, searching the darkness, hoping that the thing really had gone.

"Please God, let it be gone, please."

From the darkness the beast sprang onto the bonnet, smashing its thickset muzzle into the windscreen, ripping off anything it could get hold of. The wipers went first. The beast's eyes were transfixed on the petrified woman inside. It jumped onto the cab roof, buckling the thin structure under its weight.

The thought of driving off then dawned on her, and she was not going to wait around to be torn apart by whatever it was. She put the Land Rover into gear and accelerated. The torque of the four-wheel drive flung her back into the seat, and she kept her foot down and headed back up the track that Hunter had brought them down.

That bastard, this is his entire fault.

A stream of water now replaced the track; she was not going to stop. The beast was still on the roof, she tried to drive and look to where the thing was. It then tore through the canvas of the back tilt, dropping through like something possessed. She turned to look just at the right time to see that one of the back sliding windows was slightly open, and the creature seized its chance, just getting its nose through. The steering wheel leapt from her hands several times as the wheels hit boulders and tractor ruts amidst the mass of mud; she kept her foot on the gas.

She could smell the pungent breath of the beast as it tried to push its way into the cab. She reached for something to hit it with, her hand feeling in the dark across the seat for anything. Something cold and smooth lay wedged between the seats, she grabbed it, knowing by its weight and shape it was a small bottle. The snarling of the creature became more intense as it started chewing at the metal trim round the glass. Jenny broke the bottle against the metal dashboard, leaving the jagged neck still held in her hand. She swung round quickly and stabbed the bottle neck into the creature's muzzle. There were no screams from the animal, just jets of warm blood spurting everywhere. Jenny felt some of the warm liquid run down the back of her neck, a translucent red colour started to cover some of the windscreen.

The beast pulled back briefly, giving her enough time to slide the window shut. Seconds later, the snarling creature slammed back into the window with a vengeance, blood still spurting from its muzzle. Jenny could see those cold reflective orbs glaring at her in the rear-view mirror, her concentration not on the driving. The limb of a tree smashed through half of the front windscreen, sending shards of glass into her face and lap. The front wheels suddenly kicked off at a right angle, sending the vehicle crashing into the large earth mounds that flanked each side of the track. One of the headlamps exploded on the impact. Jenny's body thumped against the steering wheel, her head hitting the side of the door.

The engine screamed as her foot stayed firmly stuck on the accelerator, and the wheels spun in the mud. She lost consciousness for a moment, briefly forgetting everything, the beast, the boy, and Hunter. The sound of the racing engine and the whir of the turning wheels digging themselves into the mud gradually drifted into her life once more. She pushed herself off the steering column, flopping against the back windows. Something warm ran down her face. It took no far stretch of the imagination to figure out what it was, and a painful tightening of the skin made her touch the damage. The two-inch gash above her right eye cut into the bone.

Then she remembered. *The creature!*

She pulled her body forward, away from the back windows, where the beast was. Her foot came off the accelerator; the vehicle idled silently as she stared into the blackness behind. Nothing. She could not see it.

"God, let it be gone, please." She whispered.

She looked beyond the clotting blood smeared over the back partition window. In fact, blood was all over her and seemed to have splattered everywhere in the cab. Jenny risked putting her face closer to the back window, within inches, but still could see nothing. Rain fell through the now torn canvas in the roof. The moon poked out from behind dark clouds, like a torch throwing some light on the mayhem. She could not see the creature as she looked out the passenger side window. She could see nothing but darkness, wind, rain. Ghostly shadows cast by the moon played tricks with her fragile mind.

This same wind and rain were now blowing freely through one half of the front windscreen. Now the beast could get at her with ease, and fear started to take hold of her again. She knew it was there, just waiting, waiting for the right moment, waiting to play some more.

Jenny pushed her foot down on the gas pedal again. The vehicle shuddered as the wheels struggled for purchase, but both front wheels faced into the obstructing earth. "Reverse!" she said aloud at the sudden idea.

The gearbox ground in protest as she jammed the gear stick backwards without the aid of a clutch. The wheels started spinning in reverse, and slowly the vehicle began to pull out of the deep muddy ruts. Her foot stayed down: she would give it all she could; this bastard was not going to beat her. Within seconds, the vehicle managed to find some traction; it all but catapulted out of the hedge and back down the track. Jenny slammed on the brakes as she tried to get control of the steering wheel, and then pushed the gear stick into second gear, flooring the accelerator again. Smoke started to rise from the right hand side tyre. The crumpled wing lay mangled against it, but Jenny had no time to notice—she was too busy willing the vehicle up the never-ending track. However, she did notice that the beast was standing in the middle of the track, the end of the track, where the tarmac started, where civilisation started.

Blood dripped from its jowls from the damage around its nose and face, its lips curled and looking like some hideous grin. It was waiting for her. Jenny had no emotions, no tears, no pain, all she wanted to do was kill this monster as much as it wanted to kill her, and this was *war*. The Land Rover was building up speed as the track was becoming clearer, but the beast stood its ground! "Stay there, you bastard, stay there!" she hissed, her eyes wide open fixed on its shining orbs.

The speedometer read 25mph and climbing, the beast looked huge centred in the middle of the track as Jenny reached within ten feet of it. There was no stopping her now. The beast lowered on its haunches readying its jump, and she reached forward and turned off the lights.

"I'll get you, you bastard!"

It sprang into action as soon as the light went out, its eyes still glowing as it hit the bonnet, falling short of its target. Jenny turned the lights back on just to see it desperately trying to scramble up onto the bonnet, but falling off the front of the vehicle. It must have rolled underneath. A few dull thuds shook the car, but she kept going, hoping that it was dead, hoping that it died painfully.

Jenny took the battered Land Rover up on to the main road, following the road back into the village. Her body racked with pain, her head pounding, her vision double, she somehow managed to get there. She needed a phone box, a phone, anybody's phone, and she needed the police. A cloud of burning rubber from the tyre followed her into Oare, and steam billowed from the radiator. The engine sounded fit for the scrap heap, but she was not going to stop.

The little backwater seemed deserted. Not a single light shone in any of the quaint cottages.

The pub must have a phone. Her body was now on autopilot, fit to drop at any minute, but she had to get help first. She passed old Mrs Gore's cottage, turned left, and there it was, the Black Dog Inn, the grass verge lined with cars and a few tractors. She stopped the steaming vehicle and fell out of the Land Rover, her legs unsteady beneath her. Light from the grimy leaded windows was faint on the cobble path. The rain had slowed to a drizzle and the wind had grown still under a full moon. Jenny stumbled to the door and fell in through it.

"My son, please help my son, lost on the moors—need the police!" she said before she passed out.

The Black Dog Inn fell silent before this stranger cut and bleeding on the floor. Eli the landlord ordered two of the men at the bar pick her up and take her to a bench by the fire. The two large men gently picked up the wet and bloodied body and placed it where they'd been told.

CHAPTER 6

Her face now looked calm, her body at rest under a thick patchwork quilt on a large wooden backed pew by the fire. The obese landlord had somehow managed to lower his hulking great body onto its knees, but not without steadying it on a table next to the pew. He propped up the boyish head of Jenny, resting it on his thick hairy forearm as he administered a wet cloth to her cut forehead. The water trickling into the cut started the bleeding once more. Her darkened red eyes opened suddenly staring up at this beach ball faced man, her hand grabbed for the pain, but he easily held it off.

"Just you lay still, me dear; you had some bad knocks by the look of e!" He smiled, showing his rotten teeth.

Her voice was cracked and desperate. "My son, what about my son?"

He laid his thick shovel of a hand on hers. "The police are on their way, just you calm down. Some of the men have gone looking as well. They'll find the boy!"

The landlord pushed himself to his feet, feeling his cheeks flush as he did so. He gave a scowl to two men standing behind him, and then looked back at the girl.

"Aggie will look after e for a minute; I'll wait for the police to arrive, oh and the ambulance!" He shuffled away through the onlookers, followed by the remaining men left in the pub.

~~~

Aggie, a chalk-faced woman in her late sixties, sidled up next to Jenny, smiled, and sat down. The rest of the women followed suit, staring at her lying there. They were not saying or doing much, just looking, like it was a wake or a prayer meeting. Jenny wanted to tell them so much, of what had happened. She wanted to go and search for her boy again, not stay here. However, she knew that she could not move even if she wanted: her body was not ready for any more abuse. Her head pounded more than ever now, and she knew she needed to rest. But how could she? Her son was out there somewhere, and maybe that beast was still alive.

Oh God, please help. She closed her eyes tightly and prayed, the best she could.

Minutes seemed to linger for hours, and nothing seemed to be happening. Jenny threw the quilt aside and pushed herself out of the wooden pew. The old woman beside her asked where she was going but received no reply; Jenny stumbled through the group of old people, who seemed very shocked by the sheer determination of the young woman. She nearly made it to the door when the fat hulk of the landlord blocked the entire doorway. He must have been all of six feet tall and at least twenty-two stone. His belly hung over his thick leather belt like a waterfall of skin.

"Look just wait are until the police arrive, they should be 'ere in a while!" he stated in his rural dialect, his jowls wobbling as he spoke.

"I've got to go out there again—somebody's got to start looking, and that bloody thing might still be alive!" She felt lightheaded and steadied herself against a chair.

"What thing?" The fat man snapped.

Two men sitting nearby got to their feet.

"The thing that attacked me, the fucking thing I ran over!"

Jenny glanced around at some of their faces. If looks could kill.

The fat landlord grabbed hold of her shoulders. His grip was tight; Jenny could feel his fingers starting to dig into her skin. She stared into his eyes, those cold eyes!

A vehicle came screeching to a halt outside, its headlights on full, shining through the window. The mirror behind the bar reflected the light into the landlord's face. Jenny once again caught sight of those glinting icy orbs! She then passed out; her night was over.

~~~

Detective Sergeant Martin Short put two more twenty-pence pieces into the Coca Cola vending machine and lost it yet again.

"Bastard thing!" he snapped, and then slammed his fist into the red-and-white logo on the case.

The sound of his expletive and the crash of the punch echoed around the eggshell walls of the hospital corridor. A nurse stepped from behind one of the examination screens in the accident centre, glanced toward him with a scowl, and darted back behind the curtain. DS Martin Short had expected a quiet night at home with his girlfriend.

Fat chance of that. She was just as pissed about him having to work as he was. Police work was taking up too much of his private life, too much of everything, according to her. Their sex life was suffering. He had ridden with the ambulance back to the hospital, in order to get some idea from the unconscious woman of what the fuck was going on. All he knew was that a young boy was missing on the moor, not even his age or where he was seen last.

He glanced at his watch for the umpteenth time as he walked back to the waiting area, his footsteps sounding like a drill sergeant with hobnails on. Jenny Hunter had regained consciousness on the way to the hospital, but her speech was very incoherent, she spoke of strange savage beasts that attacked her although nothing in-depth about her son disappearance. He was starting to feel like it was going to be one of those cases, where truth and fantasy seem inseparable. The mention of beasts on Exmoor had become a standing joke for the local police. At first, sightings were treated seriously as if a big African cat was loose on the moor.

When the sightings became more frequent and the media circus got involved every large household cat and black dog became the beast of Exmoor. Short recalled the frenzy of hired guns that turned up with every method of bagging the illusive beast of Exmoor. He had a view that something was up there, but what he did not know what.

He pushed his hands deep into his pockets and took a deep sigh. He thought of his girlfriend curled up in the bed, naked, warm, and ready for a good time.

Damn! He looked down the ranks of seats, which were all empty, no one needed treatment at 1am on a Monday morning, a bit different from Saturday night, when all hell had broken loose in here. Short and fifteen other police officers had done a drugs raid on a small pub on his patch, ending up with half of the people in the bar being hospitalized, but they only used reasonable force!

He smiled thinking of the damage they had caused, then flopped down in one of the many tatty, beaten-to-death, PVC-covered foam chairs in the waiting room. It farted through a split in the seat. He sniggered, checking between his legs for the offending hole. Then he glanced up to see that the young girl behind the casualty check-in desk had also heard the grotesque sound. She did not look too pleased that the offender was smiling about his achievement.

Short's pale freckled face flushed. He had to explain. The girl behind the desk was good-looking, and he might meet her again, perhaps on a more personal level. He did not want her to remember him as the disgusting cop who messed his underpants in the accident and emergency waiting room.

He shook his head, about to explain that the foul sound was

not him, when a woman's voice interrupted: "Sergeant, you can see her now!"

Short straightened something, anything to hide his embarrassment. He coughed to clear his throat, smiled at the fat nurse, and followed her, glancing back at the younger nurse behind the desk.

She was not interested; she had turned her back on him.

"How is she?" he asked, walking a couple of steps behind the short, fat woman.

He smirked as he thought of something amusing about her legs. They had to be on upside down, fat bitch.

"She's a bit drowsy because we've sedated her, but she is coherent, you can have five minutes with her, and that's all!" She pulled back the curtain, stared at Short as he walked past her, then closed the curtain behind him.

Jenny had her eyes closed when DS Short stepped into the curtained room, the smell of detergents and cleanliness made his eyes water. An angled lamp jutted from the wall, its dim bulb spotlighting the small bedside table, in the middle a jug of water with no cup. Short shuffled up to the dimly lit bed, wincing on seeing her wounds. The tear above her eye was crimped, sporting whiskery strands of black thread. The stiff blankets were tucked under her arms, her body looking shrink-wrapped into the sheets. Her face was pale, gaunt and looked exhausted.

He stood silently beside the bed, eyeing up the shapely body under the sheets, the face looked nice and would be even better without all the cuts and bruises. Jenny opened her eyes slowly as if she felt his presence. He smiled thinly at her and stepped a little closer to the bed.

"Hello, I'm Detective Sergeant Martin Short, C.I.D. I came with you to the hospital in the ambulance, d'you remember?" he said in a soft soothing voice.

She shook her head. Her puffy red eyes flickered as she glanced round the room.

"Carl!" she rasped, trying to sit up, then grimaced and sank back.

"Just relax, I know it's hard." Short laid his hand on her shoulder just to reassure her. "We've got rescue services and police officers out there looking for him now." He reached for a stool, pulled it next to the bed, and sat down.

She closed her eyes tightly, squeezing a tear from the corner of each one. Short quietly cleared his throat again, he hated interviews like this.

"I've got to ask a few question, d'you mind?"

"No," she croaked.

"Good, that's good. Well, Ms Hunter, perhaps you could start by telling me just what's happened to your son." He smiled at her, reached into his leather jacket, and pulled out his black police issue notepad.

She nodded, and another tear ran down her cheek.

"I gather his name's Carl."

She grunted through pursed lips.

"Now I'm a bit sketchy on this bit of information. The landlord from the pub told us that you'd said the boy was lost around the South Common area, is that right?"

Jenny shook her head. "I never told them anything in the pub, I'm sure I didn't. My husband said he knew where we were going, but I don't know where we were!"

"Husband?" Short frowned. It was the first he had heard of a husband.

"My husband went into the pub to get a bottle of wine ..." She closed her eyes; the sedative seemed to be taking hold. "Somebody in the—" Her speech was down to a whisper, and she drifted in and out of consciousness. "—told him a good place to have the picnic."

Her head rolled to one side, her eyes closed.

Short gritted his teeth. *Shit! He whispered.*

Just when things were getting interesting, he thought. "Jenny, Jenny." He shook her shoulder softly; her head rolled back towards him, her eyes barely open.

"What's your husband's name?"

She closed her eyes again. Short gave her shoulder another shake, just as the nurse stepped in behind him.

"That's all, officer, she needs rest!"

"Yeah, all right! But I wanna know as soon as she's awake again. I've got a lot of questions, and she's got most of the answers." He looked down at the pale face of the girl, shaking his head slightly.

"When I decide she's ready to talk some more, I'll let you know." The imposing nurse was emphatically in charge.

"I hope so." Short slid past her and into the corridor. He had to tell his boss that now they had two missing persons.

~~~

The rain was now been replaced with a fine rolling mist; the kind of mist that soaked everything to the core. As Detective Inspector Bob Finch told one of his underlings for what must have been the tenth time, this was the worst kind of mist. Finch hated the outdoors, but especially any kind of weather. Most of all he hated bad weather in the early hours of the morning after a sleepless night. His forte was grumbling and kicking ass, for which he had impressive qualifications. His mood this morning was predictable: it was dark, cold, and wet, the same as the weather. The country road leading to the track was jammed packed with rescue vehicles, police cars, and a paramedic team.

The RAF search and rescue helicopter had been cancelled because of bad visibility, and anyone who could help was helping. Police and mountain rescue dogs searched, in the hope that they might find the small boy from his scent trail. Wherever that maybe a uniformed PC stepped out into the wet morning air from the warmth of his vehicle and shouted across to D Finch.

"Sir, it's DS Short for you!" He waved the car phone in the air.

Finch wiped the moisture from his face as he made his way over to the constable holding the phone, then snatched it from his grasp.

"Finch!" the detective inspector snapped, sitting down in the driver's seat of the car.

"I've had a word with the girl, and her name's Jenny Hunter. The missing boy is called Carl," Short exclaimed before being interrupted by his boss.

"How old is he?"

There was a pause before Short answered, a pause that told Finch to prepare to be disappointed.

"I don't know, she was heavily sedated and was in shock, she wasn't up to doing much talking." He raised his voice. "But I do know that it's not just one that's missing, there's two missing."

"Two?" Finch asked. "Who's the second?" He felt a bit better now; the heater in the car was on full and warming up his cold feet.

"Her husband's out on the moors as well."

The pips started to go on the pay phone; Short delved his hand into his pocket and dumped the contents on the shelf in the booth.

"Bollocks! When you need change you can't fucking find any," Short muttered.

What's the husband's name?" Finch demanded.

"She didn't tell me. Look I'll stay here until she wakes up." The phone went dead.

Finch threw his phone back in the lap of the constable who was now sitting in the passenger seat.

"Moron! And he's in the C.I.D.," Finch rasped holding the car door open with his foot and studying the array of people milling about.

Another police Land Rover started its journey down the narrow track. Torches and high-powered spotlights searched the darkness in the distance, like a chain of dancing fireflies stretched out across the moors. Lights advanced towards the forest, disappearing briefly in and out of the veil of mist.

Finch looked back at the uniformed officer.

"It seems we've got two lost out there. Her husband's also missing, must have gone looking for the boy. We'd better let everybody know, Constable." Finch took out a crumpled packet of Marlboro from his back trouser pocket, flicked a cigarette out of the packet, and put it into his mouth, while the uniformed constable got on the radio to inform the rescuers there were now two missing persons on the moor.

At 6.30 AM a sullen blue dawn replaced the darkness. The mist had cleared as if to signify a new day, but there was still a cold snap in the air. The moor was calm. DI Finch was now coordinating the search from on the moor, and the RAF rescue helicopter had resumed its search, quartering the bogs and small watercourses in the area, which was where Finch thought the bodies might be.

Bob Finch was a renowned pessimist. Mr Doom and Gloom was the nickname he had back at the station, because the worst always happened when he was around. He had just turned fifty-five but looked in his mid sixties, with grey hair that was thinning on top. He did not care about his appearance, and it showed. If cleanliness was next to godliness, Finch was the Antichrist. The smell of stale smoke and body odour followed him around like a Siamese twin, and on a hot day he worked alone; nobody wanted to work with him. He smoked about three packets a day and was under orders from the doctor to cut down; his blood pressure was too high. He drank like a fish and did not eat the right food. He put all this misfortune down to his wife buggering off with another bloke, a younger man than himself and the window cleaner to make the whole matter worse. However, he was managing; he had it all under control.

So he said.

He hated the bitch.

Finch lit his next cigarette off the butt he had just smoked down to the filter. Inhaling deeply, he had another look at the map of Exmoor stretched out on the bonnet of the police Land Rover.

"They have to be here somewhere," he said to himself. A uniformed PC stumbled towards him, thick clods of mud stuck to his feet.

"There you go, sir," he said, handing Finch a flask of tea. "Got it from a snack wagon up on the road. Any news yet, sir?"

"Thanks. No, not yet. We've got everyone out there from the rescue teams to the police tracker dogs and Exmoor rangers. If they're out there, we'll find them." He looked out over the moors, one hand pushed into the front of his coat, like Napoleon thinking out his battle plans.

08:30 AM MONDAY
A squawked message came over the radio that they had found the man, and that he was still alive. They would use the helicopter to take him up onto the road, ready for the ambulance to take him to hospital. Finch wanted to be there, so he ordered a vehicle to take him back up to the road.

The large sea king helicopter swung low over the road landing in an adjacent field. Two paramedics kept their heads low as they carried a stretcher into the fierce wind whipped up by the rotor blades, DI Finch waited by the ambulance, then piled in behind them. He needed information.

Hunter was unconscious on the way back to the hospital. The paramedics checked him over thoroughly and found nothing wrong, apart from mild hypothermia, exhaustion, and maybe shock. They would have to do more tests back at the hospital.

Hunter's hands lay at his sides, strapped in firmly for the ride back. Finch noticed the top of something orange in his hand: Looked like a large plastic ring.

He pointed it out to the paramedic who pried it from Hunter's grasp and gave it to the police officer.

"It's a child's dummy, isn't it?" Finch asked, not really needing a second opinion.

The paramedic leaned closer. "Yeah, my kids used to have ones like that." He glanced at Hunter stretched out on the trolley. "Blimey, he could do with a bath, he stinks!"

"So would you if you'd just spent all night out on the moors," retorted Finch.

Hunter regained consciousness as the ambulance pulled into the emergency bay of the hospital. His first words were "Where am I?"

"You'll be all right, son; you're at the hospital now," Finch said, pushing open the back doors of the ambulance and jumping out.

The paramedic told him to lie still; he only grunted in reply. The trolley with Hunter on it crashed through the double swing doors into the hospital complex.

~~~

DS Short was waiting for Finch as the trolley came through into the accident centre. He knew his face gave away the news that he had more information on the Hunters, but he could not keep from grinning.

"That the old man, then?" Short asked Finch as the trolley rolled past him.

Finch stopped to watch for which cubicle they were going to put Hunter in. "Yeah, found him about an hour ago, on the edge of the forest."

Short nodded slightly as he bobbed on the balls of his feet, his hands pushed deeply into his pockets. "Nice set of scratch marks on his face?"

"Yeah, I saw those." There was a moment's pause while Finch mulled something over in his head, then he carried on, still looking in the direction of Hunter's trolley. "You spoken to his wife again yet?"

Took you long enough to ask! Here it was, his moment of glory. "Yeah." He put his arm around the small of Finch's back, ushering him over to the telephone booth in the corner of the waiting room. "I sneaked in about twenty minutes ago and had a quick chat with the lady." He took out his notepad. "Apparently it was all her old man's idea to go up on to the moors and have a picnic." Short read from his notepad trying to summarise all the good bits, the bits of interest, the bits that were incriminating. "Then she told me that he went off for a stroll, on his own, and she put the boy down for a sleep in his pushchair. That was the last she saw of her son."

Finch frowned. "So what are you saying? That someone

took the boy from under her nose? Nah, couldn't have done. How far away was the pushchair from them, for God's sake?"

Short shook his head emphatically. "Not all that far, but she turned it to face away from her, out of the wind. Then her old man came back from his walk."

Finch interrupted. "Did she see him come back?"

"No, because she was in the bushes spending a penny. He sneaked up on her when he got back, and surprised her."

"Look, Short, this is all very descriptive, but what are you trying to get at?" Clearly, Finch wanted answers.

"Well, when her old man came back from his walk"—he checked his notes once again; after all, these were her words, not his—"he got a bit fresh, you know, bit of how's ya father."

Finch shook his head in disbelief. "Yeah ... skip the porn, get to the point."

Short continued, "When her husband started messing about with her, apparently he wiped blood all over her T-shirt; she said it was all over his hands."

"Did she say where he said it came from?" Finch wanted to know.

"She said he told her it was deer blood." Short allowed himself an air of scepticism.

"Of course it was." A yellow-toothed grin came to Finch's face; he pinched his chin between index finger and thumb. "Right, get a couple of uniforms down here, and keep an eye on him. No one is allowed to leave without my say-so first. Got that?"

Short nodded and wrote it down.

Finch carried on, "And find out all you can about the husband. You know the sort of thing, neighbours, friends, enemies, whether he's violent." The word *violent* had an edge on it. "Pull out all the stops on this one, Short. I want some results, and soon. Oh yeah, get the lab to have a look at that bloodstained T-shirt."

Finch strode off towards the cubicle where they had taken Hunter, leaving Short to his next move. He did not have a chance to tell him about the alleged beast attack on Jenny Hunters

Land Rover, not that Finch would have though it credible or even taken it seriously.

~~~

As Finch stopped outside the cubicle, a nurse stepped out from behind the curtain.

"Excuse me, love, police!" He showed his ID card. "Any chance of having a quick word with him?" He nodded into the cubicle.

The young nurse glanced at his identification card, then at his face. "Can't see why not, he seems OK … yes, carry on." She pulled back the curtain.

Finch stepped in. Hunter was sitting up in the bed, an Asian doctor just taking his blood pressure. He looked the policeman up and down, and Finch showed his card again. "All right if I have a quick word, doc?"

The doctor eyed first the man on the bed and then the gauge on the blood pressure machine. "That seems to be OK, Mr Hunter," He scribbled a few notes down on his clipboard. "Are you all right to answer some questions for the police?"

"Yeah." Hunter replied.

"Okay then." The doctor gave Finch the go ahead, and then left the room.

"Have you found my boy yet? And my wife Jenny! Where the fuck are they?" The thoughts came visibly rushing back into his head.

Finch perched himself on the side of the bed. "No, not yet, but we have everyone out looking for him. We'll find him, and your wife's all right. She's in here; they're just keeping her under observation for a few days."

"What's happened to her, is she all right?"

"Yeah, she'll be fine, don't worry."

Hunter swung his legs off the bed. "I've got to go and help look for the boy, he's only a baby!"

Finch grabbed his trouser leg, holding him on the bed. "Look, Mr Hunter, the best thing you can do at the moment is stay in here and reassure your wife. I think she needs you more than anything at the moment."

Hunter dropped his head into his hands.

Finch patted him on the leg; reassurance was not his strong point. "I need to know a few things. Will you help me?" Hunter nodded in agreement with his face still buried in his hands.

CHAPTER 7

Mrs Ivy Roberts placed her husband's fried breakfast on the shiny oak dining room table, like clockwork. Fred didn't need to see to know it was waiting for him. It was just after 9 AM, and he was still up in the bathroom shaving. He had a lot planned for today. After breakfast his first stop was the allotment—his peace and quiet, his sanctuary from his wife's ever-wagging tongue, his sanity. He had some earth to turn over before the onslaught of the harsh winter that he had predicted, snow for Christmas.

A shrill voice from the bottom of the stairs sent a tingle up his spine. "Fred, I'm not telling you again, your breakfast is on the table. There's plenty of starving people in Africa who'd eat it. They wouldn't wait for it to go cold, so hurry up."

"Let them bloody eat it then," he muttered, then finished wiping the leftover foam from his face.

Fred Roberts was one of life's plodders, and he knew it. Years ago he'd had ambitions that might have made him a millionaire, but he had never had the backing, especially the backing he needed most, from the dear wife. She told him repeatedly in not so many words that he was a failure. Her words rang out clearly in memory: *You are an employee, not an employer, Fred. You are just not strong enough to meet the world head on.* She told him this often, and he started to believe her. He wanted to be a whiz kid, a moneyman, but all he had been was a keg fitter at the local cider company for the whole of his working life.

Life was now a routine, a humdrum that he followed every day, every month, and every year. However, he had made his bed, and now he had to lie in it. He ambled down the stairs, a slight stoop to his walk, the walk of a broken man.

As usual, Mrs Roberts was up at the curtain. The Vigilante of Hare Lane and Mrs Neighbourhood Watch were some of the names the occupants of the street jokingly called her. Fred checked for the morning post, it was his job first thing in the morning—that and putting out the rubbish on a Thursday—but today being Monday, it was only the post.

The old man paused at the bottom of the stairs, looking towards the front door. The stained glass window above it sent a kaleidoscope of colour into the small room, giving a warm and hallowed feel to it. He liked the coloured glass above the door, it added a touch of class to the building, he thought, and they were the only ones in the street with such a window above the front door, which meant a lot to the wife.

No letters again, not even a *Reader's Digest*. He scanned the doormat for any stray letters. What was the world coming to when even the *Reader's Digest* stopped sending you junk mail? Fred glanced towards the wife up at the window as he came into the room, but she didn't notice him. She had her eyes fixed on the twins across the road, just leaving for school.

"Late again." she said, clocking them out on her watch.

"Who is?" Fred asked, sitting down to the table and staring at the burnt offering in front of him.

"Those Thomas boys from number -eight, they're late for school again, they were the same last Monday." She said, lifting the curtain and cocking an eye into the Hunters' hard standing. "I don't think those two next door came home last night either. Their car's not there, and I don't think they've ..." She moved closer to the window, her face touching the glass. "No, they haven't taken their milk in." She looked back at the old man, a look of shock, excitement, and I-told-you-so beamed across her face. Her lips puckering like the underside of a limpet, she thought of the worst.

Mr Roberts gave a dispirited grunt and started to exert pressure on his bacon with his knife. It was so crisp it exploded into hundreds of little bits, as usual. A yellow skin of fat coated the bottom of the plate—something for the egg to float on, he told himself.

Mrs Roberts turned away from the window and resumed her dusting, sending a fine spray of polish across the dining room table. Some settled on Mr Roberts's breakfast, giving him a good excuse to leave his food. He pushed his knife and fork into the middle of the plate and folded his arms to wait for the riot act.

"You haven't touched it!" she exclaimed, looking surprised, and then squirted another jet of the polish nearer his plate.

"Well, you've squirted it with that polish, haven't you? I can't eat it now," he said, then stiffened his lips like a child.

She said nothing, just snatched the plate from in front of him. "Waste not. want not. I'll give it to the birds."

She scuttled out of the dining room and into the kitchen, putting the plate on the drainer, then thinking of her next reproach.

Round one to Mr Roberts!

She came in for the attack, the only attack she knew how to do, a full-on verbal assault. Her prune-textured face confronted him across the table. She was going for the knockout blow.

"And what are you doing today then?" Her voice was harsh and almost physical.

He smiled at her. She hated that, hated seeing him happy. "Well I'd thought I go down to the allotment this morning; got some work to do down there." He stood up from his chair and looked for his shoes.

"I don't know why you bother to go down to that allotment. You have a perfectly good garden here." She followed him into the living room.

He thought about his answer carefully, he wanted to say, *To get away from you. Have a moment's peace and quiet! Let me feel like a real man again!* However, no, he needed a roof over his head. He needed to be diplomatic, or back down; they both meant the same thing. *Gutless!*

"You know our garden's not big enough, love. Besides I like the allotment." He said the wrong word, like; she did not like him to like anything.

"Huh!" Her mouth hung open ready to carry on talking just as a strange car slowly came into view. Her eyes narrowed as she automatically shifted into potential burglar mode. Neighbourhood Watch strikes again.

The old woman scuttled over to the window, peeping out from behind the net curtain. She grabbed the notepad and pen that was on the small table beside her. She had to take down the details of the number plate. The pad had many car numbers written in it, even the cars that belonged to the neighbours across the road. She logged time of sighting and which way the vehicle was driving. However, under the small column of which way the vehicle was going was always written the same: *Vehicle drove past going down Hare Lane, and then came past going up Hare Lane.* Hare Lane was a dead end street, all traffic that went down the road had to come back in the same direction, a little fact that Mrs Roberts did not care about, it just gave her twice as long at her window. Mrs Roberts jotted down the number of the blue Vauxhall Cavalier as it slowly came to a halt on the opposite side of the road. She attempted to write down the description of the man who was driving the vehicle. He looked a shifty sort of person; she said to Husband Fred, must be a thief.

~~~

DS Short turned off the engine of the car and looked at the notes he had on the Hunters. Number 4 Hare Lane had been scribbled across the top of his page. He looked across at the door numbers; there was a nice polished hardwood door with a shining brass number six centred in the middle of it, beside a persistently twitching curtain. The Hunters' house had no number on the door, in fact, hardly had any paint on the door.

Short stepped from the car and breathed deeply of the fresh morning air. He himself felt a little fresher now, after slipping home and having a shower, a change of clothes, and something to eat. He'd hoped to catch Karen before she went to work, but he was too late.

Maybe for the best, he thought. Having mad torrid sex with the woman would have killed him for the rest of the day.

~~~

"This slim, blond bloke just got out of his car, and now he's crossing the road towards the Hunter house. He's dressed smart, but he still might be a burglar.

"He's going into next door, and he's got a clipboard with him ... Maybe he's someone official!"

Fred Roberts gave her a look, but she was oblivious, her face pressed as close to the glass as she dared. At any rate, she had something else on her mind now and had stopped pestering him. Mr Roberts stamped his feet into the carpet, testing out the firmness of his new desert boots. He gave a satisfied groan as he got to his feet and lumbered across the living room floor, still testing his boots, only to be tutted at by Mrs Eagle Eyes at the curtain.

"Shush, he's going around the back!" Ivy Roberts made a dash for the kitchen.

"Who is?" the old man said slipping his arms into his tweed gardening jacket complete with obligatory leather patches on the elbows.

"That man who got out of the car." She stood at the back door, holding it ajar and peering through the crack.

Short walked down the side alley, between the two houses, not really expecting to find anything incriminating but just wanting a good look around, find out how they live and what sort of people they are. The Hunter's back gate was not so much open but hanging off its hinges. Short stepped up to the kitchen window peering through the dirt on the glass.

"They're not in!" a woman's voice exclaimed from behind him. Short caught sight of the little woman's reflection in the window and turned to face her.

"Yes, I know." He flashed his police ID badge.

The old woman's mouth dropped open. "What have they done? I always told Fred that one day he would get in trouble with the police, didn't I, Fred?" She looked around as if her husband should be beside her. He was trying to escape out the front door. She shouted his name and he knew escape was impossible now."Didn't I, Fred?" she demanded again.

Fred offered a welcome to the policeman with a frail, help-me smile. "Didn't you what Dear?" he finally answered.

She frowned at her husband she wanted total agreement. "Didn't I tell you that he would get into trouble one day?" She shunted her elbow into his rib cage. "Didn't I?"

He winced at the sharp blow to his side. "Yes you did!" he agreed.

Mrs Roberts had a smile on her face fit for the front cover of *Vogue*. Short knew this was the right person to tell him everything about the Hunter family, with no holds barred.

"D'you know Mr & Mrs Hunter well"? DS Short asked.

"We don't have a lot to do with them, do we, Fred?" She elbowed him again.

He grunted in protest but still agreed.

"That's not to say we don't know what goes on in there," she said, folding her arms and nodding with a knowing look towards the police officer as if guarding some great secret that she might disclose, if asked. After all, it was her duty as a law-abiding citizen.

DS Short smiled at her. Her husband Fred was no longer required and skulked off without saying goodbye.

"D'you mind answering a few questions? It would be a big help."

The *Vogue* smile came back to her face; she asked him in

and proceeded to tell him all, all he wanted to know and a few little opinions of her own just for good measure.

CHAPTER 8

2. 30 PM *MONDAY*

They sat in silence for a while, neither one knowing what to say to the other; maybe nothing needed to be voiced because their eyes said it all. Jock had asked the CO for the afternoon off; compassionate leave to counsel his friend. The tragedy was now common knowledge around the camp, and the CO said that he would come and see Hunter himself as soon as he had a space in his workload. Also the padre said he might make a guest appearance. Just to make things worse.

Jock sat on a chair next to Jenny Hunter's bed, a strained smile on his lips. He could see the pain in her eyes and wanted to grab her, even kiss her, but definitely wanted to hold her. However, no, this was a hospital and a public place, and he was not the woman's husband, just her lover. The silence between them at length grew deafening. The questions he wanted to ask were all rattling around in his head, and finally he said, "How d'you feel?" *You idiot,* he thought, *she feels like shit of course.* "I mean, ah ... Well, you know!" He grabbed her hand, holding it firmly in his.

She shrugged, and a single tear ran from her swollen red eyes.

"He's dead, isn't he?" Her bottom lip quivered, more tears ran down her cheeks.

Jock shook his head, he wanted to reassure her, say *No, the boy's alive, and they will find him any minute.* But he knew, if they had not found him by now, that he would be dead from exposure. He also knew he could not tell her that.

"No, they'll find him, he'll be all right, you'll see, you'll see!" He wanted to change the subject, "How's Hunter? I haven't seen him yet, is he OK?"

Jenny's head rolled first to the far side of the pillow, then back to face him, a look of hatred burning in her eyes.

"It's all his fault, you know, that bastard! He's killed my son." Her voice was full of venom; a new lease on life seemed to have entered her body, the power of hate.

"No, you can't blame him, Jenny, he couldn't have known"

Tears streamed from her eyes. "It was him, he killed Carl. Even the police think he had something to do with it. I never want to see him again." She gripped Jock's hand. "Promise me you'll look after me, promise me?" She was starting to become hysterical, and nearby patients and visitors were stealing looks at them.

"You'll be all right, I'll be here." He realised what he had just said: he had made her a commitment. *You fool! That's the perfect way to ruin an ideal set-up.* He was only in this for a good time.

"When are they letting you out of here?" he asked, then reached across to smooth her hair.

"Maybe a couple of days, I don't know." she said and closed her eyes.

"Oh God, please find him, please, I love him so much, it's not fucking fair!" She sat up in the bed, swinging her other hand across to hold his.

"Jock, you go out and look for him, please, you'll find him." Her eyes were as wide as saucers. She wanted an answer.

A nurse came over to the bed, easing Jenny back onto the

pillows. "Come on, my love, time you had a rest, I think!" The nurse smiled at Jock, and he took the hint.

"Look, I'd better go now, I've still gotta see H—" He stopped short. "Well, I've got things to do!"

She still held on firmly to his hand; ,,, she still wanted that answer.

"Promise me?" she said.

He glanced across the bed at the nurse, who had her hand cupped and was impatiently rolling two small red capsules around in it. He agreed, and she let go of his hand. Jock strode out of the ward, his pace quickening as he got closer to the door. He did not want to look back, and he did not want to come back. He wanted out, out of the whole mess. He stepped into the draughty corridor, where the air felt fresh, even though the smell of boiled cabbage was drifting in the air. The hospital kitchen must be near. He propped himself against the wall and blew out a sigh of relief.

Hunter wasn't allowed any visitors. A uniformed PC was sitting outside his room, a room usually used for private patients and those with suspected contagious diseases. He was neither, but was helping police with their inquiries. In other words, a suspect.

The Criminal Investigations Department office in the small Minehead police station was tiny and thought inadequate by most. To its occupants it had many names, such as the sweat pit, the shithole, and any name that one could call a cramped and claustrophobic place. The room was of a Victorian design as was the building, with high ceilings, sash windows, and whitewashed cracked plaster walls. The office was situated on the second floor of the red brick grade two listed building. Its vivid red colour gave it a distinctive look; in fact, it looked more like an old workhouse or asylum than a police station.

The CID team consisted of Inspector Finch (the boss), Sergeant Short, and a relative newcomer from uniform, Myles Cranbury (the pen pusher). DC Cranbury was always in the office, being the new boy with no status whatsoever.

He answered the phone, ran errands for Finch, and did the paperwork that was beneath everybody else.

Short turned another page of Hunter's military record and gave a deep sigh. His record was impeccable. He had done more tours of duty in Northern Ireland than Short wanted to count and also served in the Gulf War and had a medal to prove it.

Short read a letter written by Hunter's commanding officer.

Royal Marine Hunter P042516W has been a credit to 40 Commando Bravo Company. He has given his all to the regiment ... The letter went on to tell of Hunter's achievements and faultless conduct. *Signed Lt Col J.C. Bray, Royal Marines.* Short shook his head with another deep sigh.

He looked across at Cranbury who was sitting at the desk opposite, his head arched over the typewriter as he applied correction fluid.

"Tell ya, this bloke's seen more action than Rambo!" Short closed the file and flopped back in his chair.

There was a pause for a moment while Cranbury blew on the correction fluid then he looked across.

"Who?"

Short tapped the file with his finger. "This bloke, Hunter."

"Oh you mean your suspect?" Cranbury replied with a smirk as he adjusted the settings on the typewriter.

Short curled his top lip; he was starting to have his doubts.

"Mmm," he tutted, then grabbed his black notepad from the desk. "I spoke to the neighbours this morning; the old woman next door was very helpful—" He paused.

Cranbury hit another key on the typewriter. "Shit! Wrong one again," he snapped, Out came the correction fluid again.

There was a pause in conversation as both men were in deep thought. "What, d'you think the old woman was a little bit too helpful?" The ginger-haired recruit looked back at his work.

Short scanned his notes from his pad. "Yeah, something like that."

The slam of one of the fire doors in the corridor told them that the boss was back. Finch pushed open the door and strode into the room. Cranbury made as if he was busy, and Short studied his notes.

"Any messages?" Finch rasped and stopped in the middle of the room.

The men looked up at him, Cranbury mumbled a no, and Short did not bother to answer.

"No messages then, I take it?" Finch sank into his chair. "What a day!"

"Any luck on finding the boy, sir?" Short asked.

"No, nothing, not even a bloody trace. I tell ya, that boy's not on them moors, no chance. We've got mountain rescue out there, police tracker dogs, and now we're using those image something-or-others."

Cranbury interrupted. "Image intensifiers, sir!"

Finch scowled at him, not that Cranbury saw it because he was still messing about with the typewriter. "Yeah, that's it!"

"So where d'you reckon the boy is then?" Short asked as he massaged his temples. He could feel the beginnings of a migraine.

"Buggered if I know."

"The Rangers reckon, with the amount of rain they had that night, he could have drowned in one of those bogs. The place is full of them. My money is still on the father. Have we got the lab report back yet on that Jenny Hunter's T-shirt?"

"No not yet. I'll ring them a bit later!" Short looked across at Cranbury, he would be the one ringing.

"Yeah I reckon the husband's not telling us everything he knows. We'll go and pay him a visit later, eh?" Finch delved his hand into his Columbo-style raincoat and pulled out a packet of cigarettes.

DS Short picked up Hunter's service record, got to his feet, and took it to Finch's desk. "Have you seen this?" He dropped the file with a slap, sending a plume of ash into the air from the ashtray. The desk was one big ashtray. He took a step back, dodging the fallout.

Finch sucked on his Marlboro and abruptly gave a mucous cough. A piece of phlegm landed on the file. He wiped it away with the back of his hand, leaving what looked like a slug trail on the folder. He opened it and examined the first page, made a few snorting sounds, and shut it.

"Well?" Short asked.

"Well what?"

"Well, that doesn't read like he's the type of bloke to kill his own son, does it?"

Finch smiled, and his yellow teeth clashed with his blue-grey lips. "Does to me, son. The man's a trained killer; does it for a living. Something's gotta give, ain't it?"

Finch got to his feet and walked over to the window, looking onto the narrow road below. "All those Yanks, the ones that came back from Vietnam, the whole lot of them were round the twist, barking bloody mad." Smoke billowed from his mouth as he spoke. "It stands to reason doesn't it. Seeing your mates get killed, all them bodies, arms, legs." He held his cigarette between a nicotine-stained finger and thumb, pointing it out the window as if he was going to throw a dart. "Shit!

"Gives me the willies just thinking about it."

Short cut a glance across at Cranbury, who was shaking his head at Finch's deductions and probably thinking the same thing. Innocent until proven guilty, but not in Finch's eyes, where everybody was a suspect, and everybody was guilty until he proved them otherwise.

Finch sat on the windowsill facing his two men. "So what've we got on our man Hunter?" He looked directly at Short.

"Not a lot really. I saw one of his neighbours today."

Finch raised his eyebrows.

"She told me that they are always arguing and have the occasional fight."

Finch rubbed his nose with the palm of his hand, evidently not surprised. "And?"

"Well, she said the night before they went out on to the moors, the Hunters had a big fight, and she said she saw scratch marks on the husband's face."

"Got him," Finch snapped. "And you still think he didn't do it?"

"Granted, he has got scratch marks on his face, but that ..."

"That means he had a grudge against her. Maybe it was one fight too many for him. He wanted to get his own back, who knows?"

"Yeah, who knows, but no man in his right mind would kill his own son, would you?" Short turned his back on Finch; he had had enough of the argument.

Finch lunged forward, slamming both hands onto the desk. "No, I wouldn't, but then I'm not him, am I? And what about the fucking blood, where did that come from?"

Short had no answer. Maybe Finch was right. The phone on Cranbury's desk began to ring, piercing the silence that had just settled over the room.

Cranbury snatched up the receiver. "Cranbury CID."

Short pushed his notepad into his pocket and sat back down at his desk. Finch lit another cigarette and kept gazing out the window.

Cranbury pulled the phone away from his ear. "Guv, it's for you!"

Finch took a lung-bursting draw on his cigarette, sauntered over to Cranbury's desk, and sat on the corner of it.

"DI Finch."

Cranbury leant back in his chair, his hand held over his nose and mouth. Short had also noticed the clinging redolence of cheesy feet, body odour, and something he could not quite put his finger. He sniggered, fetching a look from Finch.

"No, I don't want to talk to the press. You give them a statement; tell them we'll let them know more as soon as we've got something." Finch listened for some moments, puffing away on his cigarette. "No we haven't got anything yet, but that'll change. We're going to see the husband in a minute, and hopefully we'll have the results of that blood on the T-shirt from the forensic boys later."

Twenty minutes later Short and Finch had arrived at the hospital. Charging Hunter was high on Finch's priorities, he told Short. He needed a result and fast before the top brass started to ask questions. The bloody T-shirt was his only card; everything hinged on the report from the lab.

In a small town like Minehead, major crime was a nonentity. Short knew Finch yearned for his big break into media stardom, just like the rest of the team. A murder would be that break. Nevertheless, where was the boy's body? That question was beginning to annoy them both.

~~~

Cranbury sat in his chair rocking back and forth on its back legs. He was now in charge and it felt good. No smelly DI was telling him what to do, no sarcastic remarks about his upbringing and most of all no orders. Cranbury sat side ways on his desk; his feet placed on Short's chair, while he read the biography of Winston Churchill. He had done all of his the paper work for the day, most of Finches and some of Shorts. He thought he was due a long break. Cranbury was the ideal type of person that the Police force wanted to recruit; highly educated and motivated, He would go a long way. Though his parents did not share his happiness in his job, they had higher expectations for him. His father was a managing director of a big chemical firm and his mother had money handed down in the family, cousins to nobility it was stated. Nevertheless, Cranbury liked his job and that is all that mattered to him.

~~~

Finch peered through the small observation window in the door into Hunter's room and could see him sitting on the bed with his knees tucked under his chin looking back at him.

"He looks well enough, Short. Maybe we can get down to some serious questioning?"

Short did not answer Finch, just raised his brows at the constable sitting by the door, as if to say here we go again. The uniformed officer was told to come into the room with them.

The hospital had given the all-clear for Hunter to be released first thing in the morning after the doctor had done his rounds. That would be when Finch would strike and take him kicking and screaming from the hospital. Maybe the case would be over. He wished.

Hunter too had thousands of questions, especially about his son. Why was a police officer outside his door? Was he a guard to keep him in or keep people out? He had a bad feeling about the whole affair. The hospital had taken DNA swabs from under his fingernails and mouth. Hunter knew that this was not a routine thing for them to do. He wanted to know most of all how the search for his son was going; No one was telling him anything.

The three officers stepped into the room, like a delegation with bad tidings. They shuffled around the bed as if to give bad news. Hunter's heart skipped a few beats, and the pulse pounding through his head drowned out their voices. They stood solemn-faced in front of him; the uniformed PC stepped to the right side of the bed. The scruffy one looked the most relaxed out of all of them, Hunter thought. He had a glint in his eye, the sort of glint that did not look like he was going to tell you some bad news.

Detective Short softly cleared his throat. Finch introduced himself again, and then introduced his underling Short; the uniformed PC never got a mention. Not that he expected one. The interview began.

~~~

The phone bursting into life on Finch's desk startled Cranbury enough to make him clap a hand over his heart and utter an expletive. He placed his book face down on the desk to keep his page, then considered whether to not answer the phone. After all, Finch was not in, so there was no urgency. He got to his feet and slowly moved towards Finch's desk, willing the instrument to stop ringing. It did not. Cranbury's hand hovered above the handset. Finch had not done him any favours, and he would probably get the message wrong anyway, or so Finch always said.

"Bastard! Fuck his calls," he rasped, turned away, and then quickly turned back to snatch it up, thinking could the call might be important.

~~~

The news that Carl was still missing enraged Hunter, a guilty rage because he was lying in a hospital and not out looking for his son. He could not sleep no matter how many of their pills he popped, and his mind was too active. He needed to do something, and repeatedly told Finch this, but neither side seemed to be listening to the other. Finch kept asking his dumb repetitious questions, but if the police were trying to implicate him, he couldn't see it. He could only keep asking if he could go and look for his son.

Finch used every trick in the book to calm his suspect, not that Hunter knew at that moment he was a suspect. He tried the old routine.

"Just relax, and tell us in your own words what happened that night." Hunter told the truth, as he had before, but they just kept asking the same questions. "Where did you go when you went for a walk?" Finch asked again.

DS Short took notes, always stopping at Hunter's answer to this question. There was not one. Hunter searched his mind, all he could remember was the woods, and he kept saying the woods.

"In the fucking woods, go and have a look, that's all I can remember, that and waking up in the ambulance!"

Finch calmed him down and they started again. This time he would use different tactics.

"Where did those scratches come from on your face?"

Hunter rubbed his fingers along the gouges, he remembered that all right, but it was no fucking business of theirs, and he told them so. Finch kept up the battle.

~~~

Cranbury put the receiver back down; a faint grin creased his face. The results of the blood analysis on the T-shirt were back, and the result was not going to make Finch's day. He picked the phone back up and dialled for an outside line, sniggering and thinking of what smelly old Finch's reaction would be. Cranbury scribbled down the hospital number and thanked the woman from directory enquiries.

He would give Short the pleasure in telling Finch that the blood was not that of Carl Hunter. Nevertheless, it was human blood ... whose, they didn't know! He dialled the hospital phone number.

~~~

Hunter had visibly had just about had enough of the questioning, after going over his story repeatedly. Short believed Hunter one hundred percent, he could not believe from the beginning that anyone would do away with his own son, just because of a row with the Mrs.

The only method of questioning left, was for Finch to go for the psychological approach. His first question: "What was the fight about between you and your wife on Saturday night then? Had one too many again, was that it?"

Short winced at the subtlety of the man. *Why not come straight out and say, You bastard, where have you dumped your son's body?*

It took just seconds for the penny to drop. Hunter at last knew what they were insinuating. He said nothing for a brief moment, his tired eyes fixed on Finch.

Then Hunter leapt from the bed, his hospital gown flung open like a cape. Finch stood no chance, and the half-naked man was on him. The full weight of Hunter hit Finch in the chest, and his tar filled lungs squashed like a couple of sponges. He gasped for breath as he gripped his attacker's hands trying to prise his vicelike grip off his throat. His chair toppled backwards, sending them both sprawling across the floor. In seconds, Hunter had a firm hold around the gasping DI's neck.

The uniformed PC and Short were taken a little off guard by the quick reaction of the patient, but then reacted as they were supposed to. The PC took out his extendable baton, and both officers tried to wrestle the commando off the detective inspector.

The action was fast, too fast for the DI. His heavy smoker's eyes bulged like golf balls as Hunter's grip became tighter. If the situation had not been so serious, Short would have laughed at the expression on his boss's face. Sheer terror. One of those trained killers had him nailed to the deck and wanted to practice his death grip on him.

At last they pulled the marine off, pinned him face down on the bed sheets, then cuffed him.

Short helped Finch to his feet, his face the colour of a blood blister. He wanted to say something, say something to the writhing Soldier on the bed, but talking looked like more than he could manage.

Two nurses and a doctor barged through the door barking orders and telling Short and Finch to release their patient. There was an expected argument between police and hospital staff, but they complied and left the room. Finch sat down on a chair outside the room and rubbed his neck. The uniformed PC slipped his baton back onto his belt and wondered what to do next, even he thought the situation funny, but dare not laugh.

"I'll have him on that, you lot are witnesses. I want full statements from both of you!" Finch's voice had a gravelly hoarseness to it.

One of the nurses came out of Hunter's room and scowled at Short as he approached, trying to explain. She did not want to know. She strode off down the corridor. Finch took out a packet of cigarettes. His hands shook as if he had the DTs, and he needed a fix.

"I want you to stay on the door, constable. He gets no

visitors, and he's ours tomorrow morning!" A yellow-toothed grin stretched Finch's leathery skin, the cigarette hung out the corner of his lips.

"Yeah things will be a little different tomorrow."

"You're not allowed to smoke in here, Guv!" Short wished he could wring his boss's neck himself.

"Ah, bollocks!" Finch snatched the cigarette out of his mouth.

The nurse who'd left the room moments earlier came back into view, stopping at the threshold into the waiting area. "There's a phone call for DS Short, in the office," she rasped, then turned her back on the men and left. Short skipped into a trot and followed, just as a doctor hove into view, shouting that he was going to make a full complaint about the inspectors' antics and make sure the right people at the top heard about it.

Short had mixed emotions as he hung up on the call from his colleague Cranbury. His assumptions had been right all the time, and he wanted to tell Finch so, just to rub his nose in it. But on the other hand the shit would hit the fan as soon as he told his boss. He had Hunter banged to rights, and the little escapade back in the room would get Finch into deep trouble, if the right people got to hear about it. Which might have been conveniently overlooked by the hierarchy if the tests had proved positive for the boy's blood, giving Finch a strong case. However, they were not, so things could only get worse from here on in.

Short now had to break the bad news to his boss. He stepped out of the building followed by the uniformed constable, thinking he might take the initiative and remove the guard from the patient. After all, he was no longer a suspect, not in Short's eyes anyway.

"There he is, sarge." The constable pointed to the tramp like figure smoking on the wooden bench.

Now it was down to Short to break the good news, not that Finch would see it like that. The PC walked off in the direction of the car park exit. Short zipped up his leather jacket and made for the garden. He stepped over the low hedge and padded across the damp lawn towards the bench,

Finch drew the smoke deep into his lungs; its mellowing effect calmed him almost immediately. He had had to get out of the hospital and have a cigarette his body needed it. The smell from the small lavender hedge surrounding the quaint lawned garden, hung heavy in the damp afternoon air. Finch hated lavender, it reminded him too much of the wife.

Bitch!

Finch pulled his raincoat collar up round his neck, then leant heavily against one of the arms on the bench. He spotted the oncoming sergeant and cocked his head to one side to face him. "Looks like rain again!" he croaked in a soft and laboured voice

"Yeah, maybe," Short answered, looking for a clean part of the bench to sit on. Bird droppings seemed to adorn every square inch of the weathered woodwork. He decided to stay standing.

"What was the phone call about?" Finch wanted to know

Short rubbed a hand over his face; the time had come. "It was Cranbury,"

"Yeah, what'd he want?" Finch straightened up and flicked his cigarette butt onto the grass.

"The results from the lab came back." He paused. "It's not the boy's blood, Guv." He waited for the reaction.

Finch sunk his head into his hands with a mumbled groan. Then he looked up. "Shit! Are they sure?" Desperation sounded in his voice; maybe they had it wrong.

Short nodded his head, his lips pursed.

"Oh, bollocks!" Finch pinched the bridge of his nose between finger and thumb. "Take the uniformed constable off the door." He got to his feet and looked at Short. "I would have bet my balls on that being the boy's blood."

"Well, it was human blood, Guv, but it doesn't match any of the family. Fuck knows where it came from."

The two of them started to walk back to the car.

"I still reckon the bastard's guilty, the bloke's a nutter," Finch added.

Short smirked but said nothing.

"Tell ya what; we'll give him the benefit of the doubt. Shall we and go and have a look into those woods? We've been over them all right, but we still might have missed something."

"Yeah, we might have done, but I think if that boy's still out there, he's gotta be dead. It's been—" Short looked at his watch."—about twenty-four hours now, and he's nowhere to be seen. I mean how long can an eighteen-month-old boy live in those conditions?"

Finch shrugged and unlocked the car, then turned to Short. "That's what I can't work out, why we haven't found the body. We've covered about twenty square miles around where the kid disappeared, and we ain't found shit!"

Short leant on the car roof facing Finch. "I don't reckon the boy's there. We would have found him if he was, wouldn't we?"

"Not if the body's been dumped somewhere. Those commandos are fit men. How far could one of them run with 100 pounds on his back? I'd say, bloody miles!" Finch opened the car door.

"Yeah I know, but what if somebody else took the child, and not the husband?" Short was not going to give up his opinion.

"Like what, the Exmoor beast?" Finch croaked a laugh, then gripped his throat. "Look, the old man can't account for his movements; I found the boy's dummy in his hand when he was in the ambulance, and there was the blood."

Short started to speak, but Finch carried on.

"I know it wasn't the son's blood, but where did it come from, eh?" Finch slid into the car, slammed the door, and unlocked Short's side.

Narrow-minded bastard, Short thought as he opened the door and got in. "All I'll say is that I'm keeping the options open. I mean she said she saw something that night, and that it attacked her in the car."

Finch started the engine. "You'll be telling me next that you believe all that media crap about the Exmoor beast." He paused and pulled out a cigarette. "You think that really had something to do with the boy's disappearance?"

Short never said a word. Maybe he could have a look at the Land Rover Jenny Hunter was driving that night, see if the attack on her might have somehow been connected with the disappearance of her son.

CHAPTER 9

9 AM TUESDAY

It was just a formality that Hunter had to wait for the doctor to check him over and then discharge him from the care of the hospital. He wished that they would hurry it up. Time moved slowly as he sat on the bed fully dressed waiting for the OK to leave. He knew the four walls of his room really well, too well for his liking. Sleepless nights had him scrutinising every square inch of each wall, and when he finished, he did it all over again.

His thoughts now were of his wife and how she was. He desperately needed to see her, to tell her he loved her and needed her, also to tell her that he was going back to the moors to find Carl. The thought of the boy's being dead had crossed his mind more than once, but he locked it away in the deep vaults of his mind. H, he could not accept it, he did not want to accept it: the boy was alive.

~~~

By 9 AM, Detective Inspector Finch and his subordinate DS

Short were on their way to the moors for yet another foray for evidence, with Finch hoping that he could finally vindicate his prejudice about Hunter. Short on the other hand thought an open mind was more to the point: innocent until proven guilty and the like. He desperately wanted to look at the Land Rover that Jenny Hunter had been driving, and been attacked in by some sort of possessed Exmoor beast creature.

The weather this morning was dry, so far, but a grey sky threatened to change that at any minute. Finch felt surprisingly chirpy; he had received a phone call from his wife last night, telling him that she had split up with the window cleaner. Short thought the mood change was an improvement and did not say anything untoward so as not to rock the boat; he preferred Finch happy. The positive mood swing also brought with it a change of clothes, a shave, and the smell of Old Spice that hung in the air like the smell of burning tyres.

Finch whistled a shrill ditty that was out of tune and unrecognizable to Short, then changed down a gear to make the climb up Porlock Hill, one of the steepest hills in the area, rising some three hundred and seventy feet above sea level.

The car grunted as Finch changed down a gear again into second gear and the pace was now at a crawl. Finally, after an ear-popping climb to the summit, the road eased to a gentle incline and levelled out onto the moors. As the car picked up speed, Finch carried on his whistling, and Short marvelled at the hands of Mother Nature.

The bleakness of the moor at times could have no comparisons, least not on this planet. However, in total contrast, the landscape would change in an instant, to rolling valleys thick with woods, streams, and scenery that had not changed in thousands of years. The car rattled as it passed over a cattle grid laid across the road. The grid was more for the sheep and wild ponies than for any cow.

Finch grabbed his packet of Marlboro from the centre console, flicked one from the packet, and thrust it in the side of his mouth, then pushed in the car lighter. Short gave him a token scowl, sighed, and then wound down the window. Finch was either too happy or too thick-skinned to notice the subtle objection to his smoking. He pulled the lighter from its holder and took three massive draws on the weed. Short hung his head closer to the window; the stale smell of the smoke that early in the morning made his guts turn. Finch glanced across at his passenger and blew a jet of smoke towards his open window.

"What, you warm or something?" asked Finch, oblivious.

"No not really, just feel like throwing up."

"Oh." Finch thought for a moment. "Well, close the bloody window I'm freezing my nuts off."

Short thought, *On the plus side, well, at least it has to smell better than his after-shave.* He compromised and wound the window up halfway.

"First stop we'll have a look at this Land Rover then, just to keep you happy," Finch said with a smile that gave Short a dazzling burst of his yellow teeth.

Finch smiling! Short could not believe it; the man must be in love.

~ ~ ~

Hunter had got the OK from the doctor to leave. He was as fit as a flea, he told him, but nevertheless asked him to rest for a few days. The doctor had also taken the liberty of prescribing him a few sleeping tablets, just in case they were needed. Hunter told him he would not need them, but brought them along just the same; he felt so tired that he could sleep for a week.

The feeling of vulnerability did not really hit him until he made his way to where his wife was being looked after. He had no bags, no clean clothes. He felt empty, alone, but at least he had Jenny.

Dear Jenny.

Hunter stepped sheepishly through the doorway that led into Ward 15. He felt nervous, but he didn't know why ... maybe apprehensive about seeing what condition his wife was in, he didn't know. To his right stood two small offices. One looked like the staff room, where the nurses made tea and took some respite from their hectic workload. The closed door to the had the word Sister written on it, in black on white lettering. He glanced through the small window and saw two nurses chatting with each other. One of them stood up and smiled at him, then opened the door to see what he wanted. She was young, pretty, and well suited for the uniform.

"Yes sir, can I help you?" she asked.

The other nurse eyed up the dishevelled commando.

"I've come to see my wife, Jenny Hunter."

There was a moment's pause from the nurse at the door. She chewed nervously on her bottom lip, and then looked back at the other nurse sitting behind her. Who just gave her a blank stare.

"Um ... yes. Well, if you can wait here, Mr Hunter, I'll see if she's awake and ready to see you!" She smiled politely at him, squeezed past him through the door, and then sauntered off down the ward.

Hunter kept his eye on her, watching to see which bed she was going to stop at. The other nurse stood up. She knew that Jenny Hunter did not want to see her husband; they were under strict orders from her not to let him in. However, what could they do? He was her husband, but they had to comply with her wishes, she was the patient.

"Mr Hunter, would you like a cup of coffee or tea?" She wanted to break the ice, soften him up, ready him for the smack in the face he was about to receive. These sorts of situations could get nasty, and she knew it, but she also knew about the tragedy of their son and felt sorry for both of them.

"No, thanks." His answer was straight to the point; he kept his eyes on the other nurse.

The squeak of her soft shoes on the polished floor stopped, and she looked to her right, behind a walled partition that blocked Hunter's view of who was in the bed. The nurse started to talk to someone, her hand came up and pointed towards Hunter, and then she moved behind the screen.

It must be Jenny.

He started to walk down the ward towards where the nurse had disappeared.

"Um, Mr Hunter, can you just wait here for a minute, a ...?" the young nurse asked knowing that Jenny Hunter had given firm directions that she did not what to see her husband.

He kept walking, not even hearing the nurse's plea to wait. She put down her cup of tea and scuttled off after him. Jenny was arguing with the nurse about why she did not want to see her husband, with the nurse trying her hardest to persuade her, but to no avail. He was a murderer, a bastard of the first degree, and she hated him. Hunter could hear the commotion as he approached the partition but as usual thought nothing of it. He stepped past the screen, followed closely by nurse number two. Husband's and wife's eyes met; hers wide open on seeing the murderer. He smiled and stepped up to the foot of the bed.

"How are you?" he asked.

The nurses glanced at each other, not really knowing what to say or do. The muscles in Jenny's cheeks bulged as she gritted her teeth. Hunter saw the contempt on her face, and his smile faded.

"What's the matter?" he asked softly.

Jenny sat bolt upright in the bed. The nurses stepped forward, expecting an attack.

"Get out!" she rasped. Now she had the full attention of the ward. Hunter glanced around at the onlookers.

"I don't want you here, I never want to see you again, you bastard!" she shouted.

Number two nurse asked Hunter politely to leave and gently cupped his arm.

Hunter shook her hand off violently. He did not understand why Jenny was acting like this. They should not be fighting at such a time.

"What the fuck's the matter with you?" he said loudly, and now both nurses were urging him to leave.

Jenny kept shouting, "Get him out, get him out, I hate him!" Hunter did not know what to do. He wanted to talk things over in a civilised way, but that would be impossible in the state his wife was in. Her shouts were now becoming screams, screams that reverberated down the corridors and into the neighbouring wards. Medical reinforcements came running.

CHAPTER 10

Finch must have been on his tenth cigarette as he swung the car into the small village of Oare—but not before he bumped over the old stone Robbers Bridge doing about forty miles an hour. The car took off, leaping some four feet or more into the air, then landed neatly on the same side of the road, leaving big gouges in the tarmac where the chassis hit.

Short gripped the seat with one hand and rubbed the side of his head with the other. He did not expect that sort of behaviour from Finch. Finch on the other hand had a beaming yellow smile on his face. He seemed to be in a reckless, happy-go-lucky mood today.

"Sorry about that, boy. You OK?" Finch asked, then started to hum a happy ballad.

Short slapped down the sunshade to look in the vanity mirror. He rubbed the side of his head, leaning in for a better view. "Yeah, no thanks to you. What you trying to do, kill us?" Short moved his jaw from side to side. Seemed okay.

"That was the Robbers Bridge! I didn't want to get robbed, did I?" Finch leant to one side in his seat and contorted his face. Short should have known what was coming next.

A whistling sound emanated from between the boss's legs, and he looked pleased with his actions. In seconds, Short was gasping for fresh air, pushing his hand over his nose and hanging his head out the window.

"Yep, three hundred years ago we would have had our throats cut back there and robbed of all we had! These moors were bad news in the old days. This place has more history and legends behind it than the Royal Family. Take the Doone family, for example, lots of bad things there. Now they were a load of bad asses!"

Short sniffed the air in the car for the rotten smell of brussel sprouts. The coast was clear; the smell had gone. "Yeah, well, that was hundreds of years ago, not now, so just take it easy, will ya. I wanna live till tomorrow!"

Finch laughed as he flicked the indicator switch and turned right, down the lane that led to the pub. He stopped on the grass verge opposite the Black Dog Inn. Both men scanned the area for the Land Rover.

"Where is it then?" Finch asked, taking out another cigarette and opening the car door.

"Good question. It was just there." Short climbed out of the car and pointed to the patch of grass in front of them.

Short looked over the hedge into the next field just in case the villagers had moved it out of the way. It was not there.

The landlord of the pub was standing on a tiny footstool watching the two policemen as he snipped back the grapevine that clung to the side of the pub. DS Short saw the large man first, but the landlord was pretending he had not seen them.

Short loudly cleared his throat. "Excuse me?" he said, then walked across the road followed by Finch. The landlord still paid no heed.

The wind stirred a little, moving the sign hanging on the gibbet above the cobbled path; Finch glanced up at it, staring the black dog in the face. "The Black Dog Inn," he muttered, then sniggered to himself.

Detective Sergeant Short stopped within feet of the fat

man, who finally glanced down at him, with a look of shock as if it was a total surprise.

"Hello, sir, I don't know if you remember me, I'm DS Short, CID!"

He flashed his ID. Finch stepped up behind him. The fat man looked over his shoulder at the other policeman. "And this is my boss, Detective Inspector Finch!"

The landlord nodded, and his whole face shook as the folds of fat around his jowls lost control. Short mused that maybe the fat man in front of him was the missing link between man and ape; he was the spit of an old orang-utan. The thought brought a smile to his lips, one the landlord seemed to notice. Finch turned his head in another direction.

"Yep I remember, bad thing that, felt so sorry for the maid!" The Landlord stepped down from the stool; it shook as his weight went on one leg.

"Yeah it was," Short answered with a look of concern on his face.

"So what can I do for you, Officers? I told you everything in my statement, can't think of nothing else." Sweat rolled off the top of his head and down his red face. He rubbed it away.

"Gonna thunder later; damn humid, makes me sweat!"

"Well Mr. ..." The name had slipped Short's mind, and he hoped the landlord would intervene.

He did. "Trout, Eli Trout!"

Short pursed his lips, trying not to laugh. To look like an orang-utan was bad enough, but to have the name Trout as well, the man must be a nature lover.

Short continued, "Yeah, Mr Trout." He smiled in apology. "Where's the Land Rover gone that was on the grass over there? The one that belonged to the girl you helped."

The landlord looked to the patch of grass where Short was pointing. The fat man scratched his head. "Ah yeah, I think Bert Smith's boy took it."

"Took it?" Finch snapped his first words since they had been there. "Took it where?" He stepped up to the large man, he did not want any lies.

"Well, he thought he'd repair it, you know, fix it up for 'em. After all that happened to the poor maid, I suppose he felt sorry for her. Good of the boy, I thought."

"Good! He's tampering with police evidence, he could be locked up for that. You'd better tell me where this, this ...!" Finch could not remember the name.

"Tom Smith," the fat man said.

"Yeah, you'd better tell me where I can find him."

The landlord pointed up the road to what looked like a cottage with a barn jutting from one side. "Up there! He's the blacksmith, that's his house."

Both men gave a brief goodbye to the large landlord Eli Trout. He watched them as they walked to their car, a thin smile on his lips, and a croak of laughter rumbled from his closed mouth. They had barely started the car, it seemed, to travel a few hundred yards, when the police officers climbed out. Finch lit another cigarette, straightened his attire, and looked into the darkness of the barn. The barn had two large doors; each one about nine feet square. Both of them were open. A large boulder held one door against the cottage wall, and the other had a lorry tyre jammed against it to hold it firmly in place. Both men stood on the threshold for a moment while their eyes became accustomed to the gloom; Finch was the first to step into the blackened barn.

The acrid smell of soot clung to everything. The walls were stone, but black smut looked painted on to them. The forge sat in one corner of the barn like a hulking black tomb. It was not lit. "Must be his day off," Finch sniped as he gazed around at the gothic looking structure. Swallow's nests hung high in the eaves, between the blankets of cobwebs and dirt.

Short spoke up. "No sign of the Land Rover, Guv, he must have it here somewhere." Short was stepping carefully over all the debris on the floor.

A shaft of light seemed to be coming out from the wall, and Short headed that way. A sudden noise, like a spanner dropping, startled them.

"Hello, Mr Smith," Short shouted, then moved closer to the shaft of light that he now saw was coming through a doorway.

"It must lead into the house," he said, looking back at the boss, who had just stamped his cigarette into the floor and was fumbling for another. Short reached for the door handle, Finch was staying put. He'd made it clear he had no interest in the Land Rover, and he thought Short's fact-finding mission would draw a blank.

Suddenly the door swung open, its handle leaping from the sergeant's grasp. He took a few startled steps backwards as daylight poured through the now open doorway, then a large figure stepped into the blaze of light and stood silhouetted. The features of the stranger were a blur for a moment; the policemen's eyes needed time to adjust to the light. Finch stayed where he was while Short took another step back.

"Mr ... umm ... Smith?" Short asked, still trying to take in the size of the giant in front of him.

"Yeah, whadee want?" the man rasped.

Short took out his identification card, showing it to the giant in front of him. Not that he could see it.

"We're police officers, Mr Smith, um, Mr Trout from the pub said that you have Mrs Hunter's Land Rover?"

There was a pause as the giant thought. "Mrs Hunter! Is that the lady who—"

Finch cut his sentence short. "Yeah, the young lady that had the accident on the moors the other night, and you have her vehicle."

"Yeah, that's right, I got it, thought I'd repair it for her."

Short now could see the full features of Mr Smith; his sheer bulk looked held together with a dirty pair of denim overalls, with his stomach looking out of control as it pushed against the threadbare cloth. Underneath the bib-and-brace and stretched over the top half of his torso was a grubby T-shirt. The sleeves had been torn off, making the giant in front of them look like an overfed hillbilly. Twenty-five stone easy, Short thought, sizing up whether his judo skills could beat this man mountain. You never knew when things could get rough, so every option was thought of, at least in Short's philosophy. All he had to do was get him on the floor, and he'd never get up again!

"We want to take a look at it if you don't mind," Finch said, stepping alongside his underling.

Smith never said a word, just waved a ham-sized arm. With Finch at the lead, they followed the large man around the back of the house and into a field that had an entrance to it from the road beside the building. There wasn't a scratch or a spot of blood on the Land Rover, at least not visible to Short and Finch as they scrutinised it. The canvas and the smashed wing had been replaced, and to make things even worse, the vehicle had been thoroughly cleaned throughout.

Smith propped himself against a near fence post, watching the two detectives go over the vehicle with a fine tooth—comb. Short saw the smug look of satisfaction on Smith's face, whether it was pride in the repair work or knowing that he'd tampered with evidence, he couldn't tell. It was too late now! There was no evidence. Short jumped into the driver's side of the vehicle and grasped the steering wheel, while Finch idly checked over the front end.

The large man came closer to the vehicle, he wanted to keep an eye on what Short was up to inside. Short slid the window open, facing the man.

"Tell me, what did you repair?" Short waited for an answer.

The large man stepped forward, within inches of the vehicle, and then slammed his hand down on the wing. "This one." He moved to the front of the Land Rover. "That glass there." He pointed to the passenger side windscreen. "And the canvas on the back."

Finch lit a cigarette and cursed as he shook the nearly empty packet.

Short stepped from the Land Rover, slamming the door behind him. "Why did you do all this, Mr Smith? You weren't asked, and you don't know the lady who owns it, do you?"

Smith smiled, and his teeth were nearly the same shade of yellow as Finch's. "No, I don't know her, but after all that has happened to the poor lady, I thought ... well I thought it would save her the trouble of doing it. Aye, that's it." Smith smiled again.

Finch stepped up beside him. "You know that this vehicle is police evidence and that you have tampered with the said evidence?"

He shook his large head; his eyes narrowed as he stared menacingly at Finch. "No, I only wanted to help, no law against that, is there?"

"No," Short answered. "But there is for touching police evidence, this vehicle could have held vital clues for us, but now—well, you've wiped the thing clean!"

Finch glanced at his watch remembering that he had a prior appointment with his boss and was now late; he insisted that they leave right away. Though first Short needed to finish warning Smith about his actions.

Smith took it all, everything Short could throw at him, and he never said a word, just kept his arms folded and chewed his bottom lip. That was until Short asked him where he had put the bashed-up wing and the old canvas that he had taken from the Land Rover. Smith's mouth dropped open, and he glanced at a tarpaulin in the corner of the field in the midst of a large clump of nettles. Short's eyes followed Smith's. Smith looked back at the officer.

"I got rid of them, didn't want to leave them lying about the yard, did I?" He raised his eyebrows and offered a thin smile.

"Mmm." Short looked across at Finch, who was not taking a lot of notice of the proceedings, too preoccupied with avoiding the cow shit with every step.

Short knew a liar when he saw one, and the man in-front of him was hiding something. He didn't know what, but he had a good idea it was under that tarpaulin. Short was about to leave when he remembered that Jenny Hunter had told him that the creature that attacked her had jumped onto the roof of the Land Rover. Short turned around, opened the cab door again, and stepped up onto the floor well to examine the roof.

Smith moved nervously. "Look, I'm sorry if I did the woman

a good turn but ..." His sentence tapered off as he saw a smile come to Short's face.

Finch was now by the gate and scraping the mud off his shoes, when Short shouted over to him.

"Guv, I think I've found something here!"

Smith stepped up to the vehicle, wondering what the police officer had found.

Finch cocked his leg over the gate and paused on the top quickly looking back. "What now?"

Short glanced down at Smith, who wanted to know what the officer had found?

"Footprints, Guv," Short called over to Finch. "Or more to the point, paw prints."

"So what's that got to do with anything?" Finch shouted back and stepped onto the road looking at his watch once more.

"The thing that attacked Mrs Hunter, she said it was a dog type of animal." Short looked closer at the huge muddy paw prints, putting his fist next to one.

"Bloody hell, nearly the same size," he muttered.

"Yeah, well, you take a look," Finch shouted back, then lowered his voice as he returned to the car. "I can't be bothered," he muttered knowing now his lateness would be noticed.

Smith watched Finch disappear out of sight, and then gave his full attention to Short.

"So what's the story here then, Mr Smith? Did you forget to clean the roof, forget to clean these bloody great paw prints off?" He glanced back at the collage of paw prints and the deep gouges where something's nails had tried to claw its way into the cab.

"Look at these scratch marks, what d'you reckon made them?"

Detective Short stepped aside, expecting Smith to look. He did not; instead he told Short a story of how his dog must have jumped up there. Short gave a cursory glance around as if to look for the dog, stating that he never saw the animal when he and Finch came around the back of the house earlier. To which Smith gave him the story that the dog wandered a lot, sometimes for days at a time.

Short did not believe him, especially when Smith did not know what size his dog was or even what breed he was. He told Smith to leave the vehicle alone, just in case the forensic boys wanted to look at the prints, and warned it was a criminal offence to touch the vehicle, and if he did, he would be in big trouble.

Finch sounded the car horn impatiently several times. Short made for the gate, his eyes still on the tarpaulin sheet that lay crumpled in the corner of the field. DS Short slid into the passenger side of the car; Finch already had the engine ticking over, and as soon as Short was buckled up, Finch pushed the car into gear and headed out.

"What d'you reckon then?" Finch asked.

"The man's lying; I think he's hiding something."

"What? Don't tell me you think he's covering up something."

Short gazed out of the window. The day was darkening over, and a black sky stretched as far as he could see.

"Maybe," he said pensively, then paused. "No, I'm sure of it!"

Finch shook his head in disbelief, and then smiled. "Well I'll give you one thing; you certainly hang on once you get your teeth into something!" He gave a chesty laugh and steered away from the village. Next stop for the two men was the moors and the patch of woods that Hunter had said was the last thing he could remember.

They made their way down the track on foot, leaving the car up on the road with a fleet of other police vehicles. Rescue teams were still out looking for the boy, as were the police and anyone who wanted to help, but still they'd found nothing, and the likelihood of finding Carl Hunter alive was becoming less hopeful by the minute, but they still kept looking.

Heading the whole shooting match now was Chief Inspector Terry Sharp, to whom DI Finch was to answer, if indeed he had any answers. Every avenue taken by Finch to get to the bottom of the missing child was drawing a blank, and his main suspect was still the father. Even though he had no proof, he had a strong feeling that Hunter was covering up something. As they reached the bottom of the track, Finch spied the colourful coachwork of a police Land Rover Discovery, and standing by the bonnet of the vehicle looking at a map was Chief Inspector Sharp. Finch grabbed Short's arm pulling him back behind a large slump of gorse.

"What's the matter with you?" Short rasped as he lost his footing and stumbled over a stone.

Finch pointed to Sharp. "That's what's the matter with me!"

Short followed the finger, "Inspector Sharp, so what?"

"And you're a copper," Finch exclaimed. He rummaged through his pockets and pulled out a packet of cigarettes and thrust one into his mouth. "Shall I tell you why we should keep clear of Sharp?"

Short expected another sermon on the ways of policing Finch style.

"Well, he's going to ask us if we have any leads on the boy's disappearance, being that I told him that the husband was a suspect, and now ... well, now we have no evidence on the husband, so we haven't any leads. That's why we keep out of his way."

Made sense; for once Finch was right. Both men headed towards the small forest, trying to stay out of sight of the chief inspector, who carried on pointing out the next line of search for the police teams.

So far the search had covered ten square mi les of the moor and not found so much as a footprint. The assumption now was that the boy had wandered off and fallen into one of the many bogs that peppered the area. If so, recovering the body would be virtually miraculous. Nobody knew how deep the bogs were but their victims, and they were not about to tell.

Finch told Short he knew of a short cut, one that would keep them out of sight and lead them into the centre of the forest. Short followed a few steps behind Finch. Soon both men found it hard to walk with the mud sticking to their shoes.

By now, men's feet were soaking wet, they had to stop every few yards to pull the clods of mud from their shoes, and the going was becoming slow and the ground becoming softer.

Short stopped to clear the mud from his shoes once again, Finch strode on; the forest was just minutes away. Short wiped his muddy hands in the grass and wondered why he listened to Finch. *It seemed like a good idea at the time.*

A cry of help from his boss had Short up and running to his call. He couldn't see Finch at first but he knew desperation in a voice when he heard it, and Finch's cry sounded desperate. He leapt over small gorse bushes, stumbling several times as he ran and scanned the area around him.

"Guv, where are you?" he shouted, and then stopped to wait for a reply.

"Over here, and hurry up.

The voice came from Short's right, beyond a bank of blackthorn. He pushed his way through the dense prickly cover until he saw Finch, up to his waist in mud and struggling to scramble out of a well-hidden bog.

"Shit, how ...?" Short looked around. The thick mud was well covered, looking like any other part of the moor.

"Don't worry about how, just worry about getting me out," Finch shouted as he struggled, trying to pull his body through the tarlike mud.

"Don't move, Guv, you'll make things worse, just stay still. I'll try to find something to pull you out!" Short remembered the old Tarzan films he watched as a boy and that was what they always said. Whether it worked or not, he was about to find out.

He looked around for a branch or anything that he could throw out on to the mud, but there was nothing to be found, unlike the Tarzan films where a branch or vine was strategically handy. However, this was no film, this was reality, and there was not as much as a twig in view. Quick thinking was needed;

Finch had started to wriggle again and was now up to his chest in the quagmire.

"Fuck's sake, Short, do something." Finch's voice betrayed his desperation and fear; clearly he did not want to die.

Short took off his leather jacket. He got down on his knees and felt for the edge of the bog. Lush green grass sank under the weight of his hand, and dirty water trickled between his fingers. He was there.

"Right, Guv, I'm going to throw this out." He showed Finch the jacket.

Finch nodded.

Short held on to one arm of the jacket and flung it towards Finch. The leather sleeve was just out of Finch's reach. Short dragged it back in and tried again. This time Finch managed to grab the sleeve. Short began to pull, hand over hand, but the bog was not giving up its victim without a fight. Short lay on his belly facing his boss, he could see the fear in his face, and thought he might look the same from Finch's view.

Slowly Finch started to move, holding on to the arm of the jacket with one hand and trying to claw his way through the mud with the other. At times Short felt himself dragged forward, but he managed to keep his grip and carry on pulling. The smell of rotten eggs coming from the decaying mud made it hard to breathe.

As Finch scrambled closer to Short, at times he seemed to have a footing on something firm and rise slightly from the mud, but then it too would sink under his full weight, and the bog seemed to take hold anew. It was then that he had the chilling thought of what might have lain under Finch's feet. Maybe it was the boy's body, his little mouth open as if to shout for his mummy or daddy. In an instant he could picture the child, his little body suspended in a sea of darkness, his mouth, eyes and nose full of the rank black mud.

Finch must have been seeing much the same terrifying image, because with one last pull by Short, he managed to scramble out onto solid ground. Both men collapsed in an exhausted heap.

~~~

They never searched the forest that day. The thought of walking around in stinking clothes did not appeal to Finch. It was not until his near fatal accident in the grasp of Mother Nature that he was really struck by the possibility that in fact the boy could have drowned in one of the many bogs. Maybe the father was telling the truth after all.

CHAPTER 11

WEDNESDAY

At 6.30 AM promptly, Mrs Roberts drew open her living room curtains to greet the dreary day. She gave the houses opposite the once-over (no one was about that early in the morning), then applied herself to her daily work. The old vacuum machine was pulled from under the stairs and noisily dragged up to the spare bedroom. She would always do the upstairs first. Her husband thought it was just to annoy him, so that he got out of bed, but really it was to have a good look at the neighbours as they left for work, or not, in some cases.

She pushed the vacuum cleaner into the middle of the floor and plugged in. The old chrome machine looked and sounded like a jet engine. She grabbed the hose poking out of the front of the cylinder and stamped down on the power switch, and the machine roared to life.

~~~

Hunter stirred from his painful sleep, with the hum of the vacuum next door bringing him back to life. His swollen eyes flickered, then slowly opened, adjusting to the gloom of the room. His head felt weighted down to the pillow, and a throbbing pain hung above his eyes. He lay motionless just staring up at the ceiling, remembering the night's terrible nightmare. He felt relief that it was just a dream, a dream that felt so real that his whole body ached, but what was it all about?

He glanced across to Jenny's side of the bed and grabbed her pillow, then pulled it to his face, smelling her perfume and hair that clung to the material. He held it close for a while, his tears soaking into it; he wanted her back. The pain of losing two people he loved was too much to bear.

After an hour of thought and soul-searching questions, he slid from the bed. The pain throughout his body was more than he had endured in any commando training. His legs ached from his ankles to his groin, and his stomach felt as if it had been used as a punch bag. He opened the curtains letting in the gloomy day.

"Fucking rain," he commented, the weather only adding to his despondent mood.

He left the window and crossed to the bedroom door, then caught sight of his reflection in the dressing table mirror; he paused for a moment, taking in his attire. His dishevelled clothes didn't bother him that much—he was used to getting pissed and sleeping with his clothes on—but his gaunt, tired face had the look of a different man, an older man, a stranger. Hunter rubbed a hand across the dark stubble on his chin, thinking that maybe he should keep the beard, to give him that distinguished look.

Turning from the mirror, he looked at the bedroom door, the same door that led him to his nightmare. His hand hovered over the handle, maybe dreading a recurrence of the dream; the thought sent an icy chill up his spine. Dismissing it as folly, he opened the door and stepped onto the landing. The first thing he clapped eyes on was one of Carl's plastic play bricks, placed on the banister by the door. His heart raced as he thought of the dream and of his son calling out to him.

The play brick was just a coincidence.

"Yeah, that's all it is." He agreed with his thoughts.

Snatching up the brick in temper Hunter opened the door into Carl's bedroom, not really knowing what to expect but hoping for normalcy. The room was as it should have been, toys scattered around the floor, Thunderbirds posters on every wall, and the little bed tucked in one corner of the room. Hunter stepped over to it and sat down. Above the headboard was a picture of Hunter and Jock with the boy, dressed in their camouflage uniforms. Carl was laughing as he sat on one shoulder of each man and wore his father's green beret. Hunter remembered the day well. It was at the Royal Bath and West Show, and the Royal Marines were giving a display. Jenny and Carl had come along to watch, and everyone had a good time.

Hunter reached up to touch the photograph and followed the outline of Carls face with his finger, around his little red cheeks and across his smiling lips. He choked back the tears, as his heart seemed to ache. There was an empty void in his life now, but why did he feel so confused? He strongly hoped that Carl was alive, but logic told him that could not be true after so long on the moors. He did not feel grief-stricken at all, but he wanted to. His feelings were so mixed up that maybe he was going mad. Maybe he did have something to do with Carl's disappearance; why couldn't he remember? Why was life playing such a cruel trick on him? He thought of others who deserved this more, greedy people that thought of nothing but money, why not them? There were no answers, just questions and plenty of them.

The nearby Church of St. Johns gave out the hour with eight chimes of the bell; Hunter counted them as he moved to the bedroom window and peered out. Mr Roberts was just going into his shed at the bottom of his garden, his sanctuary from the ever-watchful eyes of his wife. The rain had eased to a drizzle now, and the dark clouds were heading towards the town.

Stepping out of the boy's room, he went into the bathroom, turned on the shower that hung above the bath, and undressed. Within minutes, steam filled the small room, and Hunter was under the relaxing spray of the shower. He grabbed the bar of soap from its holder and rubbed it over his body. When he rubbed the soap across his stomach, he felt a stinging pain, as if he had put vinegar on an open cut. He stepped from the jet of hot water and looked down to where the stinging pain was coming from. For a moment, he could not figure out how he had come by the long thin bruise or the tears at his flesh, and then the stark memory of the nightmare hit him.

"No, it can't be," he rasped, rubbing his fingers along the wound. He jumped from the bath as he remembered the barbed wire fence in his dream, also the tear in his shirt. He picked up the T-shirt and frantically scanned it.

"But it was just a dream, it can't ..." At the bottom of the shirt was a tear. He leant heavily against the sink, still clutching the garment. "No it can't be real. What the fuck's going on?"

~~~

Detective Inspector Bob Finch and DC Myles Cranbury watched helplessly as the fire crews cut the body of DS Short from the wreckage of his car. The car had been totally burnt out inside and the front end wrapped around a large oak tree. One of the fire crew had struggled down the steep bank, pulling a length of cable behind him. He reached the crashed car and attached it to the back axle, and then a recovery vehicle had winched it to the road at the top.

Finch drew deeply on his cigarette trying to get rid of the smell of burning flesh that hung in the air. Two of the younger fire-fighters had already lost their breakfast; the sight of the charred body was too much for them. The fire crew had cut off the car door and were now in the process of removing the steering column, because it trapped the victim's legs—or what was left of them. One of the fire-fighters slipped down his mask, grabbed the cutting apparatus, and crawled in by the foot pedals; he did not look up towards the body once as the cutting tool got to work. Finished, he made a hasty withdrawal and struggled to get his breath back.

Another officer removed the steering wheel, then reeled back quickly and dropped the steering wheel to the ground. Finch stepped forward to see what had panicked the young man. He saw and turned away as quickly as the fire-fighter. Short's left leg had been burnt down to the bone, and it had fallen away from the knee as soon as it was released.

Finch took another laboured draw on his cigarette, then retreated to where Cranbury was standing. He could not understand what Short had been doing on the moor. All he could think was that he was trying to find the child's body on his own, or he had a new lead on something and did not want to trouble Finch with it.

The local police officer stepped down beside them, his hands firmly into his pockets. "Bad old business that." He nodded to the car.

Cranbury agreed, but Finch was not so forthcoming with an agreeable reply. "What time did you get word that the car was down here?" he asked.

The uniformed policeman took his hands from his pockets and slipped a mint into his mouth.

"Well, let me see." He took out his notepad and flicked over a couple of pages. "Right, here it is." He sucked noisily on his mint and then carried on. "We received a phone call at six o'clock this morning, from a Mr King. He said that he could see smoke coming from the trees, but he didn't stop to look as he was late for work."

"So what happened then?" Finch wanted to know.

The uniformed officer made more obscene sucking noises and then flicked to another page.

"Well, I came out to have a look, it's on my beat so ... when I took a closer look, I saw it was a vehicle, and the number plate on the back was still intact, so that's how I found out it was an unmarked police car, of course, and who was driving it."

The uniformed officer shook his head as he looked again at the carnage. "Was he married?" he asked with a tone of concern in his voice.

"No. He had a girlfriend," Cranbury interjected.

"Oh, has she been told yet?"

Cranbury glanced at Finch. "No, not yet!" he said softly; it would be Finch's thankless job to tell her.

The fire crew started to ease the body from the wreckage. The three policemen looked on as the blackened body was put on to a stretcher. Short's head was tilted back, and his mouth gaped open, showing his teeth. His lips had been burnt away, and he seemed to sneer at his onlookers. Where his eyes used to be, small white orbs drained of life stared into the heavens.

The local man shook his head. "Shit, what a way to go, burnt alive!"

Finch turned and glared at the uniformed man. "Just shut up, will you? It's bad enough he's dead without you going on about how he died."

There was silence for a moment as the body was carried past them and to the waiting ambulance. The fire-fighters gathered up their equipment, and the three policemen moved in to inspect the car. "What time do you think it happened?" Finch asked the chief fire officer.

The fireman took off his white helmet and mopped his brow with his hanky. "Hard to say in car fires. It was nearly burnt out when we arrived; all the seating had burnt inside, even the backseats. Like I said, it's hard to say!"

"Well, can you give me a rough estimate?" Finch snapped, looking over the damage.

The fire-fighter put his helmet back on, raised his eyebrows, and gave his reticent answer. "Off the top of my head, I'd say around 3am but I—" The fire officer stepped up to the driver side of the car.

"What is it?" Finch asked curiously.

"The clock!" The fireman looked at the dashboard and started to peel away some of the melted plastic.

"What about the clock?"

"Well it's a good assumption that when the car hit this tree and burst into flames, the clock stopped, and hopefully—"

He paused and strained his eyes at where the clock used to be, the policemen leaning in over his shoulder. The metal pin, which once held the hands, was still there, but the hands had melted, leaving blurry marks against the metal background. He rubbed his finger across the yellow plastic that was left.

"I'd say roughly between half past two and three o'clock. It's hard to tell, not a lot left here. Though your autopsy should give you a better idea."

Finch took it all in, but he still could not understand what Short was doing up on the moor in the first place, and how did he come to crash?

Cranbury called him over to the boot of the car; Finch left the fire officer and went over to him. "What's up?"

Cranbury pointed to the crumpled wing on the back, and then pulled down the boot, showing that it too had buckled. "What d'you make of that then, Guv?"

Finch called the fire officer over. "Could this smashed wing and boot have been done on the way down this bank?"

The fireman looked at the damage and then peered over the side at the tyre tracks and marks to where it had hit the tree. "No chance. This car went down here headfirst. You can see the front end took all the impact."

Finch thanked him, and he headed for his truck.

Cranbury leant into the boot and put his hand into a hole in the hardboard backing on the rear seat; the hardboard had acted like a fire stop, saving the boot from the full rage of the fire. He leant nearer to the hole and said, "What, are these teeth marks?" Finch could see the deep gouges that ran down to the carpet, which had also been torn to pieces just below the scratch marks in the board. He craned his neck a little closer, when the young detective reared away from the boot. "Blimey, it stinks in the back of here!" The two continued inspecting the damage while breathing fresh air.

"Did Short have a dog?" Cranbury asked. "A bloody big dog?"

Finch scowled at him, then thrust a cigarette between his lips. "No, I don't think so, how the bloody hell do I know?" Finch lit his cigarette. "Anyway, what the fuck's that got to do with this?"

Cranbury shook his head. "Nothing I suppose, it's just these big paw prints in here." Finch gave them a token glance then looked up the bank at the tyre tracks.

"I just can't understand this. The back end's smashed, so that means he hit something either down here, which we know he couldn't have done, or he hit something up on the road, and in that case there should be broken glass up there from the lights!"

A gathering of local reporters and TV crews had arrived and were waiting along the verge by the road. Cranbury set out cones to preserve the road as a crime scene and started the search for glass and other evidence.

Finch straightened his collar and stroked his hair vainly as the cameraman got him in shot. The male interviewer thrust the microphone towards the detective's face. "Inspector, is it right that we're led to believe it was a police officer who died in the crash?"

Finch cleared his throat. "Yes it was, but I cannot give you the name of the officer until the next of kin have been informed!"

"Has it any relevance to the case of the missing boy, Carl Hunter?" the reporter asked.

Finch shook his head. "Why should it have any connection to that case?" He faked a smile.

TV reporter: "The boy disappeared just down the road, didn't he? And talking about the boy, why hasn't he been found or even his body?"

Finch: "Look, that's nothing to do with this, and we don't even know if the child is dead yet. At the moment he's officially missing."

Reporter: "What, just like ten-year-old Debbie Summers, who went missing six years ago? She was never found either. Are the disappearances linked, d'you think?" He thrust the microphone towards Finch again.

Finch moved uneasily, trying both to smile and to hide his yellow teeth. "I agree there are similarities, but that was so long ago, I hardly think that the two cases are connected. We are looking into it, and that's all I can tell you, except that the mother of the missing boy will be giving out a statement today at the station at three o'clock." Finch pushed the microphone away and tried to get on with his job.

The cameraman turned to follow him, and so did the interviewer and the reporters.

"Is it right, Inspector Finch, that the father of the missing child is under suspicion for the disappearance of his son?"

Finch stopped dead in his tracks. "Look, I don't know where you get your information, but you've got it all wrong." He carried on walking again.

"So it's not true then?" the man persisted.

Finch swung round. "No, it's not true, and that's all I'm going to say. I have work to do. In fact, I have to inform the dead officer's next of kin."

The reporters slunk away, deterred by his last remark. Finch sidled up to Cranbury, who was crouched on his knees, scanning the grass near where the car left the road.

"Found anything?" asked Finch as he lit up yet another cigarette.

"Nothing, not even a flake of paint. The car just seems to have run straight off the road; he didn't even brake." Cranbury glanced up at Finch with a look of bewilderment on his face.

"Not even a tyre mark?" Finch asked, as he followed the line of the road to where Short's car had left it.

"No, not one, he just drove right over the edge!"

Both men walked the line that the car must have taken, scanning the ground, but there was nothing. They reached the top of the embankment and peered down the steep drop to the trees below. Cranbury crouched again, poking at something in the wet mud. It was a paw print, a possible match to the print in the boot of Short's car.

Finch rasped, "Look someone could have walked their dog along here yesterday."

"Bloody big dog, look at the size of these things, they're the size of my fist," Cranbury said. "And look at the size of those nails, they look more like claws!"

"Shit you're getting as bad as Short was. He was into nature as well," Finch scoffed, then walked away. His next job was to inform Short's family and his girlfriend of the news; he didn't have time for this fantasy.

~~~

Hunter stared hypnotically at the TV screen, but his mind wandered, searching for answers to questions that now tested his sanity. The picture changed from programme to programme, but Hunter took no heed of them. His thoughts were with his son and the nightmare of the dream that seemed to have been impossibly true. He had the bruises and the cuts that matched what had happened in the dream, also the aching body from all the running. Who was the man in the field? What was that creature that tried to get them? Nothing seemed to make sense anymore. Dreams were becoming reality, and reality was becoming a nightmare!

A blanket of grey clouds filtered out the late afternoon sun. The Roberts' kitchen light came on, flashing across Hunter's gloomy back yard, distracting him for a second. He looked to the window and noticed that the night was setting in once more, and a shiver ran up his spine. The night brought sleep, and sleep brought him the nightmare.

The six o'clock local news was just beginning with a summary of the headlines:

"In this evening's news, revelations that a southwest MP has been taking bribes for his influence on the local councils. In addition, a local firm have come up with a revolutionary new way of putting an identification mark under the skin. They say it will stamp out credit card fraud and it cannot be forged.

"But first, we begin with a tragic accident in the early hours of this morning. A police officer was killed as he drove his car off of the road about two miles from the village of Oare in the Exmoor National Park. For unexplained reasons, Detective Sergeant Martin Short's unmarked police car left the A39 and plunged down an embankment, bursting into flames when it hit the trees at the bottom. Our reporter was on the scene as the rescue services recovered the body and the vehicle ..."

Hunter stood up. He needed food, he had not eaten all day. He padded to the kitchen and slapped the single fluorescent strip to flickering life. Leaning against the cooker, he opened one of the wall units that held the tinned food; beans looked the only snack on the menu. He was dumping the contents into a saucepan when he heard the name *Hunter* mentioned. He dropped the tin into the pan and dashed back into the living room. He watched silently as the reporter interviewed DI Finch.

"Is it right, Inspector Finch, that the father of the missing child is under suspicion for the disappearance of his son?"

Hunter sat on the arm of the sofa and listened to the rest of the interview. When it had finished, the news presenter announced that the interview with Mrs Hunter, the mother of the missing boy, would be shown after the next item. Rage filled Hunter's body. Why was not he told about the interview? Why was he under suspicion?

"Bastards, I didn't kill my fucking son," he shouted, slapping his hands over his ears, trying to blank out the bullshit he had just heard. Then he remembered what they said about Short: he died in the early hours of the morning, on the moors. Could it have been Short in his dream?

No, could not have been, the man he saw got away.

His brain ached with thoughts, and nothing made sense anymore. Then he heard Jenny's voice and looked up at the television. There she was, standing outside the hospital doors with Finch to one side. Hunter smiled at her, then recalled why he was not with her. He watched as she pleaded for anyone who knew anything about Carl's whereabouts to come forward, even if they knew where the body was. Tears ran down her cheeks.

One of the reporters asked Finch if he thought the girl that went missing six years ago (Debbie Summers) and the disappearance of Carl were connected.

"Do you think Carl's been abducted?"

"We're ruling out nothing, we've done an extensive search of the moors, and still we have found nothing," Finch replied.

"What about the bogs up there? All manner of livestock have disappeared in them!"

Finch glanced across at Jenny, then back at the reporter. "Of course that could have happened, but we must rule out other possibilities before coming to conclusions like that."

Hunter watched open-mouthed as the questioning began to become more personal.

Finch tried his hardest to steer the questioning from Jenny's personal life, but they kept asking.

"Where is your husband, Mrs Hunter?" one young reporter called from the front of the room.

Hunter clenched his fists and growled, "Leave her alone, you parasite bastards!"

Finch grabbed Jenny by the arm, hoping to lead her away, but the young reporter shouted his question again.

Jenny spun around to face him, tears streaming down her cheeks. "We are no longer together!" she snapped. Finch ushered her back inside the hospital door, and the interview was over.

Hunter jumped over to the TV and slammed his fist into the controls, hitting the off button as he did so.

"You bitch! Fuck you as well, I'll find my son. I'll find him, and you lot can go to hell!" He swung his arms wildly, knocking off the few ornaments they had on the mantelpiece, and then grabbed the single chair that sat next to the sofa and hurled it at the wall.

~ ~ ~

Both Mr and Mrs Roberts looked at their living room wall on hearing the thump. They too were watching the local news. Mrs Roberts nodded knowingly all the way through the interview. Fred expected her to say *I told you so* at any minute, but she didn't; she just looked at him and nodded.

The crash of the chair against their wall had shaken it enough for one of Mrs Robert's best framed pictures to fall from its mounting. She shrieked with fright as she heard the bang, then watched her picture hit the floor. Both of them jumped to their feet, and she stood over the broken frame, her hand covering her mouth.

Fred Roberts was more concerned about what had caused it to fall off the wall. "Must have been that interview on the Telly, poor bloke."

"Poor bloke my eye, go in and tell him that he's smashed my best picture." Her wrinkled eyes glared into his.

He thought about it for a brief second, and then turned down her demand, saying that he would go and tell him tomorrow.

~~~

Hunter snatched up the phone to call Jenny's parents' house. He wanted to speak to that bitch of a wife. He put the receiver to his ear as the phone connected.

Mary Nixon, Jenny's mother, picked up the phone. "Hello," she said solemnly.

"Mary, let me speak to Jenny," Hunter said, trying to calm down. He was met with silence, then the phone went dead.

"Bitch!" He jabbed at the redial button again.

The dialling tones started. He waited for someone to answer, just as he was going to give up a male voice answered with an abrupt "Yes."

Hunter recognised the voice of Jack Nixon, Jenny's father. "Jack, I want to speak to Jenny?"

"She doesn't want to speak to you, so don't bother ringing again!" Jack slammed down the phone.

"You bastards, you shit fuck bastards!" Hunter said, then ripped the phone from its socket and threw it on the floor.

He paced up and down the room in the darkness for a long while, thinking on what he should do. It was obvious now that he was alone; he was in the wrong in everybody's eyes, but why?

He settled on the sofa and thought of his son, the only person who trusted him.

"No!" he screamed. The boy's smiling face was fixed in his mind.

~~~

Jock came around the back of the house and he stood at the window for a moment, looking unseen into the darkened room, watching Hunter sob.

He wondered whether he should leave him to get over his grief, but no, he knew Hunter too well.

The fucking idiot was bound to do something stupid.

Jock had received a phone call from Jenny telling him that Hunter had called her and had a frosty reception from her parents. Jock knew it would not be long before Hunter would take it into his head that the world was against him, and then who knew what might happen?

World War Three.

He stepped back from the window and up to the back door; he did not want Hunter to know that he had seen him crying.

~~~

Hunter heard the three soft knocks on the back door; he stood up and looked out the window, seeing Jock. The greeting between the two was brief as Jock followed Hunter into the living room. As Jock turned on the light, he noticed the upturned chair against the wall and the phone in a heap on the floor.

"Been doing a bit of tidying, I see!" He picked up the chair and turned it the right way up.

Hunter gave no reaction.

Jock sat down and looked at his mate. "You gotta pull yourself out of it, Hunter. I know it must be hard, but—"

Hunter cut him short. "But what?" He gritted his teeth. "D'you think I had anything to do with the boy going missing?"

There was a pause before Jock answered.

"Do you?" Hunter shouted.

Well as he knew Hunter, Jock jumped at the outburst. "No, I fucking don't, but don't start on me, man, I came around here to help ya!"

Hunter calmed down. "Yeah, sorry."

Jock nodded, apology accepted.

"It's this fucking house, Jock, and everything in it. It's got too many memories. The fucking place is driving me mad."

"Why don't you go away for a few days, just to get your head together? I'll look after things here."

"I don't know. I don't need a rest, I need to find Carl."

Jock leant closer. "Look, mate, everybody's doing the best they can. They'll find him."

"I've got to go up there again." Hunter paused. "I've been having these dreams ... no, more like nightmares. I was up on the moors last night, and I think I saw that copper that was killed."

Jock frowned; he wasn't sure what Hunter was trying to say. "What, you drove up there?"

Hunter shook his head. "No, this is going to sound weird, but my dream took me up there, and it was fucking real. I got the bruises to prove it!"

"Look, mate, you're under a lot of stress, and the tablets you're taking must send you as high as a kite. What you're telling me just doesn't make sense—"

Hunter got to his feet. "And you think it does to me? All I know is that I was there, and some fucking Thing tried to kill me, and that bloke ..."

"What bloke?" Jock snapped, not believing what he was hearing.

"That copper that was killed, I saw him, least I think it was him." Hunter thrust his head into his hands. "I just don't know anymore. All I know is that I'm the one that has to go up there and find Carl."

Jock sat back heavy in the chair. He feared that Hunter had been pushed too far; stress could play havoc with the mind, which both of them knew all too well. Hunter needed help!

"Look, Hunter, promise me you'll do nothing for a couple

of days. We'll see what the coppers come up with, then if they haven't found anything, I'll go up there with you and look for him."

Hunter agreed after a bit of thought. Jock had bought himself some time.

CHAPTER 12

TWO WEEKS LATER
Wednesday:
Still the police had found nothing, and the whole matter of the missing child was becoming an embarrassment for them. They had pinned their hopes on finding the body, or even clothing that might have led them to the body, but nothing! No bush or blade of grass was left unturned, and that left only two options, to the mind of Detective Inspector Finch: either the boy had drowned in one of the many bogs scattered around the area, or someone had abducted him. Finch still thought that Hunter must have played some part in the boy's disappearance, but he had no evidence. All he had was speculation, and that would not get a conviction in a court of law.

The search for the boy had now been called off; the police had neither the time nor the money to keep up their searches for any length of time. Jenny Hunter had made several more appeals to the press, but nothing came of them. The boy had seemed to disappear off the face of the earth. Nobody knew anything, or at least that was how it looked. The case of Carl Hunter was being likened to the disappearance of Debbie

Summers, who some six years before had she also disappeared on the Moors.

The media coverage was now down to a trickle. Other local stories crowded out the disappearances, but now speculation was running riot. One newspaper claimed that aliens from another planet had kidnapped Carl, or the Exmoor beast had eaten him; another told of how he must have been offered as a sacrifice to the devil.

~~~

Whatever the truth was, Hunter was now going back to find out. Jock had stalled him long enough; the nightmares were becoming worse, and now he was questioning his own sanity. Darkness swamped his mind; strange faces and people were becoming real during his hours of sleep. People he had never ever seen before, people who seemed generations away from the present. For the last two days, Hunter had not slept, nor had he seen Jock. His comfort now was a bottle of Jack Daniels, one bottle a day so far, but he was about to put it up to two bottles. The drink stopped the dreams as well as the memories. The house now had the ambience of a distillery, mouldy food clung to the pots and plates in the overcrowded sink, and the pedal bin had overflowed onto the kitchen floor, a feast for all manner of germs.

Hunter sat slumped to one side on the sofa, the bottle of Jack Daniels firmly erect on the arm of the chair, held firmly by Hunter's hand. Only a small mouthful was left in the bottle. He fought to keep his eyes open; sleep was mere moments away, but he had to stay awake. His seemed to weigh hundreds of pounds as he tried to lift it upright; he had no any strength left, and it rolled back to its original position. His eyes flickered open at a crashing sound from the backyard and then closed again. The empty bottle of whisky dropped to the floor with a thump, but Hunter did not hear it, his hands twitched and his body flinched as he started yet another nightmare.

~~~~

Fred Roberts propped his bike against his kitchen wall and bent to pick up the clothes pegs that he had knocked over with the front wheel of his bike. The small wooden objects lay all around the back doorstep.

"Stupid place to put the tin," he muttered.

He pitched the clothes pegs noisily back into their biscuit tin; Mrs Roberts stood behind the net curtain and watched, making sure that he picked up every one of them. Fred placed the tin to one side of the back door, and then glanced at his watch. He was running late now, it was 11.10 AM, and the local pub had been open for the last ten minutes. He told the wife that he was going down to the allotment so she would suspect nothing. He pushed his bike to the back gate and climbed on, then gave a concerned glance into the Hunters' backyard as he passed, noting that the dustbin contents had been dragged out all over the ground. Maybe he should see how Hunter was bearing up, see if he needed anything, he was concerned about him. No, he would attend to it when he got back from the pub; he started on his journey.

~~~

Jock stopped his Ford Capri at the bottom of Ten Beaches Road; he turned off the engine and waited. He was sure Jenny had seen him pass from her bedroom window, he'd told her to keep a lookout for him. He did not really want to knock on the front door of her mother's house; tempting fate he thought, so he would wait just down the road.

He had planned to tell her today that it was all over between them. He did not need the hassle of this sort of relationship. He wanted an easy life, and besides, the guilt trip from doing the dirty on his best mate was getting the better of him.

He watched from the rear-view mirror as Jenny came out of the house and up the road towards him. He reached across the passenger seat and opened the door. She climbed in. Jenny might have realised from his silence that something was wrong, but he didn't care; he said few words, just slipped the car into gear and drove off, heading out of town. He kept to all the back roads; he didn't want to be seen with Jenny in the car. It wouldn't have worried him before, but now he was more conscious of the affair and didn't want anyone to get unduly suspicious.

Jenny asked how he was feeling. He thought for a moment before answering. "I'm all right."

She was watching his every move, which made Jock feel as if she knew he had more on his mind.

"What's the matter?" she asked with a frown.

Jock turned the car up a forest track and brought it to a stop, then turned to her. "It's Hunter."

She snapped her gaze from his and scowled out the window. "What about him?"

"Look, I think you should talk to him, the bloke's going mad in that house all day, and now he's hitting the bottle. I can't do a thing with him, all he goes on about is these fucking dreams he keeps having."

She kept her face to the front. "I don't give a shit if he dies. If that bastard hadn't taken us up on those moors ..." She fought back the tears. "Carl would still be here today."

Jock hated seeing her cry. He reached over and put his arm around her shoulders, and she turned and kissed him, her tongue probing his mouth. He wanted to stop her there and then, but somehow the moment of passion got the better of him; he found himself giving in to her good looks and charm. Jenny reached down to his trousers and unbuttoned them, her hand massaged his testicles gently, and his erection began to grow. Following her lead, his hands unbuttoned her shirt, exposing her firm, little breasts.

~~~

Hunter's dream again took him to the same place, the moors. This time it seemed a different setting but still a familiar place, a place that seemed to jog his subconscious. As in the rest of the dreams, it was night-time, but this dream seemed to be different, he was not so much there in body as somehow present in soul. He was not walking this time but floating, floating to wherever the unknown force wanted him to go. He could see a forest outlined against the night sky; a full moon guided his way. It was not until he came to a track that he remembered: This was the small forest where he'd first looked for Carl.

Slowly he moved down the track. There were lights in the clearing, and figures moved in the shadows. Who were they?

Slowly he drifted closer. When he recognised the clearing, blind panic roared through him. It was the stone circle.

The memories suddenly rushed back, things were clear now. He remembered the thunder, the mist and the blood, but above all he remembered the lightning; the pain seemed to lance though his body once more just to remind him. He was pulled closer to the stone circle, about ten feet away from the sinister beings in their dark robes.

A tremendous power emanated from the inside of the stone circle, a power that drained the life force out of whatever it touched. The power was raw evil, and it was gaining strength by the minute.

Hunter felt a little apprehensive; he knew this dream was different, but different *how*?

Beside each of the outer small stones stood a shrouded figure carrying a flaming torch. They stood in silence and looked towards two figures in the centre. Hunter watched from the shadows, hoping that he would not be moved closer. So far, they had not seen him, whoever they were. Large hoods covered their heads and draped partially across their faces.

In the centre of the circle, two similarly dressed figures stood with their backs to Hunter. They laid their hands across something on the slab in front of them, something small under a dark shroud, but he couldn't make out exactly what it was.

One of the figures in the centre turned and started to light the torches that stood around the large stone slab. There were three along each side of the slab, and as they were lit, those standing around the outside circle started to chant.

One of the figures in the centre stood with his back to the large upright stone that was at the head of the slab. The other lifted something from the slab and stood to the side of it. The chanting became louder, amplified by the trees that surrounded them. The moon hung high in a clear sky, giving an eerie setting for the proceedings below. The figure beside the tall stone stretched his arms up to the heavens and beckoned that the beast be brought forward.

The chanting stopped.

Hunter watched as a mist arose around the stone circle, a thick blanket of mist that carpeted the forest floor but never pushed one inch into the circle. It got to knee height and simply hovered. Hunter's gaze again moved to the centre of the proceedings.

Something is moving under that sheet.

His eyes fixed on the stone slab, and there was indeed some movement under the dark shroud.

Hurried thoughts rushed his brain; he remembered the blood at the base of the stone slab.

"Oh no, don't let this ..." He cut his sentence short.

The shrouded figure that stood beside the slab raised both hands aloft, and what they held glinted. It was a knife. The blade seemed to flash like a bolt of lightning as it hung above the dark figure's head. Fear engulfed Hunters body; he suspected what was to come next.

The onlookers were now reciting words, their deep droning tones did not make sense to Hunter, the words seemed to be in a different language, and over and over he heard the world *sheol*. Then as the noise rose to a crescendo, the figure at the head of the stone slab pulled away the shroud, revealing what was underneath it. Hunter screamed despite himself and tried to move forward, but he had no control over his movements as in his other dreams. Now he was just an observer.

His worst vision was before him: there on the stone slab lay the living body of Carl Hunter. The small child was naked and made no attempt to move. Hunter screamed and shouted, but his cries went unheard.

"You bastards, I'll kill the fucking lot of you. I vow to God I'll get every motherfucking one of you!"

He watched in the most painful minutes of his life as the figures at the head of the slab held the boy's arms, and the other person brought the knife plunging through the boy's chest. The blade came down with such force that it dug into the stone underneath. The scrape of metal against the stone and the screams of his son would never leave Hunter.

Those standing around the stones were not hearing Hunter's screams or at least gave no sign that they did. He wanted someone to hear, he wanted to kill every one of them, but he could do nothing but watch. Watch the sick slaughter of his son.

Carl screamed a scream that tore the heart out of his father, the father who could do nothing.

For a few moments the boy's legs kicked as the knife was pulled down to his stomach, revealing most of his intestines. Then the boy went silent, his limbs inert and blood forming a dark pool around the little body.

Hunter's sleeping body thrashed and kicked on the sofa, and tears rolled from his closed eyes. This nightmare felt as real as the rest, yet it was as if he was only meant to watch. He could do nothing at all.

Thoughts fraught with emotion ran through his mind. *Is this a dream? Please let it be a dream. Who are these people? Why me?*

He wanted to wake, wanted to switch off from this nightmare, but he could not. The force that had brought him there now held him firm, and he had to watch. Was this a vision of the future? He would have to find out.

As Hunter watched the two figures in the centre of the circle dismember the body, he did not at first notice the disappearance of the people around the outside of the stone circle. The mist still carpeted the ground all the way around the outside of the circle but came no closer. Hunter was now as silent as his son was. Some moments later, when tore his gaze from the figures in the centre, he realised that the torches and the people around the outside had gone, but something stood in their place. Each small stone now had a guardian, a guardian that was the same as he had seen stalking DS Short, but now there were many of them; their eyes glowed like the moon itself.

The creatures moved through the mist, cutting swathes in it as they moved. They were waiting.

"Let thee, O Lord of all Sheol, take this offering for thy children. Protect us, and give us thy blessing," intoned one of the figures in the centre of the circle.

Hunter seemed to recognise the voice; he had certainly heard it before. The beasts all started to move towards the centre of the circle, their shining eyes all that was clearly visible in the gloom.

Carl's head was snatched from the table and raised high in the air. Hunter screamed, hoping to God that this was really a nightmare. Threads of tissue hung from the severed neck, and the mouth gaped open. Hunter tried to shut out the sight, but he could not. His hate seemed to swell, and rage overcame him: he wanted to kill them all.

He awoke with a start, suddenly staring with bleary eyes across his murky living room. It was early evening, and twilight was still fading from the sky. He felt some relief that all he'd witnessed was only a nightmare—he hoped. Sweat drenched his clothes, and tears cooled on his cheeks; he was trembling all over. He glanced down at the whisky bottle on the floor. Dryness filled his mouth, and he needed a drink. He rubbed his hands over his head and glanced around the room, noticing at last the smell and squalor that he was living in.

"What a fuckin' mess," he muttered, then reached down and picked up the bottle of Jack Daniels.

He stroked his tongue across his dry lips as he saw the small mouthful of liquid left in the bottle. He needed that drink.

The alcohol burnt into the back of his throat, and he grimaced at the taste, repulsed by it for once. He sat in thought for a moment as the shadows in the room disappeared and the darkness settled in. His mind was still on those moors, trying to make sense of what he had just dreamed. Was it a look into the future? He still had the feeling that Carl was alive, his visions hadn't changed that, but he knew now that he had to play some part in all of this. A force, a power that he'd never felt before was making him stronger, making him see the truth, and giving him a new lease on life. He had to go back!

He switched on the living room light and walked out into the kitchen, where the light was still on. He stood at the sink for a moment and stared at his transparent reflection in the window. He sported several weeks' growth of beard on his face, but he thought he would keep that: if he was going back on to the moors, he did not want to be recognised, especially by the villagers. They were the key to all this, he was sure.

First, he wanted to find out how many other children and people had gone missing on the moors, especially around the village.

Who could know?

He turned on the taps and thought about the question.

~~~

Fred Roberts saw Hunter come to the kitchen sink and thought that maybe now was a good time to see how he was (just to be neighbourly, of course). He left his own back door slightly ajar, just so the wife would not hear it closing. She was watching her favourite programme and had given specific orders not to be disturbed. Her wish was his command.

After grabbing a pack of four beers from the larder, he slipped quietly out the back door. Hesitantly he stopped at Hunter's back gate, thinking was worth the wrath of his wife if she found out he was colluding with the enemy.

What the hell, he thought, and walked into the Hunters' backyard. Guided by the light from Hunter's kitchen window, Fred stepped carefully over the rubbish that lay strewn all over the yard. He passed the kitchen window, where Hunter was jumbling some pans and didn't see him. Fred knocked on the back door and Hunter answered with a startled look on his face.

Fred managed what he thought was a smile, lips rolled back to expose his perfectly straight dentures. He knew they would be gleaming in the fluorescent light.

"All right, Fred, what can I do for you?" Hunter asked, ushering the old man in.

"Oh, not a lot, boy, just thought I'd pay you a visit, see if you needed anything." The old man glanced around at the state of the kitchen, and his nostrils flared at the aroma of decaying food. Hunter settled him into the armchair in the living room and began to tidy up around him.

"Here you are, son, let's have a beer." Fred pulled one of the cans from the pack and handed it to Hunter.

"Cheers," Hunter replied, and then sat opposite him.

The old man tore off the ring pull and took a few noisy gulps of beer. He smacked his lips as he set the can down beside him.

"So sorry to hear about ..."

Hunter cut him short. "Yeah." He did not want to talk about it.

The old man took the hint, but what else could he talk about?

Hunter saved him any embarrassment by changing the subject. "Fred, where should I go if I want to find out about past news, such as disappearances?"

Fred looked pensively at Hunter. "Old news." He attempted a smile. "See, my missus, she knows everything that's going on."

Both men laughed, if only to break the tension.

"No, seriously, son, try the library, they should have most newspaper records in there, especially local ones." Fred held his peace, thinking that if Hunter wanted to tell him, he would in his own good time.

Hunter smiled. "Thanks; I'll try the library in the morning."

CHAPTER 13

Miss Sarah Holly went about her usual chores on a Thursday morning. Working in the local library had not been her life's ambition, nor had it even entered into her career plans at all. It was just a job that had come along, and she happened to be in the right place at the right time—or not, as she looked at it. She did not know really, what she wanted to do when she left school, except leave home and lead a life of her own, and that she had done as soon as she landed the library job. The pay was adequate; enough to cover the rent on her small flat in town and meet all the demands for the bills, and that was about all. Sarah was one of life's dreamers, hoping that one day she would hit the big time. She had always wanted to be a writer, but found it hard to condition her mind to sit down for hours on end and get a story together. Maybe one day her ambition would come to fruition.

Three people worked in the library: Betty Williams, Paul Day, and Sarah. Betty Williams was the oldest of the workers and the most experienced. At the age of sixty-two she had accrued over thirty years service for the council at the library, and she was proud of that fact. She kept a close eye on the other two younger members of staff, especially Paul Day, she did not trust him one bit, not since she had caught him getting a blowjob in the staff room from his girlfriend. She said she was going to report the incident, but she never did. Day had told Sarah it was because the old woman fancied him, and when she saw the size of his cock, she fancied her chances too.

Paul Day was indeed the wild card in the pack, he hated working in the library, but it did have its plus side: there were always girls and plenty of them. He called it the benefit of the job, chatting up the female students who came in to look for books and to study. Day was the youngest member of the team with only six months' service behind him. At seventeen, his ambition was getting drunk every weekend and getting laid by as many girls as he could.

The library building was nearly one hundred years old and in need of some serious renovation. Cracks lined most of the walls and ceilings, with the odd patch of plaster having fallen off here and there, exposing the old wooden laths or masonry. Damp and mould gathered in most corners of the building, filling the air with a stale musty smell that mingled with the aroma of old books. Sarah stacked up her trolley once more with the returns for that morning. As it was Thursday, the library had a half day and closed at one o'clock. Her first stop was the Fiction section, where a stack of King and Hutson books needed replacing. She looked wistfully at the blurb and the picture of the author on the back of one book, hoping that one day she too could be a well-known writer. She glanced across at Paul Day, hovering around two schoolgirls who giggled continuously as he tried every chat-up line he could think of. Sarah smiled at his persistence, and then she saw that Mrs Williams had taken notice as well. With her half-rim bifocals perched on the end of her nose, she started her stalk of the young stud.

Sarah had to warn Paul, who had already been threatened with the sack once today. Quickly she snatched up a large book and dropped it squarely on the polished wood floor. It gave off an enormous bang, which startled everybody in the building. Mrs Williams stopped dead in her tracks and gave Sarah a distasteful look. Day briefly looked to where the noise had come from, then read the message in Sarah's eyes. He moved off quickly, disappearing into one of the many hiding holes that the building held. Within moments, voices were back to whispers, and Sarah carried on with her work. She could feel the flush on her pale complexion as she lifted the last two books from the trolley and set them in place, and it was then that she noticed the man at the far end of the room using the computer. She sidestepped into one of the aisles and peered over the top shelf at him. Who was he? She hadn't seen him come in. Conscious of her staring, she glanced around, only to see that Paul was watching her every move. He made sure the coast was clear of Mrs Williams before he left the safety of his hiding place and made his way across the room towards Sarah.

He swaggered across and sidled up next to her.

"What are you looking at then?" Smiling, he too glanced over the top of the books at the seated figure. "Don't let Mrs Frosty catch you looking at the opposite sex." He nudged her in the arm.

She straightened the books on the shelf in front of her. "I don't know what you're talking about." A smirk came to her lips.

"Of course you don't." He eyed up two girls seated at the tables in the centre of the room.

"Who is he, Paul, do you know?"

"Nah, never seen him before." His attention was now on the two girls, one of whom happened to glance across at him. "He asked me where we keep all the local news records."

"Oh," Sarah replied, thinking on how she should introduce herself to the stranger.

"Anyway don't do anything I wouldn't do." Day made his way over to the young women.

Sarah pushed the trolley towards the seated figure, stopping just feet from him. He was so engrossed with what he was doing that he did not see the young woman standing beside him. She could tell he was having trouble figuring out how to work the computer. "I beg your pardon. Can I help you at all?" she asked softly.

Hunter turned to face the soft spoken woman." Um yes, I can't seem to find the news records on this thing," He raised his eyebrows at her with a look of puzzlement on his face. "I've never used a computer before."

She stroked her lips with her tongue and gazed into his eyes.

"Let me see if I can help." She pulled out a stool and sat down beside him. As she reached for the keyboard, her arm brushed against his.

She did not know what the attraction was, whether it was his troubled face, or his looks she did not know, but there was definitely a strong attraction to him. "What exactly are you looking for, Mr ...?"

"The name is Hunter," he said, giving her a steady gaze. "And it's hard to say exactly what I'm after because I don't know myself." She gave him a bewildered look.

He corrected himself. "Sorry, what I mean is that I roughly know what I'm after, but ..."

She interrupted. "Well first we need a date or specific name of the item, and then we can get a reference number on where to start looking."

He took a deep breath, then gave a ragged sigh. "Where to start, that's a good question. How long have you got?" He tried to smile, but it faded in seconds.

Sarah looked at her watch; eleven thirty. She had the time as long as Mrs Mitchell stayed out of the way.

Hunter told her about Carl—she was familiar with the story anyway through the media coverage—then about the disappearance of Debbie Summers.

"Right, we should have something on Debbie Summers," she said and started to type on the keyboard.

She could feel Hunter's eyes on her. She'd been told she was plain but fancied herself as attractive—too pale by half, but her complexion, unmarked, soft, and smooth, was her best feature. How she carried herself was what made the difference, she knew. Femininity oozed from her, and she aimed to project a solitude and mystery that might make a good impression on a man of the world.

"Here we are, Debbie Summers." She grabbed a pen and wrote the reference number down on a slip of paper.

"Blimey that was only six years ago," She peered more closely at the date, then frowned. "Six years later to the day, your son disappeared," she said in a whisper.

Hunter nodded "Yeah, and the police think the two aren't connected. There's more to this than meets the eye."

Sarah smiled at him; this mystery was beginning to interest her. She rose and told him to follow her, then headed for the news records storage area. Once there, reference number in hand, she opened the door to the archives room. Around the walls stood stacks and piles of newspapers, each bundle tied with string and labelled with a small square of faded paper displaying a reference number.

"Well, finding the reference number was easy; now we've got the hard part." Sarah gave a little snort of laughter as she looked around at the piles of paper.

"Look, I don't mean to be rude or anything, but I don't want to keep you from your work."

She turned to face him. "Don't worry about it; I'd rather be helping you than, well ..." She didn't know what to say, but could feel the blood rushing to her cheeks, the telltale sign that her embarrassment was about to show again. She wanted to tell him that she was attracted to him, but it was not a girl's place to do such a thing. At least that was what she'd always been taught.

He smiled at her. "Ah, that's okay then, as long as I'm not keeping you."

She combed her fingers through her black hair, just to take her mind off what she was thinking.

They both searched for the reference number, checking the bundles one by one, now and again passing a bit of small talk. It took nearly half an hour to find the right bundle. Hunter lifted the heap of faded newspaper to a small table that sat below a large arched window overlooking a small enclosed garden. He struggled with the string binding it together, gradually losing patience and pulling at it frantically.

Sarah laid a hand on his arm. "Try this, it'll be a lot quicker," She pulled a small penknife from her trouser pocket and handed it to him.

"Thanks."

Hunter took the knife and cut the string. The split the bundle in half and began scanning the headlines on each front page.

"Here it is." Sarah said excitedly, holding the page where he could see it:

GIRL OF TEN DISAPPEARS ON EXMOOR.

Hunter too had found a paper with similar headlines, but his carried a picture of the young girl on the front page. The girl was wearing her school uniform and was smiling happily at the photographer; she had fair shoulder-length hair in pigtails and an innocent face.

Sarah gazed at the photo. "Who would do such things to children? They must be sick to take them from their parents!" She looked at Hunter who was wistfully staring at the picture.

"Yeah, who. That's what I intend to find out." He gritted his teeth and then read the story underneath the photo.

Police are baffled at the disappearance of Debbie Summers, who seems to have vanished from the face of the earth. The ten-year-old schoolgirl was last seen at a friend's house, some three miles from her home on the outskirts of Porlock. She left her friend's house at six o'clock to cycle home, but she never made it.

There were plenty of articles on the disappearance in various newspapers, all speculating on what might have happened. Hunter and Sarah Holly were scanning them one by one for more information, when an amplified voice shattered their silence.

"The library will be closing in ten minutes, thank you." The voice was that of Mrs Williams.

Sarah had forgotten the time, and even what day it was.

The announcement panicked her somewhat. She gave a quick glance at her watch, just to check.

"Blimey, it's ten to one. Oh, she's going to kill me, I have loads to do before we close.

Hunter closed the paper he was reading and looked confused over her panic. "I thought you said it would be okay to help me." She was now by the door of the room.

"Yes it was, but ... well, I forgot it was Thursday."

She could see that Hunter still didn't understand. "Thursday is half day closing, at one o'clock."

"Oh, I see. Well, I'd better get going then. I wouldn't want to land you in trouble." He stood from the table and began stacking the newspapers together.

She had to do something fast. She could not just let him leave, not like this. He stood beside her at the door; she looked him in the eye.

Why is it, when you are just getting to know someone they have to leave? she thought. The story of her life always ended up the same. She had to make the move.

"Look, I'll go through the newspapers and jot down anything that I think is relevant. There must be loads here that could be valuable to you."

"Yeah, if you could, that'll be great." He put his hand on her shoulder and gently squeezed it, then snatched his hand back. "Where's my manners, I don't even know your name."

"It's Sarah, Mr. Hunter, Sarah Holly." She grabbed his extended hand and smiled; things were looking better!

"Call me Hunter, everyone else does."

She released her grip "Well, Hunter." She couldn't help smiling at calling someone *Hunter.* "How about I try to find out all I can this afternoon and meet you tonight somewhere?" She had done it; she had actually asked a man out!

"I thought you said the library closes at one?"

"It does to the public, but I've got things to catch up on, and Betty won't mind me staying on a bit late; in fact, it might make her think I'm more interested in the job than she thinks." She laughed, knowing that when she did so, her face lit up.

"All right. Look, I can't thank you enough for this; it's really good of you to help."

"Well, buy me a drink tonight if you feel that grateful"

"I will. Where shall I meet you?" he asked.

She thought for a moment. "Let's say outside the library at seven thirty."

He agreed, and she led him through the library to the entrance. By now the place was nearly empty, with the exception of two girls waiting by the desk for Paul Day, much to the disgust of Mrs Williams, who demanded they wait outside.

"Thanks again for your help, and I'll see you tonight." He smiled.

"Yes, I look forward to it," she said, not realising that the two other members of staff were watching and listening.

Hunter pushed open the door and stepped out onto the street. She watched him mingle among the shoppers, then disappear out of sight, thinking of the evening ahead. So did Paul Day, who envied the stranger; he'd been trying to win over the charming Sarah Holly since he had started work in the library and yearned to get the innocent twenty-four-year-old in bed. Paul was grinning as Sarah turned around to face them; her tantalizing smile said it all.

She had a date!

~~~

The afternoon was bright for a change, and the air was almost warm. For once, Hunter had a good feeling inside. No doubt the weather helped. However, he was sure it had more to do with his meeting of Sarah Holly. Her hand in his had been warm and soft. He could still feel a tingle of excitement from her touch; in fact, this was the first time he had ever been aroused by a handshake.

He collected himself and straightened his civilian clothing outside his CO's office. It was usual practice when leaving the regiment to see the commanding officers before you left. Hunter's first call was at the office of Captain T.W. Brice. He found the door with that name plate, then gave a firm knock and waited. There was a moment's silence, then came the stern command: "Come in."

He entered the brightly lit room, came to attention before the officer's desk, and snapped off a salute.

"Stand easy, Hunter."

Hunter took a relaxed posture, his hands cupped behind his back.

Captain Brice laid his pen on the paperwork in front of him and sat back in his chair, looking up at Hunter.

"I'll be sorry to see you go, Hunter, you're a bloody good soldier."

"Thank you, sir."

Brice moved uncomfortably in his chair, visibly awkward in this out-of-the-ordinary situation.

"How are things at home, how's"—the captain looked down at the file in front of him, searching for the name of Hunter's wife—"Jenny bearing up?"

Hunter swallowed hard. He would tell Brice the truth, he owed him that much. "We're no longer together, sir."

Brice looked surprised. "Damn, sorry to hear that," Brice said, glancing at the family photo on his desk, of him, his wife, and his three children, all smiling, and all still alive..

"Look, Hunter, the camp was shocked to hear about your son. Myself, I can't even imagine what you're going through, but splitting up with your wife, shit, I expected Jock to tell me about that, after all, he's been with you a lot lately."

Brice noticed the puzzlement on Hunter's face.

"He has been with you during the day, hasn't he?" Brice's voice had changed to that of the commander.

Hunter couldn't figure out what Jock was up to. He'd only seen him once during the day, but he felt he had to cover up for him.

He probably has some tart on the go.

"Yes, sir, he's been around a fair bit, thanks for letting him have the time off."

~~~

With the farewells over, Hunter's next stop was the CO's office, where Lieutenant Colonel J. C. Bray would be waiting for him, and much the same conversation. This was a routine that every marine had to endure when leaving the service. Most had the option to join up again if Civvie Street was not what they expected.

CHAPTER 14

Hunter waited outside the library as arranged. He had arrived a little early, and the time dragged slowly. He stood against the library doors and watched the passing traffic, keeping just out of sight. On Thursday evening, he knew that the lads from the camp would be in town and ready for a good session on the drink, and the last thing he wanted was for any of them to see him, not that they would have recognised the smartly dressed bearded man lurking in the darkness. Hunter had made an exception tonight with his clothes. Instead of jeans, he wore a pair of brown cords, and the usual T-shirt replaced with a neatly pressed white shirt under his usual brown leather jacket.

The Church of St. Mary's in the town centre chimed in the half hour, and Hunter checked his watch.

Seven thirty exactly, so where was his date?

Taxis dropped their fares outside the pub across the road. Hunter scanned each woman who stepped from them, hoping that it would be Sarah. Repeatedly he stepped from the darkness on hearing the sound of hurried women's footsteps, each one sounding distinctive, but none of them was the woman he was expecting. Several times he startled the female passersby, seeming to appear from nowhere. One girl in a group of three shrieked with fright on seeing the bearded stranger. Her friends laughed and pulled her on down the street, to the pub across the road.

He angled his watch again at the streetlight in front of him. She was ten minutes late.

"She ain't coming, you prat, Hunter," he said aloud, then thought of the events earlier. An argument started in his head.

Did she make the date or did I? She did, so why is she late? She's not coming, you screwed up, you got it all wrong, you must have done. It was the Library at seven thirty, I'm sure that's what we arranged. Bollocks!

"Hello," a soft woman's voice said. "Sorry I'm late."

Hunter was startled. He had not heard Sarah walk up the street behind him, and somehow, he couldn't say why, he had expected her to arrive from the direction of the town centre.

He turned to face her. "Are you late?" He motioned a look at his watch. "Never mind."

She looked good, he thought, even if they were standing in the artificial light of the street. Her black hair shone in the darkness. She had put it into a platted ponytail that flattered her feminine features. Sex appeal oozed from her, even though she wore a leather bomber jacket that hid the contours of her body. Excitement and desire came over him in a rush, and he felt like a teenager on a first date. The cold breeze carried the fragrance of an expensive perfume like a scented aura that engulfed the man in front of her.

"Right, then, where's that drink you promised me?"

Hunter smiled, then nodded to the pub on the opposite side of the road. "I don't know what that place is like, but it seems quite popular."

She looked across at the pub. "The Red Lion. It's as good as the rest and a perfect place to start."

"Good, well, let's go."

They crossed the road shoulder to shoulder looking every bit an item. Sarah followed Hunter up to the crowded bar as he sidled in between two groups of people. Moments later, the barmaid sauntered over to him, seeing his outstretched hand waving a ten-pound note.

"Yes," the young girl snapped from behind the bar.

"One pint of lager, and ..." Hunter turned to Sarah, who was a few steps behind him, watching every move he made. "What do you want to drink, Sarah?"

"Just a sweet cider will do me," she replied.

By this time the barmaid had returned with Hunter's pint and was waiting impatiently for his next order.

"A sweet cider." He said, turning back to Sarah.

The server grabbed a bottle and glass and slammed them both down on the bar.

"Three pounds eight pence."

"Please," he snapped.

The girl scowled at him, she did not have time for manners, and she wasn't paid to be polite.

"Three pounds eight pence *please*, you should say," he said with a smile.

Sarah put her hand over her mouth trying not to laugh as she watched the girl's embarrassment.

"Three pounds eight pence, please," she rasped, and held out her hand for the money.

"There you are. Easy isn't it?"

He offered the ten-pound note, and the barmaid snatched it from his hand. Hunter collected his change and joined Sarah, who was still hiding her embarrassment for the girl. "Poor girl, you embarrassed her." She took her drink from him.

"She deserved it; it costs nothing to be polite."

Sarah nodded in agreement. "True. Shall we sit down? I have lots to tell you; you won't believe what I've found out today."

They edged around the crescent-shaped bar looking for a vacant table; all were full or partially occupied.

"They have a restaurant upstairs; it'll be quiet up there." She realised what she had just implied, but hinting for food wasn't what she meant." Or we can go somewhere else; somewhere we can talk in peace and quiet."

Hunter glanced up at the balcony overhanging the bar; the smell of food gave him a hunger.

"Yeah, let's go and see what they have to offer. Are you hungry?" he asked.

Before she could answer, he strode off towards the stairs that lead up to the restaurant.

At his glance, she shook her head with a smile, then followed.

The waiter showed them both to a table, the quiet table Hunter had asked for. It was tucked away in the far corner of the room, its view slightly obscured by a low partition perhaps three feet in length.

The babble of voices from down in the bar was hardly audible to the two diners; the soft piped music gave a soothing setting as they both slipped off their jackets and studied the menu. A single lit candle poked unnaturally out of a short-necked wine bottle in the centre of the table. Hardened wax clung in ripples to its sides. Hunter skipped the starter and ordered the steak, and Sarah ordered the scampi. The waiter jotted down both their choices, took the menus, and left.

"So what did you find out today?" he asked, starting the conversation.

Sarah's face lit up, as if she was guarding some great secret. She leant forward, resting her arms on the table; the candle flickered with the soft gasps of her breath. Hunter caught the full beauty of the woman; the light from the naked flame toned her skin with dancing yellows and deep orange, also casting provocative shadows. She wore a white body-hugging T-shirt that left nothing to the imagination and faded blue denims that complemented the rest of her attire. Hunter leaned a little closer to her from across the table.

"Well you know about that little girl, Debbie Summers?" Hunter nodded. "Well she's not the only one to have disappeared on the moors. I found one other quite by chance, when I was sorting through another pile of papers, and there it was looking right at me!"

Hunter frowned. "What was?"

"Well six years before Debbie Summers disappeared, another girl did a disappearing act, virtually in the same place as Carl vanished. The girl and her family were on a camping holiday, and she too was never found." Sarah's eyes widened. "The strange thing is that all of the children vanished on or around the same day, give or take a day or so. Now in one of the articles about Debbie Summers, they said that the search parties looked throughout the night, and here's the link, that they were helped by a full moon, but still found nothing."

"What about the girl who disappeared six years before the Summers girl? Was that a full moon?"

The whole plot was becoming more sinister to Hunter. What did it all mean?

Sarah carried on. "Well I looked up an old astrological chart, and yes, all the disappearances were on a full moon. I tell you, Hunter, this is creepy. I have a bad feeling about what's going on."

Hunter stared down at the table and played nervously with his napkin. "You and me both. I've been having nightmares ever since it happened, nightmares that you couldn't imagine, they're so—well, ..." His voice croaked with emotion, and he lapsed into silence.

She seemed to see the hurt he was feeling, reached across the table, and took his hand. The warmth of her grasp had a soothing effect. Part of her seemed to draw through his skin and give him an insight into her mood. He could feel her happiness, her kindness, her love, and for a brief moment he felt as one with her, as if he was part of her, knowing all that she thought. She tightened her grip.

"That's not all, I started to look deeper, through years of archives." She paused, as if gathering herself. "And ... well, this has been going on a long time. Children have been disappearing for years, every six years. As far as I looked back, children have been vanishing, and not only children. Adults disappeared before the turn of the century, walkers and such like, all said to have perished in the many bogs on the moors."

"Just like they say Carl has?"

"Yes just like Carl, and Debbie and the rest of them, but this whole story might go back before the birth of Christ and when the Romans came to this country. Apparently, they killed and slaughtered whole settlements, men, women, and children. Anyone that got in the way was killed, so many villagers fled onto the moors, an area they knew very well, and the Romans didn't. So to cut a long story short ..." Sarah took a sip from her drink, then carried on.

"After a while the Roman soldiers were ordered to quash this little bit of resistance from the peasants, which they did, but not before a druid priest conducted a sacrifice to bring forth the power of the pagan gods, so that the men in the village would have the strength to conquer their enemies. Now it said in the book—now get this one, you'll love this." A smile stretched her lips. "Well, it said that the power was given to them in the form of a wolflike beast."

Hunter swallowed hard; the word *beast* boomed into his head. Could that be what he had seen the other night in his dream?

"What did they sacrifice?" he had to ask, but felt he already knew the answer.

"A person, usually a child, and when they had done, some of the villagers were given the power of this so-called beast, but on the same day the Romans marched on their settlement and killed most of them, one of them the druid priest. And it said that because of his death he never revoked the power, never sent it back to where it came from!"

"So what good did this power do then, to those that had it?" Hunter asked, not knowing how much credence to give what Sarah was saying.

She drew a ragged sigh, maybe not believing the story herself. "Well, apparently the Romans were camped for the night, again under a full moon. Then, out of nowhere, hidden by a bank of rolling mist, they were attacked by some wolflike creatures. *Creatures from the bowels of the earth*, it said in the book. They ran into the Roman camp with death shining in their eyes. Most of the soldiers were killed. After years of Romans being killed and disappearing on the moors, they marked its boundary with small upright stones, just so that they knew not to stray too far onto the moor. Some of those stones are still there today." Sarah sat back in her chair. "Well, that's how the story goes, believe it or not."

"This is madness, that was thousands of years ago, how can that have anything to do with what's happening now?"

Hunter struggled to believe what she was telling him, yet it seemed the same sort of beasts as in his dreams. Nothing made sense to him anymore; life was a mystery.

Sarah shrugged her shoulders to his question; she was as baffled as he was.

"I don't really know, but it just seems too much of a coincidence, being that it all happened in the same place."

Their conversation was interrupted by the waiter, who had both their meals balanced on his arm. Sarah exhaled deeply in disbelief when the huge platefuls of food were set on the table. The waiter asked if they required anything else. Hunter shook his head, and the man left.

Sarah picked gingerly at her meal, and so did Hunter. Somehow his appetite had gone. His head was reeling between facts and fiction, and trying to distinguish the two.

"I've got to go back."

"Where?" Sarah asked, puzzled.

Hunter jabbed his fork into the steak. "On the moors. I've got to find out what's going on. Those villagers have something to do with it, I just know."

"Tell you what." She paused and drew a deep breath, her gaze fixed on his. "Why don't we finish up here and go back to my flat? We can talk better there, and I can show you all of the stuff I've found."

She hoped she was not being too forward in asking him back to her flat, though deep down she knew that he would go.

He agreed, bringing a smile to her face. They both ate as much of the meal as they could, with Sarah leaving a large portion of hers, much to the disgust of the waiter—who incidentally did not receive a tip.

~~~

Sarah Holly was not in the habit of bringing men back to her second-floor flat; quite the opposite, in-fact. She prided herself that she did not sleep about with men, only when they struck her as being interesting or good fun to be with. Hunter was in the interesting class, with the fun aspect hoping to come later. Her most recent boyfriend had lasted a year before he started to become predictable down to the minute and complaisant in their relationship, so she gave him the mighty push; the man had become boring.

Sarah was a great believer in fate, and her meeting with Hunter was clearly meant to be. She certainly had a physical attraction to him, more so than any other man she had ever met, but she somehow knew that it was not to be a lasting relationship; ships in the night, perhaps.

She unlocked the door to her flat, opened it, and stepped in, followed by Hunter. "Well, here we are, my humble abode." She flicked a switch, lighting up the small living room.

"Nice," Hunter commented, closing the door behind him.

The room was plain but homely; the walls painted in a pale shade of pink, dissected in the middle with a floral dado. The suite matched the top part of the walls, and the deep maroon carpet complemented the whole room, giving it a warm and cosy feel.

Sarah took the two bottles of wine that Hunter had bought on their way back to her flat, and stepped into the kitchen to open them. Hunter remained a moment longer, taking in the living room, but quickly came into the kitchen to assist her with the wine.

"This is a really nice place you have here. Did you do all the decorating yourself?" he asked. Slowly he took the bottle from her hand.

"Yep, all done with these dainty little hands." She showed

him her empty hand and smiled nervously. He was quite close to her, and they were now quite alone.

Her eyes stared into his. She moistened her lips, and her heart was beating loudly enough that she could hear it. He gave a strong pull on the corkscrew, and the cork came free.

She gave a little laugh. "Ah, well done, all it needs is a man's touch." She cringed, realising what she had just said, but it was the truth, she wanted a man's touch. She wanted *his* touch.

How long will it take him to make the first move?

~~~

Hunter placed the wine bottle on the work surface, keeping his eyes on her the whole time. Her full lips were a deep red, just the type he liked. She stepped a pace closer to him. He reached around her waist and pulled her to his body until their faces were just inches apart. He could feel the soft nervous gasps of her breath on his face; they quickened as he drew her closer. He could feel her body trembling through his; slowly he put his lips to hers. The kiss was passionate, their tongues probing each other's mouths in a growing frenzy.

Their lips parted, and they held each other for a moment. Hunter was first to pull away.

"Got any glasses for the wine?" He asked, not the most romantic thing to say, but he could think of nothing else.

She smiled at his question and drew open one of the wall units, pulled out two glasses, and handed them to him, not before kissing him again on the cheek. They both settled on the sofa with full glasses of wine, a small coffee table in front of them stacked high with books and papers.

"Here's all that I found out." She nodded to the coffee table. "But most of it is in here." She leant forward and grabbed a notepad from the top of the stack, then handed it to Hunter, who browsed through its contents.

Sarah sipped from her glass, then faced Hunter. "What d'you plan to do when you go on the moors? I mean, if you do find out anything, how do you plan to prove it?"

Hunter placed the notepad on his lap and sighed. "Well, if it has got anything to do with the villagers, they're going to pay."

Sarah fixed him with a look. "How are you going to make them pay?"

Hunter returned her intent look. "They have to die. That's what I think the nightmares are all about. They keep taking me back to the moors, and every time I see these ..." He paused, not knowing whether he was telling her too much, but he needed to tell someone, and she was the closest friend he had now.

"These what? she asked.

"Like the creatures you were talking about earlier."

"What, the creatures from the Roman story?"

He nodded. "Yeah, just like the ones in the story. They're in most of the dreams. They seem so real, and I even have bruises to prove it." He pulled up the front of his shirt, exposing the faded bruise from the barbed wire fence.

Sarah's mouth dropped open. "You got that when you were in a dream?"

"Yeah, why?"

She jumped to her feet and leapt over to a bookshelf, which was jam-packed with books. She brought one back to her seat and then opened the book to a marked page.

"There you are, astral projection. That's what I think you've been doing." She handed him the book.

Hunter studied the book briefly but still could not make out what significance this had to do with him.

"It's too much to take in; this is all mumbo jumbo, isn't it?"

Sarah shook her head. "You should know it's happening to you. Look, I know it will be hard, but d'you think you can tell me what happened that day when Carl disappeared?"

Hunter took a deep breath. He had been over this story so many times, so once more would not hurt, he thought.

He began at the beginning; it seemed the best place to start. He told her about stopping in the village to buy some food, then about the Black Dog Inn, where he bought the bottle of wine, and how Carl broke into near hysteria when seeing this woman at the shop. Sarah listened raptly to the whole story;

she topped up their glasses on occasion as Hunter carried on in full detail.

His memory was more complete now; he remembered the stone circle and the blood that lay around one of them, the mist, and the lightning. He told her everything, even the bits he could not understand, if indeed the whole story was at all believable. He still had questions that needed answering, such as being found on the outside of the forest, rather than the inside where he presumed he had fallen. These mysterious aspects indicated that maybe he would never find out what really happened.

He told her every detail about his dreams and the people in them. No matter how far-fetched it all sounded, he told her. He told her about the dream of seeing Detective Sergeant Short on the moors on the night of his death.

He was living it all again as he told her. At times talking about Carl brought emotion to his voice. He could still see his blood-soaked body lying on that slab of stone and the shadowy figures standing over him. Sarah comforted him, evidently feeling his emotion as he described his small son's disappearance. He reminded himself that she had seen the posters of Carl around the town and in the newspapers; it must be hard for her not to imagine the nightmare as well.

He finished his story and buried his head into his hands; she wrapped her arms around his neck and hugged him tightly. "So sorry, I shouldn't have asked you to bring it all up again," she whispered.

He faced her. "Well, now you know, you know as much as I do."

She smiled at him and reached for the wine bottle, draining the last of the wine into their glasses.

"May I use your bathroom?" he asked, getting to his feet.

She nodded in the direction of a door that was next to the kitchen.

For the kind of girl that Sarah was—shy and quiet, he thought—he did not expect the decor of the bathroom at all. On closing the door, he turned on the light, which to his amazement revealed a mirrored wall alongside the bath and shower. The bathroom suite was done in the same light pink as the decor in the main room of the flat, but here the feeling was glitzy, something that he would have expected an exhibitionist to have, not Sarah. She was indeed a dark horse, he thought, chuckling as in the mirrors he watched himself urinate into the toilet. *If the bathroom is like this, what's the bathroom like?* Mirror ceilings, leather masks and whips ... his mind conjured up all manner of visions. He washed his hands and tossed cold water on his face, then took a hand towel from its ring next to the sink. Dabbing the soft material to his face, he could smell Sarah's perfume clinging to it; he took in a few deep breaths of the aroma, and it seemed to cling to him as it did to the towel.

He fancied the girl and wanted to get to know her on a more intimate level. They had kissed, that was a start, but he wanted to see her naked, and began to picture her on the bed, wearing only a white basque.

"Stop it, fuck's sake. You're turning into a pervert." First things first. He needed to know everything she knew about the moors and the missing people.

He hung up the towel and opened the bathroom door. The front room was in darkness; the only light was coming from the bathroom behind him. He paused for a second, looking to see if Sarah was still in the room. *Maybe she's playing some sort of game with me.* He could see no movement, and the sofa was empty.

A sound came from the other side of the room, he peered into the darkness, but still he could see nothing.

"Sarah," he said softly, stepping towards the middle of the room.

The noise came again, and this time he could see a chink of light from under a door at the far side of the room. He stepped closer.

"Sarah," he called, but again there was no answer.

"Look, Sarah, if this is some sort of game, I ain't laughing."

His patience was wearing thin. He stepped to door, cocked

his head to one side, and listened. Music came from the room. He tapped at the door.

Sarah responded softly, "Come in."

He breathed a sigh of relief. He'd been about to think he was in another dream. He opened the door and looked in.

"What took you so long?" Sarah asked.

She lay on the bed wearing only a white basque. Her face was glowing pink, and Hunter imagined this sort of approach must be new to her.

"I hope you don't think I make a habit of doing this, but I think that you like me, and I like you, so why don't we just prove how much we like each other?" She beckoned him to the bed.

Hunter was taken aback, not just by the sheer forwardness of the girl or his dream from boyhood about being seduced by a beautiful young lady wearing only a Basque.

"Déjà vu," he said, stepping up to the bed and grabbing Sarah's outstretched hand.

"What?"

"Just something I thought of earlier, that's all." This was not the time to start a discussion on psychic phenomena or fantasies.

Sarah knelt up on the bed as Hunter sat down beside her. She flung her arms round his neck, and they kissed passionately. She unbuttoned his shirt as they both lay down on the bed, their tongues still probing each-other's mouths. His hands rubbed sensuously up and down her body feeling his way round the softness of her flesh. Their passion was only interrupted by the obstacles of his clothing. Trying to kiss and take off ones shoes at the same time was an impossibility, even for a Royal Marine Commando.

Now naked, Hunter rolled on top of her and gazed upon her plain but attractive features, her skin had a natural-looking tan to it, highlighted even more by the white lace basque she was wearing. He stroked her dark flowing hair, which followed the contours of the pillow and stopped at her soft feminine shoulders. Sarah wrapped her legs round the back of his, pushing her loins against his now erect penis. He could hold back no more, his hands searched for the fastenings that were holding the garment on, not knowing really where they could be found.

"Here," she gasped softly, taking his hand and pushing it between her legs.

Hunter then felt the poppers that fastened at the crutch. His hand cupped her firm vagina through the material, and he rubbed it gently until he could hold back no more. He pulled softly at the fastenings, and the basque jumped slightly up her body, exposing her dark pubic hair. They both moaned pleasurably as he gently pushed inside her. She gripped his buttocks and pulled them on to her. Any thoughts that either of them had hours earlier were now forgotten; their minds and bodies were as one. Sarah's gasps of pleasure became louder as she reached her climax, Hunter too was coming to a crescendo, until finally he could feel his warm fluid pump inside of her. She held him tightly as he lay on top of her, gradually getting his breath back. After a moment he rolled to one side, his body and mind filled with fatigue. The nights without sleep were now catching up.

"That was great," she said softly, sitting up in the bed.

"Yes, it was."

He smoothed his hand across her back as she made some sort of order of her hair.

"I'm just going to take a shower, I won't be long."

Sarah slid from the bed, gathered up her basque and padded naked to the bedroom door, Hunter watched with tired eyes as she pulled the door shut behind her. The light was still on in the bedroom, but the music from the record player had finished. He could not be bothered to turn it off, he was too tired. Within seconds the light started to darken, the room faded into insignificance, his eyes closed, and the perils of sleep fell upon him once again.

The loud thump stirred him from his sleep. His eyes flickered, then closed. He rolled on his side stretching his arm across for Sarah. She was not there. At first, he did not think much about being alone. Maybe she was still in the shower. How long had he been asleep? He collected his thoughts, realising that the bedroom light was no longer on.

Questions filled his head.

If Sarah had turned the light out, where was she now?

Had she gone to the toilet?

What time was it?

He shivered; the room was cold. He opened his eyes and glanced across at the bedroom door. It was still closed. He lifted his watch to his face and tried to see what the time was, but it was too dark, and his vision was blurred from the sleep. The cold bit into him once more. He looked in the direction of the record player, which was switched off; its dials were unrecognisable on the dark shape sitting in the corner of the room.

Another sound came from the direction of the front room, and this time he heard it clearly. He slid from the bed and slowly walked to the bedroom door. He felt for the light switch, found it, and switched it on. Nothing happened; the room stayed in darkness.

"Bulbs" he voiced quietly, but then thought that maybe the power had gone off.

A power cut, that's why the room is so cold, the heating is off, and Sarah has gone to find out what is going on.

His thoughts seemed to satisfy his curiosity, so he turned back towards the bed, thinking that he would get frostbite if he stood out in the open any longer. The last thing he wanted was to be halfway across the front room and have the lights come back on, and Sarah seeing him naked. Not that he was ashamed of his body, but in freezing temperatures ... well, he knew that he was not the biggest of men at the best of times. It was as he was about to get back into her bed that his curiosity was aroused again: What was the noise coming from the front room, and if it was Sarah, did she need help?

He walked back to the door and took the handle, which was freezing to the touch. He pulled down on it and opened the door; cold air drifted in from the front room. He stood in the doorway and scanned the shadowy room. By the entrance to the kitchen stood a small side table with a lamp. This lamp was switched on, but the bulb was not very bright; it lit only the entrance to the kitchen and the corner of the wall where it sat.

Something moved in the far corner of the room, the shadows cast by the lamp just suggesting its outline. Hunter strained his eyes to probe the shadowy darkness; a shape was becoming more recognisable, and giving away a reflective outline that could have only been Sarah. She sat with her back to him, leaning over the small dining room table, her naked body glowing like a beacon in the gloom. The dining room table butted up to the wall next to the bathroom door and was out of the main path through the room. By the sounds that Hunter could hear, she was obviously eating; *gorging herself* might be more apt. He smiled and came closer. Seeing her naked body again began to get him aroused. Sleep was now out of the question; he felt wide awake. Stepping up behind her, he could see that she was frantically stuffing herself on something. He placed both hands on her shoulders.

"Save some for me, then," he said, bending down to kiss her. Then he caught sight of what she was eating.

"Shit."

He took a step back as Sarah turned to face him, but not the Sarah he knew from earlier. In the dimness of the room, he could see her hideous features, her lips drawn back showing upper and lower canine teeth two inches long, and her eyes shining like quicksilver. The lower part of her face was covered in a dark substance, which could only have been blood. It hung from her lips as a thick glutinous drawl, but it was the sight of what she had been eating that sickened Hunter to the core. The small head of a child lay on the table, its spine protruding where the flesh of the neck used to be. The left hand side of the face had been eaten away, leaving the teeth on one side of the mouth exposed. The woman's fingers still pushed deep into one of the eye sockets. The head was that of Carl.

"*No!*" Hunter shouted as he backed across the room and stumbled over the sofa. She was up now and coming for him.

He fell to the floor, and everything seemed to happen in slow motion. He could feel a sharp pain in the back of his head, where he must have hit the floor, also the pressure of her hands on his shoulders!

"Hunter, are you all right? Hunter?" Sarah asked softly.

She was crouched over him shaking him to wake him up, her hands on his shoulders. His eyes blazed open, staring her in the face. He grabbed her by the throat and squeezed as hard as he could. Sarah struggled to loosen his grip, but she could not move his hands. The brightness from the light bulb hanging in the centre of the bedroom ceiling dazzled him for a second; his thoughts were still on the nightmare. Sarah gasped for breath, and he realised what was really going on and let go of her.

For one moment when he had hold of her, she looked into his eyes. Her eyes radiated hate, and he had wanted to kill her. Sarah scrambled to her feet as soon as he let go of her, and she retched, trying to catch her breath. Tears started to fill her eyes as she steadied herself at the foot of the bed. Her hair, wet from the shower, dripped on her basque, making the material translucent as it clung to her skin.

At once it came to him that he had had another nightmare.

He composed himself and viewed the room. It was the same as when he'd gone to sleep; the record player was still on, and Sarah's hair was still wet from the shower she had taken only minutes before. She started to sob, and her whole body shook in fear.

"You must have had another nightmare. I heard you shouting when I was drying myself in the bathroom, and when I came in you were on the floor—where you are now."

He wiped the sweat from his brow and realised that he had come close to killing her. The one real friend he had could so easily have died because of him.

"I'm so sorry, I really am sorry. I wouldn't hurt you for the world, you must know that, but this dream was so real, it's never been like this before, never!"

The emotion in his voice reassured her, she moved closer to him.

"I know you wouldn't." She crouched beside him and placed her hand on his. "What was the dream about?"

Hunter pushed himself to his feet and sat on the bed, he pulled the duvet round his lower body. Somehow he still felt cold. A sudden pain lanced through his skull, a sharp pain that made him clutch the back of his head. His fingers felt something warm and sticky matted into his hair; he could feel a tear in the scalp. Sarah showed concern as he viewed the blood on the end of his fingertips.

"My God, you must have hit your head when you fell out of the bed. Don't touch it, I'll get something for it," she said, then hurried out of the room.

She returned with a small bowl half full of warm water, and tucked under her arm she held a roll of cotton wool. She slid across the bed from behind him and gingerly parted the hair to view the wound.

She winced on seeing the cut. "Looks nasty," she said. "This might sting a bit."

She gently dabbed the wet cotton wool to the back of his head. He could feel a trickle water down the centre of his back.

Hunter remained silent.

Sarah asked again, "So what was the dream about?" She dropped the first of the blood-soaked cotton wool into the bowl, and the clear liquid went red.

He thought about his reply carefully. "The same sort of thing I usually get, except this one really freaked me out. I can't remember a lot about it now." He did not want to tell about it; after all, it was just a nightmare.

After a few minutes the bleeding had stopped, Sarah took the bowl back into the kitchen along with the cotton wool. When she returned to the bedroom, Hunter had already partially dressed and was just buttoning up his shirt.

"Where are you going?"

"I think I'd better leave."

She sat on the corner of the bed, confused at his actions. "Why?" she asked.

He finished fastening his shirt, then sat down beside her.

"Look, I could have killed you just now, I don't know what's happening to me, but"—he sighed deeply—"I don't trust myself anymore."

"But you didn't, it was only a nightmare!" She gazed intently into his eyes. "I can't let you leave like this."

"Please understand me, if I can't trust myself, how can you trust me?" He grabbed his shoes from under the bed, slid them on, and stood up once again.

"But I do trust you. Please stay."

Hunter faced a fitted wardrobe that took up one side of the bedroom wall. On each of the sliding doors was a full-length mirror. As he was straightening his attire, he noticed on each shoulder a few small red stains through his shirt. They were no bigger than pinpricks, but noticeable. Sarah watched as he undid the top four buttons of his shirt again and inspected each shoulder.

His heart began to race when he saw the small gouges. Each shoulder had five of these small marks, about an inch apart. They were a stark reminder of the terrible nightmare.

Sarah approached him from behind and slid her hands around his waist, then glanced over his shoulder to catch his eye in the mirror. His body went rigid on feeling her grasp around him. He stared deeply at her reflection in the mirror as she too inspected the small gouges to his flesh.

"What are those?"

Hunter buttoned up his shirt and stepped away from her.

"Looks like scratches from fingernails."

"Finger nails." She thought for a moment, a look of bewilderment on her face, then smiled.

"Of course, it was when I was trying to wake you up; I must have done it then."

Hunter didn't know the truth anymore. Was he dreaming now, or was this reality? The two dimensions were becoming dangerously close. He liked Sarah Holly. Indeed, one could say that he was struck by the girl's plain charm and personality; she was definitely more pleasure to be with than Jenny. However, his last nightmare about Sarah had felt so real, and yet it did not make sense. Just as he was learning to trust his dreams, the way he would his own instincts, they played this terrible trick on him.

Why should a relative stranger become embroiled in these dreams?

He had no idea.

He had to go back to the moors; that seemed his only salvation.

Sarah stayed a few steps behind him as he walked through the flat to the front door; he even found himself scanning the dining room table as he passed it. Maybe he wanted the head to be there, just to satisfy his curiosity, just so he knew his nightmare was correct. Nothing was there, not so much as a bloodstain. He reached the front door, and Sarah stepped beside him.

"Look, I don't know what I've done wrong, but—"

Hunter stopped her from carrying on. "It's not you, Sarah, I think you're a great girl, but I have to find out what happened to those children, and until then, I'm not good company to be with, trust me." He reached down and

took her hand.

"So what are you planning to do?" she asked.

He raised his eyebrows and shook his head. "I don't know. Maybe I'll find out when I get up there, who knows?"

She pulled herself tight to him. "Can I help?"

He smiled. "Yeah, If anything happens to me, give all your information to the police. Give it to a man called Finch at the Minehead police station, he's CID That should give him something to chew on."

Sarah grabbed a pen and paper from the telephone shelf by the front door, and wrote down the name Hunter had told her. Then she scribbled down two phone numbers and handed them to him. "Just in case you need me, ring anytime. This top one's my work number, and this is the flat. "

"Okay, I will, thanks."

They kissed briefly on the lips and exchanged smiles, then he stepped into the cold of the corridor.

"You be careful, you don't know what you're dealing with!" she said, then closed the door.

Hunter skipped down the concrete steps to the ground floor and thought about her last comment.

"Yeah, she's right about that!" He paused at the main door that led out of the apartments and glanced at his watch; it was 1:30 AM. He did not want to go home, back to that bleak, empty house that held so much misery for him. He decided to see Jock and sort out the arrangements on how he was to go back to the moors. Hunter made his way back through the town to where he had parked.

CHAPTER 15

FRIDAY MORNING: 1.45am

A thundery stickiness hung in the air, making sleep near to impossible for any who wanted it. Hunter did not. He switched off the engine to the mini and viewed Jock's house from the passenger window of the car. All was in darkness, and silence engulfed the small cul-de-sac. There was not a whisper of a breeze.

The journey from Sarah's apartment had not taken long. Jock's house was just the other end of town, the more down-market end of town. Hunter opened the door and stepped from the vehicle. The surrounding houses seemed to amplify the bang of the car door when he slammed it. A dog gave voice in one of the houses on hearing the loud noise; its protests went unnoticed by its owners, and quiet once again fell upon the estate.

Hunter walked silently to the back gate, opened it, and moved up to the back door. He listened for a second, then knocked softly. He waited; leaning against the wall, he viewed the neighbourhood. The hustle and bustle of urban life seemed so far away. Crime and violence seemed nonexistent. It was the time of day when one could contemplate the meaning of life and maybe come up with some profound answers. Hunter knocked again a little louder this time. Still there was no reply. He looked up at Jock's bedroom window, which overlooked the back garden. It was open.

~~~

Two naked bodies lay cooling atop the duvet. Jenny Hunter stretched her arm across Jock's chest and gave a contented moan. Their sex had been particularly physical that night, making the room unbearably hot, which made sleep uncomfortable, but not impossible. The first few reports from the bedroom window had stirred Jenny from her slumber. Jock also moved restlessly.

Another volley of mud and stones hit the glass, and some went through the opening and landed on the bed.

Jock opened his eyes as he felt some of the mud hit him. "What the fuck!" he said, brushing the clods of earth off his body.

"What's the matter?" Jenny sat up as another barrage of objects hit the window.

Jock slid out of bed and stepped over to the window. Jenny padded over behind him.

He saw Hunter about to throw another handful of stones and instantly drew back into the room. He grabbed Jenny by the arm and pushed her back to the bed. "What are you doing?" she snapped.

"Shut up," he whispered harshly. "It's your old man, he's outside."

Jenny sat on the bed with a stunned look. "D'you think he knows?"

Jock hurriedly pulled on some underwear. "I don't know, do I, but what the fuck's he doing here? And at this time of night."

"What are you doing?" Jenny asked.

"What does it look like; I'm going to see what he wants."

"Are you mad?" she asked, getting to her feet.

"Look, I just can't leave him out there; he'll know something's wrong if I do. Put some clothes on, will you?"

Jenny looked down at herself, then began to search for her underwear.

"Just stay in here and keep quiet, all right?"

Jenny nodded, and Jock disappeared out the door.

Hunter leant against the wall and looked into the kitchen. He watched Hunter leaning against the outside wall, watching him. He turned on the light, then plodded over to the back door.

He unlocked and opened the door, then looked frankly at his friend. "What's up, Hunt?"

"I didn't want to go home, so I thought I'd come around and see you, that's all right isn't it? Or have you got some little beauty hidden upstairs you don't want me to know about?"

Jock faked a smile and opened the door. Hunter walked into the kitchen.

"Bit late for paying people visits, innit?"

Hunter walked through to the hallway, paused at the foot of the stairs, and glanced up at the landing.

"Nah, it's already morning. How late did you want to sleep, anyway?" he quipped sarcastically.

Jock stopped behind him. "Go on into the front room, mate." He ushered Hunter through the doorway to his right, switched on the light, and quickly scanned the room for any of Jenny's clothing. It looked clear.

Hunter sat heavily in one of the armchairs; Jock poised himself on the edge of the settee, looking as uncomfortable as he felt.

"How's things going then, Jock?"

Jock grabbed a cigarette from the packet that lay on the coffee table in front of him, lit it, and took a deep draw.

"Yeah everything's okay." Smoke billowed from his mouth as he spoke. "Look, you didn't get me up at this hour just to ask how I was, what's on your mind?"

"Blimey, she must be something special, if you're that eager to get back to her. Who is she, do I know her?"

Jock shook his head. "Nah, you don't. She's just some sort I picked up in town the other night."

"Yeah. Well, sorry to disturb you, mate, but I need your help."

The floorboards creaked upstairs, Jock glanced at the door briefly.

Hunter smiled. "Seems she's getting a bit restless."

"She'll be all right." Jock leaned forward and stubbed out his cigarette. "Now what's this all about, Hunter?"

Hunter sighed. "I want you to take me back up to the moors."

"What for?"

"I know something's going on up there. Don't ask how I know, I just do, and those villagers in Oare aren't the full ticket."

Jock was puzzled but relieved that Hunter was not there to catch him at it with his wife.

"Look, mate, I know it's hard for you, especially just coming out of the marines, but you've got to let go. Carl's gone. Even the police say that the chances of finding him alive now are nonexistent, and if they can't find out what happened to him, how can you?"

Hunter leant towards him. "All I can say is that there's more to this than meets the eye. We have proof!"

"Who's we?" Jock asked.

Jock listened intently as the man in the armchair told him all about meeting the girl in the library, the plain but attractive girl who turned out to be a librarian. The very same girl he took out for a drink and ended up making love to back at her flat. Hunter left out nothing, even related some nightmares with some pretty gory details. Jock took it all in, now he did not feel that bad about cheating on his best mate. In fact he even felt jealous about this girl Sarah Holly; she sounded his type of woman. However, the information about the beasts and druids, Romans and suchlike was too much for the sceptical friend to believe. After all, this was the nineteen nineties.

"So what d'you plan to do if you find out that the villagers had something to do with Carl disappearing?"

Hunter's cheek muscles bulged. "Make them pay!"

Jock knew all too well what Hunter had in mind. To make someone pay in commando jargon was to kill them, and there was none better for the job. Hunter had done every survival course there was, even the gruelling special boat service courses within the marines He had served with the SBS many times, most being in the Gulf War.

"Mate, if you go back on those moors, that copper will have your bollocks, especially if you start taking the law into your own hands."

"Like you said Jock, they ain't looking for Carl anymore, how will they know I'm up there? That is, unless you tell them."

Jock waved away Hunter's last comment. "If you're sure, I'll take you up there, but if you find out anything, you let me know, and then we can tell the police, alright."

Hunter agreed, with visible reluctance.

"I need one other favour, Jock."

"What?"

"Your shotgun." Hunter looked him directly in the eyes; he was not going to compromise on this issue.

Jock knew there was no point in arguing with Hunter; he would have his own way in the end. So he agreed.

Hours passed as the two men reminisced about their commando days together. They talked like departing friends, telling of the good times and the now comical bad times, but neither of them talked of the future, that uncertain future only the brave and foolhardy thought about.

They would leave at 4 AM for the moors; Hunter had already packed all the necessary equipment in the boot of the mini. Jock reached under the settee and pulled out the shotgun, wrapped in an old tablecloth and taped at each end, and handed it to his friend.

Hunter put the covered gun up to his shoulder, as if to fire it. "I need a plastic bin bag, have you got one?"

Jock disappeared toward the kitchen, then moments later returned with the bin bag.

"Here you are." He tossed it to Hunter." What d'you want it for?"

"Bury the gun in, and a few other bits and pieces I'm taking up there."

Jock fidgeted nervously in the doorway. "What other bits?"

Hunter winked at him. "Now, that'd be telling."

Jock asked no more; he just wanted him out of the house. Taking Hunter to the moors now would give him time to be back to work by 8 AM.

"Right, I'll get changed, and you get the gear from your car and put it in mine. The keys are on the shelf by the back door."

Jock ran up the stairs to the bedroom, where now Jenny lay asleep on the bed. He gave a cursory glance out the window, just to check that Hunter was on his way down the garden path. He pulled both windows shut, then reached across to Jenny and shook her gently. She woke with a start.

"What's the matter?" she asked in a husky voice.

Jock told her as he dressed. "He wants me to take him back onto the moors, so I'm going to."

She combed her fingers through her hair. "He wants you to do what?"

"Take him back onto the moors."

"Why?"

Jock zipped up his trousers and tucked in his shirt.

"Your guess is as good as mine. He reckons he's going to find out what happened to Carl. He thinks the villagers had something to do with it."

Even in the darkness, Jock could see the disbelief on Jenny's face.

"Have you tried to stop him?"

"What do you think? The man's gone mad, he's ranting about monsters and all sorts of shit like that, and the worst thing is—" He paused, wondering whether to tell her about the gun. Then he realized she would find out soon enough when the shit

hit the fan. "He's going armed to the teeth. He's planning on kicking some serious ass up there, and I tell ya something for nothing, I wouldn't want to be in those poor bastards' shoes!"

Jenny sat up on the bed. "We've got to tell the police, do something. This proves he's mentally unstable. I still think that detective was right about him, he's mad enough to do something to Carl."

Jock sprang across the room at her and grabbed her by the shoulders. "Now you listen to me, Hunter might be a lot of things, but he ain't a child killer. He wouldn't hurt a hair on that boy's head, he loved him!" He let her go.

"Well he might do if he knew he was your son!" she rasped.

"Just you shut your mouth, don't you ever say that again. Besides, you didn't know if Carl was mine. He's Hunter's kid, you remember that." He didn't bother to keep the anger out of his voice.

"He is your son, and you know it," she snapped.

Jock stood at the door to the bedroom and faced her. "I want you out of here when I get back, you got that?" He left the room.

Outside, he stood with Hunter, both of them looking into the boot of Jock's Capri.

"You planning on having a war?"

Hunter pushed the rest of his kit into the trunk of the car. "Just a few basic essentials."

"What about the claymore mine?" Jock asked.

Hunter shut the trunk. "Like I said, essentials."

CHAPTER 16

FRIDAY MORNING:

The stark bleakness of the moor hit Hunter once again as he unloaded his large rucksack from the back of Jock's car and placed it on the side of the road. The morning darkness was cold and silent; the whole moor seemed devoid of life. A rolling sea mist hung just feet above the ground, cloaking the land with a visible white screen. Not even the car's lights could penetrate the moist white shield more than a few yards.

Jock moved uncomfortably as Hunter stripped down to his underwear and began to change into his outdoor clothing, most of which was army issue, apart from the blue chequered shirt that he put on. He checked one last time the contents of his rucksack, saying aloud the name of each item as he found them, and then placed them in the boot of the car, ready to be packed again once everything had been checked.

"Hunting knife, trip flares, thunder flashes, one stun grenade, dagger, hand-held crossbow with bolts, provisions, water flask, spare clothing, first aid kit, torch, cooking stove, mess tins, string, hunting knife, machete, pump-action shotgun." He paused. "Shit, forgot the ammo for the gun!"

Jock walked round to the passenger side of the car, opened the door, and then flipped down the glove compartment.

"There you go, rifled slugs, or truck stoppers as the yanks call them." He tossed the box of ten shells to Hunter, who put them with the rest of his kit.

"Nice one, mate. Now then, where was I?"

"Shotgun," Jock answered.

"Yeah, shotgun." Hunter reached deep into the rucksack and pulled out an object wrapped in a black bin liner, a curved object that he placed down gently in the boot of the car. "And claymore."

Jock sighed deeply. "You're going to get yourself killed, you know that, don't you? As soon as you start using that shit, they'll have every armed copper in the area down here."

Hunter started to place all of the equipment back into the rucksack. "Maybe."

"Look, I've got to get back, Hunter. The CO will go mad if I ain't on time this morning."

The men faced each other, and Hunter held out his hand. "Later, take care of yourself mate."

The handshake was firm, verging on a test of strength.

"If you need me, Hunt, Give me a call." They released their grip on each other.

"I will; thanks."

It was the point of no return for Hunter as he watched the lights of the Capri fade and then disappear into darkened mist. He was now alone. He stood for a while until he could hear the car's engine no more, then faced the direction of the village. In a few hours, it would be light. He would follow the road as best he could to the outskirts of the village, then work his way across the fields to the place where Carl went missing. That ungodly place that held so many cursed memories for him.

For once, he felt relaxed, calm and ready for the battle that lay ahead. His future had no meaning now. His life had been turned upside down, and he wanted answers. He had no idea what he could be taking on. For all he knew, it was a force that was as old as time itself, and forgotten by modern man, though it still lingered in the back of their minds. This force mapped out man's destiny, whether good or bad.

Hunter stepped carefully along the road to the outskirts of the darkened village, and then through the blanket of mist he saw the stone cottages. There were only five lining the main road through the village, with the rest—like the inn, the blacksmith's and a handful of other small dwellings—tucked out of sight down a narrow lane. He viewed them momentarily and wondered what sinister secrets they held. A sense of unease told him to move on; it would be light soon.

He climbed into a field opposite. He needed to pass the village unnoticed, and most of all he needed to bury the gun and other pieces of ordnance he had on him. As the dawn of a new day approached, the night sky paled into a dark blue, and the landscape was soon cast in eerie twilight shadows. Hunter saw the ideal spot to hide the weapons. No more than ten minutes away from the village was a small spinney, easy to get to and seemingly a bit secluded from prying eyes. The orange morning sun peeked over a hill in the distance, and the birds started their songs for a new day. Hunter leant against a dry stone wall and marvelled at the power of nature as the climbing sun warmed his cold face.

This could have so easily been heaven, he thought, watching the thick white mist cloak the flora, then gradually fade, leaving thin threads of gossamer hanging like glistening bunting across the vegetation. The distinctive bark of a distant red deer echoed throughout the hills and valleys, then began an ensemble of pheasant cries marking their territories. Hunter set to his task; he turned back to the spinney and pushed through the dense vegetation, searching for a suitable spot.

He placed the heavy rucksack on the ground, took out his large machete, and crawled gingerly through a fox run in the bracken. Slowly he took every object he needed into the lair; he cut at the inside of a dense gorse thicket to make room for himself and his rucksack. The gorse intertwined sharp pointed blackthorns, giving any curious onlooker second thoughts about venturing into the centre of the dense cover.

Hunter laid out his ground sheet, then cut a little further into the bush to hide the shotgun and other firepower. Once all was hidden, he placed the cut pieces of bush back into place so that nothing looked out of place. His lair in the centre of the thicket was just high enough for him to sit up in, and its roof was as impenetrable as the sides, he was satisfied that this was the ideal position.

Hunter grabbed his rucksack and crawled slowly out of the bush, following the fox run the same way as he had entered. Once outside, he replaced the bracken that had been knocked down in its original position and then set off for the fated picnic spot.

~ ~ ~

Jenny had used her car keys to drive the mini back to her parent's house. It was indeed good fortune for her that her husband had appeared at Jock's house in the early hours; it saved her from getting a taxi home. She had concluded, with great deliberation, that maybe all men were bastards and not worthy of her favours. Jock was no different from Hunter, and now she had seen his true colours.

After all those years of keeping, my mouth shut about our affair, and about Carl.

"That bastard," she said, answering her thoughts aloud, as she pulled the car into the drive of No 5, Ten Beaches Road.

There was a twitch at the net curtain of the bay window that looked out on to the drive. Someone inside was awaiting her return most eagerly. She had arrived back at about 7.30 AM just as her father was leaving for work, but not before he voiced his opinions to her. She closed the front door behind her with a slam and strolled nonchalantly into the kitchen, to where both her mother and father were waiting.

Jenny was their only child, of whom they'd had great expectations. They wanted her to have every chance that they did not. They wanted her to be a career woman, a woman with a future, someone they could boast about to the rest of their family.

Mary and Jack Nixon had mapped Jenny's life out for her since she was a baby; they had given her their best and expected her best in return. As a child, she had certainly showed promise, passing all exams with flying colours, but at the age of discovering her sexuality things seemed to go wrong, at least for the parents. She dated boys frequently and started staying out late at night; they could do nothing to stop her. If they tried, she just rebelled more, on one occasion leaving a packet of condoms on her bedside table, just so that her mother would find them. But the real nail in the coffin came when she was eighteen and started knocking around with the marines, whose reputation as womanising hooligans stunned the Nixon's into submission. It wasn't long before she married Hunter, then became pregnant.

Jenny stepped up to the kettle and felt it to see if it was still warm. She smiled at her father, who scowled back.

"Where've you been all night?" he rasped, not able to contain his frustration any longer.

"Out!" Jenny answered

Mary Nixon stepped into the fray. "Out where and who with?"

Jenny dropped her head back and looked despairingly and the ceiling. "Look, what does it matter? I'm back now, ain't I?"

Jack Nixon pushed himself to his feet.

"It matters a lot to us, because how the hell do we know where you are, you could have been—" He stopped himself from carrying on.

"Dead; why don't you just say it, Dad, I won't burst out crying if you mention death."

"Well, maybe you should." Jack Nixon shook from temper. "Carl's not long gone, and you act like you haven't a care in the world." He fumbled to put on his jacket and grabbed his lunch box. "You should be ashamed of yourself."

Mary placed her hand on his arm. "Don't, Jack."

He shrugged her away. "No, I won't leave it. It's about time she heard some home truths. I'm going to work."

Jack stormed out of the kitchen. Mary jumped when the front door slammed, though it was no surprise.

"You had to go and upset him, didn't you?"

"Me, that's rich. He was the one that started it." Jenny turned away from her mother and proceeded noisily to make herself a cup of tea.

Mary flitted feverishly back and forth in the kitchen; she still had something on her mind.

She stopped at the table. "Well you still haven't said where you were last night."

Jenny gave a ragged sigh, wondering whether to tell her the truth.

She turned to face her mother. "I stayed with a friend, OK?"

That was evidently not what her mother wanted to hear. "What friend?"

Jenny thought quickly about her answer. "A girlfriend, Sally Cotton, you remember her, don't you?"

Mary nodded half-heartedly. "I think so. Where is it that she lives?"

"On the Priorswood estate, near the shops."

Mary slowly left the kitchen thinking of whom jenny could be talking about.

Jenny sat at the kitchen table holding the mug of tea to her lips, contemplating what she should do about Jock. Her idea was that it was all Hunter's fault, he should be the one to bear the brunt of the blame, and if it were not for him, Jock would not have told her to get out. She had no love for Hunter now, and if she really thought about it, she had only married him to outrage her parents. Then Carl came along, and then it was a case of having to stay with Hunter because Jock did not want the responsibility of the child, even though she said the child was most definitely his.

She wanted to stop Hunter, maybe get revenge, and tell DI Finch that he was up on the moors again. A smile creased her cheeks. The police will think he's going to dig up the body. After all, he's still a suspect, and when they catch him, they'd hang on to him this time.

"Brilliant," she said aloud, then briskly walked out of the kitchen and ran up the stairs to her bedroom.

She opened the wardrobe door and pulled out a light brown rain mack, then rummaged through the pockets, threw the contents on her bed, then snatched up one item.

"Got it."

She scanned the small square of card in her hand.

AVON AND SOMERSET CONSTABULARY
Detective Inspector Finch
CID

Grabbing the phone on the bedside table, she dialled the number written on the card and waited for a reply.

~~~

Cranbury jabbed at the keyboard with the forefinger of each hand. As usual, Finch was out investigating, and Cranbury had been left to hold the fort. Paperwork had built up over the last few weeks because of DS Short's premature death, and the whole matter of police work was beginning to make Cranbury resent joining the force. The phone ringing on Finch's desk was a welcome interruption; he leisurely walked the few steps to the boss's desk and answered the phone, idly looking out the window.

"CID, Detective Constable Cranbury."

"Hello, this is Jenny Hunter, I wonder if I can speak to Inspector Finch please?"

"No, sorry, Mrs Hunter, he's out at the moment, can I help at all?" Cranbury tapped his fingers rhythmically on the window frame as he eyed up two WPCs just leaving the building to walk their beat.

Jenny did not want to tell just anyone. Finch would make more of a drama out of the affair, so she needed to speak to him in person.

"No, I really need to talk to Inspector Finch. Can you leave him a message to call me back?—and he's got my number."

Cranbury looked away from the window and scanned Finch's desk for a pen.

"Right, so it's give Mrs Hunter a ring. Can I tell him what it's regarding?"

"Yes, tell him it's about Mr Hunter, something he should know." She hung up.

Cranbury wrote down the message on a small piece of notepaper then tossed it into Finch's IN tray.

~~~

From the cover of the fields Hunter surveyed the length of the road. He followed its line out of the village to where it met the track that led to the area where they'd had the picnic. The once green and bumpy track was now a thick muddy slope, where obviously the police and rescue vehicles had accessed the area of the disappearance. Hunter stood at the spot where he remembered he had parked the Land Rover and viewed the surrounding area. Nothing had changed; the coarse thick grasses around him had been trampled down and muddy wheel marks crisscrossed the wet earth, but still the memories flooded back. He could picture Carl pushing the football around, and Jenny sat on the rug trying her hardest not to enjoy herself. He breathed deeply, inhaling the fresh morning air and looked over to a parting in the gorse nearby. It was the start of the track, which would lead him to the woods.

His pace slowed as he came closer to the woods, the place that seemed to be the key to the whole mystery, and the place where his nightmares nearly always brought him. Above the treetops rooks heckled and mobbed a buzzard as it cruised an updraft trying to spot its breakfast. However, below, the darkened woods lay silent; nothing seemed to stir. Beyond the woody cover lay the stone circle, perfectly hidden from any curious eyes. Hunter approached the woods cautiously, he was within yards of the edge of the trees now. Slowly he walked round the perimeter gazing into the dark twisted shadows of the woods, its deathly silence only broken on occasions by the snapping of a branch or twig.

When he reached the track that would take him to the stone circle, he had the sudden feeling he was being watched. Hunter stopped at the beginning of the narrow track, his hesitation was down to fear, and he could sense the power ahead of him, a power that compelled him not to venture any further. The nightmares flashed through his mind, and he could see his son's head being held aloft by that hooded figure. A sudden sweat chilled his brow, and a numbing ache slackened his body. He took a few deep breaths, not feeling at all well, abruptly weak as a kitten. His legs trembled, as they would have after a thirty-mile forced march in full kit. He knew it was the stone circle; its power was trying to keep him away.

"Bollocks, what's the matter with you, Hunter, are you a man or a mouse?" he said aloud, then tightened his rucksack and started down the track.

With every step he found it harder to breathe. The air had seemed to become thinner, and his fever became worse. His head ached with an unbearable pressure, and his eyes felt like they were about to spring from their sockets at any second. A trickle of blood ran from his nose, flowing through his beard and dripping from his chin. He wiped it away without looking as the stream grew fuller. His pace slowed, and his feet scuffed the wet earth. He rubbed vigorously at his eyes trying to clear his blurred vision but just made it worse. The track wavered in-front of him; seeming to snake, its way through the trees making it stretch into eternity.

Blood now rushed down his face and into the back of his throat, making him choke on the copper-tasting liquid. He struggled to keep going but he could hardly catch a breath. His rucksack felt like a millstone, and he dropped to his knees. He looked to the sky, feeling the blood clammy down the front of his clothes. With every breath he coughed more, and large red clots of the sticky fluid clung to his lips as darkness enveloped his view.

It was some moments later when he regained consciousness. The pain had gone but he could still taste the blood and feel the fever-sweat gluing his clothes to his skin. He was lying on his back, his rucksack laid beside him. The air was still and quiet. He pushed himself up on to his elbows to view the surroundings.

He was no longer on the track. Somehow, he had ended up about a hundred yards away from the woods, on a slight hill looking down at the trees. To his left lay thick gorse and bracken; to his right was a large area of grass, beyond that more gorse, and the track that had taken him to the woods. He had his bearings, but now the question was: how did he get here?

He sat upright, hawked, and spat a lump of red phlegm onto the grass.

"You'd better stay there a while," a gruff voice said from behind him.

Hunter looked round quickly to see who was approaching. The old man stepped slowly with the aid of large walking staff nearly as tall as the old man, topped with what looked like a ball of root.

"Looks like thee had a nasty fall down there, lucky I was yere."

Hunter was a bit perplexed about what to say to the stranger. He was an odd-looking person; he moved like an old man, his skin was wrinkled with age, and he had the look of many years, but his shoulder length hair was strikingly thick and jet-black in colour. He crouched beside Hunter, who was still struck dumb, and applied a wet cloth to his blood-smeared face.

Hunter flinched as the cold water trickled down his face. "It's only water, got it from the spring up the top there." The old man nodded to the top of the hill.

"Yeah, OK." Hunter took the wet cloth from his hand. "How did I get here?"

The old man stood, pondered for a moment, then said, "I dragged ee. I wasn't going to leave thee down there." The old man looked across at the trees and shook his head.

"You dragged me all the way here, uphill?"

The old man smiled. "Surprised meself too." He picked up

his wooden staff, then reached a hand to help Hunter to his feet.

"Shit, I don't know what came over me. One minute I was all right, the next ... well, it felt like the life was being drained from me. Strange!" Hunter lifted his rucksack, feeling the weight of it he thought again about how the old man had dragged him all that way.

"Whadee want in there, anyway?" The old man asked.

"Just thought I'd take a look. I'm on holiday to see the sights, that sort of thing."

The old man gave a disbelieving grunt, then started to walk down the hill.

Hunter followed. "D'you live round here?"

The old man thought about the question briefly, then with a snort of laughter he answered: "You could say that." They came to the edge of the woods. The old man stopped and looked in, and Hunter stood beside him.

He scanned the clothes that the man wore, which must have seen better days. "You don't look like one of the villagers."

The old man had a drawn gaunt face; his long black hair flowed down to the shoulders of a dirty tweed jacket, fastened at the waist with a piece of orange twine. The trousers he wore looked as if they were made from cotton, but they were so dirty it was hard to tell. His boots were leather, also fastened with orange twine.

He turned, facing Hunter. "No, I live over that hill." He gazed over the marine's shoulder and raised his staff towards a hill in front of them.

Hunter looked to where he was pointing. He had been over that hill, but had seen no evidence of habitation. "I didn't know there were any cottages over there?"

"There's a lot you don't know about." The old man started to walk in the direction of the hill.

Hunter followed him again, beginning to be irritated by the man's air of mystery. "What d'you mean there's a lot I don't know about?"

The old man pointed to a fallen tree and walked over to

it. He sat down on the trunk, and Hunter complied with his gesture and did the same.

"To begin with, you didn't know that your life was in danger when you went into there, did you?" He nodded to the woods.

"I've been in there before," Hunter snapped.

The old man looked him in the eye. "And I thought this was your first visit to this area. You're not a very good liar!"

"I never said it was my first visit, just that I was sightseeing.

The old man nodded. "Well, if you did go into the circle, it was because it wanted you there.

"It wanted me there?" Hunter wanted to know more. "The way you talk, it's as if they have some sort of power."

The old man shook his head. "And you of course did not feel that power a moment ago. You will dismiss what you felt, put it down to something you can explain." He cocked a weary glance at Hunter.

"Well, yeah, I suppose so, yet for the life of me I can't understand what it was."

"That's it, you can't understand, so you won't understand. It knows your weakness: you don't believe, and it knows it."

"Believe in what, though?"

"Let your instinct guide you. Do what you think is right and not what your logic thinks is right; the two can become dangerously close. It will use your logic against you, and if you let it, it will surely win."

Hunter was stunned. The old man talked as if he knew what Hunter was up to, and could he be one of the villagers? He did not think so, his instinct told him not, and he felt nothing around the man, nothing evil. He decided to press for more information.

"Look, you say you're not from the village, and you talk like you know me and know what I'm doing here. Now if you do, you must know I can't leave until I have found out what happened to the children and people that have disappeared up here, and if I find out that it is the villagers behind it, which I think it is—"

The old man cut his sentence short. "Why do you think that the villagers are behind the disappearances of the children?"

"I just feel that they are."

"Good, you're letting your instinct rule over your logic. You have the power to beat them, unlike the rest." The old man bowed his head solemnly, his long black hair hanging nearly to his knees.

"What d'you mean, the rest? Look, what d'you know about all of this? Too much, it seems to me. Why haven't you told the police this?" Hunter reached into his pocket and gripped his dagger.

The old man lifted his head. "Maybe you're not ready to do what is expected of you, maybe."

"What the fuck are you going on about, old man? I know what I'm expected to do. If those bastards in that village had anything to do with the disappearance of my son, they'll wish they were in hell when I've finished with them," Hunter rasped, then jumped to his feet.

The old man stood as well. "Maybe they're already in hell, as you call it. Thee must tread carefully. Remember, use your instinct. They have guardians that watch over them and the village."

The old man turned his back on Hunter and slowly walked away towards the hill. Hunter thought about following him, maybe to find out more, but about *what*, he did not know. He wanted to disbelieve the old man's stories about strange forces, guardians, and the power of the stone circle, but somehow he could not. Deep down he knew it was the truth. If he were to believe the old man's stories he had to forget now about the indoctrinations of the twentieth century, they would only cloud his mind with questions, questions that had no logical answers.

He had to find out more about this old man. Hunter looked at the tramplike figure in the distance and decided to follow him. He needed to know if he was telling the truth about where he lived. The old man was nearly at the brow of the hill now, so Hunter broke into a jog to catch up with him. He hurdled bushes and slipped many times on the wet grass but tried to keep the stranger in view. Hunter reached the top of the hill expecting to see the old man ambling down the other side, but—nothing. He was nowhere to be seen. Hunter looked for tracks in the wet grass, but there were none.

The nearest cover big enough to hide a person was at the bottom of the hill; there was plenty of thick cover there. A deep stream wound through the coarse grass at the bottom, then disappeared under gorse and other cover, but there was no way that the old man could have reached the bottom of the hill in the time that he'd had.

"Shit, where's he gone? There's nowhere for the old bugger to hide."

Hunter walked down to the stream where the ground was boggy underfoot. Clumps of thick grass stood like stepping-stones in the wetter parts of the small valley; missing one would almost certainly mean a boot full of stagnant water. He had never come across such a contrasting landscape before; so bleak, yet it was not. Everything on the moor contradicted itself, had a mystery all of its own, a mystery of depthless age.

Hunter looked for an hour for the dwelling where the old man said he lived. He found nothing, only the odd mound of earth with a few stones scattered around it. There were plenty of these, dwellings of a bygone age, he thought, but nothing that could be lived in. He glanced at his watch; it was time he met the villagers again.

"Ten o'clock. The pub will be open soon."

He started his walk back to the village, all the time thinking on the old man's words.

CHAPTER 17

All the way back to the village, he puzzled over where the old man could have vanished to. Logically, everything that he had said made no sense, but for that matter, what was logical about this whole affair? It was becoming more bizarre by the hour.

Hunter strode towards the village with a military stiffness. The hard rubber soles of his boots dug into the road surface, the sound keeping him in his step. The only time he faltered was when in sight of the village. These stone-built cottages were in a way like tombs holding the mysteries of life itself, but now the destroyer of those secrets had come, the destroyer of the villagers if they proved guilty.

His eyes followed the road into the village. Nothing seemed to stir, no cars, no people, barely a breeze; the place was like a ghost town, and Hunter felt like the gunfighter newly arrived, ready to shoot anyone who stepped out in front of him. He smiled, thinking that all he needed was a large Stetson, a cheroot, and the theme music to *The Good, the Bad and the Ugly* playing in the background.

A thin band of ghostly mist hovered level with the side of the road, cloaking the drainage ditch edging the adjacent field.

Hunter leisurely approached the first of the cottages, trying his hardest to look like a holidaymaker, or at least a rambler. He wondered whether the old man had tipped off the villagers to his presence, but dismissed it almost as fast as he had thought of it. For some unknown reason, he trusted the old man.

Conscious of being watched, he stopped outside the small cottage shop and glanced into its dusty window. Everything looked as it had when he stopped there on the day of their picnic. He remembered how Carl had reacted when he saw the woman inside. Blind terror had overwhelmed the boy, and maybe he had seen something the others could not; maybe the child had foreseen his fate.

Hunter knew that he had to go in, if only to see if the woman recognised him from all of those weeks ago. He hoped the beard would disguise him somewhat, but he would lay on a thick Liverpool accent just in case. His eyes caught sight of his own reflection in the glass, and then he pushed his fingers through his chin stubble, thinking how like a stranger he looked. He stared deeply at his transparent reflection, eying every inch of his own face. He was a stranger to himself.

A slight movement from inside of the shop caught his attention, and his eyes met those of the woman behind the counter. The motionless stare of her gaunt face sent a shiver up his spine as he reached for the handle and entered the shop. The ring of a small brass bell above the door shattered the silence of the small room. Hunter stepped towards the counter.

"Morning." His mouth had gone dry, and his voice was croaky. Sounding nervous, he coughed to clear his throat.

She nodded, casting an eye over his clothing.

Hunter looked every bit what he wanted to look like; his clothes bore the evidence of the moors. His trousers were soaked to the knees with morning dew, and his boots bore traces of the moors' dark soil. He browsed through the chocolate bars and tried to make conversation again.

"Lovely part of the country, this." He looked into her lifeless eyes and smiled. "Exmoor ... a lovely place, don't you think?"

"Aye, it is." She shuffled out of the shadows and up to the counter, putting her clawlike hands onto it.

"Yeah, I think it's got a sense of mystery about it. The place is unreal." He picked up a Mars bar and laid it on the counter next to the woman's hand, then went on browsing.

She seemed to ignore his comments about the moor and changed the subject completely. "Are you passing through?"

Hunter had her hooked now, he would play things cool. He answered, not taking his eyes off the sweet display. "No, I thought I'd do a bit of camping in the area, hang around for a while, and get a few photos of the wildlife."

She moved nervously, the tone of her voice changed. "There's no wildlife around here, not 'less you include sheep and 'orses."

Hunter faced her again. "'Orses, what are they?"

She frowned at him. "The wild 'orses, there out on the moor."

"Oh, horses." He thought about laughing at the woman's colloquial burr, but by the look on her face, she would not have taken it the right way.

"No, there's none about these parts. There's plenty further on, though."

Hunter grabbed another candy bar and placed it with the other. "Well, this morning I've already seen a herd of red deer, a few birds of prey and a couple of foxes." He paused and leant towards her. "But what I'd really like to get a look at is the Exmoor Beast." He raised his eyebrows and gave her a cheeky smile.

She rasped, "There be no such thing, you're wasting your time."

"Ah well, can't hurt to have a look round, can it?" He reached into his pocket and pulled out a pound coin, dropping it on the well-worn counter in front of him.

She snatched up the money, and then promptly sorted out his change.

Resorting to his most exaggerated Liverpool accent, he asked, "Where's the nearest pub in this area?"

She placed his change in his hand and looked him right in the eye. For a second Hunter felt uneasy. It was as if his mask had slipped briefly and she remembered who he was. Her cold bony fingers dug into his hand. He was sure that she knew, and then she released her grip and said: "Eli's Black Dog Inn—follow the road, past Mrs Gore's cottage."

He started to leave the shop, and then remembered he was not supposed to know where Mrs Gore's cottage was, as he was new to the area.

He turned to face her quickly. "Where's Mrs Gore's cottage?" he asked with what he hoped was a convincing look of puzzlement on his face.

She shuffled through the gap in the counter and followed him out of the shop.

"That cottage on the corner"—she pointed to the junction in the road—"that's Mrs Gores. Follow the road around, you'll see Eli's."

Hunter thanked her and carried on the few yards up the road until he stopped at the junction. He could feel her still watching him; he turned, and she was. He pointed towards the pub, which was just out of sight because of a large hedge bordering the field. She nodded. He waved, then carried on.

"Weird old bitch," he muttered as he came into full view of the Black Dog Inn.

He stood briefly in the middle of the small dead-end lane, looking at the pub, then back at the grass verge opposite. He could remember well stopping for the bottle of wine on that fated day and the turmoil that it had caused. He was in no doubt that the people of the village were somehow tied in with Carl's disappearance, but *why* and *how* were still questions to be answered.

His reflections were interrupted by the opening pub door to his right. Slowly the old oak door swung back, its dry screaming hinges sounding like a sound effect from a horror film as the door was pushed flush against the wall.

Eli Trout's massive body filled the porch to the extent

that, even if he turned sideways, his belly would still touch the doorframe. He was outgrowing his own house.

"Good morning," Hunter said, stepping up to the gateway of the pub.

Trout nodded, then looked to the sky. "It'll not last, rain later."

Hunter followed his gaze to the clear blue heavens; there was not a rain cloud in sight. Trout snuffled and sniffed like a congested bulldog as he swung his fat bulk towards the inner sanctum of the pub. Hunter followed.

The inside of the Black Dog Inn was dark and gloomy; an aroma of stale smoke and ale clung to the walls, benches, and stools. Hunter scanned its decor again. On his first visit to the place all of those weeks ago it was as if he had stepped back in time, but now he took a closer look.

It was not so much a public house as a village house. The inside was small, no larger than a decent-sized front room; a large exposed stone chimneybreast seemed to erupt from the gable end wall and fanned out into a huge open fireplace that nearly took up the whole width of the place. An old bread oven was built into the fireplace, and blackened pots and pans still hung from hooks fixed into the masonry, all of which looked to be still in use. There was no carpet on the floor, only cold grey flagstones that left cleaning to the imagination.

A throaty cough from behind the rustic bar startled Hunter. He turned to see the fat-faced landlord.

"What can I getee?" Trout asked with laboured breath, as if asking the question had tired him out.

Hunter took off his rucksack and set it beside the bar. Trout watched his every move.

"I'll have some of the local brew."

"Ah, cider, youm a cider man then?" Trout grabbed a glass and brought it to a barrel sitting on the bar.

"Yeah, don't mind a glass now and again."

Hunter continued surveying the decor or lack of it while Trout gave small talk and poured his drink.

"Youm sound like you're not from round yere."

"No, I'm not, just down here on holiday. I'm camping; I thought I'd try to see the mysteries of the moors," Hunter recited; his mind was on the framed photos that were scattered around the walls.

"Mysteries, what kind of mysteries?" Trout placed the glass of golden liquid on the bar.

"Oh, I don't know—folklore, that kind of thing; find out the history of the place, you know, the tribes that lived here and suchlike."

"Mmm, there's plenty of that round these yere parts, most of it being fantasy though."

Hunter scrutinised a faded yellow picture hanging in a wooden frame that looked many years old. Instead of being black and white, it was more of a faded tan colour and set onto card. It looked as if the people in the picture were wearing turn-of-the-century clothing. However, as he looked closer, he could see a familiar face. The picture had been taken outside the pub, and it looked like the whole village had turned out, but in the middle of the crowd Mr Eli Trout stood as large as life. He looked about the same age as he did now, though he had put on a lot more weight since the picture was taken. Hunter thought that the photo had been especially made to look old.

"Yeah, you're probably right about it all being fantasy." Hunter turned to face him. "When was this picture taken?" He put his finger on the frame.

Trout leant gingerly across the bar and craned his neck. "Ah, not that long ago; it was taken a few summers back."

"I thought as much, one of those fake old pictures."

Trout nodded, a bead of sweat ran from his brow.

Hunter scanned a number of other photos but always came back to the old-timey picture taken outside the pub. This time his eyes fell upon a young girl standing to Trout's right. An old woman had her hands on the young girl's shoulders. The dark-haired girl looked about ten years old, but her face looked familiar to Hunter. He was sure that he'd seen her before, but a young girl of that age ... why would her face stick in his mind?

At most, the girl would be about twelve or thirteen years old now if Trout was to be believed.

Hunter took one last look at the photo and returned to the bar. "I think I saw the girl in this picture this morning as I came into the village, the one stood to the side of you." He placed some coins on the bar and then took a sip from his drink.

Trout's sausagelike fingers scooped up the money. "No you couldn't have done, she's been left the village for a while now."

Hunter looked back at the photo. *Who is she?* He wondered whether he should try another angle to find out but thought it best to leave the matter, at least for now. He picked up his drink, walked over to the only window in the room, and looked out onto the garden, then the road. A large horse chestnut tree obscured his view of the cottages in the lane; the old tree obscured almost everything, even the sunlight into the pub. The tree grew out from the middle of the partition hedge separating the road from the pub garden. It was about where the photo had been taken in the picture he had been looking at earlier, but something was not quite right about it.

"Blimey, that tree cuts out a lot of light from in here, don't it?" Hunter turned from the window and walked back to the photos near the door.

Trout watched him, now visibly edgy.

"Yeah, for years I been meaning to cut the bloody thing down, just never got around to it."

Hunter examined the picture again. At first he could not see the obvious even though it was the most obvious object in the photograph and the biggest. He looked closely at it, but nothing struck him as odd. He walked back over to the window again and tried to look further up the lane, but the tree was in the way.

"The tree!" he muttered aloud.

The landlord seemed to start. "What d'you say, boy?"

"Nothing, just talking to myself." Hunter walked nonchalantly back to the bar; best play down his interest in the photo. "Yeah, this is a nice part of the country."

"Aye, that be right, but not for campers, least not round yere anyhow."

"You're the second one that's tried to put me off; anyone would think you don't like strangers around here."

Trout grunted. "They cause nothing but trouble, that's why. We like our village to be nice and quiet; no strangers, no trouble. My family been on the moor for hundreds of years, we've always lived here." Trout closed his eyes and seemed to reminisce.

"Yeah I can see that you're all pretty close by these photos." He had a good excuse to walk back over for another look at them.

"Aye everyone in the village has had their cottages handed down to them, from father to son, right through the generations. Everyone knows everyone else "

Yeah, and probably related to each other.

He viewed the photo again and finally saw the young tree near the window of the pub. Either somebody had planted a full-grown tree, or it had been growing there for the last fifty or more years. The tree must have grown from a seedling, in which case Trout was a liar and a damned sight older than he said he was. This just didn't make sense.

How could it be? Trout only looked a few years younger in the photo. Now if the photograph was as old as Hunter thought, that would make Trout more than a hundred years old, perhaps closer to two hundred. The woman from the shop was in the picture as well, so she'd be even older.

Hunter did not know what to believe. Logic told him this was not possible, but he remembered the old man's words about trusting his instincts instead. Nevertheless he felt uneasy and had to quell his emotions.

He calmly walked back to the bar and sat down on a stool. "Yeah, the village is certainly full of mystery. Can't wait to find out more about it."

Eli Trout frowned and sat himself down behind the bar. "Now if you really want history, you wanna getee self up to Malmsmead, to the Doone Valley, there's a plenty of history and stories there to suit you." Trout tried to put a smile behind his easy banter.

"Nah, I think I'll camp here, maybe just down the road."

"There ain't no deer around here; youm not see a thing." Trout's patience looked to be running thin.

"Who told you I was looking for deer?" Hunter asked, knowing he had told that story only to the woman from the shop.

"Umm ..." Trout stumbled over his words. "Well, that's whatee's up yere for, innit?"

Hunter would take it no further; he smiled. "Yeah, that's right, still can't hurt to have a look round, can it?" He took a large gulp from his cider, and then smacked his lips.

"Look, boy, it ain't safe out on those moors for the likes of ye, the weather can change just like that"—Trout snapped his fingers—"and all sorts can happen out there."

"Like what?" Hunter asked.

"Well all sorts. Youm got them bogs, for a start. Tell ye, boy, this ain't the place to stay."

Hunter took another drink from his cider. "Reckon I can look after myself; thanks for the concern, though. Still, now if there was a place I could stay nearby, I wouldn't need to camp on the moors, would I?"

Trout chewed his bottom lip, maybe anticipating Hunter's next question.

"How's about me staying here? This is an inn, isn't it?"

Trout shook his head; his fat jowls shook like a jelly. "Only be name it is, those rooms upstairs haven't been let in years."

"Ah, well, looks like it's a night under the canvas then."

Trout snorted and shuffled uneasily on his over burdened stool, then rubbed his hand across his sweaty face.

"How long wouldee want to stay, that's if I do have a room?"

"A few days at the most."

It took seconds for Trout to decide. Hunter could almost read in the looks on his face that he'd do anything to keep a stranger off the moors.

"Aye, all right, I'll letee have a room for a couple of days. It'll be fifty pounds a night, cash now." Trout pushed out his massive arm and waited for the money to be put into his palm.

Hunter was in. He had two days to find out what the village was about and what secrets they were hiding.

CHAPTER 18

Hunter picked up his rucksack and followed Trout out of the bar and up a narrow stairway, which was just about broad enough to accommodate the man in front of him. The old wooden treads of the stairs groaned under the fat man's weight, matching the grunts of the landlord as he climbed the steep incline.

Trout took a breath at the top, his face near a shade of beetroot purple, and Hunter waited silently for him to continue, all the time scanning his surroundings. Exposed oaken rafters twisted across the cracked plaster of the low ceiling, and at times it had fallen away to reveal a latticework of small wooden lathes. The building had clearly been neglected for years.

Trout shuffled along the narrow corridor until he reached two adjacent doors at the end. He paused, looked at both doors, and then seemed to choose the more suitable room without even entering either of them. He opened the one to his right, the one above the bar.

"Yere go, boy. It's nothing fancy, but it's better than sleeping on the moor."

He waved Hunter in and then followed.

Hunter glanced around the gloomy room. Clouds of

dust seemed to sparkle in the light that penetrated the grimy window. This room too had the stale smells of ale and damp. The whitewashed plaster walls were a faded yellow, and cobwebs cloaked every dark recess.

The landlord sent the room into a collage of shadows as he switched on the single light bulb hanging from the ceiling. Hunter placed his rucksack on the bed, then turned to faced Trout, whose pained face was sweating profusely. Hunter was sure the man was smiling, though, because the look was accompanied with snuffled laughter, as Trout switched the bulb off and on several times.

"Yeah, seems all right," Hunter said, crossing to the window and looked out over the pub's garden.

The large tree at the front of the pub obscured even the daylight reaching the bedroom window; its branches were within arm's reach of the glass. Even though the room was dowdy in appearance it looked lived in, and not that many years ago, probably by a woman. There was an old dressing table with an oval mirror, and across its dusty wooden surface lay small lace table mats. Two china dolls sat solemnly at the base of the mirror, toys once upon a time but now treasured valuables. He scanned the room quickly for other clues or memorabilia. Cheery watercolours of the moors adorned nearly every bland wall, each showing the summer or a misty fresh morning, quite the opposite of what he would have expected in such a drab place.

He faced Trout again, who was becoming impatient with this disruption of his routine. Hunter had to ask.

"Somehow I get the feeling that this used to be a woman's room, especially with the dressing table and dolls, am I right?"

Trout took a step out of the room. "Umm, aye, it was the wife's old room. Come on, I'll showee the washroom and outhouse."

Trout trundled back down the corridor; Hunter left his rucksack on the bed and followed. He knew by Trout's reticent answer that maybe he was not telling the truth, or the whole truth. Whatever it was, he knew he was hiding something.

Trout stopped at the top of the stair and looked pointedly towards a closed door to his left.

"That's my room. You don't go in there, nor any of the other rooms."

"Yeah, that's okay by me."

Trout wiped a drop of sweat from the end of his nose then carried on down the stairs. He showed Hunter the so-called outhouse, joined to a stone-built shed and of the same construction. The only thing inside was a stained toilet. The walls were bare stone and the toilet had no seat; the yellow cracked pan sat firmly on a dirty grey slab. Hunter shuddered at the thought of using such an archaic-looking monstrosity; he would rather shit in a hedge than use what Trout had shown him. The washroom was a large enamel sink in the kitchen, the same sink that held what looked like three weeks of dirty dishes. The tour was brief but to the point: Stay in your own room, and mind your own business—that was it in a nutshell.

Both men went back into the bar. Hunter finished his drink. He was on his way back onto the moor to check his hideout, and hoped that maybe he could search out the old man. He left his empty glass on the bar and tossed a wave at Trout on his way out the door. He left the sweating landlord with his large ass parked on a barstool as normal.

~~~

The beginnings of a wintry night chilled the evening air as daylight retreated over the horizon. The day shift of wildlife gathered their wits ready for night, as the nocturnal predators began their hunt. The walk back to the village was a thoughtful one for Hunter as he pondered his next move. His afternoon excursion back onto the moor had been fruitless; traces of the old man were nowhere to be found. There was not so much as a cottage within miles of where he had last seen him, if indeed he had seen him. He had also gone back to the outskirts of the woods, to look for tracks of those hideous creatures that he had seen in his dreams, but he found nothing. Then he remembered, if he would find tracks anywhere, it would be in the field where the Land Rover was being kept. That's where he thought he'd seen DS Short last—and that creature.

As twilight faded into darkness, he made his way inconspicuously past the village and to the field adjacent to where his Land Rover was parked. He crouched in the gateway for a moment, watching and listening for any signs of life; the village was silent, and nothing seemed to stir. With the stealth of a cat he straddled the gate and darted across the road pausing briefly in the gateway, then leapt into the field. The Land Rover was some hundred yards in and some fifty yards from the side of the Smith's cottage. Hunter had determined from a quick reconnaissance of the cottage that the occupant was present, and a small gable end window cast its meagre light across the field. He thought back to the dream and tried to picture where Short had been standing. He remembered the corner of the field near the house; DS Short showed a lot of interest in something over there.

Hunter's eyes became accustomed to the darkness; his night vision was becoming more sensitive. He followed the line of the hedge to the corner of the field, and then stepped carefully to the dark mound that had interested Short. He crouched beside the tarpaulin and lifted one corner of the sheet. At first he couldn't quite make out what he was looking at, but then the distinctive shape of a Land Rover wing became visible. But still he didn't know what was so interesting about a pile of old scrap. He viewed the rest of the twisted parts and could only come up with questions:

Why was Short so interested in the scrap?

What was he doing in the field in the hours of darkness?

He did not want to be seen. Why? What was he frightened of?

He pulled out a small pocket torch and shone it on the ground around him. He could see plenty of footprints in the wet mud, which he supposed belonged to DS Short, but he was looking for the prints of the hideous creature.

He turned out the torch and looked over to the gateway.

"That was where it lay in wait, just over there," he said softly, then walked within ten yards of the gate.

He dropped to a crouch again and switched on the small torch. He panned the beam from side to side and scanned the ground slowly, taking a step with each sweep of the torch. When he crossed a smooth patch of mud, he saw what he was looking for: a collage of large paw prints sunk deep into the earth. He put his hand next to one of the prints and was amazed at the size of the moulded shape.

"Fuck me! This ain't an animal native to this country, not to make tracks this big." His thoughts became a whisper of surprise.

"It must have happened! But it was a dream." The truth had him more confused now than ever before. Slowly he lifted his head and remembered the night he had ran down the steep field in front of him to warn Short, then how the creature turned its attentions away from its intended victim and focussed on him. How could he forget such a night?

Hunter looked to the top of the hill. He knew somewhere up there was a fence, that barbed wire fence that had bruised his body. He had to look, and yet his instinct told him he was in danger. He started his walk up the field, all the while alert to everything around him. He hoped that the fence was not there and that he could put his visions down to a dream, but he knew it would be there.

By now, the moor cloaked in darkness, and the only sound was his footsteps brushing their way through the ankle-high grass. He stopped briefly to look back on the village; the innocent flickering lights of the cottages looked welcoming enough. He carried on walking. Twenty yards farther on, he hit the fence, its sharp points striking the same line on his stomach as they had done in his nightmare.

Hunter pulled out his pocket torch and shone it along the length of wire. He could no longer doubt that it was the same fence and that he had been here that night. The thought numbed his brain; logic said it just wasn't possible. His senses tingled, and the hairs on his neck stood on end. Something was out here with him, watching his every move. Now more than ever Hunter could feel he was in danger and knew in what form the danger would come.

He backed away from the fence and slowly retreated down the field, facing up the slope he had just climbed. Now he was working on pure instinct. He scanned the darkness with the torch, first along the length of the fence, then beyond. The feeble light searched the blackened countryside, only illuminating objects within yards of where Hunter was standing.

Then as he cast the light further, beyond the point of ever discerning a shape, something shone back at him. The light of the torch reflected off two bright objects hovering a few feet above the ground. Even though the light of the torch revealed no shape, Hunter knew what he was facing. The eyes of the creature glowed like burning coals as it watched Hunter slowly make his way back down the hill.

Hunter kept the torch on the beast, as his stride became a lot longer. Then he had the feeling that there was something to the side of him. He quickly shone the torch to the right of him.

"Bollocks," he rasped.

There was another pair of eyes looking at him. He tried to illuminate both creatures in turn until he caught sight of a third set. Now all three of the beasts started to advance towards him, their dank breath steaming into the cold night air.

"Steady, Hunter, don't run until I give the command. *Run!*" he shouted, then turned and ran faster than he thought he could. Occasionally he looked over his shoulder to see if the creatures were behind him. They were and gaining on him fast. He knew when he passed the Land Rover that the gateway to the road would be close, but he wondered if he would make it that far.

His feet slipped now and again in the wet mud, and he stumbled, but the fear of his pursuers kept him going. He could see the gateway against the lighter shade of the road that was the only obstacle in his way now. It was as he reached the gate that the slippery mud got the better of him. He lost his footing and crashed head first into the wooden structure.

Stunned for a second, he scrambled on his hands and knees to find his torch. It was lying beside him; he snatched it up and aimed it behind him. The three beasts were now within twenty yards of him, their lifeless burning eyes bored into his very soul.

Hunter scrambled to his feet and clambered over the wooden gate. He did not stop to look back once he was on the road, and he just kept running. The first of the beasts jumped the gate, and Hunter heard the creature hit the ground. He was not about to check if the rest had jumped over. The sound of his own pulse banged in his ears, and his breathing was deep and laboured, he had to keep going.

He passed the Smiths' cottage not giving it a second glance. His goal was to reach the Black Dog Inn. At least he thought he would be safe there. Passing the last cottage before the pub, he chanced a look over his shoulder, and his pace slowed. The lane behind him was empty, and he stopped and peered into the darkness around him.

"Come on, where are you?" he whispered, trying to get his breath back.

Hunter leant on the pub fence and viewed the surrounding area. The creatures had vanished into the darkness as quickly as they had appeared, but he knew they were still there; he could feel their lifeless eyes watching him. He turned on his torch and shone it into the darkness, but those reflective eyes did not look back at him.

He gave a breathless snort of laughter. "Shit, that was close."

He bent over, hands on knees, trying to catch his breath. He knew that next time it would be his turn to hunt them. It was as he straightened up that his eyes caught sight of one of the creatures opposite him, standing on the grass verge by the road. How it had got in front of him he did not know, but the thing was too close for comfort. Its lips stretched back over its teeth, and it gave a deep, throaty growl.

Hunter knew that it could have easily sprung from where it was and been upon him; it was as if it only wanted to warn him. The warning heeded, Hunter backed up the cobbled path to the door of the pub, not once taking his eyes from the beast. He fumbled for the door handle, then turned quickly and entered the pub.

All conversation stopped when he stepped into the bar, the locals seemed disgruntled by the appearance of the dishevelled stranger. At first Hunter stared menacingly back at them, then remembered he was supposed to be a tourist and a friendly one at that. His scowl changed immediately to a smile, and he stepped up to the bar. Trout slid off his stool, and Hunter ordered the cider again.

Trout placed the glass on the counter in front of him. "Where ye been then? Talking to the worms?"

The locals, listening closely to that point, burst into spontaneous laughter, Trout grinning with them. Hunter at first could not see the funny side of the joke, which was until he looked down at his clothes; he was covered head to toe in mud. If his joining in with the joke meant being accepted by the villagers, that was fine with him. He smiled and shook his head in tacit agreement.

After a few moments, the laughter tapered off, and Hunter stood at the bar alone. Trout was back on his stool and quietly chatting with an old man smoking a pipe. Their broad accents were hardly recognisable; it was as if they were speaking in a different language. Hunter leant heavily against the bar and dared to view the people in the pub, hoping that none would recognise him. He counted eight in total, he studied each face. They all looked familiar. Each one, he was sure, was in the photo on the wall.

The old woman from the shop was sitting in the corner by the now blazing fire, watching him with her unblinking eyes. Hunter smiled at her, but her face remained motionless. Next to the woman from the shop was a middle-aged fat lady (nearly as big as Trout), who smiled at Hunter. At least one of them seemed friendly. He had to ask one of them about the picture on the wall, to find out whether they came up with the same cock-and-bull story as Trout.

He was about to make his move to the fireplace when the pub door swung open and three other villagers walked in—the Blacksmith, followed by two older men. They glared at Hunter as they stepped up beside him at the bar. The same nervous feeling he'd had on the moor stole over him again, the feeling that told him the beasts were near. Trout jumped to his feet as quick as he could and poured the men drinks without being asked. Hunter watched the whole proceeding with interest. Trout seemed fearful in some way about the men; even the other villagers in the pub hung on the blacksmith's every move.

Maybe they were feeling a fear akin to what he was feeling, and by the sheer frame of the man beside him here, the fear seemed warranted. He looked twice the size of Hunter and would take some stopping if the need arose. Trout placed their drinks on the bar, and the blacksmith summoned him with a gesture to one side. Both men disappeared out of view to one of the back rooms. Hunter was sure they were talking about him, perhaps even suspected what he was up to. If so, he had very little time. He would have to find some sort of proof that they were behind the disappearances of the children, but where to start looking?

His senses tingled with anticipation; just waiting for the two giants to come back into the bar was sending him crazy. Would they come in shouting the odds? Alternatively, play it cool and try to cover their tracks?

No, he did not think so. These people were hiding many secrets. They were not about to be coy with him.

He knew that their plan of attack would be to get rid of him, kill him, maybe get those beasts to do their dirty work; after all, they were as much a part of this nightmare as the villagers. No one here was who they seemed; the whole affair was beyond logic. The old man's words echoed in his head: *Use your instinct.* Now it was a matter of finding out a few more facts to piece together the puzzle.

Somehow, they were a lot older than they looked; the photo

on the wall was evidence. Also, those creatures on the moor ... they were trying to cover up what they were. Maybe they were killing the children? Somehow Hunter knew it went a lot deeper than that, to the realms of the unbelievable.

His train of thought was broken by the return of both men to the bar. Trout gave Hunter a curious glance, but the blacksmith's attentions were now on his drink and his two earlier companions. Even though no one was staring at him and a quiet banter once again drifted on the smoke-filled air, Hunter knew that they suspected him. His own thoughts told him to get the hell out of there, but no, he wanted to find out what these people were really about; he had lost too much to let this go. Hunter tossed back the dregs of his cider, then set down the empty glass.

"Same again, landlord." His Liverpudlian voice boomed out over the rural banter.

Trout lifted his heavy carcass from the stool and snatched up the visitor's glass.

Hunter cleared his throat. "Tell me, why's the pub called the Black Dog Inn?"

The place grew silent again; all eyes were upon the stranger. Trout faltered as he filled Hunter's glass. He eyed first Hunter, then the three men sitting behind him. The tension in the air was electric.

"It's part of the myths of the moor," a deep voice said from behind Hunter.

Hunter swung round to face the table where the three men were sitting.

"Oh yeah, and what myth is that, then?"

The blacksmith took a noisy gulp from his tankard and slammed it back on the table. If there was one thing Hunter thought all the villagers had in common, it was their pale, dark-haired men surmounted by those lifeless eyes. If the eyes truly are windows to the soul, these people had dark, sinister souls.

The blacksmith grinned. "The black dog haunts parts of the moor, sacred parts of the moor where people shouldn't go, and if yee should happen to see it, it means death isn't far away." His smile deepened the creases in his weathered features.

"Nice story. I'll have to watch out for black dogs then."

"I think yee will," the blacksmith replied.

Trout placed Hunter's pint back on the bar and retreated hastily to his stool.

Hunter picked up the glass and took three large gulps, wincing at the bitter taste. "Blimey, is this the same cider as the last one? It tastes different!"

"Bottom of the barrel," Trout said calmly.

Hunter peered into the glass. The golden liquid was cloudy this time, and powdery residue clung to the sides of the glass. Moments later a heavy fatigue engulfed his body, and he knew that Trout had added something to his cider. His first thought was to get out of here.

He set down the half-full glass and struggled to his feet. His head started to spin, and a gripping pain lance his side. His view began to grow hazy, and a burning dryness parched his throat.

"I'm turning in," he rasped.

Trout and the rest of the villagers just watched, as if waiting for him to fall. Hunter's legs felt like lead as he stumbled out of the bar and into the back room. He sensed Trout slipping from his stool to follow. Hunter staggered into the dark kitchen, steadying himself on anything that he could, then fell at the sink. His blurred thought was to make himself vomit. With sweat dripping from his brow, he jammed two fingers down his throat and vomited into the large sink full of pots and plates. He emptied his stomach in seconds, but the feeling of drowsiness was still getting the better of him. He saw Trout looking on as he stumbled from the kitchen into the hall and slowly climbed the stairs.

The corridor on the landing seemed to stretch for miles. Every step was a struggle. He slid along the wall until he reached the door to his room. When he fell through the door, he realised Trout was moving down the corridor behind him, but by now his whole body was numb, and every movement he made took all his strength and willpower.

Lock the door, a voice told him.

On his hands and knees, he pulled himself to the door and started to push it shut. Inch by inch it closed, feeling like a hundredweight he was pushing uphill. The floorboards creaked in the corridor, betraying the approach of the fat landlord. Finally the door was shut; he pulled himself up by the door handle and locked it.

He leant heavily against the door for a second and listened to Trout gasping outside. The darkness in the room was total, but he needed something more than just a lock to keep intruders out. He staggered a few paces, and his hand knocked against the dressing table. With the last of his strength, he pulled the table against the door, then stumbled over to the bed and collapsed. The room seemed to close in on him, and the drug at last took full effect.

CHAPTER 19

Eli Trout put his ear to the bedroom door and listened; he had already tried the handle and knew that Hunter had locked it. He knocked gently and waited for a response. None came, then he asked: "Ye all right, boy?"

Still there was no response, Trout was then satisfied that the drug he had slipped into Hunter's drink had done its job. He heaved a satisfied sigh, then started back down to the bar, where the villagers were about to discuss their new problem: Hunter. They were waiting for all co-conspirators to gather so they might plot Hunter's demise.

Trout entered the bar area again with all eyes on him. He calmly announced that the sleeping drug he had put in Hunter's drink had seemed to work. He told them that it should keep him out of the way until morning. A moment's silence descended on the group of eleven villagers in the bar, and the crackle of the open fire set the atmosphere of the room. Soon, though, it was over, and they were dealing with unanswered questions and unsolved problems, especially how to restore anonymity to this village. The debate at times grew heated, though Trout tried to maintain order, repeatedly stressing the need to wait until all the villagers were present.

They had already judged that Hunter must die because he was too close to their secret, but they needed to decide when and how.

The muffled voices of the villagers filtered through the floor of Hunter's room, not that he heard them as he lay silently in the darkness. His limbs twitched uncontrollably, a clear warning sign of another dream.

His mind took him back onto the moor, but this time a moor that he did not recognise. He was gazing down from a hill onto what looked like a large forest. Surrounding the forest were the usual gorse moorlands, but the vegetation was a lot thicker than he had seen before, untouched by sheep or pony. An early morning sun was just visible over the horizon, and a low white mist moistened the ground and stole up the hillside towards him.

The fresh morning air bit into the back of his throat as he took a disbelieving deep breath and wondered whether this was reality or fantasy, he had no recollection of arriving here, but as with the rest of his dreams, this one felt as real as life itself. He could feel the wind on his face and smell freshness in the air that backed up all his logical thinking that he really was living in a dream, but he knew that logic played no real part in this; all was contradiction.

He started down the hillside towards the forest, guided all the time by the now-familiar unseen force. A well-worn path cut a swath through the undergrowth and edged round the outskirts of the forest. Hunter followed it, only stopping when it branched away into the darkness of the trees. The narrow earth track twisted back among the trees; Hunter followed it with his eyes as far as he could until shadows hid it from his view.

He was apprehensive about going into the forest, but the powerful force that was guiding him was greater than his willpower to stay where he was. He had no choice in the matter; in fact, deep down he knew that he was there for a reason. As with the rest of his visions or dreams, there was a purpose for him to witness whatever the force wanted him to witness, and he trusted its judgement, whatever it was.

As he set off into the forest, he had the overwhelming feeling that he knew the place around him, but could not quite put his finger on how he knew it. Flying insects darted feverishly in and out of the shafts of light that pierced the bony wooden canopy and striped the forest floor. The squawking of rooks, nervous on the outskirts of the forest prompted him to stop and look back at the path that he had just followed. He sensed something there had just entered the forest, something that had the birds nervous enough to take wing and cry out in fear. He listened, peering down the track to the outside of the forest, and watched for any movement coming in his direction. Whatever was coming, he had a bad feeling about it. He tried to listen, but the clamour of the retreating rooks over his head drowned out everything else. He took a last cautious glance into the dimness of the forest and then pressed on, urged by the powerful force that guided him.

After another ten minutes of walking he heard the murmur of voices in front of him. His pace slowed, and he stepped warily along the track. He thought about trying to take cover but knew that the dense undergrowth would give his position away to whoever or whatever it was.

He stayed on the track and approached the voices with caution. To his right, just off the track sat two tramp like figures, both wearing dark tunics to the knee. Animal furs were strapped to their feet and legs, and each one carried a shield and a sword. Their dark hair was shoulder length and matted, and their faces were striped in red and blue. They would have put the fear of God into any mortal person, Hunter thought. He listened to the two men speak to each other in what sounded like a rural Pidgin English. They too looked uneasy about the flight of the birds from the outskirts of the forest. Maybe they also could feel the danger approaching. One of the men stood up and stepped out onto the track looking directly at Hunter— in fact, straight through him. As the man gestured to the other one sitting in the bushes to come and look at something, Hunter smiled at him. *This is when the fun starts.*

They cautiously stepped towards him. Hunter did not move, even though his senses were screaming danger, but somehow he had the feeling that it was not from the two in front of him. One of the men took a few hurried steps past the marine, seeming more interested in what was approaching their position from the edge of the forest; the other man looked directly at Hunter, then took a step straight through his body.

"What"! Hunter exclaimed, then lifted his hands to look at them.

He could not believe what he saw. His hands were transparent; he could see the track through them. It was the same with his legs, his arms, and his body: he could not touch any part of his physical body, as if he was there in spirit only. Then a nightmare really dawned on him: was he dead? Was it Trout's idea to kill him?

"That bastard, he's killed me."

Insane thoughts rushed through his head, with death being the only logical answer, but he did not believe in life after death or in God, so what was he doing here? If this was heaven, why could he feel fear?

"Shit! Maybe it's hell that I'm in." Hunter turned round and viewed the two half-naked freaks walking back down the track towards the outskirts of the forest.

"What's going on?" He glanced down at his transparent body again, and then a calm feeling came over him.

The force that guided him seemed to quell his anxiety, and a soothing voice in his head told him to keep walking, which he did. Within minutes he could hear more voices, becoming louder with each step he took. He approached a clearing in the trees; it was then as he stepped into the clearing that he knew where he was. No stone circle could be the same, its primitive structure only meaning something to its builders and to the lucky few who knew its purpose. He could see only one marked difference around the stone circle: the makeshift huts edging the forest. To all intents and purposes this was a village, with what looked like a village gathering going on in the centre of the clearing.

Hunter approached the people standing round the stone circle and watched. He still felt fear, but not his own. This was the fear felt by the people in front of him. He could feel their fear of persecution, their pain and suffering, and their wanting to be left in peace. At the perimeter of the circle stood twelve people, one at each short stone, and gathered around them in a larger circle stood the rest of the village, men women and children. The men were dressed in the same regalia as the two Hunter had encountered further down the track. The women wore black ankle-length robes, their hair was of the same colour, and their complexion was that of death itself.

Hunter moved closer to the gathering and now could see into the centre of the stone circle. Standing at the head of the large stone table was a shrouded figure wielding a dagger. Hunter stared at the man's face, and then down on to the stone he was standing over. A small child lay face up on the slab, whimpering. The dagger hovered for a second, then plunged down into the child's chest. Hunter closed his eyes before the dagger struck, but the noise of the blade hitting the stone still sickened him. The shrouded figure pulled at the chest of the boy, while the onlookers started to chant, a phrase that Hunter had never heard before.

"Ruadh Rofhessa, Ruadh Rofhessa."

The shrouded figure stood over the body and plunged both hands into the child's stomach. Blood steamed in the cold air as it poured down his soft white skin, then puddled on the slab. Then, with a sickening sound, he pulled out the child's entrails and tossed them on the ground, seeming to look at them as if waiting for something to happen. The crowd kept chanting, their voices becoming louder all of the time.

"What sort of people are you?" Hunter screamed from his soul. He had seen this bizarre ritual once before, when he had seen Carl on the slab. His heart yearned for answers, Why was he there? Why was he shown all this? Was it real? He tried to think in what way he was associated with any of this. Nothing made sense anymore. Was he alive or dead?

A feeling of calm entered his spirit once more, and he was sure he heard a voice say: *Look at the people standing at each stone round the circle. Look at the druid priest.*

The druid priest holding the dagger looked directly at him. Hunter got a good look at the man's features and knew who he was. He looked a little younger maybe, but it was definitely the mysterious old man he'd spoken to on the moor. The old man had told him to depend on his instinct rather than logic. Hunter was sure it was him, but what part did he play in all this? Thoughts rushed through his mind. Maybe the old man was the killer of the children, and maybe the villagers had nothing to do with it,

The druid priest thrust his hands in the air and looked up at the heavens. The onlookers stopped chanting, and the clear blue sky above began to cloud over. A powerful, palpable energy started to emanate from the centre of the circle. Each of the figures at the perimeter stones were fixed on the priest. Not one of then moved, but the others on the outside began to step back, frightened at what they could feel in the air.

The daylight faded quickly as black thunderclouds blotted out the sun and a warm humid wind stirred the branches in the trees. Electricity crackled in the clouds above as Hunter watched the twelve people at the smaller stones on the outside of the circle. He recognised the ones nearest to him immediately and surmised the identities of those he could not see. Nearest to him stood a younger looking Eli Trout, then at the next stone was the blacksmith, and beside him was the woman from the shop. Each member of the village must have been there. But what did it mean? Was this all happening now? Not knowing any of the answers was making him question his sanity.

A rumble of thunder shook the ground, sending most of the onlookers running into the forest. The druid priest seized a long sword from beside him and held it with both hands above his head, pointing it towards the clouds. His words were only audible between the cracks of thunder. One word boomed out as he thrust the sword towards the sky.

"*Nuadha!*"

He circled the sword above his head and uttered more strange words, but this time with every word came a clear translation in Hunter's head, as if someone or something wanted him to know what the druid priest was saying.

"*Lugh!*" the druid priest shouted, and the voice spoke to Hunter, *The spear of Lugh which insured victory.*

"*Dagdha!*" the druid shouted. *The cauldron of which none would go unsatisfied.* Then came the word *Nuadha* again, and the voice said: *The sword of NUADHA from which no one could escape.*

Hunter too was transfixed by what was going on in front of him. He was convinced that something great and miraculous was about to happen. He could sense a power that he'd never sensed before, as if he was about to witness something that only a god could do. He could feel his spirit tremble with excitement as the force from above seemed to search his whole being.

The wind now swirled around the stone circle, cloaking it in a turbulent transparent protective shield. Electricity skipped and crackled across the bottom of the clouds, on occasion reaching down to the stones below. the people now enclosed in the centre of the circle never moved, even when the stones they were standing by were hit with brief forks of lightning. As the druid priest kept beckoning at the skies with the sword, his words become clear to Hunter, answering maybe why he was there.

"Raudh Rofhessa gives these worthy warriors the power to defeat our enemy. Let their souls change to those of the beasts from the pits of the earth so that our foes may run in terror. Oh God of all Gods, I have the sword of Nuadha, the sword that you handed to my druid forefather. Give me the power to give to them through the sword." The old man climbed onto the stone slab, his legs astride the small boy's body, and held the sword aloft once more.

Thunder rumbled constantly, shaking the ground and trees

alike. Then with one blinding flash a bolt of lightning came from the clouds and struck the sword that the priest was holding. For a split second the sword glowed red, and sparks of electricity danced over the druid's body. His eyes glowed orange, then shimmered like quicksilver as the slab he was standing on emitted a tremendous light. Hunter knew that what he was looking at was the light of life itself; to him it seemed to be the power of the universe and to hold all the answers to life itself. It was not a fearful light. It was a soothing, peaceful light.

Then, with a tremendous jolt, the lightning branched off the sword and struck the nearest small stone to it, then the next as it proceeded around the circle. With each stone it struck, the power surged through its companion as well, igniting them like beacons in the night sky. Then as fast as it came, the lightning was gone, along with the wind and the thunder.

Slowly the clouds cleared, and once more a blue morning sky appeared. The forest lay silent and still for a moment as the villagers crept from the woods to see what had happened. The druid priest lay slumped over the small child's body, and a fine mist cloaked the ground at knee height. Steam rose from the stones on the outside of the circle as, one by one, each person who had stood by them dragged themselves to their feet. Within minutes, all of the villagers had come out of hiding and were warily stepping towards the stone circle. Trout and the rest of the people at the stones approached the central stone looking none the worse for their ordeal.

The druid priest pushed himself to his knees and placed the sword on the stone table, then looked down at the small boy. A gasp of disbelief came from the crowd watching as the child sat up, then stepped from the slab. Hunter felt the emotion well up inside him. He had witnessed something supernatural, something that could give life but as easily could have taken it.

He knew now that this somehow related with what he had to do. He was not alone; he was there for a reason. A force greater than humankind, maybe even the creator of humanity, wanted him there for a reason, but he knew this story was still incomplete. A flashback memory came to mind, he remembered

Sarah telling him the story of the Romans killing the villagers thousands of years ago. Could this be them?

He remembered the druid priest she talked of and the way that the villagers had been cursed because the priest was murdered, thus unable to recant the spell on his warriors.

Hunter watched, awestruck by what he had just witnessed. He sensed the relief and calm of the people in front of him, but he could also sense danger that was getting closer by the minute from all sides. His eyes scanned the forest. He knew that something was there, something that meant death to anyone that got in its way, but where was it? What was it?

Sarah's words seemed to drop into his head. "The Romans slaughtered whole settlements, men, women, and children ... The Roman soldiers were ordered to squash the resistance of the peasants on the moor."

Hunter tried to understand, but this whole affair was too fantastic to believe. He wanted to believe, but beliefs of the twentieth century just would not let him; he needed more proof. Then the thought struck him: Wasn't it enough to be made transparent like a spirit? He fought to get control of his mind, he wanted to be left alone, and he did not know how much more he could take. What did all of these voices mean? They repeated again and again until finally he screamed for them to stop.

They did stop, as quickly as he had requested them to, but the feeling of encroaching evil clogged the air like an acrid smoke choking the lungs—then a sudden cry from behind him. The whole village froze and looked to the track leading into the clearing. The call was short but enough to give a warning, and it had seemed to come from only yards away in the forest. The villagers began to run to their huts and return with their weapons; even the women carried spears and swords, and they seemed to know what was coming even if Hunter did not.

Once they had their weapons, they ran back into the centre of the stone circle and waited. The men formed a ring facing outward, with the women behind them and the children tucked away in the centre along with the druid priest. Seconds passed, and the forest seemed to come alive with the sound of branches and undergrowth trampled underfoot. The clank of armour became louder as did the rumble of something coming towards them from the track. Within moments, the bushes and tree branches shook along the edges of the clearing, revealing a shimmer of steel.

Then, behind heavy shields, with flashing gilded legends, line after line of brightly dressed Roman soldiers stepped from the forest, their swords and spears facing the villagers. In what seemed like seconds the soldiers had formed an impenetrable circle round the villagers, then stopped about twenty feet from them and waited. Not one sound came from the hundred or so soldiers, nor was there a sound from the villagers; everyone waited. The rumble from the track increased as the soldiers covering the entrance parted and four chariots raced in.

Hunter was standing between the soldiers and the villagers, he needed to get out of there, he saw the gap that the chariots had made and ran for it. Now, from the outskirts of the forest be watched as the chariots moved slowly around the stone circle. For some reason they seemed reticent to attack, perhaps due to the thunder and lightning from all sides as they approached. The old druid priest began to chant and wave his sword vigorously in the air. His chants turned to curses, and the rest of the villagers joined in the shouting, as if to goad on their attackers. The fearsome looking women screamed and waved their spears and clubs at the enemy facing them.

The ranks of the Romans faltered as if what they were watching had put the fear of God into them. The warriors on the outside of the circle began to step forward slowly. The officer in the leading chariot shouted for his men to stand firm and ordered up the bowmen. The soldiers parted to let the bowmen take up kneeling positions before the main troops.

Hunter could not believe what he was seeing. He screamed, "You bastards, you outnumber them, yet you're gonna slaughter them with arrows," but knew he could do nothing but watch.

The villagers pre-empted the onslaught of arrows and encased themselves with their shields, but the old druid climbed up on the stone slab and cursed the soldiers around him even more vigorously. With an ear-splitting crack, dozens of arrows left their bows. On the first volley, only a few of the villagers fell, but as the archers fired repeatedly, more dropped, exposing those behind them to the hail of arrows.

It was on the fourth volley that the priest was hit. Hunter watched as the old man took three arrows in the upper body, then fell to the ground. The villagers, en-raged by the leader's fall, broke ranks and swarmed for the enemy. They were engulfed in the mass of colour as the Roman army moved in from all sides. The ragtag villagers stood no chance from the disciplined Roman might, and it was like a pack of hounds on a fox. Outnumbered, one after another the villagers dropped to the ground, men, women, and children impaled and butchered, spears breaching flesh and swords cleaving bone. The coppery rank smell of blood hung heavy in the air as people fought for their lives.

Hunter felt no grief for the adults of the village, they'd lived their lives. The children that were slain he could not stomach, and each child murdered in the battle brought back the memory of Carl.

The battle ended as abruptly as it had started. The Roman soldiers took only their dead plus a few prisoners, presumably for slaves, and left the rest of the slaughtered villagers scattered round the stone circle as mute testimony to their power. Hunter stepped through the mass of bodies, some decapitated, others disembowelled, and all quite dead. He looked for each villager he knew, and one by one he found them. They had all died as brave warriors, including the women, but what puzzled Hunter was if they were dead why were they still alive in his time.

"They aren't dead, just waiting," a voice said from behind him. Hunter spun round and faced the old man he now knew as the druid priest.

"What the fu—" He quickly looked across at the bleeding body of the druid priest, then back at the same man standing in front of him.

"Aye, they got me too," the old man said as he surveyed the

bodies. "Brave people, these." He shook his head, then looked back at Hunter.

"I must be dreaming. All of this can't be happening." Hunter shut his eyes tightly, but when he opening them, everything was still the same.

"Maybe you are dreaming, but it's all for you to see. You must help me, and you're the one who's been chosen. You're the only one strong enough to help."

"What d'you mean, I've been chosen? Chosen by who?"

The old man started to walk over to his body, "There's no time to explain it all now, you'll have to be back soon."

"Back, I can't believe this; it's like something from a horror film."

"Come over yere, boy, and look." The old man was standing by the stone slab looking at his own dead body.

For a moment Hunter did not move, but his curiosity outweighed his stubbornness, and he moved to the old man's side. He looked down at the bloodied body of the druid priest, one of the arrows having gone right through the body.

"D'you see that sword? That is the sword of Nuadha, the only thing that can stop these beasts. These people have lived among mortals as mortals themselves for thousands of years, and they are in your time now." The old man sighed. "They age very little. They are now going beyond the boundaries set for them; in fact, they are going beyond the boundaries of life itself. They are taking mortals' lives for granted. The good power given to them has turned evil over the years, and it has been with them for too long. It should have been taken back by me after the battle, but as you can see, I hadn't the chance."

Hunter looked at the sword, then back at the old man. "You said beasts. Are they something to do with the villagers?"

"They are the villagers. Some of them want to die, they know that they will not live forever. They will get older, but it will take them a hundred years to your one year of ageing, and they will become more evil with passing time. They must be stopped now. The blessing that the gods gave me to give to them must be recanted before they start living and breeding with mortals."

"Breeding with mortals ... We must be talking about different people. The villagers that I know are all old, and they couldn't get it up if they wanted too." Hunter laughed. "I don't reckon you got any worries on that score."

The old man scowled at him. "Not all of them are old. One is just a young woman. She has already conceived, and she must be killed."

Hunter turned his back on the old man, trying to understand some of what he'd been told. He looked down and saw at his feet the child that had been so miraculously brought back to life after being disembowelled by the priest. The child was near naked and covered in blood. He knelt down and tried to touch the small body, but his hand just drifted through it.

Hunter glanced up at the priest. "If your God wanted to help you, why did he bring this young boy back to life only to let him die again?"

The priest stepped over to him. "That child isn't dead; she will live again, as will the rest of them."

"She!" Hunter scrutinised the face of the girl; she was familiar to him.

"This is the young girl that you were talking about, isn't it?"

The old man nodded his head.

"She must be the one that I've seen in the photos on the wall in the pub, but I haven't seen her in the village yet."

"Thou wilt, and thou must kill her."

Hunter rose to his feet and looked the old man in the eye. "So let me get this straight. You want me to kill all these villagers because they are evil?"

"All I want you to do is bring the sword of Nuadha to the stone circle." The old man had a serious look on his face. "They wilt try to stop thee, for they know who thee are. They don't yet know thee have my help, but they will as soon as thee go for the sword. thee must trust your instinct now more than ever. Thee must get that sword to the circle on the next full moon."

"When's the next full moon?"

"Tomorrow," the old man said, and then started to walk away from the mass of bodies.

Hunter shook his head in disbelief. How could he believe such fantasy? He called after the priest, "Look, I'm going to make these bastards pay for killing my son, not because of some mumbo-jumbo bullshit I hear in my dreams. Are you listening to me?" Hunter was shouting as the old man reached the edge of the clearing.

The old man turned to face him. "They will rise tonight and get revenge on those Roman soldiers who killed their friends and family; they have no emotions when they change from what they are now to the beasts that you know. All they know is that they must kill whoever is in their territory, just like wolves. The only way they can be stopped is by bringing the sword of Nuadha to the circle; otherwise they will go on killing."

Hunter still did not understand, he had so many questions but only one sprang to mind at this moment: "What did they do with my son?"

The old man's ghostly figure started to fade. "They gain power from those they sacrifice or kill. An evil power is taking control of their lives, and the spell has become a curse." The old man was still growing dimmer as his words ended.

"You didn't answer my question. What did they do with my son?"

"Thee had no son," the old man said, then was gone.

"What d'you mean I had no son? What the fuck you talking, about you crazy-ass bastard?"

~~~

1:30 AM SATURDAY

Hunter's body thrashed about on his bed, and perspiration soaked his face. Then his eyes opened wide, and he stared into the flat darkness of the room. He lay silent and still for a few moments until he had his bearings, then breathed a sigh of relief that the dream was over.

He pondered the dream for a while until he remembered Trout following him up the stairs to his room. His memory was still a little fuzzy, but he knew damn well that his drink had been spiked. He pushed himself from the bed, but a painful pressure in his head sent him crashing back onto the pillow. The pressure behind his eyes was worse than any hangover he had ever had.

He closed his eyes tightly and listened to the darkness. There was a light breeze blowing outside that made the pub sign squeak slightly on its gibbet. As Hunter opened his eyes, a cold blue light shone through the window, casting shadows round the room. He lifted himself again from the bed, this time slowly, all the time thinking on the old man's words. The blue light faded for a moment, then returned. He cocked a glance out the window. Through the branches of the tree he could see the nearly full moon high in the sky.

"Tomorrow night's the full moon," he said aloud, remembering what the old priest had told him.

He sat silently, with his elbows on his knees and his chin rested in the palms of his hands, listening to the blood pumping around his head, when he heard the murmur of voices from the bar down below. He angled his watch to the light of the moon and checked the time; it was 1:30 AM. Hunter reckoned he must have been unconscious for around two hours. He could still hear the odd muffled voice coming from somewhere beyond his bedroom door and below in the pub.

The old man's voice drifted into his head once again. *The villagers are the beasts ... They will kill anyone who is on their territory ...*

Hunter felt apprehensive now about staying where he was. If his dream was true, these people would surely kill him, sooner or later.

"Shit! What am I worried about? It was only a dream. This place is getting to you, Hunter, all you gotta to do is find out if they had anything to do with Carl's disappearance, that's all." He spoke softly, trying to reassure himself and at the same time dismiss the dreams he had been having.

An overwhelming parched throat made him momentarily forget about his dreams and impelled him to his feet and across to the door. He pushed aside the dressing table, then quietly unlocked the door and warily stepped into the darkened corridor. He crept to the staircase and stopped on the landing. He listened for the voices again, and at first he could hear nothing, then a cough emanating from the bar area told him that someone was still down there.

He was about to start down the stairs when he remembered the room that Trout had told him to stay away from. He took the few steps to his left, put his ear to the door, and listened, hoping that Trout was downstairs and not in bed asleep. The door handle, as he depressed it, made a *clunk* that seemed amplified in the darkness. He held his breath and listened through the pulse beating in his ears. There was no sound of people running up the stairs, no half-naked Eli Trout opening the door and asking him why the hell he was lurking round the pub at this time of the morning. Which was lucky for Trout, Hunter thought, because he was sure he would have killed him on the spot. Just *how* was not immediately clear, and he would be a hell of a man to wrestle to death.

A noise from one of the rooms downstairs sent Hunter springing back into the corridor, not really knowing where to go. He stayed in the darkness of the corridor for only a few moments, though they seemed much longer, then when he thought the coast was clear, he moved back to the top of the stairs. Looking into Trout's room was too risky tonight. He would seek his chance tomorrow, and this time he would get Jock's help as a lookout.

The bitter taste in his mouth and his screaming headache reminded him that he needed a drink; he remembered the sink in the kitchen and thought that it must have running water. The voices from the bar became louder as he reached the kitchen. He recognised Trout's rural tones and the blacksmith's, but the other voices he did not recognise. He did not take much notice of the talking to start with, his thirst was too great, but after he had had several mouthfuls of water, his curiosity got the better of him. The kitchen was as dark as the rest of the inn, but the back room, which joined the bar, was partially lit from the entrance to the bar.

Hunter edged his way round the room, keeping in the shadows and out of sight. The door from the bar to the back room was wedged open, casting light into the darkness as a yellow rectangle that Hunter had to avoid. He waited by the doorway and listened first to conversation that he did not understand, but soon it was clear that he was the topic of their conversation. Hunter dared a quick glance into the bar, just to see who was talking to whom. His heart raced when he saw that the whole village seemed to have turned out for this meeting.

"Tomorrow night thee must let him go on the moor," a deep voice rasped, and Hunter realized it was the blacksmith.

"Nay there be too much at risk. We can't have police looking round again because someone else has disappeared," Trout retorted.

"Don't listen to him, old man, thou hast need of killing him. He's seen too much. We caught him tonight looking under that tarpaulin, so now he's the second one who's taken an interest in that field."

"Aye, and thee killed the first one; we were lucky to get away with that." Trout had a tinge of anger in his voice.

"We got away with that because I made sure the job was done right. They'll never know what really happened."

Hunter's heart sank as he listened to their conversation, knowing now that everything he had dreamt about must have been true. By their own admission he knew that they had killed DS Short, and what the old man had told him about their being able to transform into those creatures must be true, no matter how absurd it sounded. However, he really wanted to hear what they had done with Carl. His gut feeling, since he had heard of these people's previous exploits, was that the boy was dead.

Anger started to rage inside him. He wanted his revenge now. He'd kill the lot of them. He'd show them as much mercy as they showed to their victims. He'd burn their village to the ground and kill anything that stood in his path. His life meant nothing now. He was a trained killer, and now he'd practice what he'd been taught.

He eyed up the odds once again. Just peering briefly into the bar, he counted eleven including Trout. There were twelve in the photo on the wall plus the young girl, so thirteen all told. Unlucky for them, he thought.

He remembered the twelve stones around the circle; one person stood beside each, the girl and the priest were on the inside of the circle, and the priest was on his side.

"So where are you?" he mouthed silently.

He checked his numbers again.

Seven men and four women, not counting the girl, so one was missing.

He was contemplating the odds when his senses told him that something was wrong. He scanned the room, and nothing looked out of place, but the feeling was becoming stronger. He moved from the back room and peered into the darkness of the kitchen. That room too looked no different from moments before. As he stepped back from the doorway to return to his surveillance of the villagers, he heard the creak of door hinges, then footsteps as someone walked across the kitchen floor in his direction.

Two options sprang to mind. Either jump the person and have the advantage of surprise, or try to hide, but where? He dismissed the sledgehammer approach, thinking that as soon as all hell broke loose, the villagers in the bar would come pouring through the door. The odds against him were too great, especially when he was unarmed. But there seemed to be nowhere to hide. The footsteps approached, the door opened, and a dark figure stepped into the back room. Hunter dove under a small table in one corner of the room and watched, hoping the darkness would conceal him until the man had passed. It did. The twelfth resident of the village stepped into as the silent bar; all heads turned to him, and then talk resumed.

Hunter headed back to his room. He had all the evidence he needed to bring a guilty verdict. He would see to carrying out their sentence as soon as he make contact with Jock.

CHAPTER 20

DAWN, SATURDAY MORNING.

The daylight could not have come soon enough for Hunter. Waiting in that tomb of a room felt like an eternity, waiting for those *things* from the village to go home. Hunter had now been reduced to thinking of them as things. They were human only in shape, but maybe God only knew what they really were.

He heard the villagers leave just before dawn, then heard Trout lumber up the stairs to his bedroom, and a firm slam of a door told him that the coast was clear. He leant heavily against the window frame and looked out to the beginning of a new day, a new start for some, and a joy to live for others. The night sky quickly paled into a light blue twilight. As he thought of what might have been, he sighed loudly over the good times with Jenny and Carl. The memories always seemed summery and happy, but those times were now lost forever.

His marriage to Jenny was now finished, and he could come to terms with that. But the loss of his son ... that was destroying him from the inside. He fended off the tears as anger started adrenaline surging through his body. They had chosen his demise, and now he had chosen theirs. Today was their last day on this planet.

It was only a matter of patience now. He would wait for them to make the first move and then kill them in self-defence. It sounded straightforward enough to him, and he just hoped that Jock would feel the same way.

At first light Hunter quietly and unobtrusively made his way out of the village; all seemed to be calm. He needed to find a pay phone, preferably in the next village, before Jock got his ass out of bed and left the house. Hunter jogged the five miles into Porlock. Luckily most of the run was downhill, which made it that much easier and faster.

The sleepy village of Porlock looked as if it had not changed for hundreds of years. Narrow streets edged with terrace cottages all led at last to the awesome sight of the vast rocky shoreline. What started as a bright fresh dawn was quickly changing into a cloudy autumn morning with rain seemingly imminent. Hunter found the pay phone he was looking for and punched in Jock's number, then waited as the tones sang over the line.

"Come on, Jock, get off that tart and answer the phone."

~~~

Jock lay on the bed; perspiration chilled him in the cool air. Jenny had stayed the night once again, after he'd done the crawling this time, telling her that he was sorry for his abrupt outburst when her husband had turned up unexpectedly. He knew he was a sucker for the women and could not turn away the guarantee of a screw when all he had to do was give her a call. He knew he'd regret it, but what the hell, Hunter was out of the way this time, and their marriage was virtually over anyway. Where was the harm?

Because of their early morning sex session, Jenny had taken a shower, leaving Jock to recover. He dozed off listening to the spray of the shower and woke when Jenny started to sing her top ten greatest hits in E sharp. Between the noise of the shower in the next room and her shrill ballads, he could barely hear the downstairs phone. Then Jenny at last switched off the shower and began to dry herself, and he was sure he heard the phone ringing. From the top of the stairs he saw Jenny, a towel wrapped around her, about to pick up the receiver. He told her to stop, bounded down the stairs two at a time, and snatched the phone up quickly.

"Yeah," he said brusquely and leaned against the wall.

Jenny cast her eyes over his naked body and smirked as she dropped her towel and began to fondle her breasts, watching to see if her performance would have the desired effect. Hunter's voice was better than a cold shower; the only thing that came into Jock's mind was guilt.

"Jock, it's me."

"Umm. How's it going?" Jock bumbled his words, not letting on to Jenny who it was he was talking to.

Jenny was still doing her performance at the foot of the stairs and now dropped to her knees, crawled towards him, and started to slide her hands up the inside of his legs. Jock tried to ignore her steamy advances.

"Not too good. Look, I need you up here, there's going to be some shit hitting the fan at any minute, and I need some backup."

Jock took a step back from Jenny and shook his head. "What sort of backup?"

Jenny got to her feet and sauntered up the stairs, giving her hips an exaggerated wiggle as she did so.

"The sort of backup that you're trained for, d'you get what I mean?"

There was silence at Jock's end of the phone for a moment. "So you found out that they had something to do with it then?"

"I can't go right into it now, but they've been killing people for years. The bastards have sacrifices and shit like that. I tell you, Jock, these people ain't who they seem."

"Look, Hunter, we've been through a lot together, a lot of shit, but you just can't kill civilians because you think they had something to do with the disappearance of Carl. You need proof, not a hunch.

"Right, you want proof." Hunter had a tone of anger in his voice. "There's a bloke here called Eli Trout, he owns the pub, he looks in his later sixties. We need to find out what records there are on him and the villagers. Go to the public library and see Sarah Holly, ask her to show you the electoral roll for that parish. My guess is that they aren't on it."

"So that don't mean shit, Hunter. They might not have sent in their forms, lots of people don't."

Hunter's sounded impatient. "Just do it, will you? I'll ring her and tell her that you're coming to see her and get her to sort out as much information on them as possible. Then I want you to get your ass up here. I'll show you something that will blow your mind."

Jock considered; this was the last thing he wanted. "Where shall I meet you?" he finally asked.

"The turning before the village, I'll meet you there at four o'clock, OK?"

Jock agreed, then put down the phone. Jenny was still singing up in the bedroom as she put on her clothes. Jock slammed his fist into the wall, then started to climb the stairs. Agreeing to meet Hunter meant there was a whole world of hurt out there soon to be unleashed. Jenny soon noticed his troubled expression when he entered the bedroom.

She stopped singing. "What's the matter?" she asked fastening her bra.

Jock searched out his clothes, too much was going through his mind to answer her.

"Come on, what's the matter? Was it that phone call?" she asked again. This time she stood in front of him and waited for a response.

He pulled a T-shirt over his head, then looked up at her. "It was your old man."

The room fell silent for a moment; they just looked at each other.

"What did he want?"

"He wants me to go up onto the moors. He needs my help." He lowered his head and pulled on his underwear.

"Help in what?"

"He says he's found out that the villagers had something to do with Carl's disappearance."

"You didn't say you'd go, did you?"

He got to his feet and went over to the dressing table, opened the drawer, and pulled out a pair of socks; his not answering her was as good as an answer.

"You did, didn't you? You said you'd go up there." Her voice was full of venom; this was the Jenny that Hunter knew.

"Look he's a mate of mine; we've been through a lot together ..."

Jenny interrupted. "Yeah, including me! Fine mate you are. If you think that much of him, why d'you screw me, eh?" She pushed for an answer.

"Look I don't need this now, just leave it out." He jumped to his feet and pushed past her.

She followed, she was not about to leave this now.

"Yeah, a real good mate, the kind of mate that makes his best friend's wife pregnant and doesn't have the bottle to tell him. Don't you give me that mate shit. You just feel guilty, that's all."

Jock jumped towards her with his fists raised. "Yeah, fucking right I feel guilty, guilty about betraying him, not screwing you." His voice was loud, and he meant every word.

"You're as mad as him, you'll both end up dead or in prison. Can't you get it into your head that Carl's gone, drowned in one of those bogs up there? We can't bring him back. All we can do is look to the future, a future with me and you. We can have another child." Her voice cracked with emotion, she stepped towards him. "Don't go up there."

Jock sneered at her. "You should never have been a mother; you're one fucked-up woman. You're the one that's mad, not Hunter. What sort of woman are you that'll jump in bed with another man and not so much have the guilt of your son's disappearance on your mind. You need help, lady." He stormed out the door and down the stairs.

Jenny followed. "I love you, that's why."

He grabbed his car keys from the worktop in the kitchen and headed for the front door.

"Jock, if you go up there, I'll tell him about us."

He paused at the front door. "Bollocks to you, I'll tell him myself." He opened the door and stepped out into the damp morning air.

~ ~ ~

Jock somehow knew that the dark-haired girl serving at the library counter was Sarah Holly. She had a plain but beautiful appearance that needed no makeup or false glamour. He scanned every inch of her that he could see as he stepped up to the desk and waited his turn to be served. She threw a fleeting glance at the stranger as she stamped the ticket on the inside of a book then tapped its code number into the computer.

Jock still had his eyes fixed on Sarah when a young man's voice broke his concentration.

"What can I do for you, mate?" the man asked apathetically.

Jock glanced briefly at him, then back at Sarah. "It's all right, I'm being sorted."

"Fair enough." The young man shook his head, looked briefly at Sarah Holly, then retreated to the back office.

"What can I do for you?" Sarah asked in a soft, sexy voice.

Jock thought of many things but none of them allowed in public, he would stick to the task assigned to him, for a while anyway.

"Hunter sent me."

Her eyebrows rose at his name. "Oh yes."

"He phoned you this morning didn't he?"

"Did he?" Sarah looked bemused by the whole conversation.

"He said he would, but by the look on your face, it looks like he didn't."

"No he didn't."

"Typical."

There was silence for a moment as Jock tried to remember the message.

"How is he?" Sarah asked, walking round to the front of the desk.

"Well that's a matter of opinion, but I guess he's as mad as usual."

She smiled and ushered him away from the main counter to one of the aisles of books.

"Make out that you want a book. Mrs Williams hates us talking to friends in council time."

Jock glanced towards the office behind the counter. Betty Williams looked in full flight; she was giving the young man he'd sent away the lecture of a lifetime, tearing a magazine in half as she did so. "Looks like the young lad's getting a roasting," Jock said, then looked back at the girl.

Sarah smiled. "Look, I don't want to seem rude, but what was Hunter trying to contact me about?"

"Good question. If I knew that he wasn't going to phone you, I would've written down the message he gave me. But as far as I can remember, it was something about the villagers of Oare, something about looking on the electoral roll to see if their names are on it."

"Did he give you any particular name?" she asked.

Jock thought hard. "Yeah he did, now what was it? Something to do with the owner of the pub, Eli somebody."

"Eli Trout?"

"Yeah, that's the geezer, how did you know his name?"

Sarah looked confused for a moment then answered: "Oh, I think Hunter mentioned him before, when he was talking about the pub."

"Well, you know more than me then. I ain't got the faintest idea what the hell this is all about."

Sarah took Jock to the back room and briefed him on what

she and Hunter had talked about, and in turn Jock told her what Hunter had told him. The whole concept still seemed too ludicrous to believe, but the villagers' names not being in the electoral roll seemed to confirm that something was not quite right at the quiet village of Oare.

Sarah searched for any name that may have been connected with the houses in the village, but by rights no one existed; the place should have been a ghost town. As Sarah searched the records, Jock took in the view out the window. Time went quickly as he thought about what was going to happen later in the day, and he didn't like the feeling he had. It was like death was in the room with him, as if the Grim Reaper was watching every move he made. He had never felt this jumpy before, not even in the Gulf War, but he lived by the notion that if your time was up, it was up!

Jock left the library in a sombre mood; his head awash with myths and legends that should have had no part in the twentieth century. However, what pissed him off most was that he did not even get Sarah Holly's telephone number, had no chance to ask her out. This was the worst day of his life, he decided; maybe he should kill himself and save Hunter the trouble of doing it for him. He pondered the delights of Miss Sarah Holly, thinking Hunter certainly had a talent for picking up the smart-looking women. The only conclusion he could come to on this was that it must have been Hunter's sad and harmless-looking face.

~~~

For most of the morning and part of the afternoon Hunter planned his attack, going over every detail. Nothing must be left to chance. First, he would look into Trout's bedroom; he was a big part of this conspiracy of silence and had to have something incriminating somewhere. Their guilt already proven to Hunter, he only wanted the evidence to show Jock; assumption and hearsay would not be enough.

The rain was becoming harder as it swept in torrents across the bleak moor. Hunter sat on the edge of the spinney loading the pump-action shotgun, oblivious to the rain soaking his clothes. His mind wandered back into his childhood; things that he had not thought of for years seemed just to pop into his head. He remembered his first kiss, his first fight, and the pranks that he and Jock used to get up to. A slight smile creased his lips as he remembered. The rain streamed down his face.

The smile disappeared as he drifted back into reality and remembered those bastards that had killed his son. He pumped the action of the gun, pushing one of the heavy shells into the breach. Now he was ready.

CHAPTER 21

3:45 PM SATURDAY.

Detective Inspector Bob Finch jabbed at the light switch near the door as he entered his drab and shadowy office. Within seconds, the fluorescent tubes filled the room with a wan light. He took a brief look round the empty office, grunted with displeasure, then sauntered over to his cluttered desk. Finch did not relish working on a Saturday, but now that Short was gone, it was the only way he could catch up on his paperwork. He took off his raincoat and tossed it onto Cranbury's desk, then settled into his chair. Pushing away a stack of files, he soon found the overflowing ashtray, set it on top of the files, then flicked some fresh ash into it.

Finch's last few days had been turbulent. His wife had returned home after falling out with the window cleaner with whom she'd run off. Finch naturally let her come back in the hope that they could patch things up, but within hours, they had started to argue, with Finch demanding to know if the window cleaner was better in bed than he was. Her answer was not the one that he had wanted to hear, so he asked exactly how he was better in bed, and she told him.

He grabbed a handful of files and papers from the IN tray and started to sift through them. Non-urgent ones were stacked to his left (they were for Cranbury's attention). and urgent ones he placed in front of himself. As he shuffled and restacked the files, a message slip fell into his lap.

He picked it up and started to read Cranbury's crabbed printing: JENNY HUNTER PHONED. SHE SAID IT REGARDED HER HUSBAND AND COULD YOU CALL HER BACK. DC Cranbury. Friday 9:30 AM. Finch rushed over to his coat and pulled out his notepad, then snatched up the phone as he looked for Mrs Hunter's telephone number.

~~~

Mary Nixon ambled out of the kitchen into the hall, wiped most of the flour off her hands into her apron, and then picked up the phone.

"Hello," she said softly.

"Hello, could I speak to Mrs Jenny Hunter please?"

Jenny's mother did not recognise the voice, but the formality made it sound important.

"Yeah, who's speaking please?" She was curious to know whom the strange voice belonged too.

"It's Detective Inspector Finch, Minehead CID."

Mary's mouth fell open; her immediate thought was that they had found Carl.

"Um, yes, Inspector, I'll just call her." She set down the phone and rushed up the stairs to Jenny's room.

Within seconds, her mother was hurrying Jenny down the stairs. She placed the phone slowly to her ear, took a deep breath, and then answered.

"Yes, Inspector?"

"I've just received your message. You wanted me to call you. Something to do with your husband, it says here."

Jenny closed her eyes and gave a big sigh of relief. She had forgotten about ringing the police station the day before, and it was somehow a relief that there was no news on the boy. This offered hope that he was still alive, but in other ways, it was frustrating that they still had no evidence on how or where the boy had disappeared. There was a moment's silence as Jenny gathered her thoughts, then she replied:

"Sorry, Inspector, you'll have to bear with me. It just threw me for a moment, getting a call from you. I thought that it was news about my son. You'll never know what goes through my mind in such a short time. Just walking to the phone, I think of every horrible thing I can, and I tell myself that I'm ready for anything, but I'm not."

"Sorry about that, I should have made it clear to the lady I talked to first, I didn't think." She could all but hear him cringing with embarrassment. "I wish I had some news on your son, Mrs Hunter, but we're still holding to our theory that maybe he drowned, the thing is that, without a body or even any evidence, it's hard to make any sort of judgement to what happened, but if I do hear anything, you'll be the first to know. So what was it that you wanted to talk to me about?"

"Could you hold on a minute?" Jenny asked Finch, then put her hand over the mouthpiece of the phone and looked back at her mother.

"It's nothing about Carl, it's something private." Jenny said quietly.

Mary frowned, as if in resentment that she was not wanted there, and shuffled back into the kitchen. Jenny resumed her conversation with Finch. "Well, Inspector, I thought I'd better tell you that my husband has gone back onto the moors."

~~~

Finch pulled the cigarette from his mouth; this indeed was music to his ears.

"Mmm, when did this happen?" he asked. looking for a place to extinguish his cigarette. He found nowhere, so he dropped it on the floor and stepped on it.

"Friday morning."

"Have you heard from him since then?"

"No I haven't, but he rang his friend and told him that he knows the villagers had something to do with the disappearance of Carl. I tell you, Inspector, there's going to be some trouble up there if you don't do something."

"What was his friend's name?" Finch snatched up a pen and waited for her answer.

"Why d'you want to know that?" she asked.

"What?" Finch had no patience for her coyness. "Look, Mrs Hunter, if you want my help, you'd better answer my questions. Now what's your husband's friend's name?"

There was silence for a moment, then, she quietly answered. "Jock Barnet."

Finch repeated the name as he wrote it down.

"He's a marine too," she added.

"Right, I'll have a word with Mr Barnet, d'you know if he lives at the barracks or not?"

"He has a house, but he won't be there; he's gone to help Hunter." Finch bit on his bottom lip; he was not happy to hear this. "I'll tell you, Mr Finch, people are going to die if you don't do something."

"Shit!" Finch rasped under his breath. "That's all I need, two Rambo's taking the law into their own hands." He scribbled down Jock's name. "Right, did Mr Barnet tell you anything else? I take it that's who you got all of this information from, wasn't it?"

"Well it's not that he told me this, but I think that my husband is armed."

"Marvellous, can this get any worse?" Finch muttered, more to himself than Jenny.

"Maybe."

Finch did not want to ask, but he had to. "What d'you mean, maybe?" His voice was low, and he wasn't bothering to sound sympathetic.

Jenny's voice had changed; now she talked quietly and in a submissive manner. "Well, it's a long story, but I'll cut it short."

Finch grunted down the other end of the phone.

"Well, basically ..."

"Come on, Mrs Hunter; if you've got something to tell me, just say it."

"Well it's to do with Jock ..."

Finch interrupted. "Jock Barnet?"

"Yes."

"Good, now we're getting somewhere. Carry on, Mrs Hunter."

"Well, I've been having an affair with him."

Finch interrupted again. "Jock Barnet ... you've been having an affair with your husband's best friend?"

"Yes, I know it sounds bad, but—"

Finch stepped in again. "I'm making no moral judgements, Mrs Hunter, just repeating what you're telling me as I write it down. But what has this to do with the police?"

Finch was a good liar if he wanted to be, all part of the training, he told his recruits.

"It could have a lot to do with you. Well, the affair has been going on for several years, and Hunter doesn't know."

Finch clenched his fist with frustration; he could feel the information about to emerge; he was willing her to utter those words.

"Mrs Hunter, can you please just get to the point?"

"All right." Her voice was now sharp; she was losing her temper. "Well, this morning after Hunter called, Jock and me had a row, and I told him I would tell Hunter that Carl was Jock's son if he went up there to help him." Finch's face lit up; this was what he'd wanted to hear, it was the missing link to him.

"Anyway, he told me he'd tell Hunter himself when he got up there. Hunter will kill him."

Finch shook his fist with the vigour of a celebrating soccer fan, this was music to his ears, he now had Hunter's motive for killing the boy, and he knew he was right all along. There was silence at Finch's end for a second; he was putting together the case in his head.

Then he spoke with a stern voice: "Well, I'm glad you told me this, but you would have saved a lot of my time and taxpayers' money if you had told me this at the start. So let me recap on what you have told me. Right, you say that Carl is not your husband's natural child?" He waited for her response

"Yes."

"And that he doesn't know that Carl isn't his child?"

"Yes."

"And you say that Jock Barnet is going to tell him today?"

"Yes."

Finch sighed. "I think this Jock Barnet is in serious trouble if he tells your husband that he's Carl's father. I think your husband needs help, Mrs Hunter; he's a very ill man. I'm going to sort this out right away. Thank you for this information. You'll be hearing from us; goodbye."

Finch put down the phone and whooped in triumph. He had Hunter dead to rights now, as far as he was concerned, and if he killed another psycho marine, that was OK by him, just another nail in Hunter's coffin. He wished that DS Short were still alive; he wanted to say *I told you so.*

"Your ass is mine, Mr bloody Royal Marine Commando Hunter. You're going down, you sick bastard." Finch searched his notepad again for DI Cranbury's phone number, jabbed in the number, then waited for his response.

"It's Finch, get your ass down to the station; we've got work to do.

He slammed down the phone with a contented smile.

~~~

4:05 PM *SATURDAY*

Jock was hoping that Hunter would not be at the rendezvous specified, but hope was all it was; he knew damn well Hunter would be there. The journey to the moors had taken no time at all, and he had argued with himself the whole way, trying to justify his actions. For once Jenny was right. He was only doing this out of guilt. What sort of man would he have been to let down his brother in arms in a time of need?

"Bollocks!" he said aloud. "You're full of shit, Barnet, you always look after number one, it's about time you did something for someone else for a change." He shook his head slightly. "And that's bollocks as well."

The rain swept across the moors like the beginnings of a tempest. The road seemed to bubble like water in hot fat as the rain exploded onto its hard surface. A murky sky shortened the day and made Jock no happier for his journey. He made the last turning before the village and slowed down looking for Hunter. The rain had cut down visibility, and he scanned the ditches on either side of the road.

He saw nothing, but this was the place. He sounded the horn, and Hunter scrambled from the ditch on the passenger side. As Jock drew up alongside him in the car, opened the door, threw his rucksack in the foot well, and climbed in himself.

"All right, mate?" he said, the rain dripping from his clothes.

"Yeah, just about." Jock gave him a casual glance, then faced the windscreen again. "You look like shit."

"So would you if you'd been through what I have."

Jock said nothing, just peered out onto the road in front. After a moment Hunter went on.

"Right, we've got to get rid of the car, then sneak into the village. Go straight on for about a hundred yards, then take the lane to your right. That'll take us up to some woods; we walk from there."

Jock slid into gear and continued down the road as directed.

"Did you go and see Sarah at the Library?" Hunter asked.

"Yeah."

"So what did she say about Trout then?"

Jock turned right into the lane next to the woods. "Well, first off I felt a right prick. I thought you said you were going to call her to let her know I was coming."

Hunter could hear the contempt in his voice. "Yeah I would have done if I could have got through to her, but I couldn't."

There was silence in the car as Jock wrenched up the hand

brake bringing the car to a sliding halt, and then he switched off the engine.

"So what did she say?" Hunter asked again.

"A load of old crap if you ask me."

"Like what?"

Jock moved uncomfortably in his seat. He thought about telling Hunter of his affair with Jenny and the fact that Carl was not his son. At least then it would put an end to this charade, but somehow he did not think he would live to tell the tale.

"She looked through the records that you told me to tell her about. I couldn't remember that bloke's name that you said, but she knew it ..."

Hunter interrupted." She knew Eli Trout's name?"

Jock looked a little puzzled by Hunter's question. "Yeah, why?"

Hunter thought of the conversation he had had with Sarah and remembered nothing about any villager's names being mentioned.

"Seems strange, that's all, I don't know how she knew his name."

"Well she reckons you both talked about him."

Hunter shook his head, but said no more, just told Jock to carry on.

"Well that geezer Trout wasn't on that list. Neither was anyone registered in that village."

Hunter slammed his fist into the dashboard. "I knew it! I told you, didn't I? D'you need much more proof than that?" His voice was loud and full of excitement, and Jock knew that he'd already consigned them all to perdition.

"Look, Hunter, you can't just start accusing people because they're not on the electoral list. Like I said before, it doesn't mean anything. Why not tell the police what you know and leave it to them?"

"What's the matter with you, Jock, you going soft on me or something? I ain't letting the law nowhere near this lot. It's way above their heads, in many ways. Look, it'll be dark soon. We gotta get into the village before dusk; otherwise, we might not make it at all."

Jock frowned. He did not even try to understand what Hunter was telling him. It was so much easier to take his word for it, as usual.

"Come on, I'll give you all the proof you need when we get inside the pub. All I want you to do is keep a lookout for me. I need to get into the landlord's bedroom. I tell you mate, this is one strange village."

Lookout did not sound that bad to Jock, but he still wanted to know more before taking a step outside his car.

"But what makes you think that they had something to do with Carl? I mean, the police think that the boy drowned."

Hunter opened the car door and slid one of his legs out, then looked back at Jock for a long moment. "Trust me, Jock, I just know."

Hunter stepped from the car, grabbed his rucksack, and then leant though the open door. "Coming?" He asked.

CHAPTER 22

Dusk came an hour or so early that day. The storm in the heavens was as black as Hunter had ever seen. The thunderous clouds above swirled like a sea of oil, so low that they seemed ready to engulf the whole village.

The darkness was a blessing for the two marines. They could move across the fields quickly, their footsteps in the wet earth hidden by the sound of the rain and the wind, until finally they reached the back garden of the Black Dog Inn. Hunter peered over the dry stonewall that separated garden from field; the pub was in darkness. By now, both men were soaked to the skin, but neither complained. Hunter indicated to Jock that he was to be the first over the wall; he would reconnoitre the inside of the pub through the downstairs windows, then indicate that the coast was clear. Jock nodded his understanding, and then Hunter slid over the wall. Jock watched the dark shape of Hunter disappear into the undergrowth, then re at the bottom of the kitchen window some moments later. Hunter slowly raised his eyes to the level of the windowsill and scanned the gloomy kitchen.

He then crawled along to the back room window and did

the same. He clenched his fist above his head, which was their signal.

Jock picked up the rucksack, slid over the wall, and made a more direct route to Hunter down the garden path. He crouched beneath the window next to his partner. Hunter he looked around for a way to get into the building. The only way he could see was to get in through Trout's bedroom window. The small stone outhouse was directly under it.

"We've got to get in through that window." Hunter whispered, his eyes directed to the window at the end of the building.

Jock followed his gaze. "Why go to all that trouble? You've rented a room, haven't you?"

"Yeah"

"Well, we'll both go in through the front door, and we can both go up to your room. He won't know that we're going to search his room, will he?" Jock blew away the rain as it streamed into his mouth when he spoke.

"It not as simple as that, mate. I overheard them talking last night in the pub. They're going to kill me if they see me, and that includes you if you're with me. No, we've got to do it covertly."

Jock shook his head in disbelief. "Thanks for telling me, I feel a lot better now."

Hunter gave a grunt of laughter. "Don't worry about it; it'll be a walk in the park. We get in, find the proof we need, then you can go home. Like I said, I need a lookout. That's all you have to do, I'll do the rest."

Hunter took another peep in through the window. "Trout's still in the bar. Right, Jock. I'll get on that roof, then get me ass into his bedroom. You stay here and keep a lookout for Trout, and anything else that might catch your eye. If you see anything, let me know. Once I'm in, then I'll give you the signal, and you do the same."

Hunter made his move to the outhouse but Jock grabbed his arm. "What is it?" Hunter rasped in a whispered voice.

"What'd you want to do with this?" Jock pulled across the rucksack.

"Leave it. Hide it in those bushes." He nodded to a rhododendron bush against the far wall of the toilet. "I won't need it yet."

~~~

Hunter scurried off to the end of the building, paused for a second, and looked back at Jock, who gave a quick glance through the window, then signalled the all-clear. The old dry lime mortar between the stones fell away as he got a foothold in the end wall. The outhouse comprised two small buildings, one of which was the toilet and the other a small shed where Trout kept his logs for the fire. The rain rattled off the main pub roof and down to an already full gutter, where it then over spilled like a waterfall in flood onto the outhouse roof below. Several times Hunter slipped; the green moss on the tiles had become a mass of slime making it difficult for him to keep his grip. He was within a few yards of the pub wall now, but also a few yards from the mass of water falling from the gutter above. He ducked his head into the torrent and slid the last few yards. When his hands finally touched the wall, he looked down at Jock, who gave him the thumbs-up to carry on his operation.

By now darkness was total, and the storm looked in for the night. Hunter slowly got to his feet and grabbed the bottom of Trout's windowsill. He gave it a tug, and it seemed strong enough to hold his weight. Trout's bedroom window was at arm's length even if Hunter stood at full stretch. He would have to pull himself up and at the same time see if the window was open. He held little hope that the window would be open, but there was always luck.

The weight of Hunter's wet clothes made him a lot heavier. He could feel his finger tips slipping from the wet window sill. He felt for a toehold in the masonry, and somehow just managed to pulled himself level with the window.

He rested for a second, and then leant his body weight onto

one of his elbows and his chest, while with his right hand he tried the window. As he thought, the window was fastened from the inside and wasn't budging. He glanced down at Jock and shook his head, then indicated with a clenched fist that he was going to smash the window.

The breaking of the glass was surprisingly quiet, but it was inside where the noise counted. A few heart-stopping moments passed as Jock watched the action downstairs, and then he gave the all-clear again.

Hunter reached in through the broken pane and pushed up the window latch, then tried to open the casement by pulling it from the outside. At first, it moved a little, but the wood had swollen in the frame causing it to seize solid, so Hunter pulled harder. Slowly it moved with every jerk he made.

When finally it did pull free, he lost his balance as the window swung out. He held tightly to the hinged frame, but his wet hand slipped as he tried to adjust his grip. At first, he did not feel the shard of broken glass slice through the palm of his hand, only the tightening of its muscles, then something warm trickling down his sleeve. He managed to regain his balance and pull himself in through the window, then saw the bloody handprints that he had just made. His blood was dripping steadily onto the floor of Trout's bedroom.

He reached into his pocket and pulled out a small torch. Frantically he switched it on and scanned the room just to make sure that he was alone. He was.

The severed nerves made his hand tingle, nature's way of telling him to staunch the bleeding, He searched all his pockets for a handkerchief or cloth but only found a pair of fingerless woollen gloves. He pushed one of the gloves onto the wound and slipped the other over the top of his hand, covering the other glove and the wound at the same time. Then he leant out of the window and gave the thumbs-up to Jock.

Next he moved to the door of Trout's room and tried the handle. It made a noisy clank as the catch popped out of the lining. He froze and listened for the sound of the creaking stairs, but heard nothing. He opened the door quickly but quietly, one way to quiet squeaky hinges. Now he faced the darkness of the cold, haunting corridor.

~~~

Jock climbed in through the window and noticed the dark stains on the windowsill and frame. He placed his fingertips into a puddle of the dark liquid, rubbed them together to feel for its texture, then brought them near his nose.

"Blood!" he whispered, recoiling at the coppery smell.

He searched the darkness of the room for Hunter, but could see nothing. There was neither movement nor sound near him, only the storm outside, and the muffled chink of glasses from down in the bar. "Hunter?" he called softly.

The flash of a torch into the room from the corridor told him of Hunter's position. Hunter stepped carefully back into the bedroom closing the door partially behind him.

"I thought something had happened to ya. There's blood on the windowsill."

Hunter started to scan the room more thoroughly with his torch. "Yeah, I cut myself on the window. Don't worry about it, it's not too bad."

"Fucking place gives me the creeps, Hunt, and what's that horrible smell? Smells like something's died in here."

"Yeah, doesn't smell too healthy, does it?"

Hunter narrowed the beam of the torch onto the wardrobe in the corner of the room. "Right. I'll start here, and you keep watch by the door."

Jock moved over to the partially opened door and looked out into the darkened corridor. Hunter pulled open the wardrobe and started his search.

A clock ticked noisily in the darkness. It was hard to tell where it was, but Jock had a good guess that it might be near the window. Crouched by the door, he was sorting through scenarios that could happen if Eli Trout decided to come up to his room. Each thought was replaced by another before Jock had a chance of seeing Trout's face as he came through the door, they spun round in his mind as he conjured all manner of descriptions to fit the name Trout. They all seemed harmless enough.

Presently Hunter closed the wardrobe door and sent his torch beam around the room to find the next place to search. The narrow beam of light stopped on the chest of drawers by the window where both men had entered, and he moved towards it. His foot trod on a loose floorboard, and the noise seemed ear-splitting in the deathly silence of the room. Both men froze.

"Shit!" Hunter exclaimed under his breath.

Jock cocked an ear in the direction of the corridor and waited. Hunter slowly took his foot off the loose board and gingerly stepped up to the drawers in front of him.

"All right, Jock?"

"Yeah I reckon, but don't do it again, OK? I nearly gave birth in my pants then." Jock sniggered at his own remark as he watched the dark figure across the room start to search the large wooden drawers. He began to get agitated, it seemed like forever that he had been crouching by the bloody bedroom door; he could see Hunter was not finding shit, and it was starting to look like they were wasting their time.

"Look, Hunter, um … I don't want to sound negative, but there's fuck-all here." He got up to straighten his legs. His feet were beginning to go numb. He needed to get the blood circulating again.

~~~

Hunter heard Jock say something, but he couldn't make out the words. He was too preoccupied trying to think like Trout, trying to put into practice what the druid priest had said: *Use your instinct.*

Where would you hide it, eh?

What kind of person are you, Eli Trout?

Come on, you are a simple man, where would you hide anything secret or special?

Hunter slowly panned the torch around the room.

The bed? No, not under there.

Another chest of drawers. *No, you wouldn't, would you?*

The torch illuminated Jock, who was shaking his head and pointing toward the bed.

"It's coming from in there, Hunter. That fucking smell's coming from that box." Jocks voice was a little louder than it should have been, and he took a step towards the oak coffer at the bottom of the bed.

"No. You stay by the door, Jock," Hunter rasped as his torch scanned the outside of the large carved box. Jock stepped back to the door and peered into the darkness of the corridor once again, and Hunter forgot him as he pressed on with the search.

He knew whatever he was looking for was in there. His instinct told him so, but also told him that he was in danger of losing his life. His hand stretched out towards the box, and that putrid smell hit the back of his throat like a shot of cheap whisky, like the smell of decay and rotted meat.

Hunter opened the lid cautiously. He could feel danger tingle through his body, his adrenaline pumped through his veins as if he'd mainlined heroin. As the lid opened the smell was overpowering, and he stifled a cough with the back of his hand and dared to cast the light of the torch inside.

"What's in there, Hunter?" Jock asked, taking his eyes from the door.

Hunter pulled aside a few dark gowns folded neatly on top. Then he took one out and raised it to his nose. It smelt, but it was not the cause of the problem; more likely it had just been tainted by the foulness nearby.

"So what's in there, then?" Jock asked again, a little louder this time.

Hunter choked back the stench. "Clothes, that's all I can see at the moment." He carried on looking.

~~~

"Smelly old bastard, you think he'd wash." Jock rummaged through his coat pocket, then pulled out his Zippo lighter and flicked the wheel. He wanted to have a look round the room himself, sick of standing by the door doing nothing. Maybe he could help Hunter find what he was looking for. If only either of them knew what it was.

The blue and orange flame flickered in the darkness as he slowly checked the area around him. Most of the furniture in the room was situated on Hunter's side. However, a bureau desk stood only yards from where Jock had been crouched moments before. Jock stepped over to the wooden writing surface, placed the lighter on its top, and then pulled down the front flap.

This was as good a place to start as any, he thought, and began his search.

~~~

Hunter carried on his search of the oak chest at the bottom of Trout's bed. He gripped the small torch between his teeth and scrutinised every object, one by one. There seemed to be an endless supply of dark robes, robes that were like the habits that monks wore. He pulled each one out of the box and placed it on the floor.

The rotting smell was becoming stronger as he went. He breathed in short gasps, trying to minimise the smell, but he could already taste it. He could taste death, and he was beginning to feel sick.

Hunter had taken out all of the robes, and now he encountered a length of Hessian sacking. Whatever was under the sacking he knew must be the source of the rotten stench. He took the torch from his mouth and widened the beam, as he reached for the sacking. There were dark stains splashed all over it, from mere specks to hand-sized blotches. He knew what it was and had to ask himself whether he really wanted to look under that sheet.

~~~

Jock pulled out handfuls of paper from each drawer and held them near his lighter to examine them. He had come across nothing out of the ordinary. Bills, receipts, letters, it was all boring stuff. He dropped another handful of letters onto the floor, then opened one of the bigger drawers. This time he had come across photos.

He studied each of the photographs in turn. Most of them looked many years old, but a few might have been more recent, and all were of the villagers. He chuckled to himself looking at their clothing, but the small girl who was always pictured in the front of the crowd seemed vaguely familiar. With the turn of every photo, her features were more grown up, and gradually he thought he knew who she was. At first he dismissed his hunch, but as he held a small Polaroid to the flame of his lighter, he knew it was the same woman. In the picture stood Trout and next to him the girl, both standing behind the bar of the pub; both looked happy. Those unmistakable features were too striking to be someone who shared her likeness.

Jock turned from the bureau and faced Hunter. "Mate, I reckon you should take a look at this, and tell me who you think it is." He took a step towards Hunter, who was slumped over the chest.

~~~

Hunter had found where the smell was coming from; he was just too emotional to say anything to Jock. In front of him lay a crumpled heap of material. At first he thought it was the same colour as the robes he had taken out, but as he looked closer, he could see that the colour varied. Near the outside, specks of white cloth could be seen, and near the centre it was almost black. At first he thought the centre had patches of mud, but he knew from the smell and the stiffness of the material that it was blood.

And the material was absolutely saturated with blood, blood

that was so dark that it would have come from a main artery. It was weeks old and dry now, but the whole of the material was covered in it. He started to lift the stiff ball of material not even aware of Jock's presence or even his questions. As he carefully lifted it from the chest, something underneath caught his eye. Something shining. He aimed the torch along the shape of the object. It was a sword, partially covered with another sack.

He propped the mass of stinking material on the side of the box and pulled back the sacking to reveal the whole of the sword. He cast the light up the length of the blade to the yellow coloured handle where the word *NUADHA* was clearly visible.

The unbelievable dream flashed back into his mind in a split second. This was the sword that the priest in his dream had held, the same sword that the priest told him to take back to the stone circle.

He still had trouble believing it, even with the proof in front of him. He wanted out of there; his instinct was still warning of danger, but from what? He checked the room once more with the torch. Nothing was in here, and it was the same as it had been when he had entered. The feeling was growing stronger, and as he moved the torch, its beam illuminated Jock, who was facing him, holding a picture in his hand.

"What's up, Hunter?" Jock asked in a quiet voice.

"I don't know, I just think we should get out of here. Something's wrong."

"What did you find in the box then?"

Hunter covered the sword again with the sack and picked up the blood-soaked cloth. "Nothing, just ... Um, nothing." He didn't want to tell Jock about the sword, or the dream. He could hardly believe it all himself.

Jock cleared his throat. "Well, I reckon I found something." He held the picture towards Hunter. "This picture, take a look, I think you'll know who's in it."

Hunter heard Jock, but he had difficulty following what he was saying. Something told him he had to get out of here, and now. It was as he placed the blood-soaked cloth back in the chest that the light of the torch caught something hanging from one side of the cloth. He placed it back in the chest and looked at it more closely. It was pink, fluorescent pink. He pulled on the pink material, and it started to come free. His heart began to race as he realised that his worst nightmare was becoming reality. With a sharp tug, the pink piece of clothing came free from the blood-soaked material, and he immediately dropped it, rage welling up inside.

The torch beam lay directly on the toddler's fluorescent pink snowsuit. Hunter choked back the tears. This was the evidence that he wanted, but in another way, he did not want it. He knew now that Carl was dead; the blood that soaked the cloth that the suit was wrapped in must be his.

"The bastards. They killed my boy."

Jock took a step closer and crumpled the photograph that was in his hand. "Let's kick his fucking ass," he rasped, clearly too shaken to stifle his voice.

Hunter held the snowsuit to his face. The rank smell of rotting blood clung to it, but he did not care. This was the only thing left that he remembered Carl wearing.

Hunter looked up at Jock, then at the door to the room. Something was out there. It had been there for a while. Hunter's eyes flicked from Jock's silhouette to the door, but before he could say anything, the door crashed open, and the hulking figure of Trout stepped in.

The ferocity of the door knocked the Zippo lighter into the pile of papers that Jock had left on the pull-down door of the bureau. Within seconds, they had burst into flames.

Jock spun round to face Trout, who had his gaze fixed on Hunter by the oak coffer. Trout took a step into the room; his eyes were beginning to shine like embers.

Jock shouted, "I take this fucker, Hunter," and aimed a drop kick into Trout's stomach.

Trout did not even waver as the kick hit him, merely turned and faced his attacker. "What the fuck?" Jock screamed as he recoiled from Trout's smouldering eyes.

Hunter jumped to his feet and ran at Trout, but was sent sprawling across the room with one swing of the landlord's arm and could only watch, unable to catch his breath. Jock tried a volley of punches as Trout grabbed him by the throat. Jock smashed a fist into his face repeatedly, but Trout's grip was becoming tighter, and he lifted the marine off the floor with one arm, his nails beginning to draw blood. Jock tried helplessly to release Trout's grip with one hand while pummelling him with the other, but to no effect.

By now the fire on the bureau was blackening the ceiling.

The room now cast in orange shadows as the fire raged in the corner. Hunter at last could move. He pulled a small lock knife from his pocket, threw himself at Trout, and thrust the knife into the side of Trout's neck. Blood spurted from the severed carotid artery, but Trout just swung Jock's body around and knocked Hunter to the floor again. Then, with one emphatic roundhouse, Trout slammed his fist into the side of his victim's head. The crack of Jock's breaking neck echoed around the room.

Trout tossed him aside like a rag doll and turned to his next victim. He smiled, showing hideous upper and lower canines, and started towards Hunter. Black smoke was now filling the room and billowing out the open window. Hunter glanced across; that window was his only way out.

Trout seemed to anticipate Hunter's thoughts and quickly moved closer to the window. Hunter slowly got to his feet; he was not going to let this fat bastard get the better of him. If he was going to die, he would at least take the big man with him. The top half of the room was full of smoke, so Hunter kept low. The doorway was now blocked by flames, and he knew there was only one way out. Trout's reflective eyes shone through the smoke like fog lights, and when they homed in on Hunter, death raged in them.

Trout made a grab at him and just caught the corner of his jacket; Hunter struggled free and leapt onto the bed. Trout was a lot quicker than Hunter gave him credit for, though, and he moved back to the window. Hunter ripped the sheets off the bed and partially cloaked himself in them as he moved along the wall where the fire was raging. The sheets soon ignited, and

Hunter tossed them at Trout. The fumes were now choking, and Hunter dropped to his hands and knees gasping for breath. He was going to die, he had no way past Trout, and he could only hope that Trout would die with him in the fire.

Trout grabbed him by the hair and pulled him to his feet. He pulled him closer to his contorted face. This was not Eli Trout anymore; he had changed out of all recognition. This was a monster, a freak, not a human. Trout's face was covered in blood. Jock had given it his all, but it was not enough.

"You shouldn't have come back," Trout rasped as he gave Hunter's head an open-handed slap.

Hunter landed on the oak coffer at the bottom of the bed. The side split from the impact of Hunter's body, and the contents lay in full view.

The sword! a voice said.

Hunter lay dazed on the floor, tears and blood filling his eyes. He had to move. Sure enough, Trout reached down through the smoke and made another grab at him. Hunter knocked his arm away and the words sounded in his head again. *The sword, use the sword.*

His hand dropped to his side and fell on the handle of the sword. He grabbed it and crawled nearer the flames. The room was filling with smoke, and he could see nothing. He laid his head on the floor where the smoke was not as thick. He needed to find Trout. He peered into the room but could see nothing. He was hoping Trout was dead; with all the blood he had lost, he should have died minutes ago.

Hunter got to his feet. Gagging, he moved towards where he thought the window was and caught sight of those glowing orbs to his left. Trout was there, next to the window, over by Jock's body. Hunter lunged forward and swung the sword, aiming just below the eyes.

Trout gave a choked scream as the sword sliced through his neck and chopped into his spinal column. There was a loud thud as the fat body hit the floor. Hunter hung his head out of the window and gulped a few deep breaths of fresh air. The storm was still blowing outside, and the rain had not eased at all.

He took one last breath, then ducked back into the room. He fumbled in the darkness and smoke until he found Jock's body, grabbed his arm, and pulled him over to the window. He tossed the sword to the soft earth below. Hunter then lifted Jock onto his shoulders and struggled to clamber out the window.

The heat coming from the bedroom was growing more intense. The bed was well alight, and Hunter could feel the heat on his back as he sat on the window ledge. He knew there was only one easy way onto the roof.

"Sorry about this, mate," Hunter said as he slipped from the windowsill and crashed through the outhouse roof.

The rotten rafters softened his fall somewhat, but when he had hit the roof, he automatically let go of Jock. He had a pain shooting through his right leg. He gathered his senses and pulled himself to his feet. He screamed as the pain from his leg seemed to lance through his body. Resting himself against the inside wall, Hunter felt down his right leg, reaching past the knee to the calf muscle. He found the problem and groaned. A long splinter of slate had embedded itself deep into his calf.

He tore open the leg of his trousers to examine the wound better. Rain poured through the opening in the roof, drenching him once more. Slowly he pulled the slate from his leg, all the while biting into his hand to stop himself from screaming aloud. The wound was deep and cut directly into the muscle, but it was not a bad bleeder as he thought it might have been. He did not have time to tend to it now; it would have to wait. He pushed himself from the wall and started to feel for Jock's body among the rubble.

"Where are you?" he whispered, then pushed opened the door to the toilet. "Shit!"

He came face to face with Jock, who was hanging upside down over the doorway. His eyes were wide open, and his mouth was agape, he had a look of sheer terror on his face. Blood dribbled from tears in his neck and streamed across his face. Hunter pushed him aside gently and stepped out of the outhouse, he could see that Jock was caught up in the roof rafters; one of his legs was twisted sideways. He lifted him to free the leg, then pulled Jock to the floor and knelt next to his body.

"Shit, I'm sorry, mate, this shouldn't have happened to you." Hunter's voice was but a murmur.

He stroked his hand across Jock's staring eyes, closing them for good. Sadness started to turn to anger. He stood up.

"Why me?" he screamed, glancing up into the heavens.

He lowered his head and looked around. "You murdering bastards." His voice cracked with emotion.

The fire reflecting from the blade of the sword caught his attention as it lay in the grass. He remembered the priest's words all too well. He stood up, retrieved the sword, and then limped over to the rucksack. He yanked the pump action shotgun from it and switched off the safety. He swung the rucksack onto his back and went around to the front of the pub. He did not care now what happened to him, as long as he took as many of the creatures with him as he could.

The fire had spread to the roof of the pub, and flames were shooting high into the night sky. Not even the wrath of the gods could stop him now. As he strode up the lane, a howling stopped him in his stride. It was coming from the direction of Smith's house, and then he heard another howl coming from his right, from the field opposite the pub. Then more came; they were all around him, watching him, hanging back for some reason, but they were there. Hunter kept moving. He walked up the dark lane that led to the road crossing the moors. He was heading for the stone circle, and the beasts knew it.

The hedges of the lane were high and the gardens of the cottages higher than the road; this was an ideal ambush site. Hunter needed all his wits. He caught a movement, then a flash of those lifeless eyes. He brought the gun up with one arm and squeezed off one of the solid rounds. Hunter cocked the action of the gun again, dropping the sword as he did so. They came from all directions, villagers and beasts. One old woman stepped from her front door and let go both barrels of her twelve-gauge; luckily Hunter had seen her and dived for cover, but still felt some of the birdshot rip through his legs.

He fell onto the road and swung the pump action to his shoulder, aimed it at the old woman, and pulled the trigger. The solid lump of lead hit her high in the chest, lifted her off the ground, and sent her crashing back through the door opening. Thick clotted blood sprayed the light coloured front door and the wall behind. He reloaded as one of the beasts jumped out just yards in front of him, then another behind.

Hunter frantically fired at the one facing him. He didn't wait to see if he'd hit it, but sprinted into the cottage of the woman he'd just shot, dived over her body, then spun round quickly facing the front door. One of the beasts was right behind him; it bounded up the path to the cottage as Hunter let loose another shot from his gun. The mass of led hit the beast directly in the chest, sending both of its legs buckling as its chest crumpled. The creature lay twitching for a moment in the path, then its body lay still. He quickly checked the ground floor of the cottage. It looked empty. He moved back over to the front door, switched off the hallway light and waited.

"The sword, shit, I've left the sword out there."

He glanced out onto the road; the sword was still there. However, so were they, and more of them all the time.

The burning pub now lit the stormy sky like a preview of hell.

"Come on, Hunter, what are they going to try next? Come on, think. You're a fucking marine. What would you do?"

He looked to the back of the house. "The back door!"

He kicked open the door leading into the kitchen. Still keeping the gun aimed at the front entrance, he entered the small, dark room.

CHAPTER 23

SATURDAY 5:20 PM

Smoking didn't usually bother DS Cranbury, but sitting next to DI Finch in the confines of his car was a different matter altogether. The journey to the village of Oare seemed to take forever. Cranbury did not know how much more smoke he could inhale without throwing up all over the dashboard. Finch stubbed out yet another cigarette in the already full ashtray. A few crumpled butts fell from the pile into the foot wells and Cranbury prayed silently that this would be Finch's last cigarette, at least until they stepped out of the car. Trying to be unobtrusive, slowly Cranbury stretched out his arms in front of him and made a false yawning sound, then with a flick of the wrist opened the fresh air vent. The cool jet of air gently buffeted his face, teasing the colour back into his cheeks.

"So what d'you want me to do if I see this Mr Hunter?" Cranbury asked as he pushed his finger down the neck of his shirt trying to loosen the collar. The nausea was just starting to pass.

"Nick him. Nick him for anything," Finch stated sternly.

"How about being in the wrong place at the right time?"

Cranbury had an air of contempt in his voice; he still was not convinced about Hunter's guilt.

"Just nick him, and watch yourself, the man's dangerous."

Finch had updated Cranbury on the Carl Hunter case and filled him in on the telephone conversation he had had with Jenny Hunter. Cranbury had to admit that the circumstantial evidence and motive seemed to point all fingers at the husband. However, he liked to have rock-solid proof of guilt, forensic evidence or an eyewitness, the kind of evidence that could guarantee a conviction. Although Finch did lay out a convincing case.

Hunter certainly had the motive. Not being the father of the son you thought you had would be enough to make the meekest of men kill. However, to also find out that it was your best mate that was stoking the fire of your wife … well, that should have made murder legal. Nevertheless, Cranbury was not satisfied. He felt, as did the late DS Short, that no matter how enraged Hunter might have felt, he would not have killed Carl. That is indeed if he knew about the affair all of those weeks ago.

No! Killing the child was not the logical thing to do.

Kill the wife or the boyfriend. Yes! That sounded more like it if you were the enraged husband.

Cranbury kept his thoughts to himself, so as not to upset the applecart.

"Shit! This rain's getting worse," Finch rasped, flicking the wipers onto full speed.

The rubber wiper blades seemed to have no effect on the mass of water exploding on the windscreen. Finch cut his speed to twenty miles an hour. Visibility was down to just thirty yards. The wind whipped the torrential rain in all directions, sometimes making it impossible to see through the windscreen at all.

Finch seemed uneasy at the sheer force of the storm. He leant over the steering wheel, his face just inches from the windscreen. "Buggered if I can see it," he muttered.

"See what?" Cranbury asked.

"The sign to show us the turning to the village." Finch

glanced across at Cranbury's window. "It's over your side somewhere?"

Cranbury wiped the condensation from the passenger window, but the rain streamed down the glass making it impossible to see out. "Maybe we've passed it," Cranbury said as he wound down the window

"Nah, we couldn't have done. It's just along here somewhere."

The young DC poked his head out of the window, the wind drove the rain hard into his face, and he squinted to protect his eyes as the piercing icy drops picked at his flesh. The car was at a crawl now, and Finch kept switching the lights from full beam to dim, but neither one made it possible to see more than a few yards into the downpour. Then Cranbury saw something on the horizon to the left of them.

"Stop!" he shouted.

Finch did as he was told. "What's the matter?"

"Over there, I'm sure I saw something, like a bonfire."

"Bonfire. It's not Guy Fawkes night yet, is it?"

"No, not for a few weeks yet," he answered pensively.

Finch leant across to the passenger side of the car and looked out into the darkness. The wind direction had changed.

"There it is again. Look." Cranbury pointed to the red glow in the distance."

Finch followed his indication. Well, I see some kind of flicker over there. That must be coming from the village." He drove further along the road, but still kept the car at a crawl. "The road sign must be here somewhere."

"There it is," Cranbury stated, jabbing his finger into the windscreen.

Finch turned left sharply and now seemed totally oblivious to the storm outside. The car picked up speed cutting noisily through the waterlogged surface of the road. Cranbury held on tight to his seat. Finch took the last bend before the village. The flames from the fire were clearly visible now, reaching thirty feet in the air, but a row of trees kept them from seeing exactly what was burning. They rode on in silence, Hunter the unspoken subject of their silent conversation.

~ ~ ~

Hunter sat silently in the kitchen readying his ambush by the back door. The small room was in total darkness as he wound one last strip of masking tape around the table leg and the claymore mine, then gave it a slight pull to see that it was fixed firmly. He crawled over to the opposite side of the door opening and attached the tripwire, then primed the device.

"It's all ready for ya, just come and get it."

He glanced back through the open kitchen door into the hall; the old woman's body was still lying lifeless on the floor next to the open front door.

Come on you bastards, where are ya?

Hunter loaded the rucksack onto his back and slowly rose to his feet. He drew level with the kitchen sink, then the windowsill, and looked out onto the garden beyond. It was still raining and hard to pick out any shapes, but on occasion the flames from the burning pub would cast light across the back garden. Then he saw them, those glowing silver eyes looking into his. No more than ten yards from the window stood three of the beasts. They were standing on a raised part of the garden, level with Hunter's own head; they seemed to be waiting, waiting for something else to make the first move.

Hunter took a few steps back towards the kitchen door. "What are you waiting for?" he said, taking a few more steps.

Then in the window he caught sight of his own reflection— and something moving behind him. He swung around and dropped to one knee.

The old woman he had shot earlier was up again. Now she bore those lifeless silver-blue orbs. She staggered towards him. Her facial features were changing, her hands became contorted, and long claws popped from the ends of her gnarled fingers. She dropped to her knees, blood poured from the hole in her chest.

Hunter fired two more shots at her from the hip, one of which smashed through her face and the other her neck. Grey matter and thick clots of blood splattered the walls behind her. She collapsed to the floor. Hunter fumbled in his jacket for his remaining shells. He pulled out the last four and pushed them into the chamber.

"Shit! Got to make these count, son; can't miss any of the bastards," he said, reprimanding himself.

He looked back at the kitchen window, but could see nothing. They were still out there, he could sense it. Moving back into the hall, he closed the kitchen door behind him and warily approached the open front door. The smell from the burning pub competed with the coppery stench of blood dripping from the walls. Small puddles of translucent red liquid formed near the doorway as the rain blew into the house. He needed to get out of here. He knew it would not be long before they made another attack, and this time they would be more organised. The garden in front of him looked deserted, apart from the dead beast on the path.

He looked up the lane, towards the burning pub. Burning embers fell from the sky like fiery snowflakes. The roof of the building was now gone; flames leapt in all directions, fanned by the wind. The whole village was now becoming a collage of colour and shadows as the flames leapt high in the sky. Deceptive shadows looked as if they harboured lurking evil. Shadows that danced with every leap of flame. Hunter crouched in the darkness of the doorway just watching, watching for any movement. He felt vulnerable now. They could be anywhere; they could even be upstairs. He quickly turned to face the narrow staircase; a shiver ran up his spine.

"Shit! Come on, Hunter, get a grip."

His words seemed lost somehow, forgotten as soon as they had left his lips. He had too much going on in his head, too much to think about. He quietly muttered orders to himself, trying to keep one step ahead of them.

Then over the noise of the storm came a banging from the back of the cottage. Hunter cocked an ear and listened. They were at the back door trying to get in. The adrenaline rushed his body again.

The mine! The bloody claymore mine! He had to move, and fast. It would not be long before they were in. He kept low and stepped out onto the doorstep. He knew they were close and watching, but where? He edged down the path slowly, and then heard the glass breaking in the kitchen.

The back door.

The claymore. Any second now.

He reached the front gate, all the time panning the shotgun in the direction he was looking. The sword was no more than fifteen yards from him now; it was lying in the lane next to the grass verge. He stepped out onto the tarmac of the lane and warily moved towards the shimmering blade.

~~~

Finch had a good idea that it was a building on fire as he passed the first cottage going into the village. He homed in on the massive flaming beacon then started to turn into the lane. His headlights caught Hunter carrying the shotgun. Finch slammed on the brakes. The car slid to a halt.

Hunter shielded his eyes from the full-beam headlights with his hand, peering around it, trying to see who was driving the car.

Finch was stunned at seeing Hunter; this was Finch's dream come true. Hunter was now banged to rights as far as he was concerned.

Hunter raised the shotgun and pointed it towards the car. "Shit! He's going to shoot at us," Cranbury shouted, then ducked his head into the foot well of the car.

"Bollocks!" Finch too dropped below the windscreen, his body across the centre console.

There was a massive bang and a slight shudder as the load ripped through the headlight and the adjacent wing.

Both detectives slowly raised their heads to look out of the windscreen just as another explosion shook the car again.

Cranbury reflexively raised his hands, and Finch dropped below the windscreen once more, grabbed the police radio, and frantically called for assistance.

~~~

The claymore mine had sent shrapnel flying around in the cottage, killing or maiming whatever was in there at the time. The explosion had blown out all of the windows and now Plumes of white smoke billowed from every shattered opening. Hunter saw his chance to get the sword.

~~~

Small pieces of debris fell on and round the car.

Cranbury dared a look. "The explosion came from in there, Guv," he rasped, shock audible in his voice. "Shit, what's going on here? I'm calling in the fire brigade and a couple of ambulances. I just hope to God nobody was killed." He reached for the radio mike that had been thrown near his feet.

"Already been done," Finch said evenly, "they'll be here with the rest of them."

Cranbury keyed the handset then dropped it back on the floor again.

Finch tried to stay calm, but thoughts whirled in his head.

Is this what I joined the force for? No, it was not. I saw promotion, a cushy number, not dying in the front seat of an unmarked police car.

He had to control his panic; he had to stay calm,

The soaking wind soon cleared the smoke and he viewed the carnage that the explosion had caused. The light given by the burning pub made shadows dance and small pieces of broken glass glistened like dew catching the morning sun. Then Cranbury spoke up.

"Something moved, Guv, over there by the door of that cottage that just exploded. Must be someone injured. I'm going to help."

Finch was not listening; he was watching the shadowy figure of Hunter crouched in the road.

Cranbury stepped out of the car behind the relative safety of its door. He kept low and scanned the lane, apparently having second thoughts about how exposed he would be getting to that doorway.

~~~

Hunter felt trapped; if he was to go forward, he had to get past the car and whoever was in it. He quickly viewed behind him, then to his sides. They were there he knew it, but exactly where, he did not know. The lane down to the Smiths' house seemed to stretch into an infinity of darkness, a darkness that held all manner of horrors.

~~~

Finch kept Hunter in his sights as he reached over to the glove compartment of the car and pulled out an object wrapped in a piece of cloth.

Cranbury glanced at Finch as the small light came on in the glove compartment, then watched Finch unwrap a large handgun.

"You got any bullets for that thing?" Cranbury asked.

Finch reached into the glove compartment again and pulled out a box of bullets.

"Good job I brought this today, eh?" Finch started to load the weapon.

"Why did you bring it?"

" Target practice Saturday evenings."

He got the pistol loaded. "You go help the wounded, I'll cover you." Finch opened the car door and Cranbury made his run for the cottage.

Finch steadied his hands on the open car door and pointed the .357 Magnum towards his intended target. The barrel wavered as the wind shook the door. It was a fifty-yard shot in a strong wind, and the target was not at all clear. Finch knew his chances of hitting Hunter cleanly were next to impossible, but at least it was covering fire, a form of defence against a madman armed with a shotgun and a sword.

Cranbury glanced over to the dark heap lying in the doorway then back at Finch.

"Ready, Guv?" He shouted.

"Yeah," Finch screamed back.

Hunter reached into a side pocket of his rucksack, pulled something out, and stuck it in his jacket pocket.

Finch shouted at the top of his voice, "Armed police, Hunter. Don't move, put your weapons down."

~~~

Hunter heard the word Police, but the rest of the message was unintelligible in the fierce conditions.

Police! How did they get here so quick?

Hunter watched one of the men move from the gateway and creep low up the path towards the cottage.

"You prick, they'll kill you," he muttered to himself.

He had to warn them, the beasts would kill them as quickly as they would have killed him.

He stepped forward, putting in a challenge.

"Get out of there; get back in your car and leave. They'll kill you!" he screamed at the top of his voice. Then he caught sight of those shining silvery eyes no more than twenty yards behind Finch's car.

~~~

Finch only heard part of Hunter's verbal warning, but to him it sounded like "Get back in your car, or I'll kill you." He pulled back the hammer of the pistol and waited for a clear view of the target, willing him all the time to step a little closer.

Cranbury closed up on the huddled figure lying on the path near the door. Hunter moved nervously as he watched Cranbury.

Finch screamed out his warning again, telling Hunter this time if he did not put down his weapons, he would shoot.

Hunter heard the warning and knew he had to make some kind of decision now. The best option was to jump for cover, but he knew that the two police officers would not stand a chance against the villagers.

Cranbury crouched beside the body and grabbed the wet coat that covered its features. With a hard tug, he pulled the villager over to face him. Blood ran from the open cuts in the old man's face, and a small piece of shrapnel from the mine was firmly imbedded in his cheekbone. Cranbury pulled open the old man's coat, only to see more cuts and shrapnel wounds shredding his shirt. The whole body was torn to pieces; there did not seem one inch of skin that did not have a gaping hole in it.

The thought of the old man being alive disappeared from the young detective's mind, and he just crouched there holding the body, mesmerised by the sheer carnage in front of him. He had never seen such damage on a body before. The driving rain spanked the gaunt face of the old man, making the blood seem to flow so much quicker. Cranbury could feel the warm liquid seep through his fingers, felt his stomach turn, and wanted to be sick.

Finch kept his eyes on Hunter as he put more pressure on the trigger of the pistol and shouted over to Cranbury: "Is the person alive?"

Cranbury heard the question, but somehow his mouth and throat seemed too dry to speak. He laid the old man back down on the path and covered the wounds again by pulling the coat shut.

Cranbury was about to answer when the old man grabbed his arm. "Shitttt!" Cranbury shrieked, falling back onto the wet grass as the old man sat up.

"He's alive, Guv. I don't know how, but he's alive."

Finch threw a glance in Cranbury's direction, and in that split second, Hunter reached into his pocket, pulled out one of the stun grenades, and hurled it towards Finch's car. He needed to get Cranbury and Finch back into their car and away from the area. Finch did not see the stun grenade roll within yards of the front of the vehicle; his eyes were on the charging commando, He kept the barrel of the pistol pointing at the dark figure running towards the cottage and applied the final pressure on the trigger. At the same moment, the stun grenade exploded in front of him. The ear-splitting sound and the brilliant flash threw Finch back against the car. Cranbury also rolled onto the ground, covering his head with his arms.

Hunter dived for cover as the grenade exploded. Finch's shot had missed and now Hunter jumped to his feet, ran up to the gate of the cottage, and aimed the shotgun with one hand at the bleeding villagers on the path. The heavy load smashed through the front of the old man's head, spraying pieces of skull and brain over the wall and path behind. Cranbury watched, horrified.

Hunter quickly spun round to face Finch, who was just getting his bearings again. He reloaded the shotgun and aimed it in the direction of the car. Finch fell to the wet road as he saw the gun swing in his direction. Hunter searched the darkness behind the vehicle for the luminous eyes of the creature; he could not see it anywhere. He turned the gun back to Cranbury, who was still face down in the dirt but keeping an eye on the man at the end of the path.

"Get up," Hunter ordered.

Cranbury did as directed. Slowly he rose to his feet. His eyes quickly scanned the smashed head of the villager beside him; he had never felt so frightened.

Will I be next? Oh, God please don't let me die. Cranbury hoped his prayers were heard. His legs trembled uncontrollably as he thought about what he should do.

What was in the textbooks for this sort of situation?

What had he been taught?

In those few moments as he got to his feet his academy training and exams flashed though his mind, as did his childhood, but nothing could have prepared him for this; this was anybody's worse nightmare. His mind went completely blank.

Finch pushed himself off the floor and chanced a peek through the rain swept window of the passenger door.

"Shit!" he rasped when he saw Cranbury walking up the path towards him followed by the suspect, the shotgun placed firmly at the back of the detective's head.

"Shit!" he said again, then lifted the pistol onto the roof of the car hoping that he could get a clear view of his target.

"Don't even think about it, I'll blow his fucking head off," Hunter shouted, pushing the barrel of the gun hard into Cranbury's neck.

"Yeah, Guv, he means it. Please put the pistol down."

"Shit!" Finch said again, then lifted his head from the sights of the pistol. "You're mad if you think you're going to get away with this, Hunter. You might as well give up before you get yourself killed."

"Step away from the car, and put the pistol on the road," Hunter shouted, disregarding Finch's last comment.

Finch did not move. He was not going to give it up that easily. He would try his powers of persuasion. "You'll—"

"Now!" Hunter snapped.

Cranbury jumped when Hunter shouted. He could feel the metal of the gun barrel pushing harder into the back of his neck. Instead of cold, the metal felt red hot, hot enough to push through his flesh like butter. For a brief moment, there was silence and no movement.

Finch bit down on his bottom lip and tried to think quickly on how he could resolve this matter without relinquishing his firearm. He had one option that stuck in his mind like a bad migraine: Shoot the suspect. That was the only way out—that, or give up his pistol.

Cranbury could feel his head pounding, pounding to the rhythm of his own heartbeat. Each thud of his heart blocked out any sound from the storm and all thought. He had the urge to run, but knew that he would not have taken more than two steps before he was shot, possibly to death. His anxiety spilled out into words.

"Put the fucking pistol down, Guv. Just leave it—please," Cranbury screamed as he took an unconscious step forward. A sharp dig in the back from Hunter with the gun barrel stopped him in his tracks.

Finch could see the fear in the young detective's face and heard it in his voice. He stepped away from the car, closed the door, and laid the pistol on the road in front of the vehicle, keeping his eyes on Hunter.

It was then in the shadowy light of the car's remaining headlight that Hunter realised who the scruffy figure was in front of him.

It's him. That bastard from the hospital. Finch.

He raised his gun from the back of Cranbury's neck and slowly pointed it towards Finch.

"Get in the car," he barked.

Both detectives began to walk towards the car.

"Not you, Finch!" he added.

Cranbury stopped, looked back at Hunter, then at Finch, who nodded for Cranbury to carry on.

"I told you to get in the car." Hunter jabbed the gun barrel into Cranbury's back and pushed him towards the car. Cranbury opened the passenger door, and Hunter shoved him in and slammed the door behind him. He sat motionless watching through the rain swept windscreen as Hunter stepped within yards of Finch. The passenger side headlight was still intact and now lighting up Hunter like some sort of avenging angel as he stepped into the beam of light.

"Hunter, give yourself up now and the courts might go easier on you." Finch nervously wiped the rain from his face with his hand.

The noise of the strong wind made both men shout to be heard.

Hunter wanted to see Finch squirm, just as he did to him in the hospital. As far he was concerned, this sorry excuse of a detective in front of him was responsible for turning Jenny against him.

A loud explosion shook the ground, and part of the pub wall blew out sending large stones and debris hurtling through the air. Finch dropped to his knees, but Hunter stood firm.

"Get up," Hunter growled.

Finch lifted his head; the barrel of the shotgun was inches from his face. He stood up slowly.

All Finch could keep his eyes on was the end of the shotgun, he could almost feel where it was aiming as it wavered in Hunter's hand. Thoughts of being shot in the chest with a twelve-gauge shotgun at point-blank range had Finch scared shitless. He had to do some diplomatic talking.

Talk your way out of the confrontation.

Talk to him as if he is your friend.

"Look, Mr Hunter, I know how you must feel now, I got the whole story from your wife. To be truthful, I think I might have done the same. Fuck, yeah; I think I would have done, if I would found out that my best mate was having an affair with my wife, and I do know how ya feel. My missus ran off with another bloke. I tell ya, I felt like killing the bastard, but you've had to put up with more than that. I mean, finding out that the kid wasn't yours, that must have been the final straw for you. Enough to make any man kill, I shouldn't wonder."

Hunter heard every word Finch said, every painful word. He did not want to believe it, but somehow knew that it was the truth. He stood stunned; he could only see darkness, darkness that was building into rage, rage that could take on the world. He had been betrayed by all he loved, betrayed with the worst possible deception. He tried to remember the old priest's words; they slotted into his mind like a missing piece in a jigsaw puzzle: the child was not his.

"He knew. He fucking knew!" Hunter said aloud.

His eyes welled up with tears, and his body, exhausted moments before, now felt power and strength surging through it. He was invincible now, he had the strength of ten men; nothing could touch him. He had no more fear of the villagers, no more fear of the beasts. His mind was racing with every possibility of when the affair had started.

He knew that Finch meant Jock. Jock was Carl's father.

"He knew what?" Finch asked, a little puzzled by Hunter's words. Seconds of silence passed. Finch looked over to the car, giving Cranbury a curious glance, then looked back at the marine standing in front of him.

The darkness lifted in Hunter's view, he looked into Finch's eyes and saw pain and torment, the same sort of pain that he was feeling.

"I never killed my son." His words echoed in his head. *My son.* To him Carl was still his son; nothing and no one could take that from him.

"It was this village," he added quietly, and then looked around him.

They were still there, watching and waiting, waiting for the last battle to commence. They were everywhere.

Finch stepped forward and lifted his hand, hoping that he had persuaded Hunter to give up the fight. Hunter raised the gun to Finch's face, stopping him from taking another step.

"Get in the car and leave before I change my mind."

Finch did not need telling twice. He was over to the car door in three strides. The reassuring sound of the door slamming at that moment felt better than an orgasm. He slid the car into reverse and sped back up the road. Cranbury kept his eyes on Hunter, who likewise was watching them.

"What's he up to then, Guv? Did he say where Jock Barnet was?"

"How the fuck do I know? All I know is that the bastard has my pistol. I'll be glad to see him in a body bag. Get on the radio and find out where the armed units are."

Finch straightened the car, slipped it into gear, then squealed out of the village.

CHAPTER 24

They stepped from the shadows as soon as Finch's car was out of sight, like vultures hovering for an easy meal. Three of the beasts seemed to materialize from the hedgerows in front of Hunter and skulk into the road, blocking his path to the open moor. Life meant nothing to him now; living involved too much pain. Death would be easier. However, not before retribution had been served. He slowly picked up the pistol that Finch had laid on the road, all the time watching the beasts advancing towards him. His main goal now was to follow the old priest's words and take the sword to the stone circle, no matter how ludicrous the whole idea sounded. He tucked the sword under his right arm and pushed the pistol into the waistband of his drenched trousers, then retrieved the sword.

Calmly he viewed his escape options. However, the beasts were one-step ahead of him. They were blocking every approach to the stone circle; they knew where he was headed. He had the urge to make the stand here and try to kill every one of them. He had no doubt that he could, but how long would they stay dead? If the priest was right, not long, and the sword had to be returned to the stone circle.

His heightened senses sent warning tingles throughout his body: the beasts were closing in. However, fear played no part in his thoughts now. Rage was pumping adrenaline though his body; he was the fearless warrior. The three creatures facing him were now within thirty yards; their pace was ridiculously slow. They were testing him, testing his nerve; they seemed to know that inanimate objects could not hurt them. Hunter lifted the shotgun to his shoulder, and the barrel wavered as he tried to hold the weight of both gun and sword at the same time. His arms felt numb, and his whole body seemed to be blocking out the pain and fatigue. Focussed on their eyes, which now reflected the fire raging in the pub behind him, Hunter let them move even closer. Like six burning embers floating across a darkened lake, they drifted closer to him.

The first shot blasted from the barrel, the stock bruising his tired shoulder. He reloaded. The three creatures broke ranks and moved for cover. None seemed to be hit. Hunter fired again, this time knocking one of the large creatures off its feet. It gave out an unholy scream as the round punched through its hindquarters, paralysing the back legs. He pumped the action again, pushing the last cartridge into the breach, but by now all that stood before him was an empty road.

With the howling wind and driving rain covering their advance, more of the creatures moved along the hedges on either side of the lane. Hunter was blind to their activity; he had to use his instinct now. He could feel that they were close, too close. He had to make his escape. He knew that if he stayed where he was, they would rush him at any moment, and he did not fancy his chances. The lane ahead looked too easy, with no obstruction onto the Moor.

What are they planning?

It was a long way to the stone circle on foot, perhaps too far to make it with a whole village after him.

Come on, Hunter, what the fuck are you going to do? Think!

A flash caught his eye, just yards in front of him to his left. One of the creatures had crossed a gateway on the other side of the hedge. It was stalking him.

Hunter swung the gun towards the hedge and squeezed the trigger. The heavy shot ripped through the cover and found its target. A hollow thud assured him of at least a gut shot, but no screams this time. He cocked the gun again, but after the eject, the chamber was empty.

"No more ammo. Shit!"

He quickly tucked the gun under his arm and searched his jacket pocket for more cartridges, but there were none in there, only his keys.

"The keys to the Land Rover," he murmured, squeezing the bunch of metal objects in his numb hand.

He swung round and looked behind him, back down the lane, towards the field where his vehicle was parked. He would try to get back to the Land Rover; he knew he stood more of a chance in a vehicle. He tossed the shotgun aside and retrieved the pistol. Every bullet had to count now; even though he knew none of them would kill its target, he hoped that at least it would buy him some time.

The beasts closed in from all directions. It seemed not one villager remained in human form, and they had all transformed themselves into the vengeful creatures that had stalked the moors for thousands of years. They worked like a pack of hungry lions: while a small group waited either side of the hedge at the entrance to the lane, others tried to gain the advantage of surprise. When Hunter turned about and headed away from the stone circle, however, this threw the beasts into total confusion. He ran as fast as he possibly could, past the burning pub, then into the darkness of the lane that would take him beyond the Smiths' house and into the field where he hoped the Land Rover would still be.

The beasts followed. Seeming to come from nowhere, they sprang onto the road, others backing into cover only to return; they were hunting him like a pack of hounds after a fox. Sharp pain seared through Hunter's leg as every stride opened the wound in his calf muscle. He was running blind now and could see nothing, shrouded in the blackness of the lane. He had never felt so vulnerable. The rucksack on his back had grown too heavy to carry, but he could not loosen the straps on the rucksack with both hands full. He kept running.

He sensed that the beasts were gaining on him all the time. He had to slow them down somehow. He could just make out the outline of the blacksmith's cottage ahead.

Then he had the obstacle of the gate into the field. All this would take too much time; they would surely catch him. Hunter reached into his jacket pocket and pulled out the last remaining stun grenade, removed the safety pin from it, and dropped it onto the road. Seconds later, as Hunter reached the gate, a deafening explosion and brilliant flash of light split the atmosphere.

The stun grenade had exploded just in front of the beasts, dazing them for the few moments he needed. He ripped off the rucksack and leapt over the gate. The rain had turned the terrain around the gateway into a quagmire; Hunter struggled to get a foothold in the thick mud. The Land Rover was no more than twenty yards from him now. He staggered forward, more than once falling to all fours as he tried to keep his balance.

~~~

DI Finch and DC Cranbury waited for reinforcements by the small stone bridge on the outskirts of the village. It was the main thoroughfare through the village, and Finch had positioned the car in the centre of the narrow road in order to stop any traffic going in or out. Finch settled nervously back into his seat after cocking a glance out of the rear windscreen of the vehicle. Cranbury had said the stun-grenade explosion sounded too close for comfort. His wish had been to move farther out of the village, perhaps one of the main roads a mile or so on. However, Finch was adamant that this was where the police battle lines started and Hunter's reign of terror stopped. He owed it to the poor villagers who were now being terrorised by a madman.

Finch sat silently listening to the garbled squawking of the police radio. He sucked deeply on the soothing cigarette in his mouth and thought how good it tasted. It might have been the best he had ever smoked. Cranbury, however, fidgeted endlessly and finally attracted his boss's attention.

"Will you sit still? I'm trying to think." Finch's cigarette bobbed up and down on his bottom lip as he spoke.

Cranbury huffed objectionably and pulled at the wet trousers that stuck to his legs.

"So am I," he answered abruptly.

Finch was surprised by his underling's tone of voice. However, he would let it pass this time; the situation was enough to try anyone's temper. He inhaled deeply, the end of the cigarette glowed, and then he let out a massive sigh. A long jet of smoke shot from his mouth and mushroomed onto the windscreen.

Finch glanced at his watch. "Where the bloody hell are they? They should have been here ages ago."

Cranbury was evidently preoccupied about what he had witnessed earlier. "That poor bloke, he was an old man and he just shot him at point-blank range. Shit! Poor bastard. I couldn't believe that he was still alive."

Cranbury turned to face Finch. "If you could have seen his wounds. And that bastard." He shook his head and squeezed his eyes shut. "He went out of his way to shoot him. Why?"

Finch picked the cigarette from his mouth. "There's only so much pressure the human brain can take. In Hunter's case, violence is the only way he can handle it. See, he really thinks those villagers killed his son ... or not his son, as truth would have it. Therefore, he has convinced himself that they are responsible, and now, for his own peace of mind, he's getting his revenge." The case was that simple for Finch.

Cranbury shook his head again, then solemnly looked out of the front windscreen. "Looks like your cavalry are arriving," he said.

Sure enough, distant blue lights told of a cavalcade of police cars winding through the lanes.

A broad smile creased his lips. They stepped from the car, and the rain thrashed them mercilessly. It had grown heavier, and the wind blew it in all directions.

Two muffled gunshots had both detectives looking back in the direction of the village. Finch knew all too well the sound of a .357 Magnum. His .357 Magnum. He knew he had a lot of explaining to do to his superiors. Handing over a pistol was bad enough, but seeing it used to kill innocent people was a nightmare. He would be doing paperwork for weeks, which only made him more determined to see Hunter in a body bag.

Cranbury leant across the roof of the car, facing Finch. "At least we know he's still in the village, Guv." He pulled up his collar and hunched against the storm.

Finch thought the comment was not even worthy of an answer. The blue lights drew closer.

~~~

The smell of cordite filled the cab of the Land Rover, and two neat bullet holes in the windscreen showed the exit of the two projectiles. One of the creatures slipped off the bonnet as both bullets smashed through its body. Hunter tried the starter button again. The engine fired up but stopped almost at once. Several more of the beasts had reached the vehicle by now and were attempting to rip through the canvas on the back. Hunter slammed the palm of his hand into the starter again, and this time the vehicle kicked into life.

He pushed down on the accelerator, and the engine went into a high-pitched scream. They were all around him now and throwing themselves at the vehicle. Two of the beasts had torn through the canvas and were now biting at the back of the cab. He knew he had to get out of here and quick.

Two more of them jumped onto the bonnet, their glowing eyes looking in at him as if they knew they had him trapped. Hunter pushed the Land Rover into gear, then took his foot off the clutch. Both creatures smashed into the windscreen as the vehicle shot forward. The passenger side of the windscreen shattered from the impact, and the head of one of the beasts lunged through. It tried to get leverage on the slippery bonnet but could not. Its head was just inches away from him, and the stench of death filled the cab. The beast's powerful jaws snapped as it tried to take hold of Hunter's arm.

The wheels spun in the wet earth as he turned full circle and headed for the gateway. He steered with one hand and brought the pistol up in the other. He pointed it at the creature's eye and squeezed the trigger. The bullet passed through its skull and pierced the passenger side door. Hot blood steamed as it gushed from the gaping exit wound.

"You won't be getting up again, you fucker." Hunter reached across and pushed the creature back out onto the bonnet.

He was only yards away from the gateway now, and still the two beasts were trying to get to him from behind. He just hoped the window would hold them off for a few more seconds. He struggled to keep the vehicle in a straight line as the wet earth gave the wheels no traction at all. His heart raced as he watched the second creature on the bonnet edge towards the broken half of the windscreen. Its massive body blocked out most of Hunter's view, and he could no longer see the gateway.

In desperation he flicked on the headlights, but the beast still blocked his view. Its head leered at him through the open windscreen it seemed to sense victory.

Hunter braced himself and tried to ignore the smell and the horror of the beast that was nearing him though the smashed windscreen. He had the urge to grab for the pistol in his lap and put an end to the creature's murderous existence, but the gate or hedge would be upon him at any second. The impact of the vehicle hitting the gate threw the beast off the bonnet into the darkness, and Hunter crashed against the steering wheel, but his foot stayed on the accelerator. The muddy clogged tyres bit into the surface of the man made road and briefly, the Land Rover picked up speed before hitting the Hedged embankment opposite the gate way. This time it came to an abrupt halt, with Hunter again thrown against the steering wheel. The Land Rover juddered as the tyres spun on the wet road trying to gain purchase against the embankment. Hunter's foot stayed firmly down on the accelerator pedal. He needed to focus and get the vehicle back under control. He slid it into reverse as sharp pain lanced through his chest, and he fell back in agony. A dull throb and a tightening of the skin on his forehead made him reach up to feel for the damage. Moving his arm brought more pain to his chest; he seemed to have several broken ribs.

In those few seconds while pain and fatigue racked his body, he felt like giving up. He felt so cold, as if death was already claiming his body, but his inner senses told him to keep going. *You can't die, Hunter. Come on, never give up.*

All the sounds around him merged into one, then slowly faded into insignificance. It was an effort to keep his eyes open. Shock was beginning to engulf him. His reality was now becoming a dream; he was remembering the good times, the pleasant summer days with Jenny and Carl. He could feel the warmth of the sun on his cold face. He smiled thinly as he swung Carl around in the air. The warmth touched his lips as he kissed Jenny, he could feel her saliva moistening his mouth. He licked his lips; the taste of blood struck his senses. His blood.

Hunter opened his eyes; the horror of reality was back again. Slowly he raised his hand to touch the steady flow from the gash in his forehead.

He had to keep going.

He felt for the pistol which moments before had been in his lap, and now it was gone. He began to panic.

"The floor, it must be on the floor!" He grunted from the pain in his chest as he felt around his feet for the pistol. He found it, pulled back the hammer, and turned to face the two creatures still trying to get at him from the back of the vehicle. The thick partition glass shattered as the bullets punched through it.

The two beasts let out unholy screams as parts of their limbs were smashed to pulp from the impact of the rounds. Hunter kept firing until the pistol was empty and the two creatures lay motionless in the back of the vehicle. The coppery smell of blood and death filled the cab. He dropped the pistol onto the seat.

He needed to get out of here before they attacked again.

He turned into the lane where he had confronted DI Finch.

It was empty. Not one of the beasts tried to stop him. Maybe they had given up.

No chance. They are waiting. But for what?

Only time would tell.

The adrenaline rush for now had taken the pain from his body, leaving only nagging aches.

He passed the last sinister cottage out of the village and headed for the stone circle. Now he was wondering what mystery awaited him; he hoped his visions and dreams were true. If they were, peace would not be far away. If they were not, then he thought he deserved to die.

~~~

By now the roads leading into the village were lined with police vehicles and ambulances. Finch told his attentive audience this was a siege situation, with a madman on the loose with guns and God only knew what other weapons. All of them were dressed in black and armed with semiautomatic pistols and high-calibre sniper rifles. More and more police vehicles arrived, and the whole area was a blaze of blue flashing lights. Radios garbled on all sides. Several officers in yellow reflective gear tried to make some order of the chaos. The order was given to seal off the village; the hierarchy wanted no more civilian casualties. They were hoping to contain the suspect in the village, and the carnage must go no further. The head of the firearms team asked Finch if there was any chance of the suspect giving himself up by his own free will.

"No chance," Finch abruptly answered.

Hunter's fate was now sealed.

Helicopters had also been requested for spotting the suspect, but the weather was in Hunter's favour. The conditions were too rough and cloud cover too low. This news would set the operation back hours. No one was relishing the thought of looking for a heavily armed man trained in killing techniques and able to use the cover of the countryside.

In fact, Sergeant Best, who was in-charge of the armed

response team, did not want to send his men into the village in the hours of darkness. He said that Hunter had the double advantage of knowing the terrain and being able to surprise his adversaries. In that situation, his men were no match for a fully trained Royal Marine commando.

The decision was made to draft in more officers to surround the village, then to get in contact with the military to see if they could send any Special Forces to take out one of their own men. The plan was approved all around.

Finch looked towards the village. It seemed quiet enough. The burning pub stood out like a beacon, its orange glow in the distance pinpointing the troubled village. Daylight could not come soon enough for Finch. Justice would taste sweet.

CHAPTER 25

Pain tormented Hunter as he drove the Land Rover down the rough track towards the stone circle. The steering wheel had a mind of its own, and several times it was torn from his grasp as the tyres bounced in and out of deep ruts in the mud. He gritted his teeth as his body was thrown about in the cab, agony in every jolt and bump.

The passenger side wing was suddenly ripped off by a boulder jutting out of one of the high embankments alongside the track. The remaining driver's side headlight scanned the darkness in front of him; the dirt track seemed to go on forever. The torrential downpour had turned the steep track into a stream, and the running water hid every pothole and obstruction.

He jammed his foot on the brakes to slow himself down, but nothing happened: the vehicle was travelling too fast. The handbrake and the gears were useless too; he was barely keeping control of the vehicle. Trees that overhung the track suddenly loomed from the darkness, and their solid branches punished the Land Rover as it passed. The cab took several direct hits, crumpling the bodywork.

He felt so tired now that he did not know whether he could carry on, or whether he even wanted to. The pain was almost too much. His will to survive was fading. The darkness outside was like a blanket of death, It was all around him and waiting for him to step into it. But was it that easy to die?

These questions swirled in his mind. They were questions that could be answered in time, but how much time did he have? Instantly a fond vision of Carl came to him.

"Carl," he said quietly.

His voice seemed to boom out above the noise of the vehicle. "I'm coming, son."

Again, his voice seemed amplified.

"I love you." Hunter closed his eyes.

His hands dropped from either side of the steering wheel as he fell into unconsciousness. The noise and jolting of the vehicle faded and a warm tingling sensation slowly filled his body. The anguish and the pain eased as an overwhelming feeling of love and peace radiated through him. He opened his eyes, and now there was no more darkness. There was light radiating all around him, a peaceful, loving light, with no suffering and no pain.

Where am I?

He was startled to hear a response: *You're in a place every mortal strives to see, yet finds it so hard to believe in.*

The voice was all around him, but it did not come from any particular place, unless it came from inside his own head. Hunter did not question the answer; he felt no need to. The voice seemed to cut though his very soul like a sword lancing through his heart. He knew that this voice had all the answers to his questions, but did he dare ask?

Hunter looked down at his now floating body as he drifted nearer to a brilliant light ahead. He could see through his hands, his legs, his whole body, and there was no part of his physical being that he could touch.

What's going on. Is this another dream?

Again, it was as if he had spoken.

Dreams are for the living; you must choose. Which do you want to be?

Those words echoed in his head: Dreams are for the living.

Waves of emotion flooded over him. He felt sadness that maybe his life was done, and yet moments before he had wanted it to be done. He did not know what he wanted now. He thought that maybe he was better off dead. He had no one left to love, and no one loved him. Then in an instant faces were all round him, faces of people that he had never ever seen before.

Who are they all?

Then he recognised his parents. His mother looked sad, as if she had been grieving. His father looked the same as he always did, sullen.

He felt sadness at seeing his mother; she looked so tired, so helpless; she had taken the news about Carl badly. He felt guilty that he had not seen them in such a long while, and going back to Liverpool was always the last thing on his mind.

In that second Hunter chose life. He somehow knew that all the faces around him represented those who would suffer in one way or another if he did not do the job he had set out to do.

Destroy the beasts.

His eyes opened to the cold darkness once more. The noise of the vehicle's engine and the bumping of the journey had stopped. Unbeknown to Hunter his vehicle now idled only yards away from where he and Jenny had had the picnic on that tragic day. The harsh stormy winds buffeted the cab, and cold rainwater moistened his face through the broken windscreen. He knew then that he was back to reality, back to pain and suffering, but his pain now seemed just dull aches. He had the will to survive again. Then he remembered why he was trying to survive, the business he was about. The sudden feeling of vulnerability sent a shiver up his spine. His view followed the dull beam of the headlight; it scarcely shone more than twenty yards into the heavy rain.

"Where are you?" he whispered looking for the creatures.

His heart started to race as he peered around him, but he could see nothing. The darkness was total, wrapped around him like an oppressive gauntlet. He looked through the clouded windscreen again and along the beam of the headlight. All he could see was scrubby gorse bushes at the edge of the light, so he knew he was still on the moor, but he had no idea quite where how long he had been unconscious.

Use the headlights on the Land Rover.

Quickly he pushed the vehicle into gear and started to turn the steering wheel full lock. As the vehicle moved, small gorse bushes and blackthorns came into view, but still he recognised nothing of the landscape yet. The wheels started to spin in the wet earth as the slope increased. The single headlight illuminated more thick cover as it started to scan the side of the hill, then the yellow beam of light came across the track. It looked more like a stream now as light reflected off the muddy stream and illuminated the embankments and overhanging trees. Hunter knew where he was now. The woods were not far.

He kept the steering wheel on full lock and turned the vehicle round to face the direction it had been in before. It was then that he saw them. At first, all he could see were their silver eyes glaring at him from the darkness. Those lifeless orbs that had their prey in view. Hunter jabbed on the accelerator; they were gaining ground on him fast. They bounded down the hillside towards him, their bedraggled bodies steaming as if they had crawled from the pits of hell itself.

Hunter had no time to find the proper track that would lead him to the woods, so he took the more direct route. Snipe and woodcock gave flight as the Land Rover cut a swathe through the thick cover, flashing through his beams into darkness. The thick cover slowed the Land Rover, and it laboured for traction in the soft earth.

Hunter sensed they were gaining ground and just hoped to win the race to the woods. He gripped the steering wheel firmly and gritted his teeth. There was no way these Things were going to beat him. The undergrowth began to get thicker, and he flattened saplings here and there as he tore over them. Then unexpectedly the vegetation disappeared, and what looked like flat terrain lay ahead.

The Land Rover picked up more speed without the obstacles of Mother Nature in its way. There was no stopping him now he thought. He hoped that he was putting more distance between himself and the beasts, but still had this feeling of unease.

In—fact his senses were going mad, he had the feeling that he was in serious danger, but from where he kept asking himself.

He kept his foot firmly down on the gas pedal and searched the darkness for the woods.

He thumped the steering wheel in frustration. "Come on, where is it?"

The journey seemed endless, the darkness stretched into infinity, and his instinct still told him that the beasts were near. Quickly he glanced up at the rear-view mirror, but the juddering of the vehicle made it impossible to see view anything. He would have to chance a look behind. He took a deep breath, readying himself for the pain he would feel when he twisted his body. He grunted as he turned to look behind. The darkness behind him looked devoid of life. He faced front again. Chills ran up and down his body, the nape of his neck tingled, and he felt as if he was being watched. Then a hellish thought dawned on him. He grabbed the rear-view mirror and angled it into the back of the vehicle. He saw nothing but darkness.

His breaths were low, and his pulse began to race, but he could not take his eyes from the mirror. He hoped his thoughts were not true. The red taillights of the Land Rover reflected off the inside of the canvas cover stretched over the back of the vehicle. As the clear plastic windscreen behind it flapped in the wind, it sent brief flashes of the light onto the floor of Land Rover. He could see the outline of one of the creatures that he had shot earlier, but he could not see its head. The flashes of light were sporadic. With every flap of the plastic the beast seemed to move, or was he imagining it? He glanced out the front windscreen again, and then back up at the mirror.

The flash of red light reflected into the back. The dark shapes had gone.

They were alive. Slowly he felt for the sword and grasped its handle firmly. Hunter's eyes stayed fixed on the mirror. He had no window to protect him now, no gun to stop them. He had no room to wield the sword in the Land Rover, and the beasts would tear him apart by the time he stopped the vehicle. For a second his eyes left the mirror as he reached for the door handle, then he saw the trees of the woods looming towards him out of the darkness.

You have to jump.

One of the beasts suddenly appeared just inches behind him; Hunter could feel its hot breath on the back of his neck. He pushed down the door handle and leapt from the vehicle with the sword firmly in his grasp. Within seconds, the Land Rover smashed into the trees bordering the woods. The engine immediately caught fire, and thick acrid smoke billowed from under the bonnet.

Hunter pushed himself to his feet, somewhat dazed by the fall. He staggered over to vehicle, where one of the beasts was crawling from the wreckage. He stepped up to the creature and lifted the sword. He felt no mercy for the monstrosity before him. He brought the sword down across its neck with a vengeance. The beast's body spasmed violently as the head was cut from it, and steaming blood spurted onto the cold wet grass.

By now, flames licked around the outside of the bonnet, and smoke started to filter out of the cab. Hunter peered into the vehicle to look for the other creature, but the smoke and the darkness made it impossible to see in.

"Burn in hell, you bastard," he said, looking into the cab, then calmly turned to face the darkness of the moor.

They were coming. He could not see or hear them, the raging wind and rain put paid to that, but he knew they would not be far behind him. He had no time to lose; he had to get to the stone circle as quickly as possible. He started into the woods.

~~~

There was a firm knock on the driver's side window. DI Finch wiped his hand across the steamy glass, looked outside, then grudgingly wound down the window, letting in the wind and rain.

Cranbury crouched down to face Finch. "One of our cars on the other side of the village has spotted something burning on the moor, Guv."

"Like what?" Finch asked.

Cranbury shook his head. "He doesn't quite know, but he said it wasn't there ten minutes ago."

Finch stared at him pensively for a moment. Cranbury cleared his throat. "D'you reckon it's him Gov?"

Finch was already pondering that thought. "You bet your ass it's him, and I think I know where he's heading."

"Where?"

Finch started to wind up the window. "Get in and I'll tell ya." Cranbury ran around the front of the car, opened the door, and slid into the passenger seat. He adjusted his wet clothes, trying to get comfortable in them. Finch slipped the car into gear and started to manoeuvre it away from the small stone bridge and out of the centre of the road.

"Where are you going, Guv?" Cranbury had a worried tone in his voice.

Finch decided not to point out the obvious. Cranbury could see where they were going. "Into the village my boy," he said jubilantly.

"But our orders are to stay here, least till the forces have cleared us."

"Bollocks to the forces, those bastards got us into this in the first place. We'll show them we can sort out someone like Hunter."

Finch pressed on towards the village.

As soon as he pulled away from the main body of police cars. Finch's radio started to go berserk. His call sign squawked out repeatedly.

Cranbury glanced at his boss, then back at the radio.

"I'll answer that, shall I?" he said, reaching for the mike.

"Yeah, tell them that Hunter's left the village and is now on the moor."

Cranbury picked up the mike. "Look, Guv, I don't want to sound stupid, but how do you know he's not in the village still?"

Finch quickly shot him a sideways glance. "You said yourself that one of our cars has seen something burning on the moor, and I'll lay odds that it's where we searched for the boy. He's going back to the scene of the crime, maybe he's trying to clear his conscience or something,—who knows how the brain of a madman works?"

More police cars broke ranks and followed on behind DI Finch.

~~~

Hunter blindly navigated through the dense cover of the woodland, feeling his way from tree to tree. He stumbled at almost every step. He was trying to move as fast as he could, but it was not easy. The oppressive darkness around him seemed impenetrable; pain and fatigue were sapping his energy. Branches from the trees seemed to lash out from the darkness as he beat his way nearer the centre of the woods, as if Mother Nature herself was against him.

He had to keep going.

The beasts had surely passed the burning Land Rover and leapt into the cover of the woods. Hunter's pace quickened, all but sensing that the creatures had not slackened their pursuit. He pushed himself harder than ever, telling himself he had to make it, had to do it for Carl and all the rest who had ended up as victims.

There must be no more innocent victims.

He stumbled and fell onto his knees. His whole body was wet and numb from the cold, and every muscle seemed about to give up. He started to doubt whether he had the strength to carry on. He lifted the sword and dug it into the ground, then pulled himself up on it.

He felt more alone at that moment than he ever had. He could have been floating in outer space; the darkness was just as empty. However, there was no silence, the wind howling through the trees and the rain falling on the dying autumn leaves made an unceasing clamour. He straightened up and scanned his surroundings; nothing but darkness on all sides, but as he turned to face the way he had just come, small illuminated objects danced in and out of sight. They bobbed and turned, and their destination seemed clear.

They were headed his way.

They were too close for comfort now. He banished his doubts, and his limbs seemed to gain a new lease on life. The trees ahead of him which moments before had been invisible in the darkness were now silhouetted against a backdrop of moon blue light.

The stone circle.

Above the stone circle the clouds had strangely cleared, and even the rain had ceased to fall on the clearing. It was as if there was an exclusion zone in the heavens above the stone circle, as if God's own hand had cleared the storm clouds. The moon hung high overhead, flooding the clearing in its haunting blue light, picking out each cold grey stone with ghostly clarity. Hunter could also make out a dark shape that skulked warily around the outskirts of the stones.

He burst from the cover of the trees and made straight for the stone circle ahead. He ran as fast as he could, not looking back. The sight of the stones scared him, but what was chasing him scared him more. He thought quickly on what the old priest had told him, he was within twenty yards of the first stone and the moment of truth would soon be at hand.

His heart missed a beat and he slid to a halt when one of the beasts jumped from the shadows directly ahead. He had no time to think, no time plan; he knew that in seconds many more might appear from the woods behind him, and it would sap his momentum to try to fend off such an attack. He had to keep going forward.

Hunter grabbed the sword with both hands and extended it before him, then he started his advance towards the beast. He looked into its lifeless eyes as he stepped closer, and felt repulsed by the fact that once the monstrosity in front him had been a human. The lifeless, soulless eyes seemed to deny every hint of humanity. He lifted the sword to shoulder level and quickened his pace. The beast lowered itself on its haunches, ready to spring.

"Come on motherfucker." Hunter said, trying to coax the beast into an attack.

The beast did not move, just bared its teeth, as if in derision.

"What's the matter, ya gutless or what?" Hunter growled.

A few more steps and the beast would be history.

He taunted the creature with the sword, it still did not move.

A chill ran up his spine, a bitter cold bit into his ankles, and an icy mist started to cover the ground on the outskirts of the stone circle. He knew the mist all too well: it was always accompanied by the beasts.

Had he been that stupid?

He glanced over his shoulder. His worst thoughts were right; they were stalking him from behind. He only caught sight of a few of them, but they were enough.

The best form of defence was attack.

Hunter ran towards the beast in front of him, and at the same time, the creature leapt from the ground towards Hunter. The sword severed both front legs of the beast as Hunter sidestepped and swung the large blade. The scream it gave out must have been audible for a mile. It pierced the ears and curdled the flesh.

The creature crashed to the ground in a bloodied heap, its twitching, howling body soon engulfed in the mist. Hunter wasted no time; he had to get into the circle. Within a few strides, he had passed the first of the outer stones and expected the beasts to follow him. But they only watched him as they paced around the outskirts of the circle.

Not one dared set foot inside.

Hunter moved warily to the centre of the circle, all the time trying to watch every beast as it drifted in and out of the mist. They seemed to be waiting for their moment. By now the grey blanket of mist had enveloped the entire clearing floor to waist height but also was held at the outer perimeter of the stones by some unseen force.

There was an overwhelming feeling of calm in the centre of the circle, which only came to Hunter's awareness when he realised that he could no longer feel the pain and tiredness that had racked his body moments before. He was starting to feel revitalised, as if he had tapped some reservoir of energy.

He stood at the side of the large slab and peered up at the long stone at the head of it. Now he could feel energy all around him, an energy that was surging through his body, as if he was not just feeling the energy, not just filled with it, but somehow part of it. It was an energy that brought on an immense feeling of well-being, of being loved. In this feeling there was no death, no pain, no sorrow. Hunter's body soaked it up like a dry sponge.

He laid the sword on the stone slab then steadied himself. The energy around him was like a tremendous wind, so intense that it was almost too much to endure. He did not feel worried anymore about the beasts; he was pondering the pleasures of some strange land, some paradise.

He looked up at the outskirts of the woods, still bathed in the ghostly blue light from the moon, yet beyond them he could see nothing but darkness. The trees still shook from stormy gusts, and dark thunderclouds formed a perfect circle overhead, but there was no wind or rain within the clearing.

This was like being in the eye of a hurricane.

It was when the mist started to rise above the outer stones that Hunter started to feel the energy inside the circle die off. It got weaker as the mist rose higher. The thick grey vapour was soon as high as the trees, He was now totally boxed in. Slowly it started swirling around the circle, still gaining in height. Hunter's feeling of safety was soon gone, whatever force had protected him before had now given him up. Hunter reached around and grabbed the sword from the slab. He had expected a battle come the end, and that seemed exactly what he was going to get.

The mist was swirling like a carousel around him. He stood beside the slab, poised and ready, his senses tingling with anticipation.

He threw his head back and shouted, "Come on then, what you waiting for?"

He gritted his teeth as anger once again took control of his feelings. He thought quickly about what the old priest had told him, but he dismissed his words as quickly as he had thought of them.

Take the sword to the stone circle. "Well I'm here, old man, what happens now?"

The first of the beasts emerged out of the swirling grey wall of mist around the stones and padded cautiously towards Hunter. Within seconds, another appeared, and then another, until every one of them had stepped into the confines of the circle. They had surrounded their quarry, and Hunter counted eight in total. He turned slowly, pointing the sword at each one in turn, but he knew that if they tried an all-out attack from all sides, he did not stand a chance.

Then one of the beasts lunged at him from the side; Hunter swung the sword quickly, just slicing the tip of the creature's nose. It pulled back howling as dark liquid steamed into the cold night air. Another one made a move, this time from behind. It sprang with all its might, knocking Hunter to the ground. He jumped to his feet and started to swing the sword wildly. The creature that had knocked him down came in for another attack, and this time Hunter hit it squarely with the sword. Its skull popped like a light bulb exploding.

Then another made a run for him, but the sight of the sword stopped it short. They all kept edging forward like baying jackals trying to confuse their prey. Hunter backed up against the stone slab. It was clear now that he stood no chance against these creatures.

One of the beasts came from behind again, this time jumping on the stone slab, as Hunter spun round, the beast snapped at his shoulder. He screamed in pain as the beast pulled a mouthful of flesh from his left shoulder. He swung the sword with what strength he still had, but the creature was too quick, it had already retreated.

He could tell from the look in their eyes that they sensed victory; they were just playing with him now. One by one they lunged from all directions. Hunter had all he could manage, warding them off with the sword.

He had to gain some kind of advantage.

He quickly moved between the top of the slab and the long stone and hauled himself onto the slab.

Now he was above them.

They moved closer, leaping at him as he spun round trying to fend then off. Another creature leapt onto the slab too quickly for him to respond with the sword. The beast's teeth sank into the flesh of his lower leg just before he smashed the sword through the top of its head. The pain coursing through his body was unbearable. He could not pull his leg from the beast's mouth, nor could he bend down and prise its mouth open, he had to leave it while he faced the remaining beasts. They were working themselves into more of a frenzy as they smelt Hunter's blood flowing from the open wounds on his body.

He sensed that his end was near and looked for the biggest of the beasts around him. The biggest was directly before him and had not been making as many lunges as the rest, nor did it seem too bothered whether it got into the fight. It seemed rather to be simply enjoying the sport. Hunter's plan was to just jump straight at the biggest of them and take it out before they killed him. At least then he might feel he had accomplished something.

"Lets do it you ugly bastard, let's see if you like some of this," Hunter shouted at the beast in front of him.

With a painful kick, he ripped his leg from the dead beast's mouth. He screamed into the darkness as he lifted the sword above his head and made ready to leap from the stone slab onto the beast below.

Faster than an eye blink, lightning shot from the clear night sky above and struck the sword of Nuadha that Hunter held aloft. He remained riveted to the spot as the power surged down the blade of the sword, then kicked off at a tangent, hitting the top of the long stone at the head of the slab. The ground began to tremble, and the beasts reeled back in fear. The long stone started to glow yellow, then orange as the continuous stream of power flooded from the heavens into the sword and then into the stone.

Hunter could not move. His body seemed part of the energy force; indeed, his body was conducting the energy. The beasts made a run for the outside of the circle, but in a blinding flash, the energy from the long stone emanated to each smaller perimeter stone. Those too started to glow. The beasts were trapped within a wall of energy.

Each standing stone now glowed orange, and the centre of the stone circle was beginning to fill with a brilliant light that stretched from the ground to the opening in the clouds. In the light was power, a power that Hunter had never felt before, a power that could create life or destroy it. The beasts struggled helplessly as each of them was pulled by an unseen force towards the perimeter stones. Within seconds each stood against a stone, their howls unheard. Then in a moment they were vaporized, each one now a brilliant flash of light that flowed upwards with all the rest.

An instant later it was over. The brilliant light had gone, and the cold darkness of the night was back again. Hunter dropped to his knees, letting the sword slip to the ground. His eyes blinked, and his body wavered as he battled with consciousness. Around him the wall of mist advanced into the centre of the circle, engulfing the stones like a massive wave. Hunter did not feel the icy vapour envelop him, his mind and body were now at rest.

CHAPTER 26

SUNDAY 2 AM.

The storm had calmed. The wind had slackened, and the rain was now only a light drizzle. Morale was picking up among the army of police that had now surrounded the village.

Finch had been right about Hunter not being in the village, but it had taken the armed police a good four hours to prove it. They searched every house, every outbuilding, and every place where bodies might be hidden. They found nothing alive. Jock Barnet's body was recovered and laid out in lane before the burning pub. Cause of death was still to be determined, but a broken neck was obvious even to the untrained eye.

It was still too risky to bring any sort civilian help in, so the ambulances and fire trucks still waited a mile or so away. The danger was Hunter lying in wait to ambush them, or at least that was the purported safety reason. However, Finch had a good idea where Hunter was; the fire on the moor was a dead giveaway.

By now a team of eight Royal Marine marksmen had arrived and set up observation posts around the perimeter of the village. Each marine surveyed the moors through the night scope on his SA80 rifle. Any person seen wandering the moor was to be challenged, and then if aggression was shown, the order was Shoot to kill.

Everyone seemed happy with this added protection except Finch. He thought all Royal Marine commandos were madmen. So how could he expect them to shoot one of their own? He treated the whole affair with contempt; he would not even speak to the officer in charge of the team.

Cranbury had complained that only one body had been found, and that was the body of the child's natural father, Jock Barnet. Not one villager had been found dead or alive in the village, and this he could not understand.

Finch too was perplexed at the lack of casualties. He had expected a bloodbath, and he would have predicted a bloodbath. He even searched the cottages himself just to make sure. The blood was there, and plenty of it, but no bodies. His only assumption was that Hunter must have hidden them. But where?

With each hour that passed, the weather grew milder. Soon the rain had stopped, and all they had to contend with now was the wind. A search helicopter was reordered, but the message came back that conditions were still too unstable to launch a search across the moors.

A sense of unease had pervaded the assembly; Finch could feel it. They all wondered what had really gone on and wished for daylight to relieve the tension.

Finch told everyone he talked to that Hunter was now on the moors; he knew where and pointed it out on the map. Cranbury lit the map with his torch while Finch outlined the woods and picnic area with his finger. Battle Plans were made and armed officers told of their new positions. At first light the detachment of marines would be deployed onto the moor, closely followed by the armed and unarmed police. Finch expected that, if his hunch were right, he would soon have Hunter where he wanted him.

As it began to dawn on the first day of the week, a patchy mist rolled across the moors. The storm had died with the fading night, and a crisp morning light began casting shadows once more. A light sea breeze drifted over the headland and gently dispersed the mist.

Through the thinning mist they advanced, at first just dark shapes to one another, and then with the passing of each minute their shapes were more recognisable. There were gaps of some fifty yards between the armed men. Some distance behind them came the unarmed officers, closer together and covering the ground more thoroughly. No stone was left unturned.

First to take their positions were the armed police. They scattered themselves within a couple hundred yards of the woods. Each officer had his own arc of fire; if any life was under threat deadly force was to be used. The marines were told to bypass the woods and go several miles out of their way, then to circle back and push Hunter towards the waiting armed police. They hoped in a way he would be trapped, with nowhere to run.

Finch waited back with the main force and listened to the radio messages. He desperately needed a result on this one, this whole operation had happened on his say-so, but only time would tell. It was now a waiting game, a test of nerve.

~~~

Hunter's huddled body lay at the foot of the stone slab. His fingers twitched as he started to regain consciousness, and his senses started to feel the biting cold around him. He awoke from his sleep with a start, as if still in the midst of the horrific events of the night before.

The woods were ghostly quiet. No bird song or rook call greeted the brightening day, and the wooded cover seemed devoid of life. A white frost blanketed the clearing floor, and the stone circle looked as if it were made from sugar.

He got to his knees, then pulled himself up with the help of the stone slab; his first thoughts were of his wounds. He looked down at his shoulder, knowing from the bite he had received that he should have been dead by now through loss of blood.

There was nothing, not so much as a scratch. The material had been torn away, leaving exposed skin. He felt the bare flesh with his other hand.

It's okay!

He reached to pull at his trouser leg but grimaced with pain. His whole body ached. More slowly he checked his leg; that too was all right. He seemed to be OK generally apart from aching muscles, and the aches were the only things that did make sense. He slapped his arms gingerly across his body trying to bring some warmth into it and remembered the night before. He pondered on whether it had all been a dream, but dismissed that fact because he was still there. Whatever had happened, maybe it was something that no one could explain, something that no one should try to explain or even question.

Nevertheless, whatever it was, Hunter knew that what he had seen was far greater than humanity, a force that could control human destiny, a force that could control the universe, a that used the universe like a tool. Humankind was just a mere child to it, and the planet Earth no more than a fledgling.

Was this the creator that everyone sought? He hoped it was; the feeling of love and tranquillity that emanated from its light had overcome his doubts.

Hunter glanced around at the stones and accepted that he might never know its purpose. Its secret had now gone forever with the villagers, and that suited him. He took a last look round and noticed the sword's outline on the powder white grass. He moaned as he reached and grasped it and then straightened again, dusting the frost from the blade. He frowned. Why had the sword been left? The sword was part of the mystery. Why leave it?

He tucked the sword under his arm and headed out of the circle. His footsteps crunched through the icy grass as he made for the track that would lead him back onto the open moor. As he walked through the woods, he wondered about his future.

The moors had taken everything from him, his wife, his child, his best friend. He wondered whether he could start again; make a new life for himself. He did not relish that thought; he would rather be alone for a while. Get his head together. Then the memory of Finch and the other detective flashed into his mind. There was no way the police would believe his story, but somehow it did not bother him. The worst was over.

The mist from the moor had gradually filtered through the trees on the outskirts of the woods. Hunter did not notice it until it drifted onto the track and a waist high band of the wet vapour blew gently towards him. He froze in terror and scanned the woods around him.

With the mist come the beasts. "No, you can't still be alive," he whispered. The mist was to either side of him and slowly moving towards the stone circle. He feared another attack from the creatures, but his instinct told him that everything was OK.

He had to keep moving.

The sword was now in his hands at the ready; he would take no chances this time. The end of the track was near; he could see the opening in the trees ahead, and his pace quickened. The mist grew thicker the closer he got to the woods' edge, until cautiously he stepped from the track and looked across the moor.

In places, the mist was just a haze, and visibility might be a couple of hundred yards and more. Elsewhere the sea breeze compacted a more impenetrable mist. This mist blocked out the landscape and any beasts or police who might be hidden there.

Hunter waited motionless at the entrance to the woods. He tried to scan the countryside around him, and he sensed something was not quite right.

The more he looked, the more he had the feeling that they were still alive and watching him. He gripped the sword tightly; they were close, he could feel it. But where? He took a few uncertain steps out into the open, hoping that they would make their move.

~~~

"Guv, he's been spotted," Cranbury said, passing the radio to Finch.

"Good, now we have him." Finch snatched the radio from Cranbury's hand and placed it a few inches from his mouth, then keyed the handset.

"Delta one. DI Finch speaking, where's the suspect now?"

The radio crackled, with Delta one-armed response answering. "Someone's just come out of the woods, sir. It's hard to see in this mist, but I think it's our man."

Finch punched his fist into the air in victory. "Yes."

The police marksman adjusted the scopes on his rifle, trying to get a clearer picture of the suspect. He was at about a hundred and eighty yards, which should have been an easy shot for a marksman with a rifle, but the rolling mist obscured his vision and blurred the target. He zeroed the cross hairs onto Hunter's upper body as soon as he had a clear view of him, but within seconds, the mist blocked out the target again.

Hunter could not understand what was going on. He did not know whether he could go through such torment again or whether he wanted to. A part of him was saying, *Run, run for your life, and do not look back.* His conscience was saying, *do what you set out to do. Defeat the beasts.* He had never run away from a fight, and he was not about to start. He lifted the sword and started to walk into the mist. The danger was getting closer.

Finch listened intently for more information on the movements of Hunter, a cigarette continually smoking in his mouth as the tension began to mount.

"Delta one. Over. He's gone. Over!" Squawked from the radio.

Finch spat the cigarette onto the ground. "What d'you mean he's gone? He can't have gone."

There was silence for a moment.

The police marksman scanned the mist through the scopes of the rifle, viewing his arc of fire repeatedly. The mist was too thick. He kept looking. Each armed officer was asked in turn if they could see the suspect, and a negative response came back.

Finch lit another cigarette. "1 can't believe this. One minute he's there, the next he just vanishes. Bloody brilliant." Finch snapped at Cranbury.

Cranbury was stamping his feet against the cold. "Well, Guv, the mist is quite thick. I mean how far can you see?" Cranbury looked up the line of police officers waiting to begin their part of the operation.

Finch followed his gaze. The first half dozen men could be clearly seen, but the rest paled, then disappeared into the mist.

"Well, it's probably worse up here." Finch's tone said he was always right.

Cranbury did not want to argue.

A new voice came over the radio. "I see him, sir. He's in B sector now."

Finch grabbed the map from the police constable next to him and studied the sectors that had been divided among the marksmen.

The voice came again. "He's heading back to sector A."

Finch looked at the radio. then looked back at the map.

"Sir, I've spotted the suspect again, he's still in sector A. I don't know who sector B's looking at, but it ain't the suspect, I'm looking right at him, and it looks like he's holding something, but I can't see what."

Finch keyed the handset. "Sector B, who are you looking at?"

There was silence for a moment. Then the response came.

"Sector B.I don't know who it is, sir." There was silence again as the officer tried to focus on the person with his rifle sights. "I can't see the person clearly, but I think it might be a woman, and she's heading straight for the suspect."

"Shit! That's all I need, another dead body. Can we get someone out there to stop her?" Finch looked at Cranbury for the answer.

Cranbury shrugged his shoulders. "Not from here Gov, it would take too much time."

Finch lifted the radio to his lips. "Sector B? Can you stop the woman from where you are?"

The officer in sector B lifted his eye away from the rifle scope, just to get another perspective of the distance between him and the vague figure walking across the moor. "I'm about two hundred yards away, sir. Your suspect is bound to see me if I make a dash for the girl."

Finch sucked deeply on his cigarette. He had to make a quick decision. "Go for it. We can't afford another death. Run as fast as you can, and get that person out of there."

Sector B broke cover and plunged into the mist.

Finch keyed the handset again. "Sector A, do you read me?"

"Sector A," the voice answered.

"Sector A, I want you to keep your gun trained on the suspect. If he shows any aggression or makes any sudden moves, you know what to do."

Sector A cast his eye back down the scope. He did not have a perfect view of Hunter, but it was clear enough for a shot. He hoped it would last.

Hunter stopped walking. He seemed to hear footsteps coming towards him. They sounded light, not like a man's footsteps. He sought the nearest cover and waited for the person to appear out of the mist.

Finch received the message that Hunter had dropped out of sight. He frantically radioed Sector B, who'd been pursuing the woman, but he had managed to lose her in a bank of mist. He said she just vanished, he couldn't understand it. He was right behind her, then she was gone. Finch grunted with displeasure, and then the order was given to move the rest of the armed police into the area where the suspect and the civilian had been spotted.

Hunter's instincts were screaming *Danger!* A dark shape started to emerge from the mist about twenty yards from him. The person was walking fast, with some urgency, as if heading for a certain destination. That destination seemed to be the woods. The person was more visible now, and as he scanned its small frame, he was sure it was a woman. The tight blue denims gave away the shapely contours of her legs, and a leather bomber jacket covered her upper body.

He could see her face clearly now, she was just yards away from him. "It's Sarah!" he gasped.

Hunter stood up from behind the cover to Sarah's left. She stopped dead in her tracks and stared with astonishment at the dishevelled man in front of her. There was a look of shock on her face, which soon faded to a smile.

"Sarah, what are you doing here?" he asked.

Finch received another message telling him that Hunter had appeared again, but so had the girl, and they seemed to be talking to each other.

The sector A sniper flicked the safety catch off and rested his finger on the trigger; Hunter was in his sights again.

She took a step towards him. "I thought I might be able to help you, I tried to get into the village, but the police had the road blocked. They told me that people had been killed. What have you done, Hunter?

"It's a long story, and we're not safe here; we've got to get off of the moor. Come on." He stepped beside her and grabbed her arm. "This way, it'll take us back onto the road."

He started to walk. still clutching her arm; she shrugged him off and stayed where she was.

"What's up?" he asked, facing her again.

Her face looked serious. "Did you kill them all?"

Hunter had never seen her like this before. He stepped up to her, his face just inches from hers. "This isn't the time or the place, Sarah. We've got to get out of here, we're in a lot of danger, please." He reached for her arm again.

She took a step back. "No, not until you tell me. Did you kill them." She wanted to know.

"What are they doing now?" Finch asked, speaking into the radio.

A bank of mist drifted in front of Sector A's view again.

"Shit!" He put the radio to his mouth. " I've lost them again, but he looked like he was trying to take her somewhere, he made a grab for her a few times."

Finch: "Did she look in danger?"

Sniper: "No, but she didn't look like she wanted to go with him either."

Finch: "The rest of your team should be quite close now; I want to know as soon as you can see them again, OK?"

Hunter swung the sword at a bush by his feet in frustration. Sarah took a few more steps back. She looked terrified at the sight of the sword, and Hunter noticed her fear.

"No, don't be frightened, I wouldn't hurt you. I forgot I had it in my hand." He lifted the sword to show her, as if to say he meant no harm.

She was afraid of him, and he did not like that. It looked as if she did not trust him anymore. He would have to answer her question.

"No, I didn't kill them, but I helped." He was not going to lie to her. She knew stories about the myths of the moors; she had told him about them in the first place. If anyone could understand, Sarah would. He would have to tell her.

He studied her face for some sort of reaction. She seemed to lighten up on hearing that the villagers were dead. Maybe telling her the truth had done it, and perhaps she trusted him again.

"It sounds bad, I know, but d'you remember what you told me about the myths of the moor?" She nodded. "Well it's all true. They were the ones you told me about. I can't tell you too much now, but believe me, it's all true." He smiled at her. "It would make a brilliant novel for you to write, it'll be a bloody bestseller."

She returned his smile briefly, then asked: "Did they all die?"

Such a strange question. It started him thinking. Were they all dead? His feelings told him not, but they could have been wrong.

"I think so. Look, I'll tell you more when we're out of here, if the police don't get me first." He winked at her. "Come on.

The police radio in Finch's hand squawked into life.

Sniper: "I can see them both again; they're heading directly at me. What d'you want me to do?"

Finch: "How good is your visibility?"

Sniper: "Now I can just see them, the target is in front. The mist is pretty thick in places, so I think it's better to wait until they're closer."

Finch: "Right. When you can get a sure shot at him; let him know you're there. Hopefully the rest of the team will be alongside you by then."

Hunter's curiosity was belatedly aroused. He wondered how she could have found him, especially in the mist. The more he thought about it, the more questions came to mind. He had to ask her.

"How did you know where to find me?" he asked as he kept walking.

There was silence for a moment. Then Sarah answered. "I remembered you telling me about the stone circle. Naturally when I couldn't get into the village, I headed for the woods."

Hunter started to feel uneasy again. Something just was not right, and again that *danger* feeling rose up in him. He had a good view around him, but another large bank of thick mist was being blown towards him by the westerly wind. He lifted the sword from his side and thought about Sarah's answer. He still was not satisfied.

"But there's a few woods around here. How did you know it was this one?"

Sarah's pace slowed. "Your friend Jock must have told me … Yes I'm sure he did."

Hunter scoured his mind, but he was sure he had never told Jock where the woods were.

"Jock didn't know, Sarah, I never told him." He stopped, then turned to face her. The thick bank of mist had now drifted over them, and his visibility was down to about ten yards. Sarah was nowhere to be seen.

"Sarah." He spoke quietly and received no response.

He lifted the sword in front of him. He could feel he was being watched, he could sense something stalking him. He called Sarah's name again and still received no reply. Then it dawned on him why he had been left the sword. They were not all dead. Somehow, the beasts had managed to live, but how?

A dark shape moved to the side of him, he spun round, facing it with the sword.

Sarah's face seemed to loom at him from the mist, like a freeze frame in a film her features froze in his mind.

That face. She glared at him, as the mist cloaked her once more.

"Sarah, what are you doing?" he demanded.

Her face flashed into his mind again. Then he had a vision of Jock offering him a photo. His words seemed so real, as if he had just whispered them into his ear. "I reckon you should take a look at this, and tell me who you think it is."

The picture and the words drifted away, but the thought did not. What had Jock seen in Trout's room? Who was it in the picture? Picture ... the photo downstairs in the pub. He visualized the photo again, then he realised.

"The photo, you're the young girl in the photo." His voice was a disbelieving whisper.

"You're the girl from the photo," he said again, this time a little louder. "You're one of them."

"No, I'm not like them." Sarah stepped from the mist again, a safe distance from Hunter. "They were set in their old ways, living in the past. They had to go, and thanks to you they have."

"I don't understand. I met you from total coincidence, you couldn't have possibly known I was going to the library that day."

"Nothing is coincidence. Everything is mapped out for you, but not for us. That's why we can cheat the future: we know it. But the old ones chose to dwell in the past; they were stupid and paid the price for their stupidity."

Hunter shook his head. He did not want her to be one of

those things. He was fond of the girl. She could not be one. But he remembered the photo. It was her, all right. He stepped closer to her, and she did not move.

"So if you're one of the villagers, how come you didn't die when I took this sword back to the stone circle? The rest did."

She looked at the sword, then back up at Hunter. "Because I'm carrying your baby, so part of me is mortal now. The circle can do nothing to me, thanks to you."

Hunter looked her up and down, he was still captivated by her, and he did not want to believe that she was one of those hideous creatures. She was so beautiful.

He wondered if she was telling the truth about being pregnant with his child. There could be no better thought than a wife like her and a child that belonged to both of them, but she wasn't what she seemed, and the child ... well, only God knew what that would turn out like.

"I don't want to believe this. Why me?" He said lowering the sword slightly.

The wind gentle buffeted her hair, and a few strands fell across her eyes; she flicked them away with her hand.

"Because I chose you. I knew you could do the job."

The mist thinned, bringing both Hunter and Sarah back into view of the police marksman, who radioed Finch straightaway that the suspect was now within a hundred yards and a stationary target. He asked whether he should take the shot.

Finch: "What are they doing?"

Sniper: "Looks like they're talking again, but he's got what looks like a sword pointing at her this time." The sniper focused his sights in on the object in Hunter's hand. "Yes, that's what it is, sir, a sword."

Finch shot a sideways glance at Cranbury to see if he had heard the last comment. He had, and grimaced back at his boss.

Finch replied, "Would he see you clearly if you told him of your presence?"

Sniper: "At the moment yes, but that could change at any second, the mist is very patchy."

"Bollocks!" The last thing Finch had expected was a sea mist. He lifted the radio and asked how close the rest of the armed team were. They responded by telling him that they were within range of the suspect, but their views also were hampered by the mist.

Hunter gritted his teeth and took another step towards her. "Job, you call what I've been through a job? I've lost my whole family because of you." He lifted the sword again and looked her directly in the eyes. They were the same as the beasts', they were lifeless and full of misery, and he could see the real Sarah in them.

The police sniper curled his finger around the trigger; Hunter's upper body filled the scope.

Sniper: "He looks agitated; I think we'd better make a move."

Finch: "Move, then, but don't put the girl at risk."

Finch waved the whole army of police forward; the thin blue line disappeared into the mist.

Waves of emotion rushed Hunter's body; tears ran from his exhausted eyes. He knew what he had to do, but it seemed like he was doing it in cold blood. Killing the young girl in front of him was not going to be easy.

She just stood there looking at him, as if she knew what was running through his mind and could see the pain on his face. He searched his soul for the strength he needed, but found nothing. He thought of all the reasons he should kill her: Carl, Jock, and the pain her kind had caused countless families of their victims, but looking at her face just cancelled out the thoughts of rage.

The scream "Armed Police" behind him was not totally unexpected, he did not bother to look round at the officer pointing the rifle at him, and he kept his eyes firmly fixed on Sarah.

She smiled at him, a smug smile that said she had played the winning hand.

"Time's run out, I think you've chosen your future," she said.

The policeman screamed at him again. "Put down the weapon, put it down now!"

Two more armed officers settled themselves in the cover, their rifles also trained on Hunter.

Hunter ignored the police officer's demand. He was busy considering what Sarah had just said, The word *future* was a frightening word. The more he thought about it, the less of a future he had. However, this was not about his future anymore; he could see that now. Maybe his life was over. He remembered the faces he had seen when he had entered the light. They were his future. He thought fondly of his parents for a moment, then Sarah's face came back into view.

The mist drifted across them both. Sharpshooters kept their fingers on their triggers, but visibility was starting to deteriorate.

Beyond the beauty of the girl was a monster, a beast with no feelings, a creature that preyed on the innocent and the weak, he knew now what he had to do, his desires for her had gone.

"You were right," Hunter said softly.

She frowned. "About what?"

"This was a job, and now it's finished." He lifted the sword into the air, then swung it at her with all his might.

Their dark outlines were just recognisable through the mist, and the faint glint of the blade highlighted Hunter's stance.

A single shot from a high-calibre rifle echoed through the mist. Birds exploded from the trees, and red deer barked warnings in the valleys beyond.

Hunter dropped to his knees, and the sword fell from his grasp. He coughed as the bullet took the life from his body. The darkness closed in slowly with a rushing sound in his ears as the blood pumped from his now limp body. Voices he could hear faded. He felt neither pain, nor suffering, nor emotion. His earthly body was now still and lifeless.

The sound of nature's songs started to fill the fresh morning air.

~~~

Detective Inspector Finch viewed the sword laid at his feet, next to the now covered body of Hunter. Hunter's muddy, bloodstained hand poked out from the blanket covering him, his fingers looking as if they were grasping for the sword.

Ambulance men and police carried away Sarah Holly. It was not clear whether she would survive her wounds, as she was losing lots of blood. The men and women struggled over the uneven terrain with the stretcher as they held the intravenous fluids trying to keep her alive.

Finch viewed the panorama; the mist had blown away, blue sky and thin wispy clouds stretched as far as the eye could see.

He shook his head slowly, pondering life.

"Why?" he whispered to himself.

A uniformed officer stumbled towards Finch with purpose in his step. Finch put his last cigarette in his mouth and screwed up the packet, then dug for his lighter.

"Yes?" Finch asked the young officer. He still could not find his lighter.

"Sir, we think we found the boy."

Finch frowned. "The boy ... What, Carl Hunter?" His cigarette hung from his lip.

"Yes."

"Where did you find the body?"

"In the cellar of one of those cottages. He's alive"

"Alive ...alive ..." He did not want to believe.

"Yeah, alive, a little frightened and dirty but alive." The officer looked down at the sword and the body by Finch's feet.

Finch followed his stare, looking at Hunter's exposed hand from under the sheet. He had been dead wrong about Hunter. Feelings of remorse and empathy slowly ebbed into his thoughts. He took the cigarette from his mouth and rubbed the back of the same hand across his forehead, then shook his head in disbelief. He looked at the cigarette and then threw it on the ground; he did not want to smoke anymore.

"He's alive," he whispered again in disbelief. "Poor little

bastard, what a mess, what a mess." Finch bowed his head solemnly and took a deep breath of the fresh morning air.

This was a new beginning.

Printed in the United Kingdom by
Lightning Source UK Ltd., Milton Keynes
141292UK00001B/31/P